STRANGE COMPANY

VOODOO WARFARE

NICK COLE

Published by WarGate Nova
ISBN: 978-1-949731-79-8

Edited by David Gatewood
Cover Art: Trent Kaniuga
Cover Design: M.S. Corley
Formatting: Kevin G. Summers

Website: NickColeBooks.com

LOG KEEPER'S NOTE
AFTERMATH

In those dark years of the long crossing between the world we'd cut loose of the bad contract on, and the repair facility on Hardrock, the Strange Company slept and the galaxy caught fire as we dreamed for twenty-five years of sublight.

The old order of the Monarchs, mighty yet petty gods determined to burn worlds and take humanity with them down into the deep dark graves of empire, began its final collapse. Worlds fell into shadowy chaos, overrun by the cackle of automatic weapons carried by the Simia Legions, while ring stations at Oberon and Circe burned like fiery jewels as the defense networks crumbled and ragtag collections of go-ships jumped into the darkness beyond the limits of human navigation to escape the madness of invasion and civil war.

The Ultras sent their Battle Spires into great conflicts at twenty-to-one odds, while rogue hunter-killer cyborgs carved out a nation among the stars for their own, eradicating life and silencing humanity across vast grain worlds now gone silent in the twilight. Debris fields of broken starships, Simia hulks and Monarch warships, lay twisting and drifting in the orbits of dead worlds as famine began to ravage human-controlled space.

The supercarriers were defeated at Andromeda Station. The powerful G-beams of Cerberus Gate could not hold the line, and the Rapid Jump Network for the spiral arm was gone in a single fireball moment, casting the outer frontier into permanent midnight and mute isolation for decades to come, if not forever.

It was a final game for all the marbles, or what marbles called worlds remained in the bonfire burning, consuming known space. A battle of three sides where strange alliances were made, and broken, as the table changed moment to moment in the grand game of Cheks playing out across the stars. New conquerors and would-be saviors shuffled their decks, seeking a card to play for the win, not above a cheat, a prayer, or a promise of a better tomorrow never delivered.

Into this madness and maelstrom rode the Strange Company, sleeping in an old destroyer they called the *Spider*. Determined to have their say, if even just now, at the end of all things…

CHAPTER ONE

During the long journey from the catastrophe of Crash, Astralon, call it what you will, we dreamt dreams of adventure, and pleasure, and for some, even now... conquest. And of course... a final settling up.

But those dreams were secret dreams for just one.

For the rest of the Strange, it was anything to take their sleeping minds, those that had survived the last war, off the events on that deleted world and bad contract the company had gotten itself involved in. But not everyone dreamed a ship's-AI MMO dreams of other, better lives than the ones we lived. Reality Dreams, lived inside vast fantastic virtual worlds the *Spider*'s artificial intelligence—M.O.M., or MOM as we called her. The adventures and pleasures she could dream up for us to while away the darkness of cryosleep for the long crossing of the great nether gulfs of nothingness between Crash, or Astralon, call it what you will, and the bet we were hoping would pay off on that other rock out near the edge of human expansion.

And yes... some dreamt of revenge. Payback. Call it what you will. Painting it all black. All of it. All the wrongs and not just the ones that had been done to the company lately. The Monarchs and many others had run up debts that needed settling as far as the Old Man was concerned and some who kept fire around his inner circle. They, those late-night smokers in the forward day room, they dreamed those paint-it-black dreams as they are called among the company when revenge and payback are on someone's mind.

That's the thing about the *Spider*'s forward day room just behind the docking stack. It's an old officers' lounge. It looks both forward and back. Where we have been, and where we're going. It's a dark place despite the view, and honestly, I steer clear of it. There's a serious pucker factor there I need a break from after nine months of war on Crash and a bare escape with our lives, tons of useless mem, and the dead we left behind.

But I'd be lying if contracts like that, and the bad deal and worthless mem we were promised that followed, didn't make me ache for a little payback too.

You get tired of getting kicked. Everyone does.

Even me. If I am honest with this account... honest with myself... even me. I'll smoke and think about settling up. Even a broken ruck-hump merc NCO can have such foolish dreams.

If only to give back a little of the so much that has been handed out.

Yes, even me, *da Little King*, as drunk old Stinkeye likes to crow in the lower passages whenever he finds me smoking in the dark and thinking. He always seems to find me when my mind has gone there. Like the old Voodoo warrant officer is some ship floundering on a dark sea looking for a lighthouse of revenge among the rocks and shoals to give him a purpose to haul his tattered gear and bony frame out onto one more contract.

Even me... Sergeant Orion. Keeper of the log. Brother in the Strange. Payback appeals even to me.

But that was in the weeks following Astralon as our broken-down old destroyer hauled herself up to just shy of light and the XO pointed us toward some broken rock on the stellar charts.

We're all looking for a lighthouse.

Twenty-five years later, the *Spider* eased out of sublight and settled herself into the local system traffic, not that there was much, that surrounded the desperate bet we'd made on Hardrock Shipyards.

It's an icy and storm-laden world with giant volcanic rents that add to the chaos and maelstrom planetside. No colony could survive here. But a shipyard lying along an old trade route reaching out along the galactic arm… sure. Why not. Core taps are cheap energy for the repair of starships ranging from super-freighters to old light destroyer merc transports.

Slowing from the painstakingly slow sublight crawl the old destroyer was barely capable of without her jump drive took two full months of heavy burn from the mains in retrograde just to get us set up for orbital insertion around Hardrock.

Twenty-five years didn't feel like the two weeks plus one epic rack-out our bodies were telling us had occurred. But it had. And the Monarch empire was wrecked when we popped back into current events.

M.O.M. awakened us in batches. Or at least those who could be brought back to consciousness in the waking life that seemed like a dream you hadn't had in years as you surfaced from the onboard MMO. The severely wounded were left in cryosleep. The dead, and there were always some in cryosleep this long on a ship this old, well, they were just dead now. Everyone wins the lottery, it just depends on how you look at it.

Winning that is.

I knew I was in the early batch of first awakeners because the entire superstructure of the old warship was still violently shaking and threatening to come apart as the massive mains at the back of the ship struggled to slow us for planetary arrival and shipyard entry. I spent two days in rehab with just a few of the command team, none of us saying much to one another as we tried to remember how to move, drink, eat, and just plain-old remember things.

You always lost memories in transit. And sometimes that wasn't a bad thing. You were probably going to make some new ones you'd want to forget on the next contract.

The Falmorian party girl was still inside my brain bucket, though. Her letter I'd gotten once we boarded the *Spider* after Crash. That was a good thing. She was. The dead Kid too. Not a good thing. Amarcus dead… good thing.

You add things up when you get back to your locker on the ship you haven't seen in nine months. That's a weird moment. The you who closed it is much different than the you who opens it.

On reawakening from cryo, I drank protein and vitamin slurries, pretending they were nillabanana flavored because sometimes you can trick yourself just enough to actually believe it. And all the while I'm abacus-ing up the good and the bad of my life in real time. That's why we don't say much to each other during recovery as the ship rattles and thrums all around us during the two weeks of re-entry. I was reconciling accounts and seeing what I had to live with going forward on the next contract.

And always, you're asking yourself a stupid question you already know the answer to. *Am I going?*

A casual yet constant observer would have told you I arrived at no conclusion other than that I was still alive.

I always liked moving that mental white bead to that side of the invisible abacus.

I always considered that a win. Life. Being alive one more time. Why? Believe it or not... I'm an optimist. Things can always get worse, am I right? At least I was alive one more time and no one was shooting at me while M.O.M. tried to nurse me back to life one more time for one more contract. I had that going for me.

Plus, things can always get worse.

The first sergeant, as per company standard operating procedure, was one of the first out of cryo and had been for a week before we entered recovery aboard the *Spider*. The XO, who flew the ship for the company, was out of cryo too, but now much older than he had been during the combat departure out of Astralon, Crash, call it what you will. Apparently the ship had problems during transit to Hardrock, and he'd spent eight years out of cryo keeping us alive with baling wire and bubble gum. He was now older than the captain. Older than the Old Man.

The XO looked worn out and there was no way he'd take command someday, having saved our lives alone while we were all dreaming dreams of other lives not this one. He was just the Strange Company pilot now. But we called him XO anyway because unless we could pick up a hyperdrive on this world there wasn't gonna be a company much longer.

We all knew the situation. It was grim. The galactic economy had cratered.

The first sergeant barked at all of us first awakeners as rehab injected our muscles full of minerals and nutrients, started us moving inside the dyna-cycles, and got us spun up for self-operation one more time.

"This is the first day of the rest of yer life, Sergeant Orion," erupted the first sergeant on the other side of the glass near me in recovery. "Company would appreciate it if you'd get a move on so we can go to foreign worlds and kill exotic beings for pay and fun, Sergeant."

My mouth tasted like pine nuts for the entire rehab. I tried to remember the MMO I'd just woken from. I'd spent a lot of time there, but the violence of cognition regeneration usually blanked out your mind and left you with a pretty severe hangover for a couple of weeks and little memory of what had gone on inside those fantastic virtual worlds you'd just spent the last twenty-five years in as the ship crossed the vast interstellar gulfs of darknesses between the worlds.

Something sword and sorcery... yeah, I remembered fire and steel. But there'd been world-building components and I'd set myself a challenge during the load screen requests twenty-five years ago to make something instead of killing everything like I always did. The loading screens... that was when we got to input and tell M.O.M. how we'd like to be occupied for the flight to Hardrock for repairs and may-be a new jump drive if we promised to go somewhere and kill someone. Sometimes you got your wish regarding the MMOs. Sometimes you ended up in something bizarre.

Twenty-five years later, the matronly AI would apolo-gize as you filed a complaint ticket on the experience you would not recommend inside those virtual worlds. Hoping she'd get it right for the next flight if you survived the cur-rent contract.

She thanked you in her kindly voice and told you she'd try harder to improve the experience parameters. But she always said that.

Tags got a simulation of him working inside a massive stellar insurance corporation he couldn't get fired from. No sword, no sorcery. No harem girls. It was an everyday existence and most likely the psych algos had decided he needed to calm down a bit after Astralon. So they'd sentenced him to twenty-five years of paperwork, coaching Ultraball Little League, and a wife that was pretty hot and kept having simulated children.

"After a while it wasn't so bad. I got to like it," he said to no one who cared.

But not for me. No such pastoral pleasure dome to while away the crossing from one ruined world to another icy rock no one should've ever stopped at.

"I am sorry, dear." The AI called everyone *dear*. "But the psych eval algorithm indicated you needed something a little more challenging this time, Sergeant James P. Orion. We came up with the *World of Kronan* simulation to meet your current mental health needs. The company feels you might embrace your more violent tendencies for improved contract satisfaction on behalf of future prospective clients. That's why we developed the Sack of Tulgar and the desert raider cities, and added in the fighting campaigns in the Swamps of Nethramoor against the Octoeyes of Hellbane. The horror factor of the Octoeyes has resulted in a small increase in your cognitive agility, which should serve you should the company have another contract to fulfill."

Those things were pure insanity. The whole Nethramoor was like a nightmare at three in the morning that never ended. It was haunting and the violence was desperate. Those Octoeyes could suck you down into their lairs like some crocodile taking you down into its den. Then, according to the in-game lore... it fed on you for years, keeping you alive in the watery dark.

Yeah... pass on that MMO ever again.

To be honest, I wouldn't have minded Tags's vacation. Mine had been mind-gibberingly insane and very exhausting. Like those heavy sleeps where you wake up from dreaming you're being chased by a cybertoothed bear, and you're sweating and breathing heavy and holding your sidearm out in the darkness of your tiny room down near the mains of the *Spider*. The answer I'd been hoping for from M.O.M. should have been, "Dear, I have something a little more peaceful to keep you in the SAFE PTSD matrix the company requires of its member for all contracts and insurance." A nice sim about beings some painter, or a farmer. And a hot wife.

And the PTSD matrix... that was mostly bogus though. I'd known guys who were completely sociopathic and homicidal just waiting to get their kill on planetside to see who could nail the war crimes high score on that gig. Choker, my medic, comes to mind immediately. The company lawyers always had waivers signed before we started each gig protecting those psychos regardless of their PTSD flags.

But all in all, my time inside the onboard MMO had been... *good*. I forgot about Crash and the dead we'd left behind. There had been things in there, moments of beauty amid the carnage of survival. I could still remember feeling that as I slept. Or at least the memory of that feeling as I tried to get my mobility back and forget everything that had gone down on Astralon, or Crash, call it what you will.

The Kid. Most of my platoon.

When I couldn't shake those memories, the brothers, sipping my not-nillabanana protein smoothie, I thought of

Amarcus Hannibal, dead and burning in the crawler... and I smiled, adding a white bead to the mental abacus.

There had been wars... massive battles inside the MMO I'd fought in that virtual world... and they had been... *good wars*. Noble wars between good and evil. Right and wrong. Like wars are supposed to be. Not like the kind the company fought and will fight again. In my sleeping dreams between the worlds there had been good guys, and bad guys. Evil got itself defeated. Damsels were rescued and there was much feasting. Stuff I could believe in. Reasons why I'd told myself I'd started soldiering a real long time ago in another life not this one anymore.

I felt every mile of all those years inside those worlds. I got old in some and died surrounded by imaginary families who loved me and would go on.

That kinda messes with your head.

I was getting MMO lag as real life failed to reward like those imagined fantastic worlds had. It was getting worse each time now. Harder to wake back up to the ever-darker reality I was finding myself, and the galaxy, in at the end of each long dark crossing between the worlds.

Yeah, it was fantasy. Made-up stories. But when you were in there it was as real as it gets. You could die in there. You felt what that felt like and sometimes it scared the hell outta you and sometimes... sometimes it was... *okay*. Then the entire fantasy would just reset, and you had no idea you'd died. Just some vague feeling you'd done all this before in another life not that one. But yeah, it was fantasy stuff... and I found it helped to wash the metaphorical bad taste regarding the latest rash of bad company contracts right out of my mouth after each one went the way they all did every time.

Bad.

Strange Company was on an epic run of very bad luck as far as the logs were concerned. During recovery, as you read the feeds and tried to catch up on current events and how bad everything had gotten, it got so hopeless and dark that sometimes your mind slipped back into forgotten memories of the MMO. Even memories of when you'd died, and it wasn't so bad. Like in battle saving imaginary best friends you'd made in that world. Or sometimes of old age surrounded by the love of your life and children and even grandchildren and even great-grandchildren. Some old and wise good king who'd had many adventures and lived long and well. Sometimes when the company finances, your personal losses, and the fact that half of human space had gone dark got to be too much as each of us tried to figure the state of play in the galaxy, you remembered the name of the real dead, the dead of the company, the Kid, and then you just faded into those forgotten memories and the imaginary shock took you into those deaths you were a little more... okay... with.

The real dead and sometimes the family, it was like they were there, where you were going when you died in those memories, and it wasn't such a bad place. Better than the rock they'd bought it on. Better than the galaxy torn apart by madness we found when we came out of transit and entered real time again.

A better place not this one.

It was like what you almost felt on Valhalla Day instead of the emptiness that was always there. What you were supposed to feel with the body bags of all our own all over the aft flight deck of the *Spider* on the last Sunday before we hit the cryo-coffins for the big sleep between worlds. That was what the company called it. Valhalla Day. The last party of the company before the big, long sleep and the next contract for more of us to die on. We feasted on that day. We drank too much. Then we pushed our dead off the flight deck and out into deep space just below the engines throttling up for full burn between worlds. All of us that were still alive watching as the dead caught fire in the engines and became stardust in the forever of the universe.

Then the ship's lights went down after that and slowly, within a few hours, we were all asleep once more, the ship throttling up to just under sublight. When we'd wake next, we'd be on a new contract. Or getting ready to vote on one.

And so much time would have passed, once again.

Then another sleep after that if the engines weren't fixed. Or new. Or some miracle, or disaster, had happened to us along the way we'd never know about as we became just another derelict between the stars.

There are many derelicts out there between the worlds. Lots of ghost ships.

That's what we did on Valhalla Day. Preacher called it Sunday, and none of us knew what that meant. He held a service down in the lower decks no one ever went to. No one except me.

Because... I feel bad for losers. That's my religion. And I'm the saddest high priest of all.

Preacher played music he said was from long-ago Earth. I didn't know if it was true. But it was nice, and it made me wonder who we were then when we were just humans on a world I'd never seen. None of us had. Only Monarchs go there. Only they know what Earth is. And we are not them.

So, who were we now?

On Sunday?

Valhalla Day.

Someone else during the Big Sleep between worlds.

When you get out of cryo this is what your mind is like. It's everywhere… everywhen… it takes a few days to pass.

So, I'm in central rehab drinking nillabanana-flavored regen. Pro tip, it all tastes the same. All the flavors are the same. Stale pine nuts. M.O.M. just asks you what your preference is before the restoration regime starts.

"What flavor of shake would you like for your VasOX treatments, dear?" Then she lists them. "I have peanut butter, vanilla, chocolate, nillabanana, Sommarian Mint…"

Pine nuts. They all taste like stale pine nuts aboard the *Spider*.

Now, in rehab, the first sergeant is behind the glass, barking at us first awakeners. The captain. Chief Cook. Ghost Platoon's sergeant. Hannibal should be here, but well, I killed him and left him back on Astralon inside our burning crawler as we dusted off the LZ and left that world forever.

Abacus bead shifted.

No one knows about that. Some have their suspicions. But no one knows. Right?

Amarcus Hannibal got a Valhalla sendoff into the fury of the mains too. His boots from his locker. That's all we had left of that miserable excuse for a human being. That's what we do with the ones that don't make it back to the ship.

But that's all prologue. That's the past and the problem with coming back to life is organizing it all in the proper chronological order.

I am here in rehab aboard the *Spider*, listening to the first sergeant on the other side of the glass.

And time seems to get flowing in the right direction as what happens next... begins.

"Situation is a real mess, sir," barks the first sergeant who thinks he has to yell because he's on the other side of the med glass in rehab. "Monarchs are losing the war against the Insurrection. And that ain't half the story, sir. Them Simia, those monkeys, they got war hulks and they've fought some pretty big scraps out on the frontier worlds. Parsing what's left of the galactic news networks, the quiet part they ain't sayin' aloud or nothin', sir, is it looks like the monkey people are winning out there too. Ultras have lost six Battle Spires, count 'em six, they'll admit to, and the rest are either engaged in conflicts with the Insurrectionists, or... they've gone full missing. And if that ain't somethin' then I don't know what is, sir. Six Battle Spires is..."

He didn't finish. But we all knew what he meant. *Inconceivable.* That's the word. It's inconceivable to lose six... *six*... Battle Spires.

Unthinkable.

Unimaginable.

Crews in excess of ten thousand. Multiple combat divisions of Ultras. The loss of one was death on a mass scale even by galactic standards.

Reality.

The XO in his flight officer's overalls behind the first sergeant cleared his throat. Near me in rehab and looking like warmed-over death, the captain sat at a metal table nursing his preferred flavor of stale pine nuts. My guess was... he just ordered plain. Or told M.O.M. he wanted "pine nuts" and she'd decided that we should all follow the leader.

The Old Man was not given to fantasist illusions as I was. The captain was the ultimate realist. He was reality squared.

The XO cleared his throat to speak once more. The first sergeant caught the hint from his barking litany of how much everything sucked and how screwed we were, and stepped back into the shadows on the other side of the med glass in recovery.

"XO here says he's got somethin' you need to hear, sir," said the first sergeant as he stepped away.

The XO came forward not too close to the rehab glass partition.

"Sir, flight systems for the *Spider* are failing. Current jump drive is well beyond repair as are the planetary landing engines. Reactor Three failed sixteen years into the flight from Astralon and we are low on munitions for the main gun after the running battle to evade Monarch pursuit into the deep system back at Astralon. We will make insertion in the next two weeks and are authorized orbital berthing space and a tow down to the main shipyards planetside. Conditionally, that is. As you know, the final contract on Astralon with the Seeker proved to be worthless as all mem is now valueless across the entire galactic community. What we took from that world was… is… worthless regarding payment. Our company lawyer…"

Uh-oh. I thought we had *lawyers*. Plural. More on that later.

"… she's forwarded an offer from a client, and it would remedy all of these problems including repairing and reclaiming decks sixteen and twenty-three."

Silence. The regeneration computers and medical diagnostic machines thumped and tapped silently in the silence of the rehab bay as we sat there. Our readouts on display for each other if anyone was interested in anyone else besides their own misery.

The captain gave a dry croak as he sucked at the last of his probably stale pine-nut-flavored slurry. The croak was inaudible but the look on his face, sick indigestion as usual, and the tired wave of his scarred hand, made the intention to hear it out clear to the rest of us.

Go ahead. Tell me the bad news, he seemed to say with no words at all.

The XO cleared his throat and proceeded once again.

"Our potential client has authorized currently acceptable funds for the total refit and repair of not just the *Spider*, but the company. This includes a brand-new jump drive Hardrock has in storage for us. Munitions, gear, and there are several ships moving toward our location with potential recruits. Furthermore, the client has offered us a contract once the two-month refit is complete, if we accept the terms."

Well, I thought to myself and sucked on my pretend nillabanana protein slurry… *who says miracles don't happen.*

Now, if M.O.M. had coffee-flavored regen slurry, life would be pretty downright amazing to this here beaten platoon sergeant. But the abacus says I am alive after another bad contract, and I have asked the universe for too many favors already.

"Who's the client?" croaked the captain, staring at his empty slurry cup. I was on pins and needles. Emotionally. But in real time I too looked like warmed-over death with my gray pallor and shaved head. Plus, I got a graze on Astralon and it savaged my Grim Reaper Astronaut tattoo. I was pretty chapped about the scar.

The first sergeant stepped forward.

"It's the Seeker, sir. She's the leader of the Insurrectionists and it looks like she's pretty close to winning this war against them Monarchs if the Simia don't finish everyone off first. Putting aside the wrong she did us on Astralon, sir, this could change the fortunes of the company. Radically. And I do not use that term often, sir. But… wrong is wrong and she did do us wrong, sir. We were promised mem and her plan invalidated all known galactic mem. She used us to make that happen. Bad faith contract, sir. John Strange was clear on payback for such clients. Company honor and all. So, there's that to consider. But there's also no other option available as we make approach to orbit at this time, sir."

So, there is… that. To consider.

CHAPTER TWO

Most of Strange were thawed two weeks prior to orbital insertion and hard dock with the orbital yard.

Hauser was still in deep storage down in supplies and shops. Injuries to his onboard hydraulics, internal armor, and even the operating mainframe had been so critical that putting him in cybernetic preserving gel had been the only hope of arresting some of the more corrosive combat damage in hopes that we could get him to a repair facility that specialized in cyborgs. Combat cyborgs, in fact.

Working on combat cyborgs was highly illegal twenty-five years ago when the Monarchs decided solely the difference between what was right, and wrong, and their cut of the action.

Still, there had been ways, even then, to get them repaired when they were badly damaged. Now I was down in the *Spider's* stores sections to greet the cybernetic repair facility shuttle and its MechMed drones who would be attempting to repair Hauser.

No small feat.

Dangerous for reasons I'll explain. Everyone else in the Strange was in the gym or trying to get through the shattered comm and news networks to see how much of their family, friends, and active warrants were still a concern in the post-Monarch age we were finding ourselves currently in.

"My systems indicate it has been twenty-five years, seven months, sixteen days since I was put into hibernation mode, Sergeant Orion," noted my friend the cyborg as they got him prepped for surgery. "I am currently experiencing trouble connecting with the other networks to determine the current status of the conflict, and the galaxy in general."

I couldn't tell if he was worried, or worried in his own combat cyborg Hauser way. Which technically, was impossible.

Or... did he just look so jacked-up and shot to hell despite the steps we'd taken two decades ago to salvage and save what we could of him in the aftermath of the battle at the hijacked LZ on Crash, that he seemed to convey worry? Much of his synthetic flesh was ragged and torn to pieces. Massive missing sections of the internal armor housing revealed the bullet-ravaged systems beneath. Half of his face was missing, and I was glad for my friend that he was not technically human, though he was the most human individual I had ever met, because had he actually been... he would have been in a lot of pain.

Hands down, he is the most human being I have ever encountered.

I was glad he wasn't suffering like a human would with those wounds. Still, I was feeling something and that bothered me. Made me weepy even though I don't cry. I just felt it as he looked worried. I felt worn and thin. Like some protein paste you'd spread on something you ate and didn't have enough of to go around.

Just thin and too little of what I thought I should be when I looked in the mirror and tried to be a better person, or maybe... some days, the NCO my guys deserved.

"Just Orion, Hauser," I reminded my friend. "Remember, friends use each other's names, Hause. Not rank."

His good eye shuddered visibly, something that had often been undetectable in the past. I watched the tiny damaged camera inside his iris open and close in slow motion as he tried to swallow.

If he's worried about the galaxy and what state it's in... it's because he's worried about us.

My friend was messed up and I wanted to cry. I couldn't and that had me choking as I tried to talk. Pretending my throat was just dry or something. Making it seem like the air processors down here needed replacing. Some part of me tried to just callously damage control and remind weak me that Hauser was just a machine. A combat machine. A tool we used to survive.

I told that part of me to shut up or I'd drink it to death.

"I understand, Sergeant Orion," said Hauser in that emotionless way he says things so earnestly. "But as I have told you before, Sergeant, for combat cyborgs such as this one it is... important... I have explained that before... protocols... I cannot erase. Though there has been extensive damage to my short-term memory banks. But... I remember... the important things, Sergeant... Orion. You are my friend, Sergeant. I remember other things... too... Sergeant Orion."

The MechMed ship was coming into the hangar now. Landing jets flaring. It was industrial yet still high-tech, and something about it told me help was here. I felt better but I wanted them to hurry. I'd felt anxious and omega doom all morning about turning him over to the MechMed team. Now as I watched the sleek shuttle settle onto its landing gears on the deck of the dark and ancient warship, I felt some bright spark that the universe was offering me E-Z credit at twenty-five percent. I told the universe I'd take it. I'd pay whatever. I just needed Hauser a little longer.

I don't pray, but I told whoever that I wasn't enough. I needed a little help. If there was any… I'd try to be better than I was yesterday. Or if they wanted someone dead… well, I could do that too.

The MechMed team knew what they were doing, I reminded myself. I didn't want my friend in the hands of people, machines, who were untrained. Who might hurt him. And because of his onboard micro-fusion reactor… well, if he accidentally detonated, he could hurt a lot of people, so there was that too.

I turned away from Hauser just before they came for him because my damn eyes were starting to leak even though I told them I would gouge them out if they didn't stop. This could be the last time we ever talked, and somehow, I felt like I'd failed at some mission I'd set myself regarding comforting him. Comforting the machine that was my best friend.

Don't pity me. I don't care.

I told the universe I needed just a little more time, and then I'd pay whatever asked. I was good for it. One beat-to-hell NCO. Not in good condition. Down on his luck. Various gunshot scars and other tattoos. All offers accepted.

"Like what, Hauser?" I tried to say but choked and strangled on my friend's name.

Dammit, Orion. Lock it down!

Hauser was silent for a moment. I almost thought maybe he hadn't followed the conversation. Where we were at. About him remembering the things that were important.

His mainframe was resetting at random intervals as it tried to save various partitions.

He'd been doing that lately.

He'd remembered my name. So, I was important to him.

Then he spoke. Chief Biggs was nearby as technically he was signed for the cyborg as company equipment. He was smoking one of his big fat half stogies as the MechMed drones came ambling out on their bright and shining spider legs. Chittering in Numerica to one another. Scanning lasers sweeping the darkness and vent gases that are always here on these decks. Humanoid mech torsos to make interface with biologics easier. They all had vaguely insectile appearances.

"I…" began Hauser and swallowed thickly again. A human thing the designers had needed to install for performance and operation among the still vaguely human Ultra Marines. "I remember… the desert foxes from… Astralon, Orion. The little family… of animals… you explained that humans… and their families… to me, Sergeant… Orion. You helped me… to understand… what you are. Humans." Then there was a long pause. "Everyone make… it… off-world… Sergeant Orion? I detect we are in orbit… over a world now. My sensors… interfacing with the Hardrock… docking signal. So… I assume we are… there now."

"Just Orion, Hauser."

The MechMed drones took the cargo sled we were using for a stretcher and began to move Hauser toward the softly glowing cargo deck of their shuttle. I went because I was holding his hand. His good one. The other had melted to slag. He'd reached into a burning vehicle at the firefight on the LZ to pull out one of the scouts who'd overturned a technical he'd commandeered to reach the LZ in time to make the dustoff. The vehicle was on fire. Hauser got him out.

Wolfy made it.

We were almost to the cargo deck of the repair shuttle. They would rendezvous with the surgery and repair satellite where it would take three days to restore the combat cyborg to operational status. No, I told myself... *to save his life.* They use an orbital satellite just in case he detonates during surgery. Apparently that's an issue with combat cyborgs that have hacked their own doomsday clock to escape the Monarchs' slave collar.

It's the only way they can do it.

Hauser's was set at fifty-eight seconds left of runtime. Fifty-eight seconds of life remaining in case he ever decided to self-detonate.

As I have said before, Hauser lives his entire life, what he still calls *runtime*, with just less than a minute to live.

I think that's what makes him better than the rest of us.

Makes him soak the most out of every moment of life like studying desert foxes in the night or risking himself to rescue the closest thing he has to a family. The Strange Company.

I think living that close to death, *end of runtime*, makes him different than normal humans. And in that way... he is not human.

We humans don't go through life with a clock set to the last seconds of our life. We don't have that gift. I wish we did. I wish we were aware of the score at all times. Aware of our imminent death and letting that color every action, response, and word.

We'd be different. Better maybe.

If we did, I bet we'd make different choices. Forgive more. Fight less. Watch desert foxes in the night.

That, not the killing-machine cyborg's abilities, that's what makes him superior to us.

These are the things I believe. Your mileage may vary. But I have decided, and you've heard it before from my lips… It's best to be honest about these things. So I am.

"Why are you crying now, Sergeant Orion?" asked my friend as we approached the MechMed shuttle.

The drones were indicating they had to board their patient now and I could not come because it was a clean ship. All was in order. I was unclean for their robotic ways.

I understand, MechMeds, more than you know. More… than you know.

The chief MechMed doc stepped between me and its surgery team. I tried to say something, but my voice caught in my throat, and I could not say one word. I was just choking. Strangled.

"You are… worried, Sergeant," stated Hauser flatly. "That my repairs… might not… go… well. That my doomsday… clock… may activate in the process of repair and augmentation… Sergeant. In which case… they will eject me from the satellite and activate hardened defensive… measures… to save themselves. You are worried about that… Orion… my friend. Sergeant."

I nodded and squeezed his hand tighter because that was all I could do. His synthetic-flesh-covered metal hand… I squeezed it to let him know he was real. That it wasn't just runtime, that it was his life. That we were his family. That he had one, just like those foxes he'd watched in the morning dark, as we'd fled for our lives across a world full of deserts and secrets.

What remained of his heavily damaged hydraulics squeezed back.

Then he was gone, and I stood there watching the shuttle take my friend away.

Shaking. Sobbing. Begging the universe for E-Z credit.

CHAPTER THREE

"Warhammer just lost dey core. Abandon ships order given," muttered Stinkeye in the red-lit darkness of the *Spider*'s heavy equipment cargo deck. "Battle jes startin' and thas four hundred dead jes like dat. All dead. All gon' die. Bad day, says Stinkeye. Bad day comin' like a storm fo' sho.'"

Nearby, four hulking mechs, grav-locked and strapped in tight to the deck, shuddered and groaned as our ship made the approach to Saffron City on Daystar, our target world for the next contract. Six weeks ago, we'd jumped from Hardrock to join the Seeker's Insurrection Coalition Armada in the final assault on one of the few remaining Monarch-controlled worlds. For some reason, this was a big move against our former galactic masters.

We'd taken a deal with the devil, one more time. Even if that devil was a six-foot-tall supermodel Monarch who'd double-crossed us before and run off with one of our secret weapons. The Little Girl. The Wild Thing.

The *Spider*'s shields were taking a pounding as the XO and M.O.M. flew the atmospheric approach to our primary LZ on the outskirts of Saffron City. Threading the Monarch naval ships and orbital fighters still in the battle as more and more Coalition ships jumped in-system and started shooting their way toward their LZs.

This was a big op. A big battle. And we were in it and just hoping to get planetside before we got killed.

A massive energy shot from an enemy ship somewhere out there in the dark lit up our defensive shields, penetrated armor, and savaged some of the decks just above our heads. Punch threw up down the way from me, shouting through his heaving, "Don't judge me! I always get tense just sittin' here waitin' to get killed. Be fine when I get to shoot back at someone."

Nearby, my sociopath medic smiled at me in the darkness of the assault racks as if saying, *We havin' fun now, Sergeant Orion.*

I smiled sickly at Choker. It's best to keep things friendly with him. He's dangerous and he creeps me out and there are many things I'm afraid of... and he's one of them for reasons I don't quite know why. But hey, there it is. Choker disturbs me. And his smile in the middle of ship-to-ship engagement trying to run a Monarch blockade with beam combat lighting up near-space... ain't helping.

M.O.M. announced the internal damage over the ship's comm.

"That ain't helpin' matters either," muttered Punch as the litany of damaged and off-lined systems was read off by the ship's AI. When she got to the part about decks four and five venting into open space, Punch dry-heaved like a sick dog that didn't have any more to give.

It was sad.

He swore he would kill anyone who laughed.

No one laughed. Whether this was because they knew Punch would beat them senseless when he got the first chance or getting vented into open space was everyone's worst nightmare, was hard to say.

Orbital battles, with nothing to do but sit and wait to get vented, are an infantryman's worst moments. Nothing you can do right now but die on the way into a hot LZ.

There were magazine hits and reactor cascades. Central spine explosions were quick. If you had to get it on the way to the LZ that was really the way to go.

Meanwhile we were also holed in fire control for the big main gun. So, in theory, XO would be operating the *Spider*'s main ship-to-ship defensive cannon on best-guess scenarios if he needed to fire it. Thankfully, this was a combat assault from orbit. Not ship-to-ship warfare other than as we ran the blockade, they got to shoot at us. All the *Spider* had to do was get us down to the surface, drop Strange and our new heavy mech friends, Apocalypse Outsource PMC Incorporated, then dust off for orbit and get clear of the fight on the ground.

It was the *getting to the LZ* part that was about to prove real tricky for all of us.

And then there was Stinkeye. Our drunken war wizard wasn't helping matters with his play-by-play of six million ways to die in orbit, courtesy of his mysterious witchy-powers ability to sense what was going on out there in the orbital battle. It's one thing to sit in the dark, strapped in right to the assault racks, overloaded with all the gear you can carry for the biggest battle you're probably ever going to die in, threading a Monarch blockade anchored by the last Battle Spire they've got to play with and complemented by a dozen heavily armored missile frigates, C-beam destroyers, and mercenary cruisers willing to throw in with the losers in what looked to be a last stand for all involved, having no clue what's going on just beyond the hull. It's a whole other thing to know it all as your space wizard reaches out into the void and watches it all in his mind's eye. Then cackles and crows as he narrates the violent destruction and horrible death going on out there like a bitter drunk at the end of the bar ten minutes to closing time. Spewing flammable-grade breath in every direction as he pulls at his totem flask between the horrors he's watching.

It goes like this...

"*Red Dragon*... she gonna take a shot on *Gnashing Teeth* now... Her commander orderin' all reserve power from reactors six through nineteen... chargin' now. Stand by to fire... Overseer. That's how desperate this one is, childrens. They usin' dem D-beams in orbit just to take shots at chimp ships which is everywhere and swarming the ring hull... Firing..."

A D-beam can clean multiple ships off the board in one shot. Six gigawatts of directed energy well beyond the thermonuclear range laughs at your puny shields. In fact, it plain old *snorts* at armored hull plating and then just boils everyone inside the struck vessel's hull as it melts straight through armor and decking and goes right on out the other side of the hull and into any phalanx ships riding close escort.

Or so I've heard. I'm just a ground pounder. But ships are my thing. Did I ever tell you I tried to become a scout? Quit the company and just go out into the big deep dark looking for a stake world to claim.

But then... I'd have to give up all the glamour of mercenary infantry. So...

"They hit!" shouted Stinkeye in the darkness like some acid jazz singer in the last bar you'll find yourself in, reciting spoken word poetry as the rest of the band hovers over the bass line and waits for the big crescendo to destroy themselves on.

Stinkeye wails in pain like he's boiling alive inside the hull with the dying, then hits his dented flask giving a half-hearted war whoop.

Strange Company's lucky charm. Stinkeye's never-empty magic flask. If it's ever empty… then we're all dead. Or so the religion we call company beliefs, superstitions, and SOP says it must be.

"Five tousand plus monkeez dead on that one, childrens. It's horrible to listen to. Make ya go mad like ya seen the galaxy's Heart o' Darkness. You never mind not ever knowin' that and be lucky I only tells you what I sees. You'd never sleep again if ya heard."

Then he continues with his play-by-play of the battle, seeing what we cannot see with his strange Monarch Dark Labs–bestowed magic powers, the space war wizard act in full display for the company strapped into the racks and waiting to die as the hull collapses and we're all boiled alive and venting at the same time. Except it's no act at all.

He's really who he is, whatever that is.

We are all just helpless rubes in his carnie tent, and he can tell us whatever he wants… and we'll believe.

There is only fear and uncertainty in the dark of the assault racks on the way to a bad LZ. And this is how messed up this all is… what I do for what I call a living. The heaving of Punch… it comforts me. His threats to murder anyone who laughs… it reminds me in the red-lit dark… that we're all alive.

What did the Falmorian party girl say…? I can't remember even though my lips are mumbling the words she wrote. Over and over.

The ship jumps hard and shudders across the hull plates. Decks groan. Are we hit?

Someone mutters, "We hittin' atmo. Hang on, it's about to get real rough."

But we all know that. Or at least most of us. Maybe not the New Guys or the Kids. But I've been here before.

If war is a drug… I'm done with it.

My stomach feels like acid, and I could use a smoke. I pull my smart canteen and drain some hot coffee. At least there's that.

We have many new members in the Strange since the battle on Astralon, Crash, call it what you will. It no longer exists on the stellar maps, so it doesn't matter anymore to anyone, know what I mean?

It's amazing how data can make a difference.

I remind myself that the data can lie, and that the planet is still out there, ruined and irradiated, but it's still out there regardless of what the maps and the Monarchs say.

Some things are just true regardless of D-beam strikes in the six-gigawatt range.

But the Monarchs made sure to erase Crash, Astralon, even as they themselves got erased by the Seeker's doomsday economic algorithmic weapon. And then, as Punch says, got *mollywhomped* by the Simia and the Insurrection Coalition who've decided a common enemy makes for some kind of alliance.

That's the team we're playing for today.

Insurrectionists. She's their leader. The Seeker.

Things have been real bad for the Monarchs since we dove out of the last gig, riding coffin sleep for twenty-five years on the long dark haul out to Hardrock in hopes of another contract and maybe even a jump engine on credit.

They used to rule human-controlled space. The Monarchs. Which, at the time of the release of the economic algorithmic weapon into the Monarch bank ship for upload and integration into the galactic memetic economy, consisted of roughly one hundred and fifty colonized, to varying degrees, worlds, and untouchable Earth.

Their Earth. The Monarchs' homeworld.

A *no-go* zone for the rest of humanity one-point-oh. That's us. The ancestors.

Then the Seeker's doomsday algorithm released, which destroyed the galactic economy within a matter of weeks. Mem disappeared as blockchain collapsed by either deleting verified work or adding numbers to the hash that exceeded all known verified mem, thus making the standard, and might I add, premium at the time, currency worthless overnight, basically.

Now local currencies, to varying degrees, are the coin of the realm. And of course, the Monarchs being the Monarchs and in control of everything, began immediately looting everyone's currencies summarily, once they realized their own controlled mem was worthless.

Because even they, the Monarchs, know money makes the galaxy go round no matter how many superpowers you've given yourself. There's too little of you, too much of the rest of us.

Six Monarch Battle Spires deleted. More MIA out on the frontier. The last one here, fighting us.

Red Dragon.

Or, as Fartsack in Reaper Second Squad put it, *"Oh, we're all gonna die."*

Meanwhile, as the *Spider* crawled and Strange slept dreaming dreams, as if on cue, everyone started shooting at each other and when the shooting was over, the Monarchs had lost six Battle Spires and several worlds were now smoking piles of irradiated ruin. Warlord wastelands and all.

From what I can tell, scholars are calling this, what we woke up to on the other side of the twenty-five-year coffin crawl, the New Galactic Dark Age, or the beginning of it at least. But that was just the beginning. Two years into the collapse of the economy, the chimps invaded across the frontier.

The Simia. That's what they are officially known as.

We call 'em chimps.

Turns out the Monarchs were hiding the fact that the chimps had been eating ships out beyond the frontier for years. Scouts and warships going five years beyond the borders and never returning. Our overlords the Monarchs made sure the galaxy didn't know that savage barbarians, the Simia, had a massive empire out there no one knew about, and it wasn't pretty. The chimps tore through the frontier and made straight for the Bright Worlds that ran the Monarch Empire and protected Earth. The Monarchs bled Battle Spires and Ultra Marine regiments just to keep the chimps back until the Battle for Hella, the industrial powerhouse of the Bright Worlds.

Or… it *was* the industrial powerhouse.

There are three downed Battle Spires scattered across the surface of Hella now and from what I hear, the chimps stacked Ultra battle helmets like barbarian trophies in front of their camps and burned-out battle hulks.

The chimps stacked Ultras.

That's a very hard thing for anyone to wrap their heads around.

Yeah, a D-beam strike from orbit might burn through a formation of destroyers, but the Simia have ships to spare. Thousands of battle hulks and millions of soldiers. Their ships ain't built great. But they're built a lot.

And oh yeah, they're our allies now. The Insurrectionists and the chimps have common cause to put the Monarchs in the ground and then settle up afterward.

The Strange has decided that the worlds may change, but war never does. And where there is war, there is pay. And that's what we do.

But more about that later. The wind of the world we were about to fight for was now whistling across the hull. Shrieking like a murdered banshee.

It was almost time to get it on.

CHAPTER FOUR

We were entering outer atmosphere when we began to pick up heavy chop and incoming ship-to-ship battery fire from the Monarchs' picket line of shot-to-hell destroyers guarding the upper reaches of the planet's atmo. They were using the atmospheric layers up there to deflect energy weapons fire and scramble orbital missile tracking systems within the inherent electronic interference generated by any planetary body.

Defensively speaking... it was a great place to occupy when you were fighting a defense. There was something in the understanding of that which gave me something to hold on to as our ship began to shake and rattle all around us from the beating it was taking from PDC fire and atmospheric reentry. Nearby in the cargo hold we were using as assault decks, the mighty towering mechs groaned in their gravitic restraints. Still, I held on to the bright fact the Monarchs were fighting a defense.

In my lifetime up until now... that was unheard of.

"Dis be da biggest of all da space battles you all evah gonna fights in..." barked Stinkeye in the bath of the hellish emergency lighting as the rear shields took a hit and decided to collapse. One of the *Spider's* reactors switched over to reinforce energy distribution, ablating incoming damage, throwing us into total darkness for a few seconds. "Maybe da last space battle of all da space battles that evah be, or evah were, and evah will be for all time so says I, says Stinkeye. Da end-all be-all of 'em all!" he crowed and swigged gustily from his lucky flask like we were celebrating something in the darkness.

Later I'd realize this was big for the old space war wizard. He was getting his revenge on the ones who'd made him what he was. It was like a homecoming and a hanging for Stinkeye.

He wanted his revenge. A freak who could do a kind of magic. They, the Monarchs, had taken something from him a long time ago so they could give him a trick to use on their behalf and for their ends. But he blamed them nonetheless for what they'd stolen from him in the gifting of great powers. And also, he never took credit for the drunkenness, the gambling, or any of the other vices that marked the tragic trajectory of his life. It was as though his sins were theirs too, no matter how much he committed them all on his own. Or enjoyed the committing despite the suffering they tattooed his lined and weathered old catcher's-mitt face with.

I pushed all Stinkeye's tragedies away and ran through the battle plan that lay ahead of us on LZ Heartbreak. Or at least Reaper's end of things once we were on the ground and mixing it up with the Ultras entrenched there.

The Insurrection generals had tagged it LZ Heartbreak like they knew it was gonna be such, for someone. I looked around as the emergency lighting came back on and saw no generals down here in the assault racks.

"Forget those guys," I muttered.

Punch, all out of heave, looked at me for an explanation. But I didn't have one.

Like I said, we were fighting alongside the Simia this time, and considering my last experience with the chimps it was better to have them as allies than enemies. We'd be linking up with their commander on Heartbreak to commence the assault on the commercial district of Saffron City once the LZ was secure for follow-on troops shooting the gauntlet of the orbital blockade. Which all depended on us establishing an LZ planetside.

To me, studying the plans and detailed holographic maps in the leadup to this operation, it felt like the last bid for the Monarchs before we marched on Earth and either took it back for humanity or burned it to the ground in some final act of rebellion against whoever we once were.

Like cutting off a sovereign's head.

No one had asked if we could recover from that. What the *after* of that moment would look like. Except I did. I'd asked. Smoking and drinking coffee in the quiet, darker parts of the *Spider* where I could avoid being an NCO for a few hours during the night watch. So far, I didn't like any of the answers I'd come up with.

You cut the head off the leader... then someone's got to be in charge. And I'd be lying if that didn't bother me.

The Monarchs held no cards other than their homeworld and a few others like Daystar now. Twenty-five years and the Simia had ruined them from the frontier to the Bright Worlds. Even now, saying that to myself, what the score really was, it was unreal that things had played out as they had. Hard to believe so much had changed. I'd lived my whole life, and so had everyone else for that matter, under total Monarch domination. Now all that was over forever if we stuck it to them good and hard on this one. And after that... the future was uncertain.

And that was... *scary*... if you thought too much about it.

Real freedom… real freedom scares the hell out of ordinary people. Real freedom is dangerous and uncertain. Ask any soldier on final leave before termination of service or contract. You party on that world you find yourself free on in the first days after you walk away from your unit. Drink yourself silly, get a party girl, Falmorian because you deserve it at least once in your life. Then you sleep late, wander the local beaches, and try to figure out what the shape of the universe is going forward. Maybe you even go out to the starport in the quiet afternoons, wander the hangars and bars. Try to figure out if you can scout and get off-world. If you can go out there and find something worth bringing back.

But you don't.

In the end you call the company and tell 'em you're back in for one more gig, one more reenlistment. One last time and that's a promise this time. Things will be different next time you find yourself free again. You'll have your act together then.

The first sergeant doesn't even put anyone in your slot… because they know. They know you'll be back. You just needed to figure something out. And you did. And now you're signing the e-contract again.

You always laugh a little when you sign it. You laugh when you realize they knew. Knew you'd be back.

It's safer this way for just a little while more. One more firefight and you can quit the action. But as Punch says… *Action's the juice, boss. Action's the juice.*

Getting shot at. It gets intoxicating in a way that tells you you're sick. Except it don't feel that way. Feels like the truest moment you'll ever come across and don't be surprised if you don't start looking for it wherever you can find it. Gives you a good solid look inside yourself every now and then.

"Entering atmo now," announced the XO over comm as the ship rocked and the point defense cannons erupted in *BRAAAPPPPPING* burps to knock out the incoming missiles trying to punch our armor and blow us out of the sky. Fun times, Strange Company. Sit tight. *Get it on* approaches.

Our second-in-command's voice echoes over the assault bays and across the vast internal dark spaces within our stellar home, the battle-rattled old destroyer. Reverberating off the hulking mechs waiting in the darkness above us. Within the canopies of those death machines, I can see the armor crews running through their pre-combat checklists as the cockpit lights appear almost bright and even cozy. GAU gun checks and missile pack loads.

They do bring the fun toys.

And that comforts me.

"Bet they're warm in there," says someone, one of the new guys nearby in the racks. His teeth are chattering. The assault decks have always had a problem keeping troops warm in upper atmo. Main drive is off and so it's colder here now. He's one of the guys we enlisted on Hardrock. Now he's watching me. Watching what his sergeant is watching. Trying to be hard like me when really I'm too old to be anything but scared to death. The mech crews getting ready to *get it on* in their own massive retaliation way. Armor crews acting nonchalant, even devil-may-care, like the horse cav officers of old times long before the jumps between worlds.

Shadows of something romantic about war.

It's all part of the game. I've seen mechs get hit hard and burn their crews alive while onboard ordnance cooks off like every world's Colony Day celebration. I've ridden support gun on a mech. Once. Hard pass. I like being light infantry. In the mech you're doing all that just to keep your hands from shaking because everybody on board—pilot-commander, loader, main gunner, and the two support gunners—knows you're about to be the biggest target on the battlefield when the shooting really gets going. Once those forty-ton things enter the battlespace everyone starts shooting at them with everything they've got. Every commander prioritizes fire on them for termination. A mech appears... and it's basically Final Protective Fires for the enemy. Everything anyone's got outgoing right now. Mechs either get ruined fast, or they start to run amok and then it's game over for the losers. Violently so, what with the GAU cannons, missile packs, heavy gun systems, and... stomping.

Those guys on board right now, they know it's about to get hot.

We, us grunts, we think everyone else has it easier because we're about to go out and catch fire. But there ain't nothin' easy about driving a mech into combat. Everyone sees you comin' and pulls out their anti-tank weapons because why not start shooting what you got at the thing that's coming for you, real fast, and rocking a one-forty main gun, missile packs no doubt, two rapid-fire thirty-millimeter recoilless rifle systems, two fifty-cals, and who knows what else someone's tacked on just for giggles.

Meanwhile your LT, or whoever's commanding your little ground force, is on the horn yelling for air support calling in a target, or division artillery for that matter, screaming for everything they've got to drop on their command right now.

Yeah, I see 'em up there, the armor guys with Apocalypse whatever, in their mech cockpits, and I know it ain't gonna be no picnic for them either today out there on the LZ. But hey, this one ain't gonna be a picnic for anyone. Certainly not Strange Company and especially Reaper, the guys providing infantry support for the four big walkers.

Us.

We get to bodyguard, exposed with no benefit of armor around us, protecting the dudes in the forty-ton walkers everyone's about to start shooting at the moment they make their appearance.

Yippeee, saddle up, Space Cowboy. Knew I shoulda walked away from this one back on Hardrock. But there were no ships taking on crew and no scouts heading out into the great unknown. And the company was low on NCOs.

So…

My brothers were going anyway. Sometimes you end up in a bar fight just because your friend likes to run his mouth. You can't always pick the fights, but you can do your best to finish 'em.

I return to my meditations upon actions on the LZ.

Once we're down on the LZ, a "cleared space" as they call it, where an Insurrection-crewed Mauler laid down some low-powered D-beam wattage from orbit to create a landing zone, the company will set up a perimeter with Reaper taking the twelve position. Biggs as the loadmaster will get the mechs off the *Spider* and then we'll link up with them and head into the city to start clearing a path to our objective. We move two clicks in and link up with the Simia if we can get off the X.

In the briefing it all seemed really easy. Like it always does. I've been around long enough to know that plan is already dead. They always are. My job is just to keep Reaper alive, adapt to the situation, and overcome, once a new plan happens. Get ready to implement whatever the Old Man has to get done. Kill everyone who dares oppose us.

I expect the same out of the enemy. I would do the same in their position. It's best to be honest about these things. That way there are no hard feelings.

But the gravitas of the Old Man's smoke-stained voice, and the look he gave me as he traced our line of advance, told me it was gonna be anything but easy today. He never deceived you about that the way other leaders did. He gave it to you straight in the face, in his grim yet quiet way.

But there was something about this one, the way he looked at you as he told you how awful it was gonna be in there, that told you it was gonna be a *real* rough ride, and if we didn't see each other again, well… he was sorry about that.

And the way he did that… that made you feel *respected*. Like you wanted to actually be the guy he thought you were. So you were gonna go down there with him, outnumbered, heartbreaker and lifetaker Ultra Marines all set up to get their kill on, and you were gonna try to score.

If just to be who the Old Man thought you might be.

So. What are we facing on the ground?

One Ultra Marine division that's been fighting since the Insurrection/Simia coalition force attacked this world six months ago. They've been doing a great job if the casualty counts are anything to go by.

Our side has taken the jungle surrounding Saffron City, a place of monuments and High Monarch Culture, and there in the jungles, the Simia guerrillas, they rule of late. Their guerrilla forces and mobile artillery have been tormenting the Ultras and working the edges. Insurrection mercenary dropships and the hilltop artillery were able to shell the Monarchs' last city on this world with impunity, while putting in forces to attack the Monarchs' forces asymmetrically.

But down there all over LZ Heartbreak the Ultras are fighting for their lives… and their honor. They have stacked monkey dead like they don't care if they win or lose now. They're just going for their own high score now and not doing too bad a job of it.

Die in place and Let Die.

Who knows what the supply situation is for them. But they're Ultras. They're mean, spartan, and it's a war cult. This is like religion for them.

"Best guess, sir," Chief Cook had said during the intel brief before the *Spider's* jump to this world. Using his officious tactical briefing voice like he was a sane and competent staff officer instead of the craven drug-addled psychopath I'd come to know him as. I was still burnt he'd drugged my platoon back on Crash just to attack a terminal no one wanted all that bad.

Astralon.

Call it whatever you want, it doesn't exist anymore.

"Best guess, sir… is no guess," began Chief Cook during the brief. "Standard Monarch Battle Spire come supplied to operate forever. They plan for one hundred years in day-to-day combat operations. Those things carry enough supply and ordnance to kill everyone in human space twice over. Those Ultras, if I know 'em, and believe me I don't know 'em half as much as some, salvaged everything down to the spoons in the mess halls on board that monstrosity and they will turn everything into something they can kill us with. The only thing we got goin' for us right now is they started with three divisions of infantry and now they're down to one. Them damn chimps can fight, sir. My only worry at this moment is… did the Ultra generals manage to get the thermonuclear devices out of the ordnance vaults aboard the downed Spire before she went in. Those babies, they're the one toy the Monarchs won't let their guard dogs play with unless there is, according to Ultra SOP, at least one Monarch available to enter the doomsday codes for battle-field application on the objective. And if I know those bas-tards, taking a beating from the chimps like they currently are, hell, they'd jack a Monarch just to make sure they don't put up a loss on this one. It's personal for them now. Point of honor and all. I respect them for that, sir. I'd do the same, sir. In other words, this ain't gonna be no easy day dislodg-ing them, sir. But hell… when has killing Ultras ever been easy. Not that I'd know. Nothing was ever proven and that operation never happened. Officially."

So, we got that goin' for us.

Now, as I look across the dark assault bay and the next row of racks where more of Reaper is waiting for the *down and clear* signal from Chief Biggs, I shuffle my cards and study my hand, trying to put plan and enemy together and meet the needs of Reaper surviving. All of Reaper.

I find our ex-Ultra there among my own squads. The one Hauser and I rescued on the LZ out in the desert in the Crash Waystes. His eyes reveal nothing in the emergen-cy lighting. His face is blank. Whereas the rest of Reaper from Choker to Punch are going through their own per-sonal pre-battle rituals. Reciting their prayers to gods they didn't believe in. Bargaining for a chance to at least survive what was gonna be the hottest of LZs ever. Promising death. Leaving last messages. Checking in with me to make sure the story they'd told me was in the record all good and proper in case anything should happen. Heaving. Smiling in the case of that psychopath Choker. They are all good now with whatever comes next. Or at least as good as you can be in the moments before you and death are gonna meet again to see who gets closest to twenty-one in the game of Cheks that battle truly is.

I watch the ex-Ultra down there in the racks where the rest of First waits to *get it on*. Wondering if I can truly count on him. His Ultra tag was Ulysses Two Alpha Six. Apparently, that's how Ultras get tagged during training. Like a model type... Ulysses. And the alphanumeric identifier. When he told us that, during the interrogation after the events on Crash, I saw the Old Man raise his eyes at the tag. A look of surprise, subtle for him, washing across his blown-out blue eyes. Betraying nothing in the tanned and lined face that's like a statue carved from some rock that ain't easy to carve. The Old Man nodded once to himself at hearing the rescued Ultra's tag and said nothing.

I had no idea what any of that meant. I asked the first sergeant about it, and Top just said, "It's cult, Sergeant Orion. Just like everything else in the universe. Don't know what *Ulysses* means but the CO did and... hell, I don't wanna know something. I'm just an old man, Sar'nt Orion. I don't know how much more of this I got it in me to do. But this one feels bad anyway. Real bad. Take care on this one, Orion. Take real good care. I've always liked you and you should probably take my job. Except you ain't got it in you because you care too much. And what I do... sometimes it's got nothin' to do with caring. It's just got to get done. That's all there is to it."

I passed on from the former Ultra, studying the rest of Reaper. Approach engines were throbbing through the decks of the old destroyer. We were slowing to make the LZ after the fast approach to the objective. I scanned my troops, letting the mystery of the ex-Ultra go. For now.

I saw Hauser. He was looking around at his squad. Assessing their gear, scanning the darkness. Even Hauser was more human than the Ultra who'd become a member of the company.

"Two minutes to insertion," announced M.O.M. over the assault bays. "Stand by to egress this vehicle safely."

Once we did... everyone would be shooting at everyone. So the *safely* part was funny. To me. Except I couldn't laugh at it. Might start heaving.

Beyond the hull, enemy fighters streaked in on gun runs, shooting up our heavily armored hull where they could avoid outgoing defensive fire from the PDCs. Rounds *tap-tap-tapped* along the distant upper decks, seeking to do something and instead doing nothing.

The *Spider* was built to stand up to enemy fire. Lots of it.

I patted the assault rack over my chest and whispered, "Hang in there baby."

Because... you never know. *You just never know.* This ship had gotten me out of a lot of bad situations and for all intents and purposes it was my home. But you never know. Twenty-five years since we last did battle might have produced a whole bunch of Monarch A7 Intimidator torpedo bombers with ship-killer SLMs.

Who knew what was going on out there? And if we trusted Stinkeye's insane mumblings then you might as well go to a neural witch to find out if you'll ever meet true love, or find any kind of happiness, or what numbers to pick for *La Lotteria*.

One of those ship-killer SLMs could punch armor and vent us right here and now. In the racks… nothing you could do about that but hope damage control sealed the breach or you were down low enough to the surface to get some air.

The XO came on one last time before the huge a-grav engines kicked in the *Spider's* reversers and began to howl as we lumbered in over the battle and crawled to approach-to-landing speed.

When we were slow, fat, and heavy. Ground-to-air fire's perfect opportunity to bag an old destroyer trying to make the LZ that Chief Cook and the pathfinders had set up hours ago.

"Thirty seconds to *down and clear*, Strange Company. LZ is absolutely on fire as of this moment. Get it on, Strange."

Then we were in it. And there was no going back after that in ways I never imagined when I woke up in the shipboard dark that morning from a dream of the Falmorian party girl holding me in the quiet of a long-ago better day. Whispering to me that, "There are no regrets, *estrangier.*"

CHAPTER FIVE

"Thirty seconds to the LZ and it's on fire!" shouted the XO over the ship's internal comm. The *Spider* was taking all kinds of incoming as we approached LZ Heartbreak in the last seconds to insertion. Ground fire was heavy over the outskirts of Saffron City where other Insurrection Coalition units were setting down for our "surprise invasion."

External cam feeds showed the chimp guerrillas... ha... that's funny... but it showed the Simia forces streaming out of the hot steaming jungles surrounding Saffron, making for the fractured city walls and blocky towers just now glimmering in the first of the dawn's light. The Simia were moving in cohorts, heavily armed and carrying all kinds of weapons from carbines to light machine guns to get their kill on against the Ultras entrenched throughout the arty-savaged city. Some of the Simia, the gorilla types, were even sporting what looked to be AT tubes and light mortars.

The *Spider*'s huge reversers howled into action, shuddering violently through the superstructure of the old war destroyer. That's when the rear cargo doors began to lower, flooding the assault decks with morning light, grit, and even golden-hued mist.

"Stay strapped!" shouted Punch in the role of assistant platoon leader. "Wait till the fat man gives us the order to move, Reaper. Then it's *get-it-on thirty*."

I gave Reaper one last look and wondered how many of them would make it through this one. None of them were dead yet. I was still an okay NCO. If they survived, I thought optimistically, then the next one and the one after that…

What's the old play say… how did some old hack writer put it…

Tomorrow, and tomorrow, and tomorrow,
Creeps in this petty pace from day to day
To the last syllable of recorded time,
And all our yesterdays have lighted fools
The way to dusty death. Out, out, brief candle!
Life's but a walking shadow, a poor player
That struts and frets his hour upon the stage
And then is heard no more: it is a tale
Told by an idiot, full of sound and fury.
Signifying nothing.

Trust me, I'm fun at parties.

Yeah. I look at First. Then Second. Then Third. That's my whole platoon. All of them. Those are my squads right now. And that's who we've got to get through another day that promises in no way shape or form… to be easy.

Fine.

I'm good with that. I just like to know the score. Then, I can play to win. Or lose less.

In First I've got Punch as the squad leader. I'm not taking a squad on this one because I've got a lot to do including interfacing with some multi-ton death machines soon to be stomping all around us and unloading hot death in mass dosage on our enemies and hopefully with none of us in the way.

Mass dosage... yes, well beyond the physician-recommended allowance. Helpful... yes. But it promises to be a whole new level of danger I haven't had the pleasure of in quite a while.

Most of our contracts of late have been as light infantry because, as it's been stated, the company has seen better days. We are not top shelf or even well. We are... you'll do. Even though we got topped off on a new hyperdrive, courtesy of an ex-Monarch and current supreme commander of the Insurrection Coalition, the Seeker, our gear is still the gear we've been humping for three contracts now, surplus from Biggs's never-ending stash of cheap and mostly reliable weapons hidden somewhere aboard the *Spider*.

There are gems among his arsenal. And there are some real dogs.

Each Reaper is kitted in an S16 light battle rifle, a plate carrier, TEC chest rig (tactical equipment carrier), CRUNCH combat helmet, ballistic pauldrons, or at least one. Combat tanto on the rig. Plus all the other knives all of us carry. Of course, you know about my karambit if you've read this far. The one that gutted my worst enemy back on Crash, and no, I sleep just fine about that knowing a nightmare is pushing irradiated daisies back on that ruined world. We each carry an assault ruck and all that can be stuffed into it because the *Spider* is dusting off for orbit. Ballistic shin and knee guards. Assault gloves. Gear can be personalized but because we got a lotta new hires not so much.

All the grenades of all the types you can carry and want to be responsible for.

Of course Choker, our medic, has begun to collect his own totems. A new and very weird thing for that psychopath, which is saying something. One time, for a week, he started talking with his pinky finger. As in, perfect ventriloquism and he made you think his pinky was doing all the talking. I PT'd him to death, which is hard because he don't smoke easy, when I found myself lighting up the pinky about something. So, his weird is pro compared to others in Strange. Now he's started making a voodoo necklace of strange objects that seem meaningless. They dangle around his scrawny neck, draped over his plate carrier between the straps of his chest rig. Like's he's joined the resident space-wizard-combat-vet-from-every-war-that's-ever-been   cult. With the one and only Stinkeye as their glorious leader even though he despises everyone and anyone and cheats at Cheks every chance he gets, still managing a loss eighty percent of the time.

Thankfully, your parsecs may vary, weird medic and even weirder space wizard are going in with First. They're left of me on the assault racks as the *Spider* settles toward the LZ. Trailing down the line from them are Tags, Goods, Itchy, Ulysses, or the Spartan. The Ultra. Then New Guys One, Two, and Three who simply are called such and respond to their numbers if they know what's good for them. They have not earned their tags yet. There's one Kid this time and I try not to care about him. Signed on in the last few hours before we pulled out of Hardrock. I haven't gotten to know him, and I realize that's a shortcoming on my part as a leader. But in my defense… I've known enough *Kids* who've ended up dead before we could officially get them blind drunk and reward them with the tag they'd gotten one way or another. And a bad tattoo.

I can only learn the names of so many dead Kids.

And of course, Stinkeye is attached to First because who knows what the hell we're going to face on the ground and he'll probably come in handy or cause enough mayhem to let us kill some OpFor. Fifty-fifty he ends up getting drunk and being utterly useless.

Still, he is a Voodoo warrant and the oldest surviving member of the company, so that affords him a certain amount of... as they say, *He gets to do whatever he wants.*

Before the insertion, Stinkeye simply walked up to me on the assault decks of the *Spider* and muttered raggedly, "Goin' wit ya, Little King. Dis one's gonna be bad and you probably gonna get killed."

That's some pro-level motivation, Chief. Thank you.

"Then why go with us, Stink?" I said nonchalantly because I would never ever call him by his rank or give him the respect due that position.

Nor would he expect me to. It is understood.

That would be just too weird for either of us.

Stink said nothing and just took a long gusty pull from his flask and walked off to find a last game of Cheks to get into before everyone got killed.

He will tell you that everyone gambles wildly, and badly, before a battle in hopes of not having to settle up on the other side.

"Most people survive, Little King. So dey gonna owes old Stink when they real surprised they make it. Thas how I retire. Thas my savings plan."

It's a smart plan. I'll give him that. Except, as I have observed, it's usually Stinkeye who's gambling wildly, and very badly. Like he knows he might not be around to settle up.

His dark prophecies never bothered me, though. He always said that stuff before every op. It woulda been weird if he hadn't.

Across the way in the opposite assault racks are Reaper's Second Squad. Jax, who'd been hit pretty bad back on Crash, Astralon, call it what you will it doesn't exist anymore as far as anyone's concerned. Jax is the primary EOD specialist for our platoon and gets the running of Second. I'd been given an extra EOD guy, Dusty from Dog because the Old Man, and especially the first sergeant, had both expected the need of such boom wizards. "Yer gonna have a lotta debris problems with them walkers, Sergeant Orion," lectured the first sergeant. "So you got two idiots who don't mind runnin' around in the middle of a firefight loaded with all kinds o' high-ex. Consider yourself unlucky. I envy their huge balls and reckless youth."

First would be acting as the assaulters with Third as support under Hauser. Second would be tasked with clearing obstacles for the walkers. And acting as assaulters when needed.

So we got that goin' for us.

Second was comprised of Jax carrying all the high-ex he could do with a bunch distributed throughout the rest of the squad. Hustle and Hoser were on the Pig as usual. My experience indicated that guys working with explosives to clear obstacles needed a lot of cover fire. And nothing did that better than the Pig as worked by those two pros.

Second was also carrying Wolfy on loan from Ghost's shooters acting in the SDM role as squad designated marksman. A good sniper was great cover. Again, I was thinking of the clearing and demo work they'd been doing out there under fire, staying in front of the walkers. The rest of Second was rounded out by Solo, Two Times, Rockstar, Fartsack, Foxy, and Klutz.

All of them including Klutz, thought his sergeant optimistically and ironically, were carrying enough explosives to crater several city blocks. Even now, as the rear hatches on the *Spider*'s assault decks slid open and the huge landing gears of the ancient destroyer cushioned the weight of our huge ship as we set down in the middle of a crossfire hurricane firefight on a new world, maybe giving a guy who'd been legitimately tagged Klutz enough explosives to vaporize all of us wasn't a great idea.

In my defense… *I had none.*

"Needs must, Sar'nt Orion," as the first sergeant had crowed and gone off laughing to himself.

At the end of the racks came Third, led by Hauser. They'd be following us out onto the LZ with orders to clear the dustoff area, identify a superior overwatch position, and start laying down suppressive on everyone they could until we got the walkers clear of the *Spider* and into action. Then we could start cutting a path to the *oh-be-jay, as they say.*

Third was probably the most rock solid of Reaper's squads. One… it had Hauser. An Eight Series combat-model cyborg. Game-changer in anyone's lineup. The rest were established killers who'd either come with experience in other militaries or had been poached out of Dog. Back on Astralon, Reaper had been savaged. Dog had taken heavy casualties but not as many deaths. Now Dog, under the leadership of Player, had a lot of new guys and I'd had high hopes that possibly the Amarcus death cult would have died like he did back in the burning ruins of Biggs's crawler. Instead, he was now revered as some sort of death god for Dog that had taken shape in various iconifying and disturbing ways. Basic was quoting his catchphrases like they were reciting holy writ. Pro was the Amarcus tattoo glaring at me from their shoulders and forearms somewhere among their ink-sleeved arms.

"Burn in hell," I'd whisper when I saw it there.

"What, Sar'nt Orion?" someone would ask in response.

"Burnin' Belle. Nice place on Dusk to get a drink. If we ever go there, I'll buy you one."

"Oh thanks, Sar'nt. That'd be straight!"

"Burn in hell, Amarcus," I'd mutter as I left the conversation.

"You bet. Can't wait, Sar'nt."

To be honest though… in the back of my mind all that death cult stuff didn't bode well for me eventually. I'd heard that not all of Dog were cool with how their death god died *not mysteriously*. Plus, I've written all of it down in the records here and I'll redact these parts until my company-noted death occurs, but some can override that given their data clearance level. I'd know if they did. So, when it happens, I'll be ready with an explanation. And a gun. Always with a gun. Just in case that's how they want to go. And the knife. But only because sometimes there's cake and I like cake.

Some in Dog already considered the circumstances very suspicious. Because they are. Or were. And of course, there was my known proximity to their glorious dead god when he got dead-ed. I wasn't about to tell them the circumstances weren't just downright shady, they were pitch black. But I had a feeling… an itch that something was coming my way whether I liked it or not.

So, the explanation.

The gun.

And the knife because maybe there was gonna be that cake.

And Punch. He'd figured it out and he just said, "That thing… I got ya covered."

What thing, I asked.

"Hannibal. I got it when it happens."

So… Sergeant Orion has that in his pocket. It's going to get messy someday, and hopefully not in the middle of a firefight, or on a bad LZ.

If only just for their sakes.

I'm cool with whatever regarding me.

Under Hauser, Third was good to go. I could count on them even if there might be one or two that wanted me dead. He had Runs and Slash to work with and so far, they'd soldiered on point. Both were shooters despite the fact that Runs earned that tag because he ran his mouth. Constantly. Slash. I had a bad feeling about him for no reason other than he didn't say much and over in Dog he'd earned the tag because whenever he got cut up on op, he never allowed it to be stitched up until he made an actual fire and poured the ash into the wound. Whether he did that to be hard, or it was some religion, I had no idea. But it gave me the creeps. Man, if I could come out on the winning end of a contract, I'd have all my scars and tats smoothed over in some high-end gene-editing facility. I was tired of looking merc ugly. You shoulda seen me when I first started out. Unblemished by gunshots and tattoos. I was good-looking. Or at least some girl I once thought I was gonna spend forever with thought so.

Slash also had a lot of knives. Which is saying something for this bunch.

Eights was also in Third over from Dog. Eights because he always played that card in Cheks. It was his power move and word had it Stinkeye was into Eights for a large amount of hard currency now that mem was useless.

Stinkeye had been muttering all week, "Man, I got a real bad, bad, feelin' Eights gonna die on Heartbreak. My voodoo be a' sensin' somethin'."

Eights just laughed.

Duster was the other guy from Dog who'd be acting as our backup EOD. He was tight and I'd worked with him before, and plus, he'd never much cared for Amarcus if I remembered correctly.

So… I could trust him?

Ha. No. I don't trust anyone. That's how you get to be an NCO. You believe everything that can and will go wrong, can and will.

The only thing you have to do is laugh on the inside when someone comes up with a plan of how things will go on the objective.

You know better. And you learn to know better by trusting no one and nothing.

We drew Mad Max as the squad's secondary gunner with Bad Bet as AG. They were Dog purists. I'd keep my eye on them. Then came Bender and Blender and there was talk of changing their tags because of the confusion. But there had been a million things to do before the insertion and I hadn't had the time. If someone's had to be changed then the one getting changed got to pick it. Company rules going back to John Strange, our mysterious and legendary founder. And spoiler… if you let some dude pick his tag it was gonna be a real big hassle. Ace. Killer. All the usual heartbreaker and lifetaker stuff. Like he was some spectacuthriller hero from back in the day that they don't make anymore because galactic civilization has up and collapsed while we were taking the long sleep.

Ain't no one got time for movies anymore. Especially the time or money to make 'em. If you haven't noticed, it's a fight for our very existence right now.

Once someone wins… maybe.

Priorities. Gotta have 'em. So says the Old Man. So it must be. I attend and know wisdom for I am but a lowly, broke, ruck-hump NCO with grand dreams of being left alone forever and never again having to deal with anyone else's problems ever again.

I have many of my own that are long overdue in their need for attending to.

Bonus round… I scored Yahtzee in the SDM slot on loan from Ghost. Then there is Nether and no one is much happy about that because he bothers them in that he doesn't actually exist as far as existence is concerned. But he is attached to us and not only is he actually someone I call a friend—Sergeant Orion, friend to the friendless—but he can do some crazy whack on your behalf when you are seriously pinned down and the enemy is talking about breaching and clearing your favorite fighting hidey-hole.

In this I consider myself lucky. To have him as a friend. And the fact that he can make things disappear from reality.

These are mine and even though some of them might actually be trying to kill me for a past and very legitimate wrong, I will do my best to keep them all alive today as best I can. And tomorrow. And for all the tomorrows that follow like the old hack says until some bullet finds my skull and I too push daisies on a foreign world.

Strangers to the universe.

Brothers to the end.

CHAPTER
SIX

The first to die was a kid we'd started calling Hotsoup. Mainly because he burned his tongue on some soup one time and it was so bad, he sounded like a baby for a week afterward whenever he tried to talk. If he said anything, someone inevitably began to laugh at his injured lisp. This was all as we trained up for the contract on this one. Then he'd invariably make the mistake of explaining why he'd suddenly started talking with a lisp. "Hoth thoop burnth my thung." In his defense, sometimes the *Spider's* food dispensers did that and made the food either too hot or, sometimes, too cold. Hotsoup couldn't help using the words *Hot Soup.* As in… *I burned myself drinking hot soup at the range we'd been training on that day.* But with a childish lisp. Everyone knew you needed to let soup from dispensers cool.

But when the kid said, "Hot Soup," with the burn on his tongue and all, it came out like *"Hoth Thoup."* And of course, that was even funnier to everyone involved.

So he got a lot of grief and we collectively decided he should be tagged Hotsoup.

When Punch, as we crawled forward through the apocalypse glass of the Mauler D-beam-cleared area of LZ Heartbreak, our fatigues and gear, and yeah, skin, getting cut to shreds, told me we just lost Hotsoup to an Ultra mortar strike, I barely heard him over the incoming and outgoing violence.

Machine-gun fire. Emplaced and light.

Rifles.

Grenades.

Someone was firing missiles at the *Spider* still on the ground and trying to get the mechs offloaded. The comm was alive with frantic chatter as squad leaders called in enemy positions and wounded already. Hunter-killer teams coming in on close-air gun runs against the Ultra bunkers all over the far buildings along the LZ they were shooting at us from turned the noise level and chaos up by orders the hearing pro couldn't block out.

Everything was loud and violent, and it made you feel small and targeted.

"Sarge…" said Punch, again trying to get through to me as I tried to get Reaper into some sort of organization on the LZ. Incoming from two Ultra positions on the west side of the devastated plaza firing at us drowned out whatever it was he had to say.

"What?" I shouted back at Punch, who was dumping fire from behind a torn chunk of street that had been up-ended by some previous explosion, then remelted by the recent LZ-clearing D-beam strike.

We had Ultras attacking our LZ because of course that's how surprise insertions are supposed to go.

"We just lost Hotsoup, Sarge. He rushed and landed over there…"

I looked *over there* and saw the drifting smoke of a recent mortar that had come in and landed right where Hotsoup had gone for cover. Which had been smart, considering everyone was shooting at us from multiple directions and getting cover was a good move. The debris had stopped raining by the time I'd looked over and saw what remained of Hotsoup.

"Mortar?" I practically mouthed at my assistant platoon leader over the blare of incoming heavy fire.

Punch nodded in business-like fashion, hunkered down, swapped in a new mag for his shorty, then shrugged and gave me a look, satisfied he was locked and loaded and ready to roll.

"That kinda day, Sarge," he shouted. "Know what I mean?" he mouthed as an incoming missile streaked across the battlefield and slammed into the *Spider*'s upper defensive shields, which exploded in a rage of white noise as the shot was deflected.

I did. I knew.

But what I didn't know was… his story. Hotsoup's. Other than the fact that one rainy afternoon on Hardrock, out in the barrens of that misty and inhospitable world no one should have ever built a shipyard on, he'd had the misfortune to drink some soup that was too hot and subsequently burned his tongue on it, marking him for what remained of his life with a ridiculous tag.

He got angry about it and that just encouraged everyone to use it even more. If I'd had more time, I would have had a quick walk and counseled him on how to get out of a bad tag. Let it go. Let them have fun. You'll either get used to it, or they'll forget it.

But I didn't. Once the company took the contract, it was twenties for weeks. I had six things to do all the time. I never took that walk and told him how to shuck a bad tag.

And so, we never let him live it down. That's how a tag is in the Strange. We veterans know that in the end, survive long enough and a guy will own a tag, no matter how whacked it is, and start calling it out when he's mag-dumping on some ambush.

"Hot soup, bastards! Come and get some."

If he'd survived, that totally would've happened. But he didn't live long enough to own it. And so, it didn't.

Sergeant Orion failed to…

Added to the list of things I'll feel bad about later if I survive this firefight and the next one. Until then… it has been noted.

We gave *Hotsoup* to him anyway, which was our way of saying he was one of us now. Forever. He just didn't see it that way yet. And now he was dead, and he was no longer my concern, except to make sure he got his burial and was noted in the company logs for all time. I had one last job as an NCO in the company. One last duty. And if I survived this battle, I'd see it got done. If not, Punch or whoever got Reaper, they could get it handled then.

Not my circus. Not my monkeys anymore.

Or at least that's what I tell myself when I think about the vacation from being an NCO that a violent death will eventually provide. Hey… it's enough to get to the next bonfire that needs to be put out, so don't judge me. Some days are just that way. It comforts me to put a little perspective on my responsibilities, and the relief that violent death by fast-moving lead or sudden explosion will provide.

It's best to be honest about these things. And so, I am. I may not be the best sergeant. But I'm the one you got.

I know this seems callous, but I'm not writing this all down, this account, just for you to think better of me. Remember, this is sliced out of the main logs because it involved the Seeker. This is about her, and what happened to us. And what was feeling more and more like a tragedy to me the more I thought about what the company had gotten itself involved in this time.

Hotsoup was the first to buy it at the Battle for Saffron City on LZ Heartbreak.

Strangers to the universe, brothers to the end.

Let your soup cool, kids, if you want a better tag.

CHAPTER SEVEN

It's readily apparent, even to a poor dumb tired ruck-hump NCO like me that things are not going... immediately... according to plan as far as the Insurrection's assault on one of the last Monarch strongholds is concerned.

How do I know this, having just crossed the line of departure?

Well gather around the supply cage and let ol' Sarge download an axiom that has got to be as old as Martian legionaries in the first Solar War. Here it is, kids.

No plan survives contact with the enemy.

None.

I know, officers want it to be different. Other officers I have worked with. The current warlord of the Strange, the Old Man, he's different. But yeah, officers are generally so in love with the special best-ever plan they made all by themselves, that they cannot conceive it will fall apart in seconds.

NCOs on the other hand... not their first rodeo. The question is... how long will it take for the plan to fall apart, come unglued, or just no longer be relevant to the situation, courtesy of bad intel or no intel, we find ourselves in?

Same stuff, different day.

A lot of young guys come lookin' to merc, or just join any of the local planetary militaries, thinking it's going to be exactly like the thrillers and games they watch and play.

Inside ultraball tip, boys: those shooter games and thrillers are all financed by the Monarchs' psyops divisions to recruit young men and women to get all excited about combat and then join and serve the cause, also known as the Current Thing. What's the cause? Keeping the Monarchs in power as humanity slowly expands outward.

That. Has. Always. Been. The Current Thing.

I got that from Chief Cook who worked for over a year, back when he was with Monarch Psyops, developing a "shoot-em-up," his words, called *Hero Warrior: Call of the Ultra Marines.*

"One of the best, and might I add here, weirdest years of my life, Sergeant Orion," Chief Cook once told me over cold beers in some jungle shack cantina back on Pthalo. "Far better than this forsaken flying snake-ridden hellhole we find ourselves in now. Boy oh boy, Orion, I'll tell you… working with the simp-betas all day telling them all these lies about war so they code for the glory of the Monarchs… it felt like I'd arrived at what I was truly born to be. A liar. But for a cause, know what I mean?"

I did not.

"That's what psyops really is: lying, Orion. But for the right, if not sometimes…" he made air quotes at this point, "*good*… reasons. You're a professional liar. But… a hero too."

"Are you?" I asked drily over the bottle I was nursing, hoping he hadn't slipped anything into it when I'd gone out back to piss in the spider-ridden pit they called the latrine.

"Droll, Orion. Very. That's why you're not Special Ops. You… don't understand… the game. And it's not your fault. You're just a simple grunt. We point, you break their stuff and kill. You have no idea what's at stake, regardless of whatever side you happen to find yourself on one dark and stormy op. It's not about them. It's about you when you're us. And how big of a con, a sweet, sweet con, Orion, you can pull on all the phonies. That's what makes us Psyops guys tick, regardless of the uniform we put on that morning. It ain't just job satisfaction. It's a point of honor, that is if we had any. Which we don't."

His eyes were wild like some desert prophet seeing the interconnections in the universe. He sloshed his beer everywhere as he waved his hands, sermonizing.

"Why the lies?" I said. "Why not tell them the truth, Cook?"

The chief gave me this sudden look, jerked out of his beer and possibly other stimulants, driven by religious fervor that seemed to convey his disbelief that I would ask such blunt, pedestrian question of such a true believer as himself.

Really, Orion? he seemed to smirk. As if he were some beatific angel, and I nothing more than a ground-bound sinner who would never know anything other than the entrenching tool and cold chow forever in the hell that was my chosen profession.

"Oh, Sergeant Orion," he tsked, "…you sweet summer child, you. You think kids wanna play a digital game where you sit around and bury your feces so the enemy can't stalk and kill you? Sweat until you can't, then get crotch rot or sand sickness from the biters if that's the kind of world you find yourself about to die on for… the Current Thing. 'Cause there's always sand sickness, ain't there Orion. There's always biters. There's always the Current Thing. That's a feature, not a bug, and your kind never question that. And how exactly do we, say… optimize rations… Sergeant Orion, for gameplay? Digging through some box the first sergeant dropped off hours ago to sit in the heat or soak in the dirty mud. Leeches, or again the biters, crawling all over it. You, digging through the box with the bad date, looking for Chicken Smash or Scrambled Egg and Baff. Remember, it's not beef. It's *baff*. And... you'll be baffled by whoever would mistake it for anything even remotely approaching meat." He swigged his beer and seemed to look for shadows in the room. "What's the gameplay for that, Orion? What're the power-ups there that the kids will want to play so bad they're down there at the recruiters signing their best years away to the Monarchs and... the Current Thing? The loot crates? The strike packages?

"Nah, they don't want to play your game, Orion, your life. The kids want weapons that don't go dry, and pushing some little red button to just garrote a guy when seconds ago you had your carbine out and were dropping tangos right and left with all kinds of dropships going down, making gun runs, explosions, and dead comrades gazing at you like the hero you'll be. And *oh*-fficial... military chatter, Sergeant Orion," he hissed. "That's what really gets 'em joinin' up. Not how it really is. No one wants to play *this* game. Get the hell away from me, you bastards!" he shrieked, batting at nothing I could see.

Or at least, that's how it was twenty-five years ago before the Monarchs decided to take Crash or Astralon and the Seeker wiped out their whole financial empire. Back then they did run the game, and the Current Thing. But now...

... Now, everyone's strapping a rifle because it's do-or-die time. Seriously. Everyone's just trying to survive or get revenge. That's been abundantly clear since Blackrock.

I'm not totally sure which one the Strange is here to do. That's above my pay grade. All I know is right now on this LZ, I got two KIA: Hotsoup and New Guy Number Three.

Three got shot dead by an Ultra sniper way back off in some building on our four o'clock.

Bang, just like that. Guy domed him straight up. For the next minute that followed, New Guy Three just lay there because... what we were gonna do? He was dead and we had incoming, and we were returning fire to save our lives. It wasn't the standard infantry call to final protective fire only because I didn't call it, as I was too busy shooting every Ultra I could to maintain the integrity of the LZ.

Hey! What about those mechs that were supposed to be ruining everything in every direction? Our job was to keep Ultra AT killer teams off them.

So far... not happening. They were still stuck on our ride.

It's not that we were taking fire from every direction there on the LZ all along our sector. We were, but it's not just that. It's that everything is going badly and we're making mistakes. Twelve o'clock to four o'clock was Reaper. Dog twelve to eight. Ghost four to six. I've got all three squads down in three wedges and good cover except for Choker and Punch who tried to save New Guy Three's life by hustling him back on board the still-grounded *Spider* whose engines are still howling just below liftoff power.

His brains are leaking out, guys!

The heat those massive engines are throwing is starting to make me sweat.

Punch gets back and tells me New Guy Three is dead, after dodging plunging fire from an emplaced Ultra belt-fed we can't seem to knock out to get back. Hauser's Third is suppressing another emplacement. And Jax and Second are hunkering, sensing I'm getting pissed off enough about getting shot up sitting here on the LZ to go out and start punching, Ultras or not, right in the face.

"They can't get the mechs off the bird, Sarge," says Punch breathlessly as more incoming splashes into the soot and burnt dirt or ricochets the twisted wreckage we're using as cover.

I knew that. I knew he was dead. His brains were leaking out. You should've known that, Punch, I don't say.

Also, Biggs should have had those walking tin cans off in five. Twenty minutes in and we're still not off the LZ and I can tell that was the problem back there on the cargo deck.

Too much incoming and too many shoulds.

"Ogre lost a motivator on her right hydraulic and the mechanics are all over her trying to install a new line, fast," continues Punch as I try to figure out the fight we're in.

"And…?" I prompt after I motivate the platoon out of a pause in our return fire.

That's when the mortars start. And just in case you're thinking we got mortar support because our indirect specialist, Chief Chungo, got his fat act together and started the mortar bots up on our behalf… that didn't happen.

Ultra mortars began to rain down across the LZ we were holding. The first ones that had tried to nail us as we "hit the beach" all around the ship, those got knocked out by the chimps when they pushed through the streets two blocks to our west and overran an Ultra eighty-eight-millimeter mortar team. The chimps are in full savage mode now out there in Saffron City, and if you listen you can hear automatic gunfire and screeching. It sounds like the hells various enemies have told me to go to. All around the LZ we can see teams and clusters of the chimps swarming into the tall buildings surrounding our LZ, to root out the Ultras trying to defend there.

Traffic from Chief Cook indicated they were trying to take out the entrenched Ultra Marines who'd just happened to get lucky and set up near our LZ.

"My guess, Sarge," said Punch when we discussed our position between six- to eight-round bursts incoming from the Ultra emplaced gun that we couldn't seem to hit, "is they saw the D-beam strike go off, Sarge. And then they went and got the hustle on thinking this is where we were coming in. Smart, huh, Sarge?"

Nearby, Ulysses, our reformed Ultra, simply nodded at me to confirm this was something our enemy would do. Then he returned to scanning his sector and made ready for whatever order we gave him to go out there and kill his former brothers.

We catch a break, and the mortars start slamming into the *Spider* where, as I look back just before beginning to suck dirt and avoid jagged fast-flying shrap, I can see they've turned on the massive floods inside the cargo deck and there are small figures there scrambling all over Apocalypse Solutions' biggest baddest mech. The Ogre.

Punch and I crawl under a melted piece of once-building, courtesy of the D-beam strike prepping the LZ, and I won't lie here, I still feel exposed as mortars rock all sectors of our LZ.

Squad leaders are yelling at their men to do the same as indirect explosive rounds fall all over the *Spider*.

She's currently got no shields operational on the ground so the impacts of what feels like one-twenties, against our starship, are direct hits on her armor and hull.

That's gonna be expensive to repair. As an NCO I sign for equipment, and I feel the pain.

"Feels like one-twenties!" shouts Punch despite the ear pro the company spent money on back at Blackrock. The large rounds come in at a high angle and slam into the upper armor of our ship. Shrapnel and debris rain down across the hull, and all over us hunkering out here in the LZ.

"I'm hit!" shrieks New Guy Number Two and passes out.

Choker crawls through the mud and debris, checks the wound, and shouts out, "It's just a cut, Sar'nt. Bringing him around."

Choker has zero bedside manner.

"You ain't dead yet, slug!" he yells over the artillery as the multi-shot adrenaline injector revives the kid right there in the middle of his worst day ever.

This ain't like the game, I bet he's thinking.

"Crawl deep under that bar," advises Choker, laughing like a socio- or psychopath despite the fast-flying shrap slamming into the ruin and wreckage we're hiding in. "Don't forget your weapon, idiot! C'mon! It's just a scratch! The fun hasn't even started!"

The mortars continue to fall and just as soon as they've started, they stop.

I've fallen for this trick before. Stop mortar fire and wait for us to crawl out from under our hidey-holes. Then drop more rounds and catch us out in the open.

"Hold your positions!" I shout. Nearby, Ulysses taps his ear and hand-signals me to switch channels to my private comm. I do.

"What?"

"Sergeant Orion... Ultra tactics in this situation, if we were facing one of the line units, would have been to move forward during the mortar fire and attack now, thinking we're waiting for more mortars. Permission to pop up and scan for targets."

I nod and switch back to general comm watching this kid as he does what he does next.

I gotta tell you about Ulysses Two Alpha Six. Our Ultra. It's a story. And it's a story I'm not altogether sure about as of right now. But the Old Man came to me after the first sergeant put him with Reapers and had a conversation with me.

"You can trust him, Sergeant," said the captain.

"How do I know that? Sir."

The Old Man looked at me with those washed-out blue gunfighter eyes of his, eyes that have seen more than I can ever imagine, I imagine, a half-burnt cheap cigarette smoldering between his fingers. He only smokes cheap cigarettes and he smokes them endlessly. Then he looked away and stared off toward the ships in the yard under refit. This was back on Blackrock. Before Saffron City.

"Because I said so, Sergeant." Then, "I hope that's enough."

I have strong feelings and at least impressions about most guys in Strange. I know the villains and the heroes. Yeah, they're all my brothers. But I know who you can trust, and who you can't.

The captain... he's the one you don't doubt. He is one hundred percent for every man in the company. I've seen him stick when it was time to go just to make sure someone got every chance they could to get out of the bad situation we were in.

And I've seen him go in after that guy, and if that wasn't enough, carry out the body. I'd doubt the stars and their courses in the galaxy before I'd ever doubt that man.

His credit is good with me.

Having said that, he was one of the big reasons why I didn't know exactly what we were after here in this fight at Saffron City or dealing with the Seeker when she'd crossed us. Money, or revenge.

I was cool with either, I just wanted to know which one was the reason we were gonna spend brass.

And yeah, despite the Seeker screwing us on the pay... I got her. I respected her. A little. As much as I can any-one. And maybe I even had a little thing for her. But not enough to ever take it seriously. I see myself in the mirror every morning there is one. It's more like this... she's just some hot actress in one of those thrillers that I'll see every time just 'cause she's in it. She ain't like the rest of us. She doesn't have scars and bullet puckers. Or slashes and cuts. Or... I don't know. But she don't got what us... mortals... have. The folds and coffee stains, the cuts and tears, on the map of our lives across the stars.

Sometimes, when you ain't got nothin' but messages from across time and the galaxy from a party girl who re-members you once... maybe a crush ain't such a bad thing to have if just to give you a fantasy that you've got a reason to be out here.

So, you can see where my loyalties might have... prob-lems. In this situation.

But if the captain says I can trust the Ultra we picked up off the ground back on the bad LZ at Crash, or Astralon, call it what you want, then... I do. His word is enough for me to extend credit on this one.

Ulysses Two Alpha Six, or just Ulysses as the Strange calls him, the only guy to come with his own tag, is an ultra-high-speed cool guy after all. He slithers through the mud, and seems to just ooze up through some debris and get a good field of view, without exposing himself, of our sector.

Pro.

He's got scout sniper training for sure. But it's the way he moves. Like a natural athlete. Everything he does, he does... competently. We all see it. He's the kind of soldier, or warrior, you aspire to be and maybe even allow others to think you are. Sometimes. But we can all see this guy is just naturally gifted, and well trained too.

But it's that *naturally* part... that's something like the Monarch. The Seeker. Something that ain't us.

"If he weren't an Ultra..." the first sergeant is remarked to have once said to someone in passing. "Then he reminds me of a younger me in the batts."

The Saturnian Batts are as close to Ultra as it can get. The first sergeant is given to embellishment. Or his *There I Was* stories are really that hairy.

There's chatter on the comm in the lull that follows the falling mortars the enemy has seen fit to lay on us. I have a real bad feeling as I watch Ulysses take a good look at our sector. The news... will not be good. I shoot back a quick look at the hulking mechs inside the *Spider*'s cargo bays.

Our ship is smoking from the indirect fire damage. One of the engines is on fire, internally, and black smoke is bubbling up and boiling out of the housing there. That's not good. Fire suppression systems should be kicking in.

I can see Sergeant Angry, the platoon sergeant for Apocalypse Solutions, shouting at someone hanging from one of the Ogre's massive hydraulic articulators.

Punch taps me, sensing I didn't track the latest flash report over the comm coming from the XO.

"Ship says we got Ultra gunships inbound, Sarge. It's get-it-on thirty or my mom raised a beautiful little girl."

At that moment I'm wishing those mechs would get it together and get on the battlefield to support our hung-out-in-the-wind ruck-busted humps.

It's too quiet.

Then…

Ulysses begins to fire at someone, shouting, "Contact front!"

CHAPTER EIGHT

"Damn!" I swear and hustle out from under my hidey-hole in the D-beam-created debris, feeling fat and overweight in my battle rattle because I am tired and scared. I don't have a spare ounce of fat on me and even my own troops make fun of how rail thin I am. But I am always scared of what can go wrong next. Someone's got to be.

And the thinness...

The NCO diet plan will do that for you. Coffee, all of it, all the time. Cigarettes constantly as you stand in the cold at the range, or doing some inspection, or long night watches. Throw in never a real full meal all at once. Just random rations stuffed in your pockets and stolen while you're always doing something, watching someone do something, or getting someone out of, or into, trouble, constantly.

"Damn," I say again as I hunch-run over to Ulysses and slither much less adeptly than he did up through the rubble he's fighting from to get a good look at what he's shooting at exactly.

Half of me, at that moment, as everyone watches and wonders what to do next, is hoping our former Ultra is just way too gung-ho and engaging some small recon team come to get too close to our road show.

The other half of me is wondering why all these dumb bastards aren't shooting back right now.

Then I get a look at what's about to be a real big problem for Reaper in the next two minutes, maybe less.

I can see several two-man teams of Ultras out there and all through the D-beam-blasted debris field. And they are close. Real close. Those crafty weasels used the mortar strike to get close.

I envy them. I would not trust our indirect specialist enough to attempt that maneuver. Chungo has fired dangerous munitions danger close to Strange just to see if the cheap deal he got was worth it. I don't see the logic, but he's done it.

As one, seeing me see them, the Ultras out there rise without signal and start bounding overwatch forward engaging as they close.

One team moving, one team covering. Rounds are now coming at our position.

They're literally attempting to overrun us right now.

Hauser opens fire with the Pig and cuts three of them to shreds using accurate fire off to our right. Good, Hauser, I needed that right now. In moments via commands, he's got his men oriented and supporting by fire Ulysses's attempt to engage the closing Ultras at extremely close range.

He switched over to holosights and is shooting as fast as he can acquire targets. The former Ultra is also shooting semi-auto and I'm pretty damn sure his marksmanship is excellent. There's a professional economy in everything he does that feels brutally competent. One time on the range with him back at Blackrock, testing him, we instead learned stuff that improved our game.

The Old Man swooped in and had Ulysses teach some classes on gunfighting and CQB, even though we didn't have a lot of time in the run-up to the mission. I'll be honest and say I'm not so old that he didn't fix some of my garbage technique. Though I made sure no one knew that actually happened, and just quietly made the improvements to my game without making a big deal about it.

Now there are dead Ultras drilled right through their armored helmets out there in the black ruin of the D-beam-blasted LZ. But there are more alive and getting ready to pull a raid on us. One group is surging forward and coming for us, while another sets up a base of fire to keep us occupied.

I have a real bad feeling grenades are imminent.

"Second… flank left and set up a base of fire on our anchor!" I shout into the comm, hearing my own breathlessness as everything goes kinetic everywhere at once and I realize I'm in it once again and that we, the Strange, are indeed getting it on.

The emplaced Ultra guns open up again in the middle distance, but we have the cover provided by the debris field of the beam strike. Still, one of the guys in Third manages to catch a round. Bad Bet the AG gets tagged, swears, and goes right on doing his job muttering hardboy talk and daring anyone to dispute.

Later Choker will tell me the Third Squad medic, Blender, related that Bad Bet just looked at his shattered arm and swore, saying, "Well this might as well happen." Then he kept feeding bloody belts to the other Third gunner, Mad Max, who didn't seem to mind much due to all the quiet anger everyone suspects drives him. The blood that is. Mad Max didn't mind that.

The gunner had a good field of traversing fire, and he was killing Ultras for the high score which was why he'd joined the Strange. But this was only known to me as it was part of his story.

"Why the spite?" I asked him one time before he told me the story.

He thought about it and then quietly replied, "Everyone's got to have a hobby, Sar'nt."

CHAPTER NINE

Burst fire at close range, just after dawn, is a hell of a way to start your day on a new world, but the Strange was in it once again.

And that's why we get paid.

As I have said before, when there's nothing left to do but fight... then you fight like the third guy in line for the escape pod rated for two.

I dusted an Ultra Marine at twenty meters who was moving to close, hunched and weaving through the D-beam-blasted ruin. I fired, dropping that bad guy as hot rounds punched smoking holes in his battered and dirty armor. He was down on one knee when I squeezed again, landing rounds in his bucket and the blasted grit behind him.

He went down and I had to hope he was good and dead. There wasn't time to confirm. This was a brawl, and it would be for the next five minutes. Or over if you got killed before that.

Ulysses grabbed my drag handle and jerked me down suddenly, savagely pulling me under cover as the emplaced gun out there in the shattered and torn-apart buildings tried to range us with a targeting burst.

Huge rounds smacked into burnt concrete, twisted by nuclear-heat levels of bombardment fire.

I landed in the blackened dirt as char and crust blossomed all around me. Then more rounds from the Ultra heavy machine gun started to work the area we'd just been fighting from.

"Shifting," grunted Ulysses as he slithered off through the charred dirt and ruin to find a new shooting position to smoke tangos from as more rounds passed overheard with neither remorse nor hesitation. There was final brutality in their passage that felt real in ways I hadn't felt in a few months twenty-five years ago.

"Reaper Actual, this is Reaper Three-Six…" It was Hauser over the comm. I could hear the hot blare of the Pig he was working in the feed of the transmission. Grenades went off close by and one of the Ultras came inside the "wire" of our passion, spraying fire everywhere. Low and prone I dumped the rest of the magazine on him and watched him take rounds, then turn and get ready to shoot me even though I'd tagged his armor with at least a few shots. I had no idea who shot him straight through the bucket a second after that. But the resulting trauma show was terrific.

Someone's fast-moving seven-six-two round struck the Ultra's bucket, entered, and then redirected straight out the top of the protection.

The Ultra pitched over and another grenade went off along our defensive line.

"Go for Reaper Actual, Three-Six…" I said, keying my throat mic.

"Estimating platoon-sized element…" reported Hauser in his typical combat cyborg efficiency and calmness with just the right amount of urgency as he was designed to do. "They must have a microwave scrambler that interfered with my sensor algorithms…"

At that moment Jax, running Second, who'd shifted left, set up an interlocking field of fire for the platoon of Ultras hitting our center and beginning to catch the infiltrators in a brutal crossfire between both Reaper elements. Third had two Pigs suppressing while the squad designated marksman worked the crawlers and shooters supporting the enemy push into our center.

That timely seven-six-two that had just saved my life had to have come from the Second SDM we tagged as Wolfy.

Why?

He had wolf tattoos, of course. And not very good ones either. When asked why all the tattoos, and with no distinction as to quality or artistic ability, he simply responded, not offended in the least, "I like wolves." That was all the quiet dude who'd been shifted from Second would say on the subject of his garbage wolf tats.

The odds that he was—even now in the middle of a firefight with some of humanity's best killers—wearing a really awful wolf T-shirt… were one hundred percent. Wolves. Wolves under a full moon, or several moons, or wolves with some hot alien chick. This guy did not discriminate. Wolves were his jam and that really only seemed to bother me.

You have to be honest about these things. There was more to this than just *I Like Wolves*. I knew there was some really jacked-up twisted story he wasn't telling me and that bugged me on levels I couldn't let go of.

I know… issues.

He wore those cheap wolf tees under his fatigues and plate carrier, and if he got shot and I had to needle-D him, I'd probably have to cut through a really awful yellow tee with a bad print of wolves in the forest baying at the moon.

Just for the record… I prefer nothing underneath and will sometimes just wear my plate carrier instead of a shirt. But I'm hardcore, or lazy, like that. Whatevs. Plus, I get hot when people are trying to kill me. So it's best to take off your gear before the shooting starts.

Now, small digression in the middle of this battle... the wolf thing... it's weird. It's like a cult out here on the edge of human expansion. No one, unless you've spent big money to ride transport into one of the really high-mem Bright Worlds, has ever seen a wolf in real life. Wolves are from Earth. Yeah, there are species that the colonists, scouts, and exploration vessels have catalogued as "wolves" out here in the new worlds, but they are not actually wolves as humanity knew them once and long ago.

There's a rat-like creature on Blossom, indigenous. The locals call that a wolf. But it's not a wolf. I know. I looked 'em up because the whole cult, and everyone who's into them, it really bothers me because it makes no sense.

Still, even though most of the people on most of the worlds have never seen a wolf, the bad tattoo, the cruddy T-shirts, and general wolf merchandise can be found in every hard-luck starport you'll ever cross. It's the surest sign you have no class and never will.

Wolfy wears his tees despite these galaxy-wide accepted norms and my obvious irritations. Well, maybe not *galaxy*-accepted, but one hundred and thirty-four human-discovered and colonized worlds all agree that wolf stuff is weird and cheap and crappy.

Digression over.

The first Ultra drop enters the battlespace above our heads over the LZ we must fight for.

"Predators inbound!" shouts Punch and starts pulling trigger on the lead drop, landing rounds in the canopy and engines which are heavily armored. The clunky gunship streaks over the battlefield as the door gunner unloads on someone not us.

I am thankful for this.

"Tags… deploy the Jackhammer!" roars Punch over the battle. He's walking and firing at the gunship making a right turn out over the attacking enemy to give the other door gunner some action on our position. Brass flies away from his shorty in tight quick intervals as he continues to put rounds on the enemy drop out there and above.

Meanwhile, Ultras on the ground are still shooting at our tight little perimeter.

I've counseled Punch on this before. The chance of bringing down an armored hunter-killer-style dropship, or any drop, with a carbine… it's rare. Really it only happens in the movies.

But he goes nuts when they're involved, and he can't be talked out of this course of action.

None of my hard-earned advice or shouting has convinced my second-in-command squad leader that he has a less than ten percent chance, given the latest battlefield statistics relevant twenty-five years ago, of effecting a kill on a dropship with a rifle.

He is not dissuaded or convinced otherwise.

"Gives 'em somethin' to think about, Sarge," he finally said when I asked him why, after all the rational evidence I'd presented, he still insisted on engaging the threat in this manner as opposed to other effective means of dealing with airborne threats of the hunter-killer dropship variety.

"Gives 'em somethin' to think about, Sarge."

At least this time he's actually moved to the best possible course of action while still doing the worst course of action regarding this particular threat to our continued existence, and ordered our anti-air assets to engage.

Each squad is carrying three one-shot Jackhammers. The man-portable anti-aircraft guided rockets are for the protection of the mechs that have yet to come out here and give us a hand killing the enemy. Mechs are great at destroying other mechs, or even infantry when they can catch them in the open, or just destroying hardened positions. But they're weak against close air support, or hidden infantry with anti-mech armor rounds. In fact they're downright weak as kittens.

Tags, one of the Dog guys transferred into Reaper, shoulders his slung Bastard and gets the Jackhammer ready to deploy. Then he promptly takes a round from one of the Ultras now danger close and gets knocked on his butt right there in the burnt debris and mud of our fighting perimeter.

He took it right in the carrier and I can see he is, right at that moment, pretty sure he's about to die because it hurts like hell and you either can't believe you've just been shot or you're kicking yourself because you've finally been shot and you knew this was coming and you're wondering why you didn't bail on this contract when you had the chance.

We've all been there. You can read that look from a mile away.

I'm trying to run the battle and get New Guys One and Two to effectively engage the enemy with that perfect amount of both encouragement and vulgarity. One's smiling like an idiot and rocking the Ultras out there on full auto. This is not a good use of ammunition, but I don't want to dissuade the killer instinct he clearly seems to have. I will work with him on select fire should we all survive right now.

In fact, I thought I had done this already. But maybe that was someone else.

Actual combat surprises most people. Even me.

Two isn't doing anything. He's not hiding, which is good. He's also not running. Better. But he's just crouched there in the low ready and waiting for me to tell him to go ahead and expend some rounds on our behalf so we can all sleep on some muddy street later tonight.

So I don't have time to run over to Tags, get the Jackhammer deployed, and fire it. Plus, there's a whole bunch of incoming between me and my downed anti-air guy.

"You're okay!" I shout at Tags across the incoming fire.

Tags has gone bone white under his warpaint. He looks at me in stunned disbelief, unwilling, but desirous, of believing the truth.

I turn to New Guy Two and direct him to engage Ultras on the right. He's still not moving.

Back to Tags. "You took it in the plate! You're good. Deploy that Jackhammer and fire it!"

Tags slowly nods his head, face still bone white, hands shaking, and reaches, trembling, toward the anti-air rocket lying in the charcoal grit of the D-beam-ruined block that was once here.

He's on his knees, a horrible position to fire AT in, but hey, I'm working with what I got here.

New Guy Two takes a shot and I count that as a win for my NCO soldier development skills.

"Get some!" I yell like I'm all worked up and care. I do care. Honestly. But I'll have to be honest... I don't get war rage like some. Punch does this bit great. Anyone fires a weapon and he's right there whooping and yelling "GET

SOME!" like he's had too much in the wrong kind of bar, or he's at some thundermetal concert that's so loud you can barely think straight.

Punch is killer motivation personified.

I don't go to thundermetal concerts.

Coffee, cigarettes, sitting in the dark, that's me. My thing. That's how I like to spend my free time. I mean, come on... the next disaster is headed my way shortly, we all know it is. I know that. NCOs don't get to have fun like normal people. That's what NCOs are for. The opposite of normal people fun. When you're having fun, they're standing by to get you out or fix it. They're smoking, drinking coffee, trying not to be found, and waiting for the next call from the local police, the first sergeant, or... oh hells no... the Old Man.

But New Guy Two believes my bad acting enthusiasms and begins to engage the enemy like he means it... sorta. He's still not sure.

It's something to work with. Returning fire is really important in war. Otherwise it's just getting shot at by someone else. One supernova. Would not recommend. Highly.

By the time I turn back to Tags, he's got the anti-air asset deployed into the firing config and he flips the holo-reticle for the tracking and targeting algos to take over, acquire, and let him know he can fire.

That's probably, in hindsight, what got him killed next.

Ultras run some high-speed fancy software. If those drops were tricked out, and I'm betting they were, as soon as the weapon locked and Tags got tone, one of the gunners aboard the enemy dropships overhead was fed an alert that an anti-air asset was in play. A real danger for the dropship and crew. Being an Ultra, the best soldiers in the universe despite their down-and-out condition here twenty-five years later in the second-to-last battle for all the marbles...

Earth would be the last.

And that's too unthinkable to even imagine. So I won't tangent here. But hey... where did the company think this was going?

All the way, that's where it was going.

And that scared the hell out of me. Why it didn't scare everyone else I have no idea. Maybe everyone's just braver or doesn't care. Don't know. But taking out Earth... there was something primally wrong about that.

Yeah, wars were something, but crossing that line... that was the thing. You couldn't come back from that.

Tags got tone, and the drop that was on its second orbit of the field, gunners laying the hate on anything and everything they could spot, got an anti-air lock warning as the sensors updated the possible target location for the anti-air asset inside their fancy Ultra helmets and one of them dosed the whole area where Tags was with as much outgoing lead as possible.

Tags got it. The launcher got it. The entire area around Tags turned into a sudden charred dirt fountain display of horror and death.

Punch swore, we all hunkered, and two more drops swooped in, reversers howling inside the massive engine housings as they took control of the battlespace.

That was when XO back on the *Spider* got a bright idea, armed the point defense cannons on the ship, and blasted all three Predator dropships in the space of less than thirty seconds.

Clearing the LZ.

Larger ships like the *Spider* carry PDCs. Point defense cannons. These generally aren't used for ship-to-ship combat like the heavy main gun the *Spider* carries. PDCs are used to take out incoming missiles and sometimes slow-moving fighters armed with ship-killer missiles of various types. Or even the ship-killers themselves like the ASM-46. A huge, fast-moving snub-nosed AI-guided ship-killer missile with a warhead that'll punch shields, armor, and crack a spine. Your ship gets hit with one of those and it's game over, son.

So PDCs are great against those because they don't move missile-, or direct-fire energy weapons, fast. They're faster than fighters that aren't operating on full burn for an intercept vector. If they've slowed to attack speed, then the PDCs can engage fighters.

Ship-killers are slower.

But here, on a bad LZ getting worse, with drop-ships which range from slow-moving troop transports to slow-moving hunter-killers… slow comparative to the fast speeds in space and orbital combat, but slow enough… here the PDCs had all the time in the world to light up the swarming Predators within seconds.

The first Ultra hunter-killer dropship that had made its gun run over the top, door gunners spraying everything they could while the pilot gunner laid down targeting fire with the forward thirty-mil from the blister forward of the pilot, got the attention of the PDCs first. The *Spider's* dorsal PDC, a twin thirty-millimeter GAU gun optimized for space and orbital combat, swiveled to life and dumped a brief stream of depleted uranium fire into the bird just completing its second orbit over our heads.

I know the numbers.

About three thousand rounds ate up that bird, chewing it to pieces in less than a couple of seconds. The biggest *BRRRRRRRRRRRRRRRRRRRT* I'd ever heard in my life spat out a tight cone of fire right into the Ultra drop amidships as I turned away from where Tags lay dying, or dead already. I was still covered and the black dust of the fire he'd received drifted away between us on the heat drafts off the *Spider*'s howling engines.

I followed the swarm of dark fire from the turrets atop our old destroyer and watched angry hornets tear up the cargo deck of the orbiting Ultra drop, the rear empennage, and something, and how could it have not, caught the main engines on board and detonated them as well as the fuel and munitions. The rear half of the drop exploded and the front section, where the pilots were no doubt wondering why suddenly none of their controls responded to command, nose-dived off into the destruction the D-beam had left in its fiery wake. Where it fireballed.

Seconds later the smaller PDC that protected the forward bridge went active and decimated the second of the three Ultra Predator HK dropships that had been dominating the battlefield as more of their shock troops swept forward across the rubble on our position.

The bridge stack PDC is smaller. Most ship-to-ship missiles don't target the bridge. They go for the heat and energy signatures, engines and reactors, in swarms along the back of any ship. That's why the back of the ship has the bigger better PDCs and the sandcasters. Only smarter, lighter, more agile missiles are used against bridges. So the PDC defensive calibers used here are smaller. I know there are those of you reading this account, reveling in all this battlefield comeuppance against the Ultras, who are thinking

I misused the word decimated. No, I didn't. Decimation is to reduce by a tenth, technically. The smaller bridge stack PDC opened fire and caught my attention as it targeted the second Ultra HK's engine and lit that one up in one long, but lighter, burst.

The pilot's controls must've flared like a celebration on Celestron, bright in the Bright Worlds by anyone's standard. I hear the chimps arrived and now Celestron is a ghost-haunted ruin where one can journey for days across a vast wasteland and not hear another sound, man nor beast.

The galaxy has changed much in twenty-five years. But… that's all well beyond my pay grade. Front side forward, Sergeant Orion. And maybe there's a found scout ship out there somewhere on the other side of this mess to take me off and away from all of this.

Or maybe, impossibly… the Falmorian party girl. But more about that later.

So, the bridge stack PDC lit up the second drop's engines and the bird broke off from the attack, already trailing black smoke as the pilot, who must've survived, who knew about the door gunners, broke off and tried to get out of the fight as quick as possible now that PDCs were being used against them.

That wasn't good enough for the PDC. It paused in its lighter, more lady-like chatter of outgoing rounds, compared to the GAU twins that had fired first, reacquired, and fired again. Its AI preferred engines because that was the best way to shoot down a lot of micro-pack missiles, the kind that usually got used on bridges, and then, as it fired again, decided in its logic-driven computer brain that the pilot was the problem that needed to be addressed for an optimal kill.

The next burst was a longer stream of outgoing fire that hosed the cockpit canopy. The pilot must've already been fighting a wounded bird when suddenly the entire cockpit got ventilated by high-power AP from the PDC.

Armor-piercing'll do it.

The bird heeled over and just drove into one of the blasted buildings along the perimeter of our LZ. It was an underwhelming crash with no giant explosion. But it would burn there for the rest of the day.

I know it's the enemy. I know they were trying their best to kill us just seconds before But you get a sick feeling watching a drop go in knowing that could just as easily be you and yours.

But, as the first sergeant likes to remind me, "Try not to personalize the enemy, Sergeant Orion. You'll be a lot happier and live a lot longer if you don't get attached and all."

Can do, First Sergeant. Tryin' my best.

The third drop exploded when the main engine PDC, the big eighty-eight, opened fire and blasted that thing from the sky like it didn't exist in the minute after the shooting started.

But by that time I was on Tags, realizing there was nothing I could do for him. He was already gone.

Can I personalize my guys, First Sergeant?

Then someone blew the sandcasters aboard the *Spider* and obscured the whole LZ, giving us cover for an hour until the winds shifted.

Twenty minutes later, the Ultras dead and dying out there in the black rubble, the sand drifting and hanging in the air, we were in shemaghs, or gas masks if you thought to bring them, and the captain was there with orders for

Reaper to go out and smoke some mortar teams who were targeting the LZ and the now heavily damaged *Spider*.

The mechs were stuck on the ride in. The ride was stuck on the ground. This contract was already bad. And it was day one.

For now… nothing was going according to plan. Same stuff, different day, Sergeant Orion.

CHAPTER
TEN

We had to hold the integrity of the line guarding the LZ until the mechs got up and ready for action. Once the Old Man and the first sergeant came out to check our wounded, reorient our defensive posture, and reposition the medium machine guns to support the perimeter, I got the mission to go out and kill the Ultra mortar team.

Search and destroy.

"Here's the deal, Sergeant Orion," began the first sergeant. "These Apocalypse boys… I got a real bad feeling this is their first time in it and all. Knew that when we got the contract to attach them and act as a support force for the mechs. But… the Seeker's paid for our engine and all… so sometimes there's that. We can't let those mechs get out in the open with that Ultra team ready to drop steel on 'em… so while we got all this damn sand in the air, I suggest you get your combat infiltration cyborg, turn everything over to Corporal Punch, and get out there and dust them boys good and proper. Ship's last radar contact plots them in this area but I suspect they'll shift to here…"

The first sergeant was holding a flexy with the battlefield in holo-display tactical green. I had my mouth and nose covered as I bent forward to study the battlefield. The electromagnetic sand from the ship's sandcasters was still hanging in the air and as Choker had said when it was time to either mask up or get shemaghs on, "You guys don't want to breathe that stuff for too long. It'll kill you dead faster than I would when you're sleeping, and I stand over you in the night and just watch you breathing."

That's our medic.

Meanwhile the first sergeant went on with what he wanted out of us. "They probably got a good look at them mechs on board and they know we're gonna drive on this avenue of attack once they get in play. Their main force and command structure is over here gettin' hit by the chimps. So… if I was back in the batts… that's the way I'd expect the mechs to come and hit me in this sector here."

The Old Man, no gas mask, no shemagh for protection, cigarette smoldering between his index and middle fingers, stood nearby and watched my men get the perimeter ready for defense. Positions were improved. Smart mines went out. Then we were in the long halt defensive posture. Half watching, half getting their gear ready for whatever came next.

Nearby, Tags lay wrapped in his poncho. What could be found of Hotsoup, mostly his bloody gear, lay there also. No one had wrapped what remained of him in a poncho as his poncho had been shredded and destroyed in the mortar impact. And they would need theirs for later.

So it has always been with soldiers. There is no place more real than a battlefield.

Bad Bet from Third had gotten his arm shattered. But he could still hump belts and feed. We had three KIA so we needed every dirty boot. Choker shot him up with painkillers, duracast the arm, and made a sling. It would do.

The Old Man burned the last of his smoke and flung it off into the hanging sand in the air as he listened to me tell the first sergeant who I was gonna take with me out there to kill the Ultra mortar team.

Hauser. Wolfy. Duster. Me. Two teams. We'd find them and smoke them. And yeah, the fact that they were Ultras, much feared twenty-five years ago, was not lost on me. But things had changed since the time of Monarch supremacy. That was then, this was now, as some writer once wrote.

"Take the Ultra with you," said the Old Man, and then he and the first sergeant were gone, off to check Dog and never Ghost.

Ghost took care of themselves. Ghost was pro.

CHAPTER ELEVEN

We stripped down our gear to the bare minimum of what we'd need to get it done quick and still hit hard. Because I was bringing Hauser, literally a killing machine without par, I left the anti-armor killers behind. We were leaving our rucks loaded with everything we'd need to live on the ground inside the LZ perimeter. Stinkeye came out of whatever hole he'd been hiding in during much of the firefight and indirect fire strikes we'd walked into upon landing, cleared his ragged throat, and took a quick hit from his totem flask.

Quick hits like that told me he was getting down to business. Which was something he hated to do as that involved work and exposure to danger. Two things he seemed to maintain some arcane religious belief against despite being a member of a private military contractor outfit.

He stumbled up, dusting black char and debris off himself and his faded old cammies, his face caked in the black stuff making his mud-brown well-used catcher's mitt leather skin seem somehow... younger? Which, in hindsight, summed him up. War and horror seemed to make him... if not younger-seeming, then busier. Like he had troublemaking to get done and was behind the mayhem scheduled. He was hitting his totem flask fast and quick as I briefed my kill team on what we were gonna do out there.

This usually meant he was gonna hijack my brief.

I finished and glared at the Voodoo chief warrant, thinking to myself, well, this might as well happen. Then with little ceremony, listing slightly, weaving back and forth, Stinkeye cleared his throat, which was a horrible sound to hear, and announced, "Best I be goin' along with yas... Sergeant Orion. I'm good at findin' things don't wanna be found."

Great. I expected nothing out of him. Which was a mistake. There was every chance he'd make things worse for us. So I should've, as a good NCO, at least expected that. But, in my defense, I had just been shelled and shot at.

Stinkeye never carried a ruck so there was nothing for him to leave behind, and as a chief warrant officer in the company... he could do whatever the hell he wanted to do. Who was I to stop him? I'd found Stinkeye to be almost-useful many times. Other times he was either completely useless, or a real liability. Sometimes, when your bacon was really in the heat stove... he came through and straight-up game-changed with the incoming hurricane heavy and zips in the wire.

The odds were ten percent he'd be a combat multiplier. Eighty percent he'd watch and hide. Ten percent he'd get some of us killed. Caution and fear of the dreaded Ultras out there, the galaxy's tip-of-the-spear killers, reminded me that even though I was taking the combat cyborg in, I probably needed our Voodoo Platoon wizard powered up straight by the Monarch Dark Labs long, long, ago... just in case the going got weird and all.

And if the going was, in fact, going to get very weird... then Voodoo Platoon was as weird as it gets. Take that, tac-plan AIs! Sar'nt Orion is one crafty hobo.

Or, as the first sergeant likes to say, "If you want to win any conflict, give a bunch of teenage boys as much firepower and explosives as they can carry, Sergeant Orion, and let them be led by a wily old hobo for a platoon sergeant. They will show you how creative violence can get. At the small unit level, that is."

And while many of Strange Company are, technically never mind coffin-sleep, in their twenties or thirties... all of them are emotionally teenage boys.

I can attest to that before any Inquisitor war crimes tribunal and not lose an ounce of sleep. Even though I wouldn't.

As I have stated before, deep dives in the company logs mention a "Stinkeye" in battles long, long ago. Was there someone else that went by that tag? Or are the logs to be trusted at all? I have asked myself this on many occasions. Sometimes, when you read back to the wars on Centauri, or even the Halfway Station Battles, there's someone who can do exactly the same things the old drunk Voodoo space war wizard can do. But in these other accounts those seemingly same individuals go by other names. And so... who knows.

Suspiciously, the records files of these, and a few others through company history, are corrupted and so no image or biometrics scan exists.

Some might say *oh well* or *go figure*, and leave it be. But me... I smell flak over the target. Otherwise, why would there be flak?

I put Hauser on point with the Pig because he's Hauser and he has an advanced suite of optics and targeting sensors we'll need. This is like putting a scout mech on point, but better, because Hauser gets it done quietly instead of all Stomp Stomp Stompy like a ten-ton scout mech tends to do. I put Ulysses Two Alpha Six behind him and organize them as the support team once we pick up the enemy on the way to the objective. My wily combat hobo thinking sees it like this…

We make contact, they pin the enemy with suppressive with Hauser acting as the primary base of fire and Ulysses running rear security on the gun. Myself and Duster flank and try to overrun the pinned enemy once we've used our frags, and the platoon sergeant, me, has ordered Hauser to shift fire. Wolfy will hand back on our six, take rear security, and then, once we make contact, begin to support in the squad designated marksman role, going for any leaders or other side marksmen.

Hey… it's a plan. Not the greatest plan. But it's mine and it's better to have one than not. It's why they give me the stripes and rockers. And believe me, they don't just give these things away. You gotta be wily. And… I'll admit, it's probably not the plan that will be used in any way, shape, or form once everyone starts shooting at everyone else. It rarely happens that way. But it's in place, and that satisfies the requirements of my job. We may even get lucky and things might actually go down that way—the way I have a plan for. Imagine that, I think with all the wistful foolishness of a tac-plan AI, instead of having to think for ourselves on how to get creatively destructive. With incoming and wounded screaming and me supposed to be leading effectively.

What if I get domed? What's gonna happen to them? The only comfort I have is that Hauser is there and if I go down, he'll get it done while I bleed out.

Imagine if Choker took charge. Stinkeye always mutters about the galaxy having a heart of darkness and all… well, if so, that sociopath Choker's found it and he's holding it open to see what comes through.

Trust me, I like Choker. But he creeps me out.

Then there's our space war wizard warrant officer who's currently drunk, in the middle of a battle not going according to anyone's tac-plan AI. But, in his defense, Stinkeye's always drunk. So, operationally he is… war wizard, one each. Use as directed. Hey, wait… there's no field manual for this guy's job position! So of course, Stinkeye will do what he always does: stick close to me until he gets all serious about getting ready to make his particular brand of mischief. Then, generally according to past predictive behavior, he'll disappear from our zone of control and get out there among the enemy so he can do what he does. Make trouble.

Hopefully for the other side. That would be nice, Stinkeye. The company would appreciate your stare-into-the-void efforts on their behalf.

I mean… he doesn't actually disappear. Not like Nether, fading from existence and all. But he'll just say something like, "Headin' out, Little King. I know what you gotta get done… I go make them guys some trouble now."

Then he just wanders off, hitting his dented totem flask one last time and beginning to walk with a purpose toward where he's got to go next and what he's got to do now.

I always feel… a little bad when that happens. Bad when I see him go off on his own because I think it's the only time when I really understand him. Understand why he's Stinkeye.

He's alone in the universe. Going out there alone, again, and scared to death because Stink never acts brave about what he does. He's not a hardboy or skull stacker. Not his jam. Yeah, he's a braggart about Cheks and a mean drunk most of the time, and seriously one day he and Cook will kill one or the other, or each other at the same time. But he ain't brave when the shooting starts. He's scared. And yet, despite that, he goes out there into the middle of fights, away from the fellowship of our company of heavily armed emotional teenagers with guns and high-ex, one war hobo in charge of the whole mess, to do what he's got to do.

On our behalf.

Which, now that I frame it all... is a kind of bravery.

He's not fearless. He's scared to death. But he goes anyway.

When I see him walking off as it's about to go violently down, tension in the air as thick as the too-much lube on your bolt carrier group, I understand how alone he is in those moments. How alone he's been all along. Even in the Strange. Where we have no one but ourselves to depend on, and we've sworn to one another to do that, even to the death. Which is often the case.

He's alone because of what he's been through, and if those company logs, even the parts that have been corrupted, are true in what they say about him, or someone like him... then he's seen more dead Strange than I ever will. More ghosts that never seem to stop watching from the edges of every fight, waiting for it to be your turn so you can come and find out what they know.

And maybe that's why Stinkeye does the drunken-bad-gambler-space-war-wizard act. It keeps all of us eventually-to-be ghosts from bad LZs and unfound IEDs... at distance until it comes time to find out what the others know.

I could see how it would be easier that way.

Just before my little kill team departs the perimeter, I see Tags lying under his poncho as the electromagnetic sand in the air begins to fall now that it's ionizing and gaining mass in the local atmosphere, no longer effective at hiding targets or deflecting and destroying inbound missiles trying to kill our ship in deep space.

Nether is nearby and he lets me know via our private comm that he's heading out to get some work done on our behalf.

"There are some Ultra snipers I spotted, Orion. I'll go drop the building they're in a few stories and they won't be a problem for us anymore."

That's one way to put it, I think.

Just before we go, as Punch takes over and begins running my platoon, I pull "our Ultra" aside and ask him why the captain ordered me to take him with us on this one.

"Old Man says we need you on this. Why?"

Ulysses studied me for a moment in the sandy morning light. In the distance there were more chimp artillery strikes booming out and arching unseen overhead. Then falling down with great crashes and explosions among the Ultra-held blocks of the city. I'll be honest. I felt *less than* under Ulysses's gaze as the war got underway all around us. It didn't feel like it had reached any pitch. It was still just getting started. Opening moves. Probe and feel. But you could feel the real fight shaping up. And the slaughter that was coming with it on this one. I could feel that crawling under my skin. I'd been there before. And this time felt the same.

Ulysses standing there, it was like standing with a real soldier. An actual lifetaker, maybe not a heartbreaker. Just a lifetaker. And there was something cold about that. Colder than the hardboy lifetaker and heartbreaker line. Standing there and being judged and found unworthy to stack at his lifetaker level.

If we hadn't just called him by his name, then we would have almost surely unanimously tagged him *Lifetaker*.

Benefit of the doubt—which is a thing I've been trying to do lately—I don't think he was doing that on purpose. Making me feel... less. And I've stacked more than my fair share. But it's all been for survival. Him... different in ways I'd never understood until I met him. And I began to know him, if anyone could.

It's just this. He really is, actually, a real live Ultra. The premier warriors in the galaxy. Everyone is less than him and that's not just because he feels that way even though the Ultras are a semi-fanatical death cult.

He knows that because they are the best. They eat, drink, and breathe... war.

So, I tell myself as he begins to answer my question, it's not unusual to feel less under his gaze. He's younger than me. Handsome in a rugged way only physical athletics and genetic perfection can achieve. He's not a war-weary, scarred, bad tattooed, doesn't eat enough, too much coffee, chain-smoking merc NCO with ghosts of his own.

He's young and perfect.

Ultras are both devout and Spartan. In the truest sense of both those words. Believe me, I looked them up.

Devout. Committed or devoted to religion or to religious duties or exercises. Or, devoted to a pursuit, belief, or mode of behavior. Serious. Earnest. For Ultras their religion was the conduct of warfare.

And Spartan. A person of great courage and self-discipline. They live for their profession and I don't think, or have never heard, there is much else to their existence.

So, consider this... if the circumstances were reversed, he'd be killing all of us right now. Very quickly.

"Ultra light infantry indirect fire teams are most likely maneuvering out there to start dropping steel once they get a fire mission from the spotter close to the lines and most likely co-located with the crew-served teams ringing the LZ. The company commander believes, I can surmise, that is what we are facing, and what he wants terminated, Sergeant."

Sergeant, not Sar'nt or Hey Sar'nt Orion like everyone else says in the Strange. Sometimes I can't tell whether what they really mean is Hey Grandpa, or are they talking to me like I'm some hard-of-hearing Golden retriever that'll just do whatever's got to be done because that's my job and it's what I've always done and nothing else would ever be expected of me.

I don't know. It's not so much of a rank, not that I care, as something else they've attached to the compass points of all our collective lives. Something familiar.

Sometimes, when I haven't had enough sleep and too much coffee and way too many cigarettes, I wanna shout, "Hey, Strange bums... I'm a Class Three suborbital pilot. Class Two and I can become a Scout, and when that happens," I lie even to myself, "I'm outta here, losers!"

It's weird telling yourself a lie you both believe and know is a lie all along, being told to you by a scoundrel. The worst scoundrel of all. Yourself.

As Stinkeye sometimes says, "No one lies to ya like yas lie to yaselves, Little King."

But I digress.

Our Ultra was telling me what Ultras did in situations like the one we were facing out there.

"Ultra light infantry indirect fire teams," Ulysses went on. "Which is what we're facing, Sergeant. They come with two overwatch groups providing security. In essence, if they're operating as we used to twenty-five years ago, and I have no evidence to suspect this has changed under General Arkadees, then we're facing three elements involved with the indirect fire team. One team of snipers on overwatch, usually elevated. One gun team to suppress any counterattack against the mortars, concealed. Then the mortar teams themselves. Three two-man teams with three perimeter security total to cover. I surmise the captain knew I knew this, as any Ultra would know it, and felt it best that you take me along to make sure we neutralize this threat effectively with as little loss of friendly forces as possible."

Ulysses spoke concisely and clearly. His communication was effective. I would have killed for a platoon, or even a squad, of this guy. Remember most people don't know how to talk without a lot of extraneous words or slang, or just *umm*s and *aw*s and *you know*s or the one Sergeant Orion beats out of all comm traffic every time it surfaces, *It's like, ya know...*

I will not digress. I really should on the subject of *It's like, you know*. But... I will not.

I shoulda been an Ultra, I think as this kid lets me know, concisely and clearly, exactly what I need to know to get done out there what we're being sent to do. He's answering my question completely and efficiently without extra words. What a paradise, never mind the death cult, pain worship, and various weird stories I've heard about the Ultras. Imagine how stuff gets done in that organization, I think wistfully.

Only a platoon sergeant would appreciate such a crisp effective organization where not only everyone does their job, they know their job, and seek, at every possible moment, to do a better job, at their job.

Half of Strange wants to be Ghost for various dumb reasons like you don't get shot at as much in the back there and they do all the cool stuff.

Never mind that these statements are in direct contradiction with one another. You can't hang back and do cool stuff. Cool stuff usually means fast-roping in behind the enemy and cutting throats or working fast suppressed, metaphorically holding your breath the entire time because technically you are surrounded by the enemy when you're running amok in the enemy rear. Doing cool stuff and all.

And in an effort to actually get recruited for Strange's high-speed, low-drag platoon, the Ghosts, the makers of these asinine statements, rarely do anything to actually convince anyone they're Ghost material.

Before I was the Reaper "plat daddy," I was in Ghost for a while. I got real good at working point to get noticed, and as has been admitted to in these log slices, very good with the karambit in order to take out sentries quick and deadly if we were doing it that way. In Ghost I got better at these things and learned the dark arts of high explosives and general dirty tricks.

I did those two things before the Reaper Platoon leader at the time came and thought it might be nice to come and hang with them for a while.

We're ready to head out now and I comm with the first sergeant and tell him we're crossing over the line of advance.

"Good to go, Reaper Actual. Come back with all your fingers and toes, and make sure them Ultras is actual dead.

They got hang-back-and-play-dead protocols when they're losing. Doghouse out."

I catch myself looking away at the dead under their ponchos over there, or what remains of them in the case of Hotsoup who caught a mortar round coming in. So there's that, I think to myself. Away from our dead, Choker is poking one of the downed Ultras with a burnt stick he's torn out of the apocalypse-blasted rubble of our LZ.

He sees me watching and tosses the stick away. Then walks off to do his job and make sure everyone is hydrating to be ready for whatever comes next. There're probably injuries he should check on.

If I'd asked Choker what the hell he was doing with that stick, poking a dead enemy who'd managed to make it inside our perimeter, he probably would have said something like, "Just wanted to see if they're any different than us, Sar'nt. You know... for intel or something."

But that would have been a lie. He was doing it because he's a psychopath, or a sociopath. Regardless of the constant distraction psyop he's running against me that he is indeed a sociopath, he's a psycho. I know it. He knows it. That's why he lies about it.

But he's *my* psycho or sociopath. And that's the fun of being a plat daddy in the Strange. Every boot in this outfit is the same as Choker on some level. None of us is an Ultra.

Again, I say that almost wistfully. Like I've stumbled into some better resort with a bunch of my drunken, ugly, lowlife friends and seen other fine and beautiful people not us eating chilled shellfish on silver platters full of ice, sipping cold white wine, and murmuring polite conversation.

I turn back to Ulysses and study that handsome face, noticing a tiny scar under his chin. It comes up just over the top of the chin from under the strap of his helmet. I take a deep breath and I'm glad I spotted it on him. It means he's not perfect. Take that. You're one of us now, loser. It means that... and that there's no such thing this side of eternity. Perfection, that is. That he, Ulysses the super soldier, and believe me he really is based on skills and all, never mind the spectacuthriller good looks and natural athleticism, is flawed just like us, even in some small way. He's just like Choker, and even Punch who will fight anyone or anything any time. And me. Whose flaws are many and well known.

And those Ultras we gotta go kill now... they ain't perfect either. And that's why I haven't been breathing deeply, or at all, since the captain gave me the op to go out and waste them. But now I know, they ain't perfect. Even in some small way. They can be killed too.

I hit my smart canteen and suck cold coffee as I ask Ulysses how to kill his former brothers, wondering why he's here with us now. Wondering if I can trust him. Remembering the Old Man stood credit for him. Then I stow my smart canteen and gather my team.

"Listen up, Strange... this is how we're gonna do this. And... no one dies on this one. Got me, idiots?"

They're *my* idiots. They ain't perfect, but they're mine. And I need all of them for reasons I haven't quite figured out yet. I just know... I can't be like Stinkeye.

That way... lies da heart of darkness, Little King.

CHAPTER TWELVE

Movement to contact, for me, is as tense as it gets. Some people like offense better. I get that. I like having the advantage of surprise. Getting to choose the time and place of the fight and naturally you get the upper hand when you got the numbers because doctrine says so. You only get to be the aggressor when you got at least three-to-one odds.

Trust me, seven-to-one is the way to roll.

But I don't mind defense as much as the next guy. I've seen guys in Strange get all itchy about that. Listening to the gunfire out there rolling their way as units forward of your position and all along the line get probed and engaged by the enemy. Sitting there waiting, you start thinking about how little cover concealment, armor, and ammo you got to work with for the sounds of what's coming your way. It gets in your hard drive. Then there's the fact that the enemy can plot fire and start dropping indirect all over you... and it gets to you for a minute as you sit there and wait to get it on.

Me, I really don't mind defense. You have some time to plan some dirty tricks. You know the terrain. Or at least a little better than the guys coming at ya because chances are they've only got drone or map recon going 'cause you iced all their scouts and shot up their probes. One time I jumped out of the trench with Punch and just went after a probe. That surprised the hell outta them. The regulars we were facing on Pthalo decided not to come at us for the rest of the day after that little stunt. Hey, I'm not sayin' defense is great. Believe me, seven-to-one and mortar support any day, every day, all day. That's the way to roll. Maybe even tac air on station. But I'm just sayin'… I don't mind defense.

Having said that, I'd just added up what we were likely facing out there once we found the Ultra indirect team that would start shelling the LZ, and our ride off this rock, and reached the conclusion that Hauser, Duster, Ulysses, Wolfy, and me, and don't forget Stinkeye because… maybe and all… that we most likely didn't have seven-to-one odds to roll them.

One crew-served. Two guys. Sniper team. Two guys. Three mortar teams. Six guys. Three security for the mortars. That added up to me as not even being remotely in the neighborhood of seven-to-one. In fact… they outnumbered us.

To give the Old Man the benefit of the doubt, a thing I'm doing lately, we had a combat cyborg, massive combat multiplier there. An Ultra. Technically that equaled one of them, but I had a feeling, and I don't know why here, just that maybe it was the way our usually unimpressed captain raised his eyebrows slightly when Ulysses gave us his name. Ulysses Two Alpha Six. Apparently all Strange is whispering about this, and both Chiefs Cook and Stinkeye have become opposite factions, of course, in this game, that Ultra names are actually job designations.

That Ulysses Two Alpha Six means something important. Something big.

And we had Stinkeye who could occasionally do something incredible, for us even sometimes. Or, get us all sucked into the big black hole at the center of the galaxy. A thing he'd drunkenly claimed to be able to do one night when

Scooch over in Dog beat him so badly at Cheks that Stink had to eat rations for a week while we were planetside at some refit facility because he had no mem for the bars or meat on the street.

Still, the odds were not in our favor, doctrinally speaking. But I am a wily old hobo. And I have a combat cyborg.

We made our way out to the hit location, moving quickly along carved gashes and piles of D-beam-blackened glass melted into bizarre doomsday shapes. Sometimes, within these strange structures you'd see the possessions of the people who'd lived here prior to the strike. On this second-to-last Monarch-ruled world.

Which was still an amazing thing. I've never been on a world the Monarchs called one of theirs. Just colonies. Marsantyium was one of a handful they'd once called their personal homes.

Earth… was their home world. Not ours. Rumor was that Earth was all they had left now that we were ruining them here in Saffron City and across the rest of this hellish jungle paradise.

I don't know what I was expecting to see in the melted glass structures. I guess something other than what I saw. But what was frozen there, melted as though transformed only a little in the intense heat of the orbital strike, was so common it seemed like it shouldn't be here on a Monarch world. Everyday items, now seemingly forever frozen in the act of dark destruction when someone had fired the D-beams from orbit.

And there were also corpses in there, baked in the apocalypse glass forever.

Around and above us, the misty sand from the *Spider's* sandcaster defensive armaments was beginning to fade by the time we made the ring of structures that marked the limits of the orbital strike that had cleared LZ Heartbreak for us to come in and not get much accomplished so far in the now zero plus two hours since the Insurrection invasion began on this last of two remaining Monarch worlds.

Across the vast sprawling jungle city out there, the cackle of chimp automatic weapons broke out in sudden demonic choruses that mixed with the shrieking of the Simia as they tried to overrun another entrenched Ultra position somewhere along their collapsing line.

Of course, the Ultras replied in a more businesslike and murderous fashion. The sounds of their lethal responses were much more measured, controlled, brutal. Something workmanlike in it as it all went down out there with the wild shrieking of the chimps rebounding and reverberating off the city walls and avenues as both forces collided and pushed to see who'd be alive five minutes from now.

In those sudden explosions of combat, my little kill team would pause and listen as one, without anyone even giving the halt. Hauser would quietly identify the weapon systems being used as he scanned our route through the rubble forward, watching for Ultra snipers and possible sudden ambushes of brutality that would settle our service records finally. We listened as the combat cyborg assessed and analyzed the battles we were hearing out there in a city being overrun by death and madness. That was one of his functions. Battlefield tactical and combat analysis on the go.

Very helpful.

Monarch Ultra hunter-killer combat cyborg teams, of which Hauser had been in one, consisted of three Hausers who could devastate entire companies of regular infantry when all three were carrying complete heavy weapons packages, sensor and analysis suites, and heavy anti-personnel support launchers in the form of either heavy one-twenty mortars or recoilless rocket launchers.

"Yalli and Kocher firing 7.92×57mm Mauser," whispered Hauser as we halted, and he scanned the spreading debris for ambushes. "Fifteen-round bursts indicate they're suppressing beyond the recommended parameters."

A second later: "Degtyaryov machine gun firing seven-six-two. Simia squad automatic gunners are carrying those. Dumping the drum, Sergeant Orion. Rounds fired inaccurately but at high volume. Effective in close quarters battle if the Ultras are using bunkers to defend from. My sensor analysis would suggest the Simia are pushing… and winning, Sergeant Orion."

He'd note sniper fire when it rang out, small arms fire when it erupted in sudden long bursts, and differentiate between types of explosives being used. Mines being detonated against the invaders or frags being used by the Ultras to keep the screaming nightmare monkeys back.

Then Hauser noted the Ultras were going to final protective fires on one battle we were hearing out there. That fight had gone utterly frenetic off to our west a few blocks. The rest of the kill team had already figured out that whoever was defending was down to their last few meters and were dumping everything they had. The Ultras were getting overrun, and their commander had ordered everything fired to hold the collapsing line.

For a moment the chaos was insane as machine guns chattered, grenades were used with abandon, a string of mines detonated like rippling chain lightning, and still, on the other side of all that, the junky Simia weapons continued to chatter and bark in reply, competing with the angry psychotic screams of the chimps surging forward to overrun the last of the Monarchs' guard dogs.

Then I remembered they, the Ultras dying out there, they were just like us as I watched Ulysses scanning the heights for snipers. His eagle eyes scoured every shadow and potential recessed shooting hide. His brothers were dying amid the demonic monkey screaming... and that didn't distract him from his constant scan. He wasn't grieving in the least as I, standing there and already tired in my boots of this long day getting longer, listened as the last of the Ultras in that position out there... died violently.

A kind of silence followed the last string of mine detonations being used in the final defense. For a moment the soundscape was blown out by the fading explosions, and as our hearing came back, you could detect the small *pop*s and the underwhelming *bang bang bang*s of carbines and pistols getting used with precision at the last defense.

Then a final wave of junky, rattling, overwhelming monkey gunfire... and silence. You could imagine the chimps out there, hulking, hairy arms holding smoking weapons with drum mags seated atop the barrels. Casting looks of murder about the silent devastation they were standing in as the dust cleared and the morning turned toward burning noon. Dead Ultra infantry everywhere, spent brass in piles.

A future horror no one would have ever imagined.

Then some Ultra pulled his last grenade and blew himself up as the chimps got close enough for that guy to take a few more to Ultra Valhalla, or whatever they believe in.

Then the monkeys beginning to scream and shriek in victory.

It was insane when you stopped and thought about what was really going on out there.

We were stopped. Stopping in the shadow of a building that had been raggedly sliced in half by the D-beam strike as if that was an ordinary thing.

Believe me, a building cut in half by a D-beam strike is utterly mesmerizing. And they're not just buildings like you'd see on every human colony world. They're... amazing.

"Hell, Sar'nt," said Duster who was right behind me and just off to my left watching the fractured remains all around us for shadows and ambushers in crevices as the chimps' victory-screeched. "Don't know what's worse... going after Ultras, or the fact that those things are on our side some-how. That's pure nightmare fuel right there, Sar'nt. Anyone think what's gonna happen when we all kill our mutual en-emies? What're them chimps gonna do then?"

Yeah, I felt the cold shiver walk up my spine too.

We'd taken a knee, everyone covering behind chunks of rubble that were the former lives of a people we never knew. The shrieking and screeching out there of the mon-keys was cacophonic as it echoed through the streets of the ruined city. That was when I felt some cold river run down my spine as I got a vision, or just a nightmare, of what the universe was going to look like going forward now that the chimps were players in the big galactic battle for all the mar-bles, and what remained of human-controlled space.

We were beyond the wire now. Beyond the protection of the defense guns of the *Spider* or supporting fire from Ghost or Dog. The city all around was fantastic and silent despite its ongoing destruction. If there had been people here, they were gone now. It was definitely war-torn. Craters and hell-holes punched into the facades of great and ornate walls. Piles of red marble collapsed in the streets in great dusty mounds. Shattered windows on the tall faces of the monumental buildings that made me feel small and insignificant.

And then there were those grand buildings themselves. They weren't just buildings. They were more. Words like temple, palace, and other bigger words seemed more appropriate as we stared up and around at all the greatness that had been denied us. In the runup to the attack, we'd gotten a briefing on what types of structures we'd be moving through once the attack commenced. Briefings regarding breaching and fighting into and from these types of structures. I'd merely listened and studied photographs and reports and thought of everything in military terms.

Thinking I knew what I was getting into. What I'd see once we were on the ground. Instead... it was jaw-dropping.

Almost universally the architecture of Saffron City was marble. Red marble veined in gold. Sturdy stuff that would stand up to small arms fire and even rockets and heavy machine-gun fire. Great stuff for both cover and concealment.

As an NCO leading infantry, I liked that. As an NCO leading infantry supporting mechs, no go. I had concerns. Why? Mechs had a hard time with structures, and I'd often seen their pilots and crews just try to punch through obstacles because they'd picked up that bad habit by getting away with it on other, cheaper worlds where the construction was little more than disposable colonization habs and what had been erected in recent years.

Not these buildings. These were built to last a thousand millennia. Or at least that was the thought as I stared up and tried to take it all in.

Send a mech combat team into a fight on a world with some history and good solid building materials, and that mech was most likely going to get hung up in some collapsed rubble, or have the entire structure come down on it when it tried to punch through.

In the defense of the mech crews, it's good to remember that as soon as they enter a battle, everyone, and I mean everyone, starts shooting everything they have at them immediately. Mechs are kill on sight and kill right now. Thus, mechs often tried to overrun structures either to eliminate the teams firing anti-armor at them from the cover within, or because they were trying to get enemy fire off them and the mech crews would use the cover to absorb some hits the armor was taking. Then the enemy could detonate planted explosives and bring down the structure on the mech with a chance of either deadlining it or taking it out of action completely.

And even if the mech was just stuck for a few, the enemy could get close with incendiaries and light up the heat sinks with burning fuel. And that was bad.

Mech crews didn't just get all battle lust and go romper stomper... they had their reasons for trying to plow through structures. But here... they'd have a difficult time with that. We knew that going in.

So, as an infantry small unit leader I'd been thankful for the sturdy cover and concealment provided by these monuments, gained from images I'd observed during the map recons of this, the Monarchs' second-to-last held world, but I had concerns regarding the mech crews.

If the mechs started taking fire from these structures, I had to get my guys in there, breaching and clearing to keep the anti-armor fire off the big boys. I'd ordered my guys to take double flashbangs to get the jump on entrenched defenders. Also, each platoon had a Carl gunner carrying the ancient fabled recoilless rifle launcher that had followed humanity out into the stars so we could kill each other.

Correction. Each platoon had one Carl gunner. Strange had been low on MeGoosae plural slang for the Carl, singular MeGoosa, and so Biggs, go big or go home Biggs, had dug out an old relic from Earth's ancient past that had been sitting deep down in the dark of the ancient weapons stores of the *Spider*. The old clamshell markings in Numerica labeled it simply an M67. Whatever that was. Like the Carl it was a recoilless rifle firing rocket rounds. Unlike the Carl it was a ninety-millimeter launcher and we had a ton of HEAT and anti-personnel rounds to use for it.

Goods was the gunner. Itchy the ammo carrier. Both were back in the defense on our sector of the LZ. I'd wanted to move fast and hit fast.

Now, actually moving through the urban terrain we would be fighting much of the battle in, I was overwhelmingly impressed with how immense and permanent it was. The architecture was something I'd only ever seen in movies. It was… impressive. Repetitive I know, but… it stunned you and made you feel stupid in its grand Monarch glory. The streets were wide as though for the parades of divisions of snap-and-starch Ultras in triumph that would be seen on any given day. Great for the mechs. Bad for the infantry. Wide open and exposed to excellent fields of fire, infantry would be sitting ducks out there. I'd known that going in. I'd keep the guys close to the walls. That was my plan. As soon as we got contact, we'd react appropriately. If they were entrenched, we'd stack and breach with flashbangs and go in shooting high-dosage to eliminate the threat.

Strange might have lacked many things, but when it came to door-kicking, we knew what we were doing.

If the entrenched teams were elevated, then we'd use the recoilless rifles with anti-personnel rounds while the rest of the squads suppressed that position. Open fire and the gunners would launch a dialed-in round that'd send a shotgun of tungsten balls speeding away in every direction all over the bad guys trying to kill our big boys going romper stomper in the streets.

But back to the amazing city all around us. It was… I know… words fail… but it was monumental in ways I'd never imagined actually seeing in my lifetime. Most of my life has been spent on dirty, cold, haphazard colony worlds, or burning sand-blown colony worlds that aren't all that old. Very few things were made to last. On those worlds you could still see that most things were built out of need, as opposed to… opulence. Like this world. Things built for some primal human desire to create something so immense in a vast universe that does everything it can, every day of your life, to make you feel small and insignificant.

And in some way, it all felt like I was a part of it, despite the Monarchs' desire to insist *they* were true humanity, and that we, the rest of us out in the dark of the stars, were something other. Every building was familiar. If that was because of all the spectacuthrillers I've seen, or something unknown inside my genetic memory, I don't know. But it was like looking into a humanity I'd known was there all along. And discovering that it was grander, richer, and more beautiful than I ever could have imagined.

Even as it was being destroyed all around me.

As we began to take fire from the Ultra crew-served weapon guarding the mortar position we'd stumbled upon most likely, I have to confess in that instance that I was… proud. Proud something like this had been built by humans.

Humanity. Even if that humanity rejected its one-point-oh version.

The buildings, many of them on the street we were moving down, keeping to the blue shadows being thrown by the enormous structures, were so grand and immense they seemed impossible in their construction. They were faced by huge, fat with permeance, scalloped columns that had to be multi-tons in and of themselves. The gold-veined red marble was swirling and beautiful and so sturdy that where these columns had been hit by indirect chimp artillery fire, they hadn't collapsed. Instead they were pockmarked or had large sections of their fullness torn out of them by the falling screaming rounds. But they were still upright. Still holding the grand temples they fronted aloft, daring the universe to challenge them. To challenge the human spirit among the stars.

Temples. They were like that.

I've seen a lot of temples in my time across the worlds of the outer expansion of humanity. I've seen them on all the worlds I've traveled to. I pay attention to them when I encounter them. I've seen all kinds. Reed structures climbing into the sky that seem like they're about to fall over in a strong wind yet according to the alien locals they've been there a thousand years of recorded history. Or incense wafting out of frog-shaped piles of green dark stones where one crosses giant sturdy moss to enter the temple and descend down into the sacred grottos, seeing strange gems that glow within and sometimes, according to the locals, whisper deep truths about life and the universe if you'll meditate long enough and pay out enough mem, back in the day when mem was worth anything, to recompense the local priests for enlightenment.

But… I've never seen anything like the massive structures in Saffron City. Even remotely so. Maybe in the spectacuthrillers that center on the opulence of the beautiful life of the Monarchs, our betters. A life of incredible luxury and excessive excess without restraint, and of course the constant drama no one ordinary can relate to. *Whose noble firstborn child is the Chosen One to save the Galaxy? Which world rests in the fate of a Hero's hands? The love of a woman who has the cold beauty, and powers, of a Goddess.* In those entertainments the Monarch stars are always fighting over piles of fantastic mem, or just wealth beyond imagining of the simple like me. Or murdering their rivals and enemies for grand wrongs done in ancient times.

I'm just looking for a cheap used scout ship to head out and try to make a little for myself.

But who does that? Murder your enemies? In real life? I mean every person on every world has got an enemy. Of course they do. Rarely do they plot and scheme to get the guy down the block who bugs them because he's always playing his music a bit too loud during the off-hours. Most people just seethe and hate in silence. Not Monarchs. They launch wars of a thousand ships over some slight. They weave intricate schemes and plots to steal their rivals' wealth as some kind of justice due. These spectacuthrillers are fun, but apparently that's all there is to do in the lives of the wealthy and powerful. The Monarchs, that is.

Ordinary people… seethe hate and maybe look to do a little better this year than they did last.

But wait… as I think on it, as I put this all down… you did murder your rival, Orion. Remember… back on Astralon, Crash, call it what you will. There are the remains of a burnt-out crawler on a desert LZ in the middle of nowhere. Inside that roasted ruin is a certain NCO who used to be your nemesis.

It was self-defense?

The incoming fire is from the crew-served weapon Ulysses hipped us to in the quick brief before we got sent out here to wipe them out. The one on overwatch for the no-doubt nearby mortar teams. Ulysses said there would be a sniper team too. And a crew-served on overwatch. Then the mortar teams. Three of them. Each with one perimeter security gunner using some level of squad suppression weapon. Most likely high-cycle belt-fed with a nanoconductor-cooled barrel.

The odds are nowhere near seven-to-one.

"Contact!" yells Wolfy, who returns fire with a shot from his rifle. The rest of the kill team scramble for cover as Wolfy calls out the crew-served gun's position and elevation. I suck dust and hear that they're three stories up inside a giant's head that is the fantastic facade of the building that faces the wide and once-beautiful street. Massive urns line the center of the wide avenue here. An avenue that must have once thronged with cars and a-grav vehicles. Or divisions of Ultra Marines marching in triumph and another colony world smashed for the glory of the Monarchs.

Definitely a-grav vehicles would have driven this road as I crawl for cover while rounds smash into urns and streak overhead. This is a Monarch world after all. Nothing but mammoth red clay urns for them. Giant bougainvillea-overflowing urns must be used for we are not men, we are gods among the stars!

Every brick, and I don't even think they use bricks here, but still bricks is all I can think of… but every brick on this world screams the message of gods among the stars.

And yet it is their second-to-last world and we are here to ruin them on it. It's time, Strange, to get it on good and hard.

The giant's head high above seemed like the face of some god from an elder age glaring out over the city. Carved in the local red marble, its features are fine and beautiful, the pinnacle of human perfection writ large, as I slither on my back behind cover and see bright red tracer rounds streaking overhead. The soulless eyes of the giant head god are nothing more than blank spaces. From one of these eyes the Ultras have detonated the marble, blowing it outward from the empty eye socket when they set up the kill zone to overwatch the nearby mortar teams that must be setting up behind the piles of rubble further up the street. From the empty eye socket of the strange human god the machine-gun team is traversing us with plunging fire.

Good for them, I think and then mutter, "Got somethin' for you, bastards…"

The Ultra's powerful crew-served weapon sends hot rounds streaking down at us. They ranged badly in the first burst and came up short. Perhaps because of the way Hauser patrols, he'd gotten us close enough that they were surprised when they spotted us, or the ground sensors went off, and they had to lower the gun to engage us fast. That had jammed their chi. As my team scrambles for cover, I see one of the bougainvillea-filled urns in the center of the street get hit and shatter as a round smacks into and then through it. Red dirt pours out as the pottery shatters and crumbles in the beautiful parade-ready street. More rounds smack the street, chew up the paving of the road, and ricochet toward us and off in other directions all at once. Tracers alternate and streak away like lasers in the misty morning rising as the day promises heat.

More rounds come in and I'm wondering where the snipers are as we begin to reply with gunfire of our own. No doubt the Ultras are calling targets to one another over their comm. Instead of coming out to hunt and kill them, we've walked right into it.

Good going, me.

Regardless, assessing the situation, it looks bad for us instantly. I slither for more cover behind a white-marble-veined-in-red-and-gold abutment that indicates the limits of what must've been some kind of café on this street. It's just enough cover if I keep low and close to it. A huge round knocks stone away from it and while it scares the hell out of me and makes me swear, I'm safe here.

"Look for the snipers!" I shout above the chaos and chance a look to see what's going on when there's a break in the crew-served action. Hauser's moving forward, using the urns as cover, suppressing the Ultra machine-gun team with short bursts of fire on the move. Staying mobile and moving fast with a high-cycle light machine gun is classic combat cyborg tactics. It's a total blitz.

They can also do this with medium machine guns.

But Hauser prefers the Pig.

"It's effective at close quarters, Sergeant Orion, and acceptable engagement parameters at range," Hauser has told me more than once. "I have found my speed and accuracy can often put me in a position to surprise biologics at close quarters due to their inability to determine that I am not one of them and instead a combat cyborg unit with a much higher strength and mobility rate. The shorter barrel length allows me a higher effective rate for termination at the standard gunfight range of seven to fifteen meters. Anything larger would be… unwieldy, Sergeant Orion. But not impossible. But that type of weapon would allow more of them to escape my maximum effective kill window."

Remember all those recoilless rifles I was just talking about? The MeGoosa or the 90mm M67… yeah, one of those would be great right about now. But Sergeant Orion didn't think we were gonna get the chance to use one and instead left those in the defense.

He did, on the other hand, attach the grenade launcher to the lower barrel of the tried-and-true Bastard he seems to keep carrying into all these conflicts on all these worlds instead of spending some of his hard-earned mercenary pay on a good rifle system like much of the rest of Strange in Reaper doesn't.

Punch could. He saves everything he gets paid. But he likes the shorty Bastard he carries and swears by it. Even though he lost a couple of fingers on the last one. Still, he stands by the S16 as being the best weapon humanity ever produced to go out and kill their enemies among the stars with.

"Duster!" I shout, unsure where my EOD guy managed to find some cover as more six- to eight-round bursts dose our current position. The distant crew-served gun goes *dumba dumba dumba dumba… dumba dumba* at regular intervals as gunner and AG try to engage the sudden monkey scramble my kill team has become below their engagement window.

Hauser is charging and firing at them. If I were them, I'd be afraid. Unlike other biologics on other worlds we've faced, I'm sure the Ultras' helmets and armor systems can identify combat cyborgs and all kinds of weapons. Meanwhile I can hear Wolfy get off another shot. He's good. I mean he's none of the shooters in Ghost. But he's good. Ulysses… no idea. I can only see so much, pinned and taking fire and all.

For a moment Duster doesn't come back to me in real-time or over the comm.

Uh-oh, I think. Another dead troop.

"This might as well happen," I mutter and get ready to adjust my own fire as, lying on my back, I heft the Bastard up at an angle where I roughly think the crew-served position might be if I land a forty-millimeter grenade on them. I see the lip of the concrete wall I'm covering behind and remind myself not to send the launched grenade right into that. I raise the launcher barrel mounted beneath my rifle a little higher after I pat the wall for no reason at all.

Good luck, I guess.

Maybe I'm telling it to be nice and not get in the way of the high-explosive round I'm about to send with all the love in the galaxy at my enemies?

They'd do the same to me.

But then Duster is there, yelling from just behind me up the street we're fighting on.

"Comm's bad, Sar'nt. I'm here. Whatcha wanna do, Boss?"

To Duster everyone is *Boss*. There's a story there I bet, but now, being shot at and all, now ain't the time.

"Work your way up to the end of the wall, hang out and keep your face down. Need to see where this thing lands," I shout back at him as more incoming fire works someone else on the hot street.

The crew-served weapon is firing on Hauser, farther up the street, running and gunning faster than they can traverse and target, as he opens fire on them.

It's a race. If he can make the building the Ultra machine gun team is in, he'll do them quicker than they can imagine. Imagine a deadly animal running at you with no wall, or barrier, or protection between you and it. Now imagine that fast-moving deadly animal has a machine gun. That's Hauser.

I hear an Ultra sniper rifle go off. It's a thunderous crack that echoes out over the street. The rumor is, and I've really only ever faced Ultras back on Crash… is that Ultra line units don't like to work suppressed. Even the squad designated marksmen and snipers.

"Da terrah…" Stinkey once told me, meaning terror. "Thas the weapon they like to use da most, Little King. Dey want yas to know it's comin' right for yas and all. Them big snipes go a'firin' and they wantcha to hear the boom."

Then he hit his flask and wandered off drunkenly mumbling some old-guy song none of us knew or had ever heard on all the worlds we'd ever traveled to.

"Here come da boom, childrens," he crooned raggedly. Then he'd just laugh like it was the funniest thing in all the worlds. If he sang it once, if it somehow got into his hard drive, he'd sing it for the rest of the day. And eventually everyone got annoyed by this because there was no way to figure out where the old song came from as it wasn't on any of the services or streaming libraries.

I asked Nether if he'd ever heard the song.

Nether merely told me, "It's not the classics from Earth, Orion. It's not Bach. And that's all I listen to. That's my last tether to the universe."

Nether had talked about tethers. The things he needs to anchor himself to our present reality after what had been done to him in the Monarch Dark Labs. And *that*—

the Monarch Dark Labs—that was real Heart of Darkness stuff if what Nether sometimes had to tell me was true. Apparently Nether, due to these experiments, needed time tethering himself to reality, to do what he did for us, or even just to exist. Otherwise… he'd actually disappear and cease to exist. At night he was a shadow. During the day he was invisible. As I have said, this creeped everyone in Strange out. Except me. I found his presence, even if unseen, comforting. Honest. He'd get one pull of my cigarette as we sat there, talking or not talking, before he made it disappear. Just like the foundation of the building he was about to make disappear on another Ultra sniper team out there menacing us on the LZ.

I thumped the first launched grenade out and waited for the explosion. The crew-served weapon continued to fire and Duster shouted adjustments above its thunder.

I loaded another fat round and prepared to fire.

CHAPTER THIRTEEN

"Adjust… two clicks up, left a smidge, Boss!" shouted Duster over the thud of incoming fire from the heavy machine gun in the dead god's eye. Duster had observed the impact of my launched grenade, something I did on my back and without a clear visual on what I was lobbing at. The Ultras didn't seem to appreciate my attention and responded by patiently dosing our position to the rear of their perceived enemy contact with a couple of long bursts from the crew-served they were operating. Duster covered as hot rounds and bright tracers streaked down at us. I was already behind cover, so we were good as they tried to murder us for having tried to murder them.

We were doing war. Nothing personal. Just business. How 'bout another forty-millimeter fragmentation grenade, Ultraweenies! Having said that, even with a good amount of concrete between myself and the impacting rounds they were sending at my position, I was still getting the feeling I was being pulverized by some kind of shock wave from these rounds even through all that thick cover.

I swore and felt like I was gonna barf. For a moment I wanted to go all Puncher and scream that anyone who laughed was going to get punched in the face, but everyone else had problems of their own at that moment.

Intel briefs in the runup to the assault on Marsantyium, second-to-last of the Monarch worlds, had indicated some

Ultra Marine units were now fielding high-energy relativistic kinetic rounds. Later, after the fight there in the middle of the street, I'd get a close look at the effectiveness of my first encounter with HERK rounds, and why I needed them in my life.

They were a game-changer when it came to suppressive fire.

Squad automatic weapons like the light machine gun we called the Pig, which Strange had in abundance on board the *Spider*'s weapon racks and stores, were excellent at suppressing and pinning the enemy so other friendly elements could flank and wipe them out with grenades and automatic gunfire. The one concept that neutralized effective fire, regardless of whether a squad suppression weapon was being used, was cover. If the enemy had it, you had to defeat it so you could start putting rounds on target. There were munitions that did that. We didn't have them in my little ad hoc kill team. Cover defeated most standard carry rounds depending on thickness, durability, and construction.

Generally, seven-six-two defeats cover, is the basic rule of thumb. But not concrete like most hardened positions and bunkers use. Or in the case of a wily old hobo sergeant currently pinned down by a heavy crew-served Ultra machine-gun team, myself in fact, the concrete abutment near the grand roadway where café drinkers must have once sat and watched passing parades of the spit-and-polish Ultra Marines on their way to the temples beyond the canals that guarded the city center, to deliver their triumph, their treasure, and their slaves.

Yeah. I'm hoping readers of this doomed account in the future think I'm lying and making that part up. Actual slavery. But yeah, in Monarch society, slaves were a thing. And if

I was glad about anything other than the long-time-coming general payback against those who'd been uppity enough to declare themselves our betters, I was hoping it was an end to actual slavery.

Removal of free will from any intelligent species is worth dying for as far as this old murder hobo merc sergeant is concerned.

I go all in on that.

But as I was saying, after the battle, when I'd see that the HERK rounds chewed through the concrete I was covering behind as more attention on my position came from the crew-served weapon firing out of the dead god's eye three stories up, down and across the street from my fighting position, I was on the hunt to find as much of these sweet rounds as I could and put them to work for my team.

NCOs, even while pinned and getting shot at by rounds that would tear you in half, are always thinking about supply. Ammo, rats, and sleep for them.

Rats as in rations. Not rats. Rats are everywhere on all the worlds. They came with us from Earth a long time ago. And they've flourished, whereas we're on the verge of destroying ourselves.

When we're gone the chimps will blame us for the rat problem. I can live with that.

Small impacts turned to sudden spreading craters against the other side of my solid cover. Debris sprays scattered the street where the belt-fed rounds had impacted my defense and exploded outward in ways I'd never seen incoming do. What I was feeling as I mentally adjusted my grenade launcher two clicks, was something akin to being vibrated to death by incoming fire. The launcher was fixed to my barrel so there were no adjustments to actually be made other than noting the sights and trying to remember where I'd landed them last time on a target I was guessing the general location of.

The launcher on the Bastard is a best-guess scenario most days of the week. I've learned to do without the sights and when I've gotta use the launcher attachment enough I get fairly good with it.

I hadn't used it in twenty-five years and change. But to be fair, I'd been asleep for most of that time.

When I need to carry an indirect weapon, I'll usually go with something more effective like the Savage Lone Wolf. It's a pump-action grenade launcher that looks a lot like a heavy shotgun. Heavy as all can get but it gets the job done when you gotta drop a lot of frag.

But, with shadowing and ranging the mechs, making sure they didn't get jumped by enemy AT teams, I figured I needed to cut down on my carry and went with the Bastard's launcher attachment.

And the job wasn't getting done.

I made a mental note I probably needed to hump one of the Savage Lone Wolfs for the rest of the battle if we made it back to the LZ and the *Spider*. Once we got back, I could have someone run into stores and grab one from Biggs before the mechs were ready to roll and get involved on our behalf.

If they were ready to roll.

"What the hell is a smidge, Duster?" I shouted angrily as shock waves from the impacting HERK rounds made my voice sound all tremulous. The impacts were vibrating through my body, and I was feeling sick to my stomach and ready to hurl. My eyes were uncontrollably blinking.

I usually feel sick way before a battle, but never right in it. And sometimes occasionally afterward depending on how many body parts are lying around in the sand on the objective.

"Fifteen degrees *left*, Boss! A smidge!"

I made the adjustment, muttering to myself that fifteen degrees didn't sound anything close to a smidge and shouted, "Frag out!" then pulled the trigger for the launcher hanging under the barrel of my scratched and battered but clean-as-a-whistle battle rifle.

I mean there was probably a fine grit of electromagnetic sand in the chamber and barrel from the deployment of the *Spider*'s sandcasters. So, there was that. NCOs think about weapons maintenance and changing socks when they're not thinking about ammo supply, rats, and sleep.

Now you know why I find dark places on the *Spider* and just zone, drinking black coffee and waiting for the next disaster to come looking for me. Technically I'm thirty-six. But I feel eighty.

My launched frag round thumped out as my cover got pulverized and I started getting angry because it was better than being sick.

Now, I don't know if I was actually getting angry at being sick, and tired of getting shot at behind good cover… or Stinkeye was already starting to make his damned mischief. But that was coming…

I just can't blame him for it yet this far in.

"Way off, Boss!" shouted Duster over the blare of the machine gun. He readjusted my fire, and I was having to restrain myself from literally getting on my knees and taking a shot with a clear view of the machine-gun nest. Bet I could hit them then. Also, I'd get ripped to shreds by a highly trained Ultra gunner who was no joke with the weapon he was employing against us.

I made the adjustments from my back, basically blind, and missed again.

So that was the growing anger talking.

This was fine by me, I tried to reason as the shock-wave impacts grew more violent and my trembling fingers struggled to get the next round off my chest rig.

Now I was angry at my fingers. Ever been angry at your fingers? I have. It's weird, man.

Anyway, classic mistake. The Ultras were making a classic mistake and I started chanting that to myself, calling my fingers cowards like the little weasels they were as I opened the launch tube and pushed in the next fragmentation round. The classic mistake... the Ultras were paying attention to the guy with the handheld artillery shooting at them... when they really should've been paying attention to the killer cyborg who'd just made the temple of the dead god and had begun murdering his way right into their machine-gun nest.

Later, as I walked the battlefield slaughter, Hauser talked me through how it all went down as he breached their defenses and began to terminate them.

"I reached the front entrance of the Plague God Temple..." said Hauser in his staccato yet softly calming crisp voice. Apparently, the accent is Germanic as he has told me before.

Have I told you I just like listening to Hauser talk? Sometimes I invite him down to the dark parts of the ship where I hide from everyone and just ask him to tell me everything he knows about something.

Usually it's just mundane technical data. Sometimes he'll tell you things he's learned.

The Germanic tone… it's very calm yet quietly confident. I bet Germans were really cool, whoever they were back on Earth. They sound peaceful and meditative.

Yeah. It was Plague's Temple. If you're reading this log slice after the time of the Monarchs, and I hope you are… Plague was one of the Elder Monarchs, the first to subjugate humanity. I was only dimly aware of his history but knew he'd been some kind of early player in their rise to power. Apparently, Plague was once the ruler of the Monarchs and if you were part of the various cults that made the focus of their lives worshipping these gods among men, then you know all the trivia.

Good for you. I'm glad a large percentage of them were dragged down and done to death by the chimps and the Insurrection that arose across human space during our flight time to Hardrock.

Relativistic travel is a hell of a time machine. The trick is not to pay too much attention to the gaps and just keep gluing your life together in patches and fragments. Telling yourself one day you're gonna find the perfect world to just stay in timeline and end your days with some understanding of current events and the local calendar.

I'd just like to experience seasons for about twenty years and feel them coming before the calendar says it's so. Fall, especially.

Before my lifetime, Plague had fallen into disfavor within the greater Monarch society. But that didn't concern me as I mounted the steps, counting the dead that Hauser had machine-gunned his way through to reach and breach the temple. This was after the battle. I got the logos and symbology stamped in the veined red marble, the letters filled in platinum and written in standard Grand Monarch script and their official font. Of course, they called it High Monarch, and it was forbidden to speak it unless addressing them personally, but you had to learn it as a kid anyway even though you'd probably never use it.

The "conspiracy theorists" who now seemed to have formed the backbone of the Insurrection had always said there was more to it than just learning a language you'd never use.

As I looked back on all this during the flight out to the battle, now having lived as a free man for most of my years on the edge of a vast and yet still growing stellar civilization, making my living as a paid warrior trying to collect enough scratch to maybe scout someday, I realized how much of my "education" was little more than blatant indoctrination by the Monarchs and those who fawningly served them.

Let me put it this way. Going to other worlds and fighting alongside other dudes who had strong and even wrong ideas sometimes, showed me how much of what I thought was true... was just a big ol' lie.

Mind control really.

So, yeah. The Insurrection was long overdue.

Human space had tired of the Monarchs' Current Thing manipulation as Chief Cook had put it, and decided all on its own to start stringing them up.

Hauser showed me the remains of his attack on the Temple of Plague to take out the Ultra Marine crew-served he deemed a "priority threat to mission accomplishment."

Even though they were soldiers just like me, slaughtered by Hauser on the bloody red marble steps leading into the temple, they were still the Monarchs' guard dogs lying there shot to death, much ventilated by Hauser's Pig.

And I was glad they were dead. Them or us. They'd chosen to be the guard dogs of tyrants. The Monarchs were being wiped out to the last. And that I'd had some small part in that… gave me comfort. Even if it was just expended brass and missed grenade shots.

So, what had happened as I was launching ineffective indirect fire, badly at that, with the help of Duster, with Wolfy keeping up the fire on their snipers he'd glassed at distance down the street, was that Hauser had managed to breach the temple, devastating a Monarch combat team stationed there to provide security for the MG team above.

"I took three rounds to the chest…" noted Hauser with little emotion. Just an update of operational status. "… but my internal armor deflected the hits, and all my current onboard systems remain unaffected by the damage, Sergeant Orion. I am operating at expected maximums for this type of warfare."

Just Orion, Hauser, I thought to myself because I was tired of repeating it.

He ignored my unspoken words and continued with his account of storming the Temple of Plague and eliminating the machine-gun team.

I was calmer then. Coming down off what Stinkeye had done to us.

"I identified three Ultra shock troopers reacting to the sudden contact of our force entering the objective. The first trooper was running from the temple, three- to five-second dash to make a position my combat sensor analysis identified as a possible fighting location. I fired eight rounds and achieved seven impacts on target in one point seven eight seconds. Target was effectively neutralized."

I'll bet. Seven giant seven-six-two holes suddenly appearing in your body will do that to you.

I'd seen the dead kid halfway down the steps as we began. I could tell the dead Ultra knew he needed to get forward so the two coming out could alternate covering fire and maneuver. He just had no idea the hulking brute with the chattering Pig was an actual killing machine.

Hauser looks human. And he is. To me. But… he ain't.

"This engagement resulted in a round impacting my chest armor just above the micro-core. It came from the Ultra NCO initiating covering fire from the door to this building. He fired several times. I was moving as I brought my weapon up and engaged with twenty-five rounds. The first impact to strike this target went through the throat six rounds into the spread. The target was dead but continued to fight even though I hit him nine more times as I began to advance on the portal they were firing from."

The arch cut into the Marsantyium marble was the entrance to the temple of the dead god Plague. Rounds from the Pig had scarred the marble and I wondered for how many hundreds or even thousands of years after this day people would wonder how that had happened and never know.

And in time, accept as fact that it was always so. I have seen many such scars like that on old blown-out buildings across all the worlds I've fought on and wondered the same.

Whoever they are, we'll be distant relatives just because of these bullet strikes. I'm cool with that.

The morning was getting hot, and we passed from the developing heat of the day into the cool red shadows of the temple within. The two dead Ultras, and the NCO who'd managed to actually and ineffectively shoot Hauser center mass as the combat cyborg began to advance and murder like the walking death machine he was, still lay there with a ragged bullet hole in his throat.

His helmet was off, and he was just some guy who was done with this whole mess now. He was looking at something I couldn't see, but I was sure one day I would. Maybe one day soon.

This felt like it could go that way. But then again, it always did. Every time.

It was the dead god on the throne at the far end of the room which was little more than a hollow cylinder inside the massive statue of Plague that had fronted the street, that drew my eye next.

Again, I haven't in this account done justice to how overwhelming and awe-inspiring it was, and believe me, I feel dirty even describing a Monarch temple that way because it's pure Monarch sickbags in all their boorish elite piggery, but I have sworn to be as accurate with this account as possible. It's so other than anything you've ever experienced that you keep wondering if it's kind of a dream you're walking through. Unsure that it isn't a nightmare, but still... it's... *that*... epic. In the middle of the sudden fight we got into on the street out there as I launched grenades, badly I will admit again for the record, seriously I wasn't even getting close to nailing the crew-served team, but as it all went down out there at first contact, I wasn't focusing on the fact that the image of a strange Monarch god, Plague himself but writ in colossus, had fronted the street all carved in the local Marsantyium marble. Gold-veined with black flecks. Like the color of dried blood. And yet swirling and beautiful instead of dead and turning to rust. Instead, I'd seen the machine-gun team laying the hate from his gouged-out eye three stories up. I was focusing on that and trying to get my team out of this.

What I was seeing at that first moment of startling gunfire was the battle we were suddenly in. Machine-gun nest engaging us from elevation. Hauser rushing because his combat analysis protocols told him to neutralize the biggest threat to save our hides. Ulysses, I would find out over the comm as Hauser cleared the temple, was flanking right to find the mortar teams and hopefully draw them away from getting involved in the unexpected ambush we'd just walked into.

Tactically brilliant, of course Ulysses would do that. Except we'd walked into a hornets' nest too because there was more going on off to our right there than we'd expected.

Now, after the battle, as Hauser walked me through the killing streak, droning on about the efficient savagery and ruthless termination in his usual Hauser manner, focusing on kill strikes and fatality ratios, listing off the litany of violence he'd carefully measured out against our ambushers to ensure maximum efficiency intersecting with utter violence, all I could do was stare at the dead Monarch god Plague who'd been shot to death on his very own carved red marble throne.

It was like witnessing the assassination of some historical figure you knew of, but didn't know much about in truth, in real-time right in front of you.

On the throne where the body was slumped, it was hard to tell what was local marble and what was the dead god's blood.

He was… smaller. Smaller than you would have ever thought given the images you suddenly started remembering seeing throughout the constant programming of your life. Or even the colossus that was the very building he'd been murdered in. Thinner and slighter than the robust, almost jolly annihilator of humanity who'd liberated the Monarchs from the burden of humanity long, long, ago before there was jump, or even dumb thrust, for the stars. He was slumped on the throne, alone. The blood ran down onto the mosaic floor showing all his achievements across the centuries of our time among the stars.

What was there, on the floor, along with the dead Ultras thanks to Hauser, was history in some form even if it was a lie. It was there with the remains of a blackened spreading frag detonation that had gone off when Ultra Number Three, as the Ultra NCO was getting ventilated good and hard in the defense at the portal by Hauser's Pig, rolled a grenade on Hauser.

Who… had promptly kicked the explosive right back into the temple and continued to fire like it was the most natural thing in the world.

Never mess with a killing machine. They don't call them that just for fun and advertising.

What was there on the mosaiced floor of the Temple of Plague was the history of us all, humanity, but from his point of view.

Of course.

The Monarchs write the official histories. Wrote, that is.

As I've said before… history, real history, was illegal under the Monarchs for at least my entire life. But the reason the Old Man gave me the job of Log Keeper was he knew I had a thing for it even though it was banned and all. He'd seen me around the cities and starports when we were on leave in between contracts, haunting the old forgotten libraries for books that had been declared officially banned for centuries. Or taking the local tours of out-of-the-way historic spots, finding out the real truths of human expansion into the stellar void in dusty old shrines or lonely barely curated museums where the docents dozed and played cards, unaware of the wealth of forbidden truths they kept watch over.

That's how I got the job of Strange Company Log Keeper.

I'm a history junkie, and while I fully accept my picture of the span of human history is vastly incomplete—how could it not be, and also I believe that's a massive understatement—but even given that, I could tell from the brief moments I had with the bloody mosaic floor where Ultras had been shot to pieces as Hauser began to control the room, that Plague had recorded our history as he saw it, and it was access to information on levels I'd never even dreamed of finding.

Even though it was as *he* wanted it to be, I could triangulate, I told myself as I got ready to capture it in the seconds I had with it. I could learn something hidden within the lies. Protected by the lies.

I popped my smart device and took a picture. Then several pictures as fast as I could, attempting to record it all despite the spreading blood of the dead and the dying in this silent and faux-sacred place. If I survived today, and all the days that came after this battle that history will record as the Sack of Marsantyium, then I could study it all after, and hopefully, by detecting the lies, and sensing the flak over the real targets, find out what the truth of all of us has really been all along.

We might finally know, humanity, who we really were. And maybe that will help us become who we are. High-minded. Even I didn't believe that.

I'm just curiously obsessed. That's the truth and sometimes you have to be honest about these things.

The part that caught my eye in the first snapshots from my device was at the center of it all. As though my eyes and mind told me it was important even though my consciousness wasn't recognizing it at first. The part about Plague's development of the bioweapons that had brought humanity into submission. Calling them "medicine" when really they were control and genocide. That was, if you took the impressions and emphasis of the whole mosaic there on a floor being consumed by the spreading blood of dead warriors and their dead god, and according to the one the pretty pictures captured on the floor, it conveyed that this moment had set the Monarchs free to lead humanity to their destiny among the stars.

That's the story Plague would have you believe. The story he had decreed created on the floor of his dusty old forgotten throne room.

There were other achievements there. Other crimes some would call sins. Some I knew. Some I'd heard of. Some I'd only ever suspected. Some that seemed, in fact, simply unbelievable. All of them, each, was portrayed as some immensely great leap in Monarch culture.

All the ones I could recognize had come with incredible death tolls for the mass of humanity.

My prizes captured on my device, I tucked it into my carrier and returned to Hauser's narrative of the battle that

had taken place. He confirmed he'd stormed the stairs leading up to the machine-gun nest, surprised the gunners, and
carefully terminated them with extreme violence of action.

I turned the dead god on the throne.

"You do that one too, Hause?"

I wonder if Hauser even knew who that was, pale and
bloodless, tiny and frail and looking nothing like the god
he'd portrayed himself to be. Even with the Monarch-only
longevity treatments that made him seem young across all
the centuries of outward stellar expansion. The implants to
give him stronger features, and hair even.

It was hard to look at the corpse and not wonder who
he really was. Who he'd really been when the Monarchs had
sought their own destiny at the expense of humanity in the
long mists of a history they'd so thoroughly destroyed to
cover all of their crimes. I doubted we'd truly ever know
where, or how, we'd come to our present moments for the
rest of our future.

But these are just the musings of a ruck-hump hobo
NCO who just happened to be a part of the shenanigans
that overturned the old order and gave humanity a chance
to carve its own destiny out here in the dark.

We'd see how much better we could do, but even I didn't
have high hopes for us. I'm an optimist that way.

"Negative, Sergeant. The Ultras did that. Entry and exit
wounds are indicative of their current armaments on site."

Above the dead god slumped on the bloody throne I
saw words carved in High Monarch. A language I'd never
honestly used, but had been forced to learn long ago with
numbers and phonics and so many other things that came
along with the learning.

I sounded them out in the dead silence of the place having no idea what they meant anymore. The knowledge of such things was dying with the Monarchs.

"Optimus Maximus Gates."

CHAPTER FOURTEEN

So, the dead god on the bloody red throne, that would come after the fight we'd just walked into when I was lying on my back and trying to contribute indirect fire. Let me step back a bit in this account because I had to put Hauser's actions down first for the official company account before I got to the next part we got involved in.

It's too bad we don't give out medals in the Strange because Hauser definitely earned one. If our combat cyborg hadn't pushed on the machine-gun nest initially at first contact, running and gunning at full speed to neutralize the threat an entrenched crew-served weapon with elevation and a good field of fire for both traversing and plunging fire, then my little kill team and myself would have been wiped out in fairly short order.

But we don't give medals in the Strange. Generally, we just hand out lots of good-natured scorn. And to be honest not all of it is good-natured. Some of it's just downright cruel. I know, I'm skinny as a rail and I got no hips. But finding stick figures drawn of yourself with the words "Lifelike Representation of Orion" hurts. It stings, guys. Maybe we could find something else to do like get good at fire discipline and other useful warfighting skills.

So, do something like Hauser did, if you're a regular guy in one of Strange's line platoons, then everyone's gonna call you "hero" for the foreseeable future. And not in a

146

good way. Like, "Hey Hero, you got guard duty oh-three to zero-six. That brave enough for you?" Or, "We need some ammo from supply… send the hero because all of us are too scairt to go!" Then much laughter from everyone. So you're gonna get a lot of cruddy jobs to do because you're *a hero* and all.

You'll learn better if you live.

In the Strange we don't want anyone to ever think they're better than us, due to the fact that we all hate ourselves so much.

It's a sort of weird way of staying humble. But it works for us. Go change someone else. We got a contract to fulfill.

But Hauser is different than the rest of us in ways that are obvious, and not so much.

Everyone likes our combat cyborg on a personal level, like the company dog if we had one. They like him even though most of them only view him as a thinking-killing machine that can game-change hard when it needs to get done and we're not getting it done. For them, to have him around for rainy days when the lead is thick and hot in the air and the LZ isn't just hot, it's on fire… that's good enough for them. They appreciate him in that way. As I have noted before, they will not hesitate to sacrifice him to get their bacon right out of the heat stove at the drop of a hat. Especially if the situation is particularly dire in the nature of what looked to be a few last stands we've been unfortunate enough to participate in on recent contracts. You should've seen us back in the day.

But we don't do medals in the Strange.

We just do jokes to keep grim mortality at bay and pass the time.

So, Hauser's prompt and violent elimination of the gun team that would have shot us all to pieces allowed Ulysses to counterattack three two-man mortar teams including their security located off to the right of our line of march at first contact, all by his lonesome.

He correctly surmised we'd walked into it, and that they, our enemy and his former brothers, had two options they could pursue in response to our incursion. It was conceivable they could have started dropping steel, danger close, all over our attack. Ulysses didn't give them time to figure out where we were exactly, and that there might not be more of us than they were picking up from observation and whatever local radar sensor they were running.

So as Hauser charged and I thumped, the rest of the team got engaged with their specific skill sets. As the NCO who has trained them much, I'd like to take credit for all this. But no credit will be given. Wolfy engaged Ultra snipers who had taken up a position on a rooftop with a clear field of fire down another intersecting avenue. Those enemy snipers still had the ability to shift to cover the mortar teams. Ulysses Two Alpha Six, a former Ultra, went wide right behind the debris piles created by a collapsed building farther up the street toward the intersection where the mortars were setting up to attack the LZ as the dust-filled skies began to clear and their spotter got ready to request a fire mission no doubt.

Ulysses covered behind the debris piles further up the street and kept working to the right, away from the Ultra gun team above in the dead god's eye.

So, to lay out the battle. The dead god temple was at our ten o'clock of our primary objective, the mortars. Those were at our twelve up the street where two avenues intercepted one another in a Y intersection.

The snipers were at one and taking fire from a guy in a real awful starport kiosk wolf T-shirt.

As spit-and-polish Ultras, the galaxy's tip-of-the-spear killers, I bet that had to bother them on some level. I'd like to think that, but I'm so black-pilled on humanity, I bet the Ultra spotter working alongside the sniper sporting the massive HEX long-range engagement system with the vented fat hexagonal barrel and Zeiss-Oro cyberscope optic was like, "Yo, this guy's got some sweet wolf shirt on! Gotta see…" while Wolfy engaged and domed the both of them.

The debris piles of the building that had been previously hit by chimp mobile artillery strikes in the weeks leading up to the battle, lay along the twelve-o'clock radius to the target. Using these dusty red piles of former Monarch high culture as cover, Ulysses continued to shift right as the fire from the machine-gun team began to scan for more targets. Meanwhile Ulysses came out on the mortars' flank and spotted them getting ready to do their thing.

Which was probably a fire mission on little old me lying prone on my back and not contributing meaningfully due to bad accuracy with indirect weapons and an Ultra MG team giving it their all to hole-punch me. A lot.

Two Ultra mortar security went forward to the debris piles while one hung back to pull rear and watch the other avenues of approach on the mortars from the opposite direction.

Like I said, Ultra Marines are pro. They don't panic. They just work their game plan.

The two Ultra Marine grunts pulling security that had gone forward toward the debris piles, strapped with

SturmTech squad automatic weapons, didn't see our won-derboy Ultra off their left at the end of the debris pile as they tried to spot the contact coming their way from where the MG team was no doubt position-reporting me. The Ultra version of spotrep. The SturmTech SAWs are the nano-cooled barrel kind that can go high-cycle and dump high-explosive five-five-six all day long.

Oh mama, those are sweet. Sergeant Orion likey-likey.

The two Ultra security got their laser targeting up and were getting ready to dump hard on anyone that pushed the mortars in any way, shape, or form. I have analyzed the sit-uation after the fact, conducting my own little after-action review as I began to obsess about this Ultra among us called Ulysses Two Alpha Six and Ulysses for short, and I want to know why he's so… good at what he does. Why he is… better.

I have to admit, half my guys would have opened fire right there and gotten themselves killed instantly about six different ways to Sirius.

First off, you got two stone-cold killers, Ultra Marines strapping the Sturms no less. They didn't get that job because they were new or won some lottery. Half of my guys would have engaged them first because they would have immedi-ately freaked out and thought what I would have thought. *Oh hell, two stone-cold killers.* Put up a wall of fast-moving lead between me and them and hope for the best.

And I'm not kidding, contrary to events so far today, we're pros. We've stacked on more worlds than most. But you have to be honest about what the average guy with a rifle is going to do in any given situation.

When they give you those sergeant stripes, reality kicks you right in the balls. Every day. Forever. Again and again.

You become a master of the human condition even if you've never read a book or been to some fancy off-world academic crèche. CQ when the company gets a weekend pass will disabuse you of any faith you ever had in humanity. You will always only ever expect the worst, and never be disappointed.

I'm an optimist that way.

It's not a bad idea at face value to engage the two Ultras strapping the Sturms. You've got the drop after all. You might get lucky and punch armor on the spot, take them down and... Winner Winner Chicken in Gross Sauce Rations Dinner.

But there's the Ultras in the mortar teams, all of them specialized light-infantry killers in their own right. Watching you go kinetic on their two sentries. So, they go to primaries and start shooting. You're dead.

All six of them. Plus, don't forget the other guy on rear security strapping a Sturm also. He'll probably engage. A lot in fact.

Or they could cover and use frags on you. Like six grenades all at once. The Ultra equivalent of what Killer Joe who bought it on the last contract used to sometimes yell instead of, "Frag out."

"Good luck with all your problems over there!"

We got used to it and made the mental adjustments to cover when we heard him say it. Grenade going out, boys!

Either way, unlike in the Monarch spectacuthrillers, you're dead if you make any of those choices in the situation Wonderboy Ulysses suddenly found himself in. Seven-to-one odds are perfect. For them. That is if you managed to kill the two killers with the Sturms in the first place. You still got seven more heavily armed Ultras to get through to see the other side of this.

Like I said, half my guys would have gone for the two Ultra security and that would have gotten them killed instantly.

The other half…

They would have gone for the mortar teams. And then ended up wasted by the security team.

Who knows what the hell Choker would have done?

He might have won. Seriously. I'm not kidding. He may be a psycho or a sociopath, our medic that is, but he's got psychopath killing powers.

We keep him as the medic because nothing grosses him out and the last thing you want when you're gut-shot and your intestines are leaking out all over the place is a medic losing his lunch in your contract-related injury. Especially if it's Winner Winner Chicken in Gross Sauce Dinner.

Actually, the rat packet calls it *Chicken Galactica Supremo*. Like it's fancy and not gross.

But seriously, don't mess with Choker. One time we were door-kicking on Pthalo and he stepped into a room with six locals working for the wrong side. All of them had automatic weapons and they didn't know any other setting but kitchen sink. So they started blasting as the door got kicked in and Choker came in pie-ing the room. What was our medic doing door-kicking…? He gets bored and we have to let him do one. He got hit twice right off the bat and according to the guy next on the stack, it didn't seem to faze our psychopath medic in the least. Instead, Choker just kept calmly shooting until all four were dead. The whole room is getting destroyed in the process by the bad guys mag-dumping wildly in every direction. Second guy in engages number five and kills that guy. Then local guy six shoots Choker again as he pops out from another room no one had spotted and covered, but this time right in the thigh. Choker swore quietly, and according to someone who overheard it, that was the beginning of the disturbing things he would start saying all the way to the casevac. He started growling and muttering like a dog as he swapped mags and then shot guy six a whole bunch even though he was clearly dead and Choker needed immediate attention for the several wounds he'd just received over the course of fifteen seconds.

We lost him to the rear hospitals for two months, but he came back with three puckered bullet scars and that smile of his. Like nothing had ever happened that weird.

When guys would ask him about it, he would act like it had never happened.

"I ain't been shot. I have no idea what you're talking about," he'd reply and walk off or talk about the weather even if it was awful.

"Bro… I was a carrier on your litter to the drop. You were bleeding out and babbling."

"Musta been someone else. Nothing missing from me. I'm totally normal."

You know who says that? Says, *I'm totally normal?* You know who? *People who aren't totally normal.*

Again, the guys on the litter and the medics on the drop got a mild case of PTSD when they shot Choker up with painkillers and everyone got a look inside his mind and what was going on as he turned into a raving lunatic.

I am thankful I wasn't there to hear it. Seriously. He already creeps me out enough. I can barely sleep as it is. I don't need him and the things he said running around in my head.

But hey, he's a good medic. I'd never badmouth him.

So, most of my guys would have died finding themselves in the exact same situation Ulysses had just maneuvered into in order to get us off the X and accomplish the mission.

I don't hate him. But I'm struggling with jealousy. No one reads the logs. I can admit that. He's perfect. He does everything perfectly. He's the kind of soldier you want to be. But aren't.

And I realize what I'm feeling could easily turn into hate for a soldier I'm tasked with leading. So… stow that, Sergeant Orion.

The universe finally dealt you a good card. Don't question things, you'll be happier.

Ulysses had the advantage of surprise and a target-rich environment at that moment. He was a skilled shooter. And obviously he's a good tactical tactician. That's not a repeated word that means the same thing. Tactical tactician. You can be a good strategic tactician. Meaning you're good with the big picture. Or a skilled tactical tactician. You're good at assessing the small fight you're in and you've got a pretty good grasp at what needs to be done to not just get out of it, but to actually kill the other guy. Add an *in it to win it* attitude and you might just come out with all, or most of, your fingers and toes.

Some people think being good at Cheks means you're a tactician of any kind. It doesn't. Cheks is a game. Gunfire is for keeps in the same way that true love is. Also both are fatal. Ulysses could have shot many of them right there, but not all of them. If he'd gone that route as Hauser began to storm the Temple of Plague at almost the same moment in order to conduct his own little killing spree, Ulysses would have gotten shot a bunch by all the other Ultras involved in the mortar team. But that's not what Ulysses does right at that moment of uncertain opportunity. I know I'm obsessing over this but I think it's key. In a fight, some people just fight like a mad bull. Other people think. I've found the thinkers usually turn it into a bullfight.

Note... the bull never wins the bullfight.

Of course, being violent is a given.

No, he doesn't make any of the easy bad choices. Ulysses rolls off his belly because he's high-crawl-slithered up along the debris pile to spot the force he's about to engage and not get spotted because he's closer than most gunfights ever get. Again, he's a pro even in this ambush.

Remember it's an ambush. We got ambushed, and Ulysses is actually going for the kill on our original target regardless of what the enemy had planned and kicked this whole show off, taking the momentum of the battle for their own and forcing us into a reactionary posture. Amazing. Seriously, if you don't get that then we can't be friends. In this... he's even better than Hauser. My friend yes. But also yes, a state-of-the-art Dark Labs–designed killing machine on levels that would leave normies horrified. Hauser is pure predator when he goes into that mode. And Hauser is reacting to enemy contact instead of staying on mission. But he has to because otherwise we're dead. The Ultra, our Ultra, is pure predator regardless of ambushes and enemy momentum.

He's going to kill what he came to kill. Regardless.

When I think back on the moment, and that contact, I shudder. Seriously. That's next-level stuff, and for a moment I wonder if he's some kind of Ultra cyborg maybe. Next-gen and better than Hauser?

On his back, Ulysses starts pulling frags and sky-hooking them over the debris pile down onto the mortar teams spaced out in the intersection getting ready to drop steel on us.

Concussion and fragmentation give him the advantage immediately and now as he pops up, hunkering down for as much cover as he can get, he begins to carefully engage both SAW gunners off to his left, both of whom are eyes forward and ready to lay down suppressive on the attack they think is coming from their twelve o'clock when Ulysses is at their nine.

Both die because Ulysses is a shooter.

I didn't inspect the shooting. We were on the hustle to secure the site, grab any intel, and get back to the LZ, but I'm betting both gunners died with an economy of outgoing rounds.

The mortar teams, those who haven't been maimed by the fragmentation blasts of the grenades he sky-hooked into their midst or knocked senseless by the concussion of those sudden and close blasts despite the fancy HUDs in their armor, are easy targets in their disorientation for his rapid yet controlled fire.

He got issued a company Bastard, added a minimum of things he wanted on it, and turned it effectively into a rapid-fire battle rifle even though he's only firing on single shot. Now he's firing armor-piercing seven-six-two which is quite a bang for your pull. But not him. He might as well be firing a lighter caliber he's engaging so fast, and yet patiently, as he shoots as many of them down as he can in a very small space of time.

I heard the tightly spaced fire go off on my right, knew the sound of the Bastard, and knew Ulysses's firing pattern. Someone was getting all the hate they could swallow.

Some of this part of the account came from Wolfy our SDM. He'd dusted both enemy sniper and spotter and shifted to support Ulysses who he had eyes on forward and almost up on our objective with a view to a kill.

Weird wolf shirt flapping beneath his chest rig and carrier, Wolfy had taken a small set of steps at a run to an overhead sidewalk on the other side of the street. This gave him some elevation and a new firing position to engage from.

Snipers are always looking for the next place to shoot from.

Wolfy sees Ulysses dust both gunners with an economy of gunfire, then pivot to take in the devastated mortar teams reeling from the sky-hooked grenades. Ulysses's rifle is at low ready before he begins to fire on the mortar teams.

Watching Ulysses work his carbine reminds me of how Hauser, an actual killing machine, works his weapons, or any weapons Hause picks up.

"I have detailed files," he's told me before when I've seen him have to go to a pickup on a battlefield. Instantly it's being used more effectively than by the dead guy who humped it, swore by it, and operated with it.

Ulysses Two Alpha Six has that same feel when I've watched him fire on the Ultra in this battle.

Low ready with his Bastard, instead of wasting the grenade-devastated mortar men, Ulysses engages the third Ultra SAW gunner at seventy-five meters who's only now shifting away from rear security watching the avenue he's been charged to watch. Hot smoking rounds find center mass on that Ultra and the gunner goes down on his back, legs doing the *kickin' chicken.*

Wolfy's engaging the mortars and periodizing anyone who seems like they're gonna smoke Ulysses at close range regardless of the fact that many are wounded, have lost limbs, or must be bleeding from the ears. Almost at the same time all threats are neutralized, Ulysses, dry on ammo, doesn't mag-swap and instead pulls his sidearm, walks down into the ruined Ultra mortars with sniper support behind him, and starts handing out headshots to the wounded and dying to make sure they all achieve KIA.

"Coldest thing I ever saw, Sar'nt," Wolfy would tell me later as he rubbed one of the awful wolf tattoos he had on his arm like it was a lucky charm of some kind. Maybe it is. "And I've seen some cold things in the Strange out here. Remember... he's one of 'em, Sar'nt. Remember that."

I can't forget it. It's like some puzzle I can't solve yet, but I know I've got to... for some reason that eludes me right now.

And for a moment, as I think about the problem of Ulysses, I hear ice and crystal and the warm flow of scotch that smells like burnt autumn leaves... flowing. Just as I'd heard in the Bar at the End of the Universe before I hallucinated meeting the founder of the Strange Company.

But the fight wasn't over just yet. Five psychotic moments lay ahead. I should have known... I was feeling unreasonably irritable. Mistaking what was happening, what Stinkeye was doing, for my anger at Ulysses being so perfect a warrior. But... it was something else.

A moment later Ulysses is urgently, yet not frantically, letting us know there's a fast-attack ORF inbound on us from the avenue at the one o'clock.

On my back, thumbing in another frag to the Bastard's launcher, after hearing Hauser waste the crew-served team high above, and the Ulysses sky-hooked grenades detonating and then the very one-sided gunfight that went down after that, I heard the engines of the multi-vehicle QRF that's been called in to support the mortar teams we'd caught.

We are in very big trouble. That was my first thought.

But by that time Stinkeye had crawled out of whatever hole he'd been covering in as all the incoming rocked our contact, and then he was chanting at me.

"Ain't no way outta dis one but da hard ways, Little King. Now youze a killah! Listen to the red rage a'comin'... listen to da unquiet wrath thas been there all along inside yas..."

Then he *berserked* us.

CHAPTER FIFTEEN

I was covered in wet blood when it was over. The madness Stinkeye *whammied* us with to get through five minutes of hell was fading as I walked away from burning wreckage, heading toward more carnage. More fire. More wreckage.

It was like waking from a binge. Or maybe fading into one...

Anger and peace exchanged places, resuming our normal viewing channels. Returning control of our lives to us once more.

Listen, our space war wizard has been in more fights, if the ancient logs of the company are even vaguely true, than all of us currently strapping and humping in the Strange put together will ever be in, collectively. I get that. But listen, it doesn't make being suddenly turned into a rage-filled space Viking with nothing but violence and an unquenchable murderous bloodlust filling your mind... it doesn't... make it *okay* to do that to us.

I was shaking like I'd been on that binge for too long. Or hadn't eaten, living only on coffee and cigarettes until my body said feed me or you fall down. I held up my blood-covered assault glove and willed my hand to stop shaking. For a moment I considered eating a protein bar to stabilize myself. But there was too much blood and I couldn't. Plus there were actions on the objective, and the smell of burning fuel washing across the hot day turning to noon didn't bode well for consuming calories.

In Stinkeye's defense, and as I walked the battlefield after our mindless slaughter of the Ultras… I had to confess there really hadn't been a lot of choices open for my kill team at that sudden moment before our raid went pearshaped. I was, even as Stinkeye's *rumma-dumma-ding* nonsense rhyme-chanting began to make my blood boil, my testosterone boosting, no really spiking dangerously, the anger within also spiking like I'd just killed a case of rage-ohol all by my lonesome, images of easy and total carnage suddenly overwhelming any kind of rational thinking I was in possession of at that point in the fight, I was already realizing we were in a very bad situation at that moment to react to an inbound Ultra QRF suddenly coming in hot to rescue their murdered mortar section.

Inbound hot to make someone pay. And the only someones there for them to collect the blood debt from was us.

I've said it before… when there's nothing left to do but fight… then you fight hard.

Here's how bad it looked at that moment as I began to lose my mind to the battle lust Stinkeye was chanting on us. We were on foot, spread out after the battle. Uncertain of our ammo status or even casualties. I had no control of my element at that moment as we heard their a-grav engines and the Little Raven drop coming in through the high canyon walls of the dead red city. Ulysses had just called in the sitrep letting us know we had two inbound armored a-grav fast-attack transports and an armored hunter-killer drop flying low and close to the streets. They'd be up on us fast. We had seconds to make our play and then see it out to the bitter end. The only thing I could think of to do, at that moment, was to get a message off to the first sergeant advising him of the hot water we currently were in.

"Doghouse… I say again we have two Bulldogs and one Little Raven inbound. Reaper Team consolidating on the *oh-be-jay*… we will pull back ASAP. Requesting immediate fire mission to cover our retreat. Gimme anything you got, Doghouse!"

The first sergeant said something. Probably telling me arty wasn't available. I mean it never showed. Sergeant Chungo never made it rain. If he had… we'd be as dead as the dead I had to step around and over in the aftermath of the madness.

As it went down, me running and trying to comm, while my mind went rapidly battle-mad, Stinkeye was already chanting. I was running forward to the debris piles just shy of where Ulysses had wiped the Ultra mortars out with sniper support from Wolfy. Stinkeye followed me, singing nonsense words and I hated him for that.

Wun two, dey comin' for you. Tree four, open da door to darkness. Five six, Little King, gonna make a real big mess. Seven eight… da MK Ultra she is great. Taste and see, nine ten… we gonna kill, again and again and again… Wun two…

He'd done this to Strange before. Another time, another platoon. Not Reaper that War Crimes Massacre time. But with Dog. Early on when Hannibal had first taken over as platoon sergeant during a contract we were working. Dog had been out on a search-and-destroy mission on that world. They'd gotten into a really big ambush and two of the riverine attack craft they were using on that contract took RPGs with casualties. Then they started to sink within incoming 7.62 filling the air. Hannibal had two more craft under him, and they tried to get to the other sinking craft.

The attack was coming from marshes near a Froggo reed village. Multiple emplaced machine guns firing and loads of Skula RPGs were suddenly thick like insects in the air. Skulas are unreliable and more than likely to detonate on the trigger man if fired, but when they hit, they exploded shrap in every direction and that had torn up the two riverine boats currently sinking in the lagoon between the reed marshes.

With the loss of the miniguns on those boats, Dog was suddenly outgunned and trying to pull their own out of the muddy waters of the marshes as rounds fountained everywhere and more RPGs were coming out. Stinkeye had gone along that day because as he put it later, "I like boats, Little King. Nothin' bad ever happens ta ya when yas on a boat. 'Cept today."

So now the platoon is in it and bad things are indeed happening to Dog on the boats when Stinkeye starts his murder chanting thing.

Taste and see, nine ten… we gonna kill, again and again and again… Wun two…

Within a minute the two remaining gun-laden boats under Hannibal's direct command do the most unexpected thing ever. Instead of laying down massive suppressive with the remaining guns, they charge two of the six machine-gun nests, miniguns chewing up reeds and Froggos as they go in full throttle and beach. Driving right into the heaviest concentrations, everyone shooting everyone they can.

Froggos was slang for the local natives when we were on that contract. A warlike humanoid frog species that didn't like paying taxes to the Monarch Empire. We were working for the Monarchs on that one, so we got the good gear and got to be the "winners."

Anyway, Hannibal goes nuts as Stinkeye chants and Dog beaches both riverine craft right there in the reeds. The gunners still working the minis lay the hate in every direction. Reeds explode, Froggos are torn to shreds, but more are coming in to support. RPGs go skirling off into the water and explode. But Dog abandons the boats, and then launches into a killing spree inside the reeds. A huge chaotic firefight erupts. No lines. No tactics. It's tag with guns inside the marsh and there was serious friendly fire. For twenty minutes it's an insane firefight in every direction and spent brass flying everywhere. The reeds catch fire and most of the Froggos are dead and retreating but Dog isn't done.

Still under the influence of Stinkeye's *berserking*, Dog isn't done in the least. They go Ultra. Guys are shot and bleeding out and shoving mags into smoking weapons as they head to the next kill zone. No one is in control of anything and Amarcus is in front, swearing murder and shooting down retreating Froggos. No one is assisting the wounded. Hell, the Old Man and the first sergeant didn't even know about it until it was over. The first clue they had something was wrong was seeing the village on fire from the pontoon base as the horizon filled with black smoke.

That whole world was nothing but endless horizon. It was oceans and seas of reeds and the occasional small island hill rising from the whole stinking mess.

When the Monarchs sent in their Maulers, the Froggos finally surrendered because the Maulers can fly atmospheric and let go with their ten-gigawatt plasma beams. In one day they could have set the whole world on fire and left it to burn.

The Froggos got the point when they saw the Maulers making high-orbit passes and surrendered, choosing to become slaves of the empire.

The Inquisitors charged us with war crimes and the company took it hard on that one. Contracts with the Monarchs don't cover war crimes. Yeah, it was really Stinkeye's fault. But we always blamed Amarcus for it anyway.

Stink had just freaked out when it got bad and used one of his more powerful weapons to get them out of there. But there was something about Amarcus that made it worse than it should've been. Stinkeye would avoid Hannibal every chance he got after that. Something inherently wrong inside him that we'd suspected all along, had bloomed in full that day.

After that, it never fully went away.

And in time, we became enemies.

Amarcus Hannibal had never been far from that kind of savagery Stinkeye had awakened in him. It had taken the merest of pushes from Stinkeye's Dark Labs powers to let it loose, and once it was loose, it stayed.

It was bad. Stink was afraid. Even though the old drunk never said so, I could tell. Whenever Hannibal was around, a good game of Cheks or not, Stinkeye got quiet and faded into the shadows as soon as he could.

After Astralon, as the *Spider* ramped up to sublight, Stinkeye cornered me one time, drunk and his breath stinking.

"Ya done good, Little King," he gasped.

I told him we were just trying to survive down there. We'd all done our best.

Stinkeye smiled and got all serious, raising his head and looking down at me with what he called his *Eye of Truth* look.

Again, it's all an act. But if you don't know him and you're a little child easily frightened… it's worth the ticket at the cheap carnival on the edge of the starport.

"Not that, Little King. Da other thing. Ya sent the darkness back where he belong now. Universe got a chance now for a little while more."

Then he wandered off drunkenly singing some old song about having something to believe in.

Another classic none of us would ever find in the entertainment streams. Another mystery. Another cheap bit of costumery for the space war wizard act.

That was the day we pushed the dead into the engines.

Now, incoming QRF and seconds to react to contact, he was gonna do to me, to us, what he'd done to Hannibal. What had ruined Dog.

I wasn't cool with that because I knew of it and had always feared it being done. And I was powerless to stop it so I ran and tried to be a busy NCO who could actually get his studs out of this one.

I didn't feel very wily old hobo at that point. But I did feel it, what Stinkeye was doing to us, coming on like bad food poisoning or a real bone-chiller flu. Where you feel it deep down inside of you and you know it feels very wrong and it's barely even begun. Like something seriously toxic inside of you that's going to take you some places you don't want to go right now, or ever.

I was thinking… *I don't have time for this right now.*

I remembered afterward, I think I was chanting that very thing as I came down off the *berserking* on the other side of it when I was covered in wet blood. I was backing away from the flaming wreck of the Ultra Little Raven then, a light armored fast-attack drop specializing in suppression with six minis chained together. You get on the wrong side of one of those on a gun run and your day just got a whole lot worse.

I hope you like having a thousand holes in you.

But I remember chanting *I don't have time for this* afterward, coming down off Stinkeye's Heart of Darkness juice, thinking, but mumbling really, "I don't have time for this."

Like that had been the anchor that hadn't worked as the murder roller coaster began to climb for the first drop.

I was only dimly aware I'd been saying that in the moments it all began to start, as I turned and saw the weird, crazed look on our space war wizard's face beginning to consume all my attention as I ran from him, heading for the debris piles, shouting orders to my team that seemed meaningless because no one was going to listen now.

But I was still trying to avoid what was coming because that's how Dog lost her way. How Amarcus became who he really, really wanted to be standing there in that burning village full of shot and gutted Froggos.

Hauser. Hauser wouldn't listen to Stinkeye's murder chanting because he's immune. He wouldn't listen, *he's a machine*. I remember that being important as I tried to resist the tendrils of madness taking hold of my mind.

Wun two, dey comin' for you. Tree four, open da door to darkness. Five six, Little King, gonna make a real big mess. Seven eight… da MK Ultra she is great. Taste and see, nine ten… we gonna kill, again and again and again… Wun two…

Then the rest of us… we were gone off on a murdering spree like nothing you've ever experienced.

I knew the stories from Amarcus's genocide on Koogar Village. Dog had butchered those Froggos. Fighting-age adults. Younglings too.

It was bad even by the standards of war.

All the time after that, after what Stinkeye had done to Dog that day, I would always think back that that was when they'd lost their way. All the soldiers in Dog. Good guys I'd once known had become mean, and sullen, and began to behave in ways that made me think I'd never really known them. Hannibal, like some evil spirit, had been let loose that day. He'd taken control of all of them on the bloody red afternoon out in the marshes, burning villages and cutting up Froggos for more than just payback.

It had crossed a line than cannot be crossed back over.

When the first sergeant made it out there that afternoon with the Old Man, the whole platoon was dry on ammo. And they were still killing Froggos. Knives out.

It had taken the anger and iron will of the Old Man, a real live Ultra commander, if the rumors are true, to rein them in and stop the madness.

I gathered all the stories as the Log Keeper on the other side of it.

They're horrible.

But… the truth just is. So, it's in the main logs if you ever wanna see what we're capable of. What we did out there. And why sometimes I think our story is a tragedy that hasn't seen its final act yet.

But I can feel it coming. I can feel it most days and always late in the night. Like there're some sins that just can't be let pass. Like there's no good thing left in the universe.

I could feel Stinkeye's witchery taking hold of all of us, Duster, Wolfy, even Ulysses, as I ran forward, battle-rattle rattling, gunshots still ringing in my ears despite the ear pro. Insides beat to death by the HERK rounds.

The chanting was already filling me with rage as I tried to run from it, as I made it to Ulysses who already had a wild look in his eyes and was on one knee, sketching out our defense in the dust. Normally he has the calm cool of a pro soldier. Hard. Filled with quiet hate just waiting for a target to lay it on with all the fury and malice he has trained to be the best at. Now he had this dangerously energetic look in his eyes as he laid out how we should take on the incoming Ultra QRF. Almost like we were long-lost friends, reunited on some wild night when the winds were high and dry, the liquor cold and burning, and no rules to hold us back from the trouble we could get up to in the dark.

"We got two Bulldogs comin' in hot, Sergeant. That'll be a driver, a gunner, and four to dismount. Two of those each. Standard is they'll have a drop ready for suppression by air on their six and riding overwatch. Sounds like one of the little Ravens coming in with 'em now, Sergeant Orion. We can take these guys!"

When I responded to this, Duster was already there saying, "Yeah, we got this, Sar'nt. We can do this."

He had the look of a bad bet junkie gambler who's got a system this time.

And Stinkeye, deadly serious, lips moving in his chant as he faded and let the mischief run. Even at that moment I was still resisting him. This was exactly how Dog had lost their soul, I kept telling myself. This was how Amarcus Hannibal became what I'd begun to think of, picture really, whenever Stinkeye raved and muttered about there being an actual Heart of Darkness to the galaxy.

I didn't want that. Not for my guys. Not for me.

I was trying to respond to Ulysses, but my lips were moving through gun oil gone bad. Sluggish and dirty like it'd been reused on a bad op downrange and beyond the love of constant supply. Thick and slow and dirty.

I was shaking my head, fighting it with reason I no longer possessed as my shaking hands did the trick of checking my mags, knowing, wanting, to use them a lot. Knowing the killing was coming. We were hunkered there in a rough circle as the QRF came down the wide road from the Y intersection, on the other side of the debris. No short halt for us. No patrol clock to watch sectors. No one thinking anything but murder and rage as two armored fast-attack a-gravs throbbed silently into our area of operation. Having no idea what they were getting into. No doubt they were seeing their murdered dead in the red chalky debris of the weeks of constant shelling that had failed to mar much of this fantastic city. Realizing the perpetrators had come, killed, and maybe gone.

Ulysses, like the combat leader I'd never be, assault-gloved finger tracing our lines of attack in the red dust as we got ready to make an attack that was our only option, outlined the simple pincer. I was fighting the madness with all I had. Shutting my eyes and gritting my teeth as my guys turned into ghouls, jittery and laughing about what was coming.

They were… *highly motivated.* Imagined wrongs were suddenly shouted out, courtesy of Stinkeye. Vows to punish and pay back were used in response.

It was like some religious service for a religion of violence.

No, I wanted to shout into the dead streets and tall Monarch monuments. *This is how we lose our way. This is how we go where Amarcus went. This is where things go bad!*

And maybe, whispered the galaxy, *Amarcus is waiting for us where he went…*

I looked around as I lost it totally and became just like them, feeling the red rage take me. Now, later, I realized I was looking for the Little Girl at the last second. The one the Seeker had taken with her when she left us to the twenty-five-year haul to another world for an engine she had waiting for us. The Little Girl who'd been, impossibly, a part of the company.

I was looking for her friend, really. The Wild Thing.

But she was gone…

I may have imagined I was smelling the smell of burnt leaves on an autumn wind. Power chords of some hellish guitar stoking all our hatred to life in the distance that had nothing to do with Stinkeye's mischief. Hatred for the Monarchs. Hatred for the Ultras. Hatred for… just plain old life.

"Good… Little King," hissed Stinkeye from across our tight circle.

The Ultra drop was howling close and coming in now. We'd get some kind of jump on them on the ground force. The drop would kill us a whole lot and there wasn't a damn thing we could do about that. The pilot would spool up the guns and we'd be dead. We were running into our own kill zone, and we were helpless to do anything about it.

So, there was that.

"You are da darkness now…" said Stinkeye as he drew his ancient scarred and dented 1911 I've never seen him do a lick of maintenance on. Or load it. Or even fire it unless he was drunk and just wanting to make noise and trouble after getting beat bad at Cheks.

"Les get it on now, childrens," he crooned. "Only way tru dis is to let go and let da hate flow…"

CHAPTER SIXTEEN

The one thing we had going for us as we lost our minds and went berserk in a sudden battle rage, was that Hauser had taken control of the crew-served gun in the dead god's eye three stories above the fight. When I'd gone up there after seeing Plague dead on the throne there were piles of brass from the huge fifty-cal shells littered all over the place.

But there were still belts and cans of fifty-cal orange-tip HERK rounds ready to go. If we'd had time, I would have taken that gun. But we couldn't do it effectively and pull back to our line. So I left it. Could've ruined it with thermite, but maybe there was a part of me hoping we could get back and commandeer it later.

Ever the wily old NCO, I am always looking to work smarter and not harder, if just for the amount of paperwork when you do it the hard way being more, and having to explain mistakes that were made and could have been avoided.

Like I said, the one thing the lunatics we'd become had going for us as the Bulldog a-gravs came throbbing into the kill zone and the Ultra cav troopers dismounted to secure the area, was Hauser on the gun.

It was Wolfy who lost his mind first. He never made it to the planning circle where a feverish and wild-eyed Ulysses was showing us how we could do this right now instead of running like we should've. Wolfy had continued down the overhead sidewalk, sticking close to the shadows from an overhang, when he engaged and fired first on the Ultra QRF.

He hadn't totally lost his mind before his first shot, he'd tell me later. He domed the gunner on the lead vehicle as they came in. Bonus round for us. Hauser, who'd heard my insane babbling about *not having the time for this* and "rally on me," but spoken by some snarling beast who was swearing he'd rip the heads straight from these Ultras' mangy corpses, opened fire on vehicle two. The a-grav gunner there was torn to shreds in the turret with a perfectly ranged and on-target burst from the Ultra crew-served Hauser had just swiveled to orient the gun sight on the arrived QRF.

Remember… *detailed files.*

We were on the move as the a-grav Ultra troopers dismounted with short hops over the sides of snub-nosed disc ships levitating off the ground six to four feet.

Both gunners died within seconds of each other, and you'd think we had the advantage immediately. But remember, these were Ultras. No easy day. Ever.

What I can remember about what happened next are snapshots covered in a blood-red haze of battle. All I know is that I wanted them, the Ultras and anyone who opposed us, dead. I wanted to kill them myself. All of them. And… everything.

I was tired of the state of the Strange Company and the hard times we'd fallen on as of late. It was payback now and the galaxy had obliged a guilty pleasure.

The first trooper to hit the ground got rag-dolled by several sharp bursts from what had to have been all of us shooting that guy. Ulysses had gone wide right again around the debris pile and was engaging immediately. Stinkeye had followed hooting and hollering, waving his relic sidearm and probably flagging all of us.

Who cares?

We were a-murderin' now.

Duster and I were supposed to go left. This seemed like a rational plan. Pincer attack supported by a heavy weapon.

Except no one was communicating with the heavy weapons, and we were all rushing in like breathless junkies rushing on the drug of their choice. Breathing heavy, gasping for hot dry air as I just ran straight over the top of the debris instead of going left because why wait? Scrabbling up through the ruined scree, cutting and slipping on shattered shards of High Monarch Culture, one assault-gloved hand barely controlling my battle rifle. I remember seeing my own spit drooling out on the dusty red marble and brick that formed the pile. Then I was up and mag-dumping on that first guy I could sight.

Meanwhile seven other Ultras in complete control of their faculties took cover, or tried to, and began to return fire at less than fifty meters. Hell, this gunfight might have been at twenty-five.

It was that close. The very definition of a real knife-and-gun show as you're about to see.

At the top of the pile, I swapped mags because I'd just burned thirty rounds on a dead guy and so had Duster. Ulysses might have even engaged that guy. I had no idea. All I knew is… he was the first down, even as the others leaped over the sides, we shot him a whole bunch.

I had the presence of mind to try to get another magazine in, but my feet wanted to move at the same time because I needed to get close and bleed them. I got the next mag out of my carrier, slipped, and went face forward, who cares, and then started burning rounds from the prone on an Ultra who'd taken cover behind one of the blown-apart mortar men and was getting ready to lay some in our direction.

He was my next target. I shot him in the helmet and kept shooting, not realizing his twitching meant he was dead. I thought he was still in it to win it.

In the meantime, Ulysses was moving straight up on the four that had come out of the rear a-grav. Like a madman. No cover. Nothing. Just working the Bastard we'd issued him like it was his own personal precision death machine. He was shooting the Ultras down and probably killing them in the first few rounds. But there were some shots that had to have tagged armor. So extra shots were needed to make sure they were dead.

Stinkeye followed, blasting away on his six to clearly no effect.

I remembered, later, seeing that happening off to my right. Then, off to my left, Duster got hit and spun around spraying blood.

That made me even angrier than I was. They'd shot one of my guys while I was trying to kill them. Bastards!

Duster, who'd been shot, fired wildly on the driver of the lead a-grav, despite being hit, smashing rounds into the driver in the vehicle's forward bulb. Armored glass took impact rounds, spider-webbing, then one got through due to the extreme violence of the excessive shooting and splattered the driver's brains all over the back of the canopy.

I saw that.

You can't unsee that.

I remember thinking... *good*.

Then I was on my back, feet tangled, my rifle miraculously empty again and realizing I'd tripped over one of the dead Ultra Marine security gunners Ulysses had wasted on first contact.

The ones with the SturmTech SAWS. The SAWS with the nano-cooled barrels.

I spotted it, jerked it up angrily, and unloaded as fast as I could, creating a sudden line of dirt fountains amid the Marsantyium debris, barely missing Ulysses who was so far forward now that my drag fire had almost cut him in half.

Duster, shot, ditched his primary, laughing wildly, and shucked the kukri he always carried, jamming it right into the next Ultra he ran into even as that guy tried to shoot him. Duster kicked the carbine wide and jammed his huge knife in that guy. Then he was hacking, driving the curved blade in and in again and again.

The Little Raven came in and went to guns fast. The pilot must've seen the friendly ground units getting overrun and decided he had nothing to lose with excessive fire danger close. He wasn't worried about paperwork. Two bright lines of outgoing fire chewed up the battlefield, but no one got hit. The gun run was late and as the fast-moving matte-black gunship swept over the fight, the pilot leaned forward, helmet pivoting to track us as he passed overhead. Hot brass rained down on all of us and I took one on my arm where normal people wear sleeves. It burned and blistered but I didn't mind it at the time. I was going high-cycle and disintegrating Ultras in my cone of death. Two to be specific.

It was, at the time, a beautiful feeling of violence fully realized, and I wondered how I would ever repeat this feeling again.

If the blazing light machine gun would have been a girl, I would have made an honest woman of her.

I unloaded so hard on them, they turned to nothing but flying body parts and bloody spray mere meters away. Meanwhile, two more were covering behind the rear Bulldog when Ulysses surged on that loc and killed them both with accurate yet insane point-blank fire done violently.

I could hear him double-tapping them as he passed over like some familiar angel of death.

Everything I'm relating here... it's all snippets. Insane snippets of mad carnage remembered. Like I'm only seeing every other frame now when I try to think back about it all. If there's a soundtrack, it's more a *soundtrance*. And it's Stinkeye's words he spoke at the beginning and was no longer speaking, weaving through the folds in our brains and causing chemicals to go into mass production. Rage-inducing chemicals. Pain-killing chemicals. A cessation in frontal lobe activity regarding reason and self-preservation and better judgment.

We didn't care now. We were lost to the killing.

There's a frame I can see but there's something missing in between that one and the next. The frame before is me blasting the last Ultra I was engaging into nothing but red mist and pieces with the Sturm.

The guy's bucket blew off and I'm pretty sure most of his head went with it as the Sturm's barrel barely climbed. The weapon fired so smoothly. I remember roaring with delight, putting pressure, too much pressure, to drag the *blaarrrrring* gun down and hit center mass. Willing the black cone of seven-six-two to not just stay down, or stay on target, but to go through that guy and make him dead.

I pushed on the barrel, grinning like a madman, and his legs disappeared as his torso came apart, falling into the voluminous cone of my outgoing blur of fire.

I stood in one swift yet psychotic motion, screaming, raging, gun dry now.

I flung my new favorite weapon aside because it had nothing further to offer me.

That's the snapshot of the madness I get before the next one. But there's definitely something missing in between.

The Little Raven went over the top of us. I saw that. Then what happens next? If I block everything out, and listen to the *soundtrance*... I think Hauser was engaging the Ultra close air support from the dead god's eye.

It must've climbed and turned on that wide triumphal parade street behind us. The pilot jerking back on the collective and mashing the right rudder to get the bird turned around with no room to spare, morning sun glaring through the canopy as suddenly the engine and hydraulics panels lit up in damage response from a burst of Hauser's fire.

Remember... *detailed files*.

Don't mess with combat cyborgs. Ever.

The Little Raven spun in and went down in the street over that way. Breathlessly like some psycho killer I ran toward it, feeling like my chest was gonna burst at any moment. Like I was gonna have a heart attack right there and keep on going, sucking hot dry air, and never feeling or thinking anything but war and violence and slaughter ever again. Feeling my karambit slide from its sheath on my carrier as I approached the crash. The bird was on its side and the pilot, who must've been injured but was still in fighting shape somewhat, had crawled out of the top of the Raven, flames already rising from the main turbines and along the rear empennage.

He tried to rack the sidearm he'd shoot me with to defend himself, but his wrist was broken from the crash. I pulled him down onto the street like some Saurian amphibian pulls a swimmer in a dark river down, smashing him into the red stone of the road.

Then I stabbed him a bunch.

Like I said, when I came to, walking back up the street, the QRF handled, I was covered in wet blood and breathing heavily. But I was calm now. In that way you are after an intense workout.

Peaceful.

Cleaned out.

Different now.

Stinkeye came toward me, totem flask out, apologizing like a pitiful beggar seeking nothing more than not to be beat. Some distant part of me wanted to smash his face in. But then I saw Duster still hammering the dead Ultra with his broken kukri. Both Bulldogs on fire now as flames and black smoke began to boil. Someone had dropped an armed thermite grenade in each a-grav troop assault carrier. Dead Ultras, and pieces of them, were everywhere. Black smoke rising over the objective.

"I hads to do it, Little King," whimpered Stinkeye. "Yas didn't have the numbers. Was the only way, Little King."

I nodded, feeling a smile on my face. Wondering if I was cursed now. Cursed to become like Amarcus Hannibal. My devil. And the devil I'd killed.

I swallowed thickly.

Stinkeye handed me his totem flask. Rounds were cooking off in the burning Raven behind us. The smell of burning bodies was in the late morning air.

Hauser was crossing the street, Pig held at port arms. Ready to annihilate on command.

I drank and felt the madness leaving me.

I turned to Stinkeye, knowing I should beat him to death right there, or sometime soon. Knowing I couldn't.

Because he was a friend.

And a brother.

Strangers to the universe. Brothers to the end.

I nodded for no reason and walked toward the destruction as one of the a-gravs became fully engulfed and began to burn greedily.

There in the center of it all, like some savage warlord from long ago, stood Ulysses, satisfied with what he'd wrought.

And for a brief moment, I realized what the shape of the future would be now that the Monarchs were dead and dying.

It would be just as terrible.

And what about me, myself… me. I was just some small player in this tragedy. Nothing more.

Nothing less.

CHAPTER SEVENTEEN

The day had already passed its zenith on the falling world of Marsantyium when we finally made it back to our lines by a circuitous and different route than the one we'd taken in. Ultra hunter-killer teams were on the move and drone recon was beginning to pick up a surge headed our way. We followed Hauser on point who took us back using buildings, tunnels, and underground parking lots that weren't shattered from the chimp shelling of the past few weeks.

The going was slow and cautious and at times we crawled or duck-walked to stay less visible. Our faces and fatigues were caked in the constant red dust of the ruined yet still fantastic city.

In these dark and cool places where we stopped, as Hauser scanned the silent darkness like some malevolent sentient willing to do maximum violence on our behalf, we downed water and chewed a protein bar each.

No one said a word about what had happened back on the objective, and I was reminded of something Punch used to laugh and say when things went haywire.

"Hey, what happened on the oh-bee-jay, stays on the oh-bee-jay."

If you are a chimp historian reading this six hundred years from now, trying to figure out how we got as far as we did out into the stellar neighborhood despite our obvious handicaps... *oh-bee-jay* is military speak for *objective*.

I am aware the company logs may be for the benefit of another species not us humans who solely comprise the Strange Company. Interestingly, no alien has ever served in the company that I know of. But six hundred years from now, after we've smoked the Monarchs, I'm betting the company will be mostly alien by then.

Standing there in the dark of the parking garage where we'd made our halt in a shadowy recess with an escape route all planned out, I had no idea how long the fighting would last before we got a break. The plan was already *canked*. Things weren't good. And as I listened to comm traffic with one ear open, two things became rapidly clear regarding the situation back at the LZ.

The mechs still weren't off the bird.

The Ultras were on the move and getting ready for their counterattack.

Apparently, the other player gets to make a move in this game of galactic Cheks for all the marbles.

I inquired of Ulysses regarding this new development, hoping his life as a former Ultra would provide some insight. Then again, our company commander had once been one, if the rumors, myths, and really legends, were to be believed.

Honestly, Ulysses and the Old Man could have been brothers in character, demeanor, and chisel, if separated by time, or coffin-sleep.

Ulysses listened to me in the cool shadows underground as I relayed what I'd heard over the comm from Ghost Platoon's spot-repping the Ultras out there beyond our lines and starting to stage for a major attack.

Ulysses listened quietly in the cool underground darkness as I made everyone change socks in pairs. One ready to go with their rifle and on the scan, the other swapping socks, good NCO that I am. First Sergeant would be proud. Nearby, Hauser watched the darkness, his head also on a constant slow swivel, scanning for potential threats.

I'd been here before with him. His rifle would suddenly engage and then he'd announce contact and call targets as he suppressed. It scared the hell out of you the first few times it happened… and every time after. It was so sudden and mechanical. So automatic.

And then there would be incoming. So you got un-scared and got down to getting it on for the company and your brothers.

The lower garage beneath the city was clean and orderly and it was hard for me to believe this place of massive monuments and temples had ever been a real, live, active, dirty, swearing, loud, honking, hooting, angry, and beautiful city full of life and vice like so many along the worlds I'd visited, imagining I might be something other than a constant tourist.

That I might find a girl, a student or an artist, in a café… and stay awhile. Long enough to call it home and grow old with her.

This world felt more like… a diorama, a model, a hobbyist's vision of what a perfect stellar city should look like.

That was a feeling I couldn't shake and once I'd articulated it in my mind that I was having it, the realization that it was more of a model city of what a city should be, then I realized I'd been having that thought all along in the background apps of my mind since we'd departed the LZ and made our first foray into enemy-held territory within Saffron City.

A distant explosion rocked the underground walls for a second and I was suddenly aware that being buried alive was a distinct possibility.

No one said anything. We were still all, I guess, processing the oh-bee-jay. And what had happened there...

"Standard, Sergeant," answered Ulysses of my question regarding the Ultras' next tactical move. "Their commander wanted to see what you'd bring to the fight. If it's Arkades, the Imperator General himself, then he wanted our side to show what we were bringing before he committed in any way meaningful. He's cautious. That was always his reputation. He also never lost a fight and not all Ultra battles were as one-sided as you think. The expeditionary forces out on the frontier... we faced overwhelming numbers in battles no one knows about out there. Now, like other battles he has commanded, Sergeant, he'll fight where you aren't. Hit you where you're hurt bad. Strangle you where you're having trouble breathing. In other words he's going to be where we don't want him to be."

I thought about that and chewed my bar, trying not to hurl as I did so. My hand had stopped shaking and the blood I'd been covered in was mostly dry now.

"So, they hung back beyond our insertion points and now they're being moved forward where the intel says we need to be hit?"

"Negative, Sergeant. General Arkades buried them. They dug in deep using crater charges, and then combat engineers covered them with the battledozers."

Okay...

My level of respect for the Ultras just grew ten feet. Infantry, soldiers in general, don't like being buried alive, or even confined spaces. We don't even like boarding actions on starships. Choker goes nuts when we gotta do that. I mean… more nuts than he already is. But… it's everything we can do to keep him functional and not fetal when outer hulls and airlocks become a thing for the Strange.

Go figure… there's probably something in that to explain Choker. But I don't care. I'm sure there's a whole bunch of other dark stuff I don't wanna know in there too.

Hard pass. Good luck with your therapy, Choke. That is… if you don't skin the noggin doctor first and then try to see his patients with a flesh mask on.

That's totally something he'd do. I know it.

Some deranged psychopaths are best left sleeping. Trust me on this.

"How do they get out?" I asked, fascinated at the concept of being buried alive for a combat operation. I mean not *fascinated*… sorry. I meant *totally horrified*.

Also… *hard pass* on that one.

I'd stopped chewing my bar. I didn't feel hungry. I'd roll it up and save it for the next break in the action. Maybe I could enjoy it then. Maybe I could digest it. Still, it stayed there halfway to my mouth as Ulysses related how buried-alive Ultras popped out right in the middle of your fight and started slitting throats.

Fun, huh?

"Shape charges planted by the engineers and controlled by the buried unit commanders can create tubes to the surface for a quieter deployment into the enemy's rear or flank. That's an orderly assault evacuation from an improvised sub-bunker, Sergeant. But if we—*they*—need to get in it fast… then we blow the main charges and dirt-fountain everything on top of our heads. Immediate access to the surface and a large trench to fight from in the process."

Still holding the uneaten protein bar in silence, I asked the next most obvious question regarding my enemies, who, as my eyes flicked this way and that in the subterranean darkness Hauser was scanning with his enhanced thermal vision, could easily be walled up and ready to blow charges and come screaming out of the walls with tomahawks and Sturms.

Ultras. And yeah, I said it like a swear word. I really didn't need this, man. This was gonna be my last contract.

I wasn't even breathing.

"What about overpressure from the charges detonating?" I asked, because surely that would be suicide to bury yourselves alive and then detonate high explosives in what had to be a significant amount of earth and debris on top of you. Seems like a great way to get even more buried alive, and turned to nothing but crushed bone and bloody pulp at the same time.

"Ultras have blast blankets. Plus our armor has a shock-gel layer between body and ceramic. We still lose about twenty-five percent in that maneuver, but the surprise multiplier adjusts the odds in our favor in most combat scenarios. It's extreme, Sergeant, but it works and that's all that matters to an Ultra. Getting it done. That's how we measure our lives. Failure is worse than death for an Ultra. So we are, as we chanted in the old hymns and cadences go… *in it to win it*, Sergeant. There is nothing else. Either do, or do not." He paused and seemed to think better about what he was going to say next. Then he said what he had hesitated about. "I've ordered it done, and executed it before."

So, he was some type of combat leader. But he looks so young. At best he seems like he could be a just-christened buck sergeant.

Highly motivated, peak physical shape, lots to learn.

I don't know that I was ever that guy. But I wanted to be.

"Did you ever fight under this General Arkades, Ulysses?"

He nodded once in the darkness.

I finished the bar and watched the garage and the shadows. Composing my comm to the first sergeant regarding what I'd just learned. What we might be facing.

Then it was time to move again.

CHAPTER EIGHTEEN

"That was really cool of you, Sar'nt."

Wolfy had stalked up next to me as we crossed back into our lines at the LZ. The radio traffic is increasing. Ultra armor is on the move out there. Other districts controlled by Insurrection forces and chimps are being shelled in prep for the big fight coming our collective way. The day is hot now but there are great storm clouds beyond the city, over the emerald-green jungles and among jagged red granite mountains out there in the distance. There are no birds in the air, and everything feels lifeless, tense, waiting for something terrible to happen.

But I'm an optimist that way.

Wolfy isn't tall. Not taller than me. But he has this way of walking that's almost like ranging over hills and through fields where you need to take long strides to get anywhere anytime soon. That gives him the appearance of someone who is tall but isn't.

"What you did there back at the oh-be-jay? That was cool, Sar'nt."

I feel some small pit in my stomach open up because much of what happened under the influence of Stinkeye's berserking is… missing… in our minds. So this feels uncertain. And I don't like it.

But I cover anyway. 'Cause I'm a pro NCO that way. Never let 'em see you sweat or see you breathe through your mouth. If you have to hurl because you drank too much the night before, or the PT was too brutal that morning after all the drinking and smokes, then just swallow it and find a dark tree-lined stretch to get it done in when no one's looking.

"Die on someone else's time," the guy who'd taught me to NCO had always lectured me. It was good wisdom. And yeah, I'd used it to effect on some occasions.

Don't ever let them see it. Don't let them ever see the weakness. You'll lose them after that, and they need you, whether they know it or not.

"We were all just doin' whatever it took out there, Wolfy…" I offered cautiously. "… to get through that one. That's just our job in Reaper, man."

"No. I don't mean that, Sar'nt Orion," said my squad designated marksman after a short pause. He was serious about something. "What you did for Hotsoup. When you went all forbidden popsicle with that Sturm on those two Ultras from the QRF. Right out there out front, Sar'nt. When you did it for Hotsoup."

Did I?

I wasn't following but I had a feeling I wasn't going to like where this was headed.

"I was blasting away and closing, Sar'nt," continued Wolfy, "and then I just saw you go all high-cycle and start screaming *Hot soup!* And I was like, man… *that's beautiful.* He woulda loved that."

I have no memory of that.

"Who?" I asked, trying to be cagey.

"Hotsoup," said Wolfy almost beatifically. Emphatically, like I needed to believe what he believed. Or assuming blindly that I already did…

Wolfy is off in another world as he lowers his sniper rifle and holds it like I was holding the Sturm. Which I'd strapped to my ruck, found as many belts as I could, and humped back here because finders keepers.

Daddy got a new toy. Sorry, Bastard. But you always knew I was a cheater all along.

"You were like... *Want some of this, losers?*" Wolfy is doing that whisper-scream thing shy people do when they imitate someone yelling while recounting some story or incident or action movie they've seen. "*You want some of this, sickbags? Come get some! This is for Hotsoup! Hot soup, sickbags! Hot soup for every one of you! Hot soup! Come and get some!*"

Wolfy's eyes are glazed over as he recounts my "heroism" and apparently... *tribute*... to our fallen brother.

Of which... I have no clue.

Wolfy's back there in it with contact on the QRF. Reenacting *me*, vaporizing Ultras with my own personal death machine on high-cycle. And also... the Sturm didn't go forbidden popsicle thanks to that sweet nano-cooled vented barrel.

I think I'm in love. With the light machine gun.

I also have no memory of ever doing that weird *Hot soup, losers!* thing. Berserking, it's a helluva drug. Thanks for that, Stinkeye. Thanks for making a mindless massacre even worse by now having me have to deal with... something uncomfortable. Like what, are people gonna think me and Hotsoup were gay lovers or something because I screamed out his name in a firefight? I really don't need that now in my life. No one will ever let me live that down. What the hell else other embarrassing things did I say?

Hotsoup. Barely knew him. Seriously. If I had to be honest, I'd say I probably didn't even like the guy. He was small about his tag when the pro move is to own it. He went around bitter about it, and I liked him less for that.

I had a tag once. But somehow everyone just kept calling me *Orion* along the way, which is actually my name. I think Stinkeye calling me *Little King*, which no one else does, at least to my face, reinforced *Orion* over the light years and bad contracts. But I don't know.

There are mysteries and not everything has an answer, Sergeant Orion.

Still, I wasn't bitter about my old tag like Hotsoup was. And no, I'm not telling you what my old tag was here. You can dig around in the company logs and figure it out for yourself. But it wasn't flattering, and they gave it to me when I was dumb and new and needed the money.

Scumbags.

Wolfy was staring at me with an actual tear running down his dirt-stained face. Clearly he had some kind of ties to the now-deceased Hotsoup.

What I'd done under the influence of Stinkeye's space witchery had meant something to him.

"*Hot soup* is my new *Yahtzee*, Sar'nt. Thanks for showing me the way. He was the best of us. He was my best friend."

I nodded. I had no idea. I thought everyone kinda hated him. Who knew?

Snipers say *Yahtzee* whenever they dome a guy. It's like an ancient good luck saying. No, I have no idea what it means. Cavemen on Earth must've once uttered it when they smashed the brains out of enemy cavemen with a big heavy rock.

So, there's that.

Wolfy's feelings are making me feel… *uncomfortable.* Which feelings do in general. That's why darkness and cigarettes. And I have things to do now that we're back at the LZ before the big push from the enemy. But clearly, one of my soldiers is grieving over a comrade and I should… do… *something?*

"Yeah…" I faux-sigh like the weight of Hotsoup's death actually bothers me. I try not to grieve on a contract. Front sight forward until we make it back to the *Spider.* Then smokes and darkness somewhere where no one can find me in the lower decks. I probably maybe might have grieved for Soup then, when I was entering him into the permanent record of the logs.

Trust me… I hate me too.

Wolfy is staring at me like I should say something… comforting.

"He was…" I can't think of anything to say about Hotsoup who got shot to death on a bad LZ because I encouraged him to stay in the fight and get that anti-air weapon system operational.

Do I feel bad about that?

No.

That was his job. We were under fire. We all have jobs to do.

"… he was the best…" I parrot what Wolfy has just said, feeling awful. For parroting. "… of us."

There.

Wolfy looks at me and puts his hand on my shoulder.

He nods and chokes back a sob and I wonder if he's gaslighting me.

Because I'm a people person that way.

But his grief seems legit and so I continue my discomfort in order to keep my sniper operational. So I stand there waiting for this to be over.

Soon, hopefully.

Wolfy chokes out a soft, "He really was…" and then whispers because it's all he can muster, "Hotsoup, man. We're gonna do this for Hotsoup, Sar'nt. We're gonna do it for The Soup!"

He wipes angry tears from his eyes and it's then I notice he has dried blood around his mouth.

Oh hell… he went full berserk. That kinda stuff happened at the Froggo village.

Berserking is a helluva drug.

Damn you, Stinkeye.

I bet he's laughing his mangy old brown butt off right now. And like all warrant officers, he's disappeared and nowhere to be found as we get ready for the next fight headed our way as sure as those clouds are boiling up into thunderheads out there in the early afternoon of a red sky.

War.

CHAPTER NINETEEN

In full view of my platoon, I stripped out of my chest rig, battle belt, and plate carrier, then shucked off my blood-stained fatigues. They were ruined. Then I got my tightly rolled backups out of my ruck. Socks too.

Every NCO knows… you got two you got one. You got one you got none. So it was good to have a backup set of fatigues to get into whatever came next.

And I had a feeling something serious was definitely headed our way by the echoing sounds of gunfire and explosions raging out to our flanks. The monkey screeching, and their cacophonic gunfire, had mostly disappeared.

For some reason, that felt more ominous than I would have thought at first.

I got out my microwipes before getting into my fatigues and gear and took a field bath as more enemy artillery went off like thunder in the skies. Lightning flashes presided over destroyed blocks to our west. We were targeted by enemy indirect but the PDCs roared to sudden *burrppping* life and knocked out the incoming rounds with swarms of outgoing fire and resulting brief fireworks displays.

I walked over to Wolfy and handed him a microwipe once I had my pants and boots back on. Fresh socks too and honestly, at least my feet felt new.

I needed coffee and a smoke, but I never smoked during an op. Unless it was looking bad. And so far it was, but it was too early to admit it to myself, and by doing so, to the rest of the unit.

I cast a quick glance and could still see the hulking shapes of the mechs immobile on the lower cargo deck. Sergeant Angry was over there, waving his hands and screaming at someone. His rants had become a source of joy for the Strange Company and reminded many of them of their initial basic training drill instructors they'd had in the various services they'd first started out in before deciding to private military contract.

"What?" asked Wolfy as I handed him the microwipe. His cordite and red dust-covered cheeks still held the tracks of the tears he'd wept over his dead friend Hotsoup.

"You got somethin'…" I said awkwardly, motioning to his face where the blood was caked, "…there." He badly attempted to wipe away whatever had gotten out of hand on the LZ.

I had dark visions that Wolfy had gone… wolfy… at some point.

"Oh," he said, wiping his mouth and face and seeing the dried blood. "That…" he whispered, trailing off, his eyes going to some old friend, or darkness. Snapshots he possessed of Stinkeye's shenanigans on our behalf.

I hoped for him those particular snapshots were missing in some way.

I walked back to my ruck, leaving Wolfy to clean up the mess on his face, and whatever had happened there, glaring at everyone and wondering how much they knew about what had gone down out there. Did they know I'd done it for Hotsoup?

Yikes. I'd never live that down. I could see them changing my tag, unofficially, and starting to use Hotsoup behind my back in reference to me. Yeah, I'm in the middle of a fight, a full-on invasion against the Monarchs themselves, but these kinda things can get out of hand. I'm not saying I have a lot of respect around here. But I have some. And I'm trying to hold on to what little I have if just so I can keep them alive when the incoming starts… you know, incoming.

I am a petty and prideful man. Small and wicked too.

I'd set up my smart canteen to brew hot coffee while I got myself ready, and now as more artillery and gunfire started up once again to the west, I got called back to the CP on the back deck of the *Spider* for a command team briefing.

So it was a good thing I didn't look like a gunshot victim. Like Duster, who'd actually been shot in the fight but who'd been so out of his mind on Stinkeye witchery that he'd just gone on shooting and closing to point-blank range with real live Ultras. Imagine that.

The round went through his arm, tricep actually, and took out a huge piece of flesh in the passing. But really, it was a big scratch and there may have been some muscle damage. Choker was busy spraying bacto-cool and laughing as Duster screamed and growled at the psychotic medic. The prognosis after that was duracast the upper limb but remain operational as our demo. Duster would ditch the carbine shorty he carried and work with his sidearm until we could get access to Cutter, who was apparently still on the bird and running an aid station that was currently not taking casevacs.

I had no official comm on that… but I had an idea why.

My guess was our combat surgeon was still drunk. He usually drank when the fighting began and started to sober once we took casualties. I know… he sounds awful, but it actually worked for us. Truth was, Cutter was a bad drunk. We knew it. He knew it. And I knew his story because that's what I do around here. Honestly, I'd be just as drunk, all the time, if I'd been through what he'd been through.

Seriously. I'm just being honest about this. Your mileage may vary. Perhaps you're better than the rest of us.

Yeah, that's an excuse on how to deal with pain. And not a good one. Cutter's life would have been a lot better sober, but he'd chosen drinking like an animal as a way to cope, and he was flat-out miserable for it. But when it came to meatball war-injury-related surgery and care he was a flawless surgeon. Crabby, angry, impatient. Sure, all those things. But he took pride in his work and saving your life like he really meant it. He sewed you up better than any Bright World doc, which he'd once been and a very well paid one at that, way better than anything you were likely to get in a PMC out in the Third Worlds. He did all this sweating alcohol out of his pores and cursing at you for being stupid enough to get wounded. But, if you made it to Cutter, you were probably gonna survive. He was very good at what he did.

It's just that he was drunk a lot too.

But we'd worked out a system!

He got the drinking done when the fighting started. Then, after that, he was all business. When it was over, he'd binge to the point of death.

Every NCO had taken their turn sitting with him in those dark times as the company rotated off the line, our company surgeon shaking and raving in the throes of the delirium tremens. Crying for mercy as he violently shook, raging with violent anger at hallucinations we could not see. He had saved every one of them, and their men, at some point. They were happy to do it.

Three days later, on the other side of the detox, trembling and thin, Cutter would start seeing patients again. Preacher would come and pray with him, as he'd done throughout the detox. I'd see Cutter's shoulders shaking as he sobbed and the old soldier we called our chaplain whispered words I could not hear. I could hear Cutter swearing softly though, swearing he'd never drink again, and even Preacher knew this was a pretty lie that the sinner seeking salvation wanted more than anything.

But we all had some kind of blind faith at that moment, that this time… this time it would work, for Cutter.

Even me. A jaded old ruck-hump NCO who doesn't believe in anything anymore. Except the Seeker had caused me to believe just a little on the last op with promises of a better tomorrow if I did. Made me tell a lie to the company for a noble cause. Challenged me to believe in something, just once. At least for a little while.

And look where that had gotten us.

I took Punch and left Hauser in charge to go attend the meeting at the CP on the cargo deck of the bird.

"What happened out there, Big Sarge?" asked Punch as we hustled back to the rear, a hundred meters away or so.

"Nothin'," I answered. I was all geared up and ready to go now. I didn't have time, or room, for shame. I left the Sturm I'd commandeered there next to my ruck, and I had the Bastard with me. That felt right. Like I wasn't cheating no matter what had gone down during that hot forbidden moment of high-cyclic passion wasting Ultras and screaming nonsense.

Hot soup, losers!

I shuddered and said nothing, ignoring my assistant squad leader as we raced for the *Spider*.

But... I was gonna use the hell outta the Sturm until I was outta HERK rounds. That was for sure. Bet on anything you like, but that one's easy money.

"Chimps and Chief Cook came in while you guys were out doin' nothin', Sarge," continued Punch, ignoring my omission of facts, ignoring my feigned obliviousness to embarrassing questions, carrying on in the ASL role. "So... I'm betting whatever meeting we're walking into is gonna be weird."

I could feel the understatement in that. And I didn't like it. Not one bit.

But hey, what was I gonna do. I was summoned. I'd be there. Told to go kill... I'd do that too.

That's why they paid me the big bucks.

But I am allowed a small pontification on the matter. Comes with the stripes. And hey, they don't put these on just anyone. You gotta be stupid enough to hang around long enough, and some kind of weirdo who digs the pain, to wanna sarge.

"Punch, for some people..." I paused grandly like I was really doling out the secrets of the universe here in the way some mobster peels off hard currency from his wad. Don't spend it all in one place, kid. "For some people, total warfare with the Monarchs, with drunken psy-users like Stinkeye and Nether on your six, or whatever madness Chief Cook's gonna cook up on our behalf, pardon the pun, and the possibility of the whole world getting lit on fire by a Mauler strike, is literally the very definition of weird. There ain't much you can do about it when it starts to rain thermal plasma in the nine-trillion-degree range, no joke, man. But for the Strange, Punch... it's just Tuesday. Cheer up. Things can only get worse."

CHAPTER TWENTY

Yeah, I'll have to admit. That was a weird meeting. Forget the fact that two months ago in company time, and really twenty-five years in real-time, the chimps had been a raving, screaming, living nightmare horde trying to kill us on Astralon, Crash, call it what you will. Now they were standing there on the deck of the *Spider* in all their tribal madness.

As allies. And it's weird, man.

The chimp foot soldiers were dressed like your average guerrillas, pardon the pun. Ragged clothing. Patchwork gear from rando chest rigs that had done service in various second-rate armies. Then there were the vintage war-surplus plate carriers. Some of the chimps have even got assault gloves, but none of them are wearing combat boots. They're brimming with weapons and anger. They all seem to be strapping old Frankensteins of various generational AKs to the drum-fed light machine guns that seem ancient beyond identification. No uniformity of weapons. Some have unexplainable tacticool attachments, others are wrapped in tape or bloody bandages for better grip. The chimps don't do advanced sights. Iron sights and I'm not sure they even use those unless they're taking their time, which they don't seem to do as they move, sweeping forward over their enemies and firing wildly, coming at the Ultras out there like a living nightmare fully realized.

I've been on the receiving end of monkeys with guns. It ain't fun. One star. Would not recommend a lot. Cannot emphasize that point more.

I even felt bad for the Ultras out there. A little.

Those are the chimp "foot soldiers" who came with their general, who was surrounded by a much more impressive "praetorian guard" of hulking six-hundred-pound gorillas.

Among the chimp foot soldiers, I couldn't detect any kind of military discipline, much less organization as we stood there in the chaos waiting for the meeting to get underway as enemy shelling across our lines continued, growing in intensity as the moments passed. The chimp foot soldiers moved like any gang or mob or Third World army. Just a cluster of grinning psychos ready to do murder on the big man of the moment's behalf. Most of these foot soldiers were monkeys of the chimpanzee or orangutan type. There were a few gorillas among them, acting as heavy machine gunners was my guess. I kid you not, these were carrying modern-make MG42s. The new designs made by some of the high-speed weapons developers who'd been supplying the rebelling colonies out along the frontier, the ones who had the mem to pay, back in the days when the company had been fighting on various sides during the Monarchs' suppression and domination wars of the outer worlds. The old designs with new improvements had been big sellers.

The media had referred to those outer worlds as the Third Worlds. But that's all over now. Or at least it is for the Monarchs.

Then came the praetorians who ringed the chimp general and stood like menacing sentinels, heads and shoulders above all. These hulking, black-furred gorillas radiated pure animal menace, and honestly, it felt dangerous to be near them. Like they could just grab you with their leathery hands and tear your arms out of your sockets before you could do a thing about it.

They wore armor. It was slick and ornate and that contributed to the tribal weirdness. It was modern combat armor, ceramic, but it had been cut and patterned to look like something out of Earth's ancient Bronze Age past where the Monarchs claimed to have begun their imperial rule over the home world we all once came from. The protection wrapped about the immense frames of the gorilla praetorian guard was like something Roman legionnaires must've once worn.

But all in black with little bits of gold flaking here and there. They carried huge giga-spears and slung sub guns.

It was weird.

Did I mention they have fangs?

"Lemme know when you wanna fight one of those things, Punch. I'll get that arranged for morale and all, ya know. I'll even lose money on you winning."

Punch said nothing and I couldn't tell whether he was seriously considering it, or just pretending it was he who hadn't heard the indelicate question this time.

And then there was Chief Cook near their general. Nodding and talking rapidly with our command team as the small chimp general, a humanoid monkey or chimpanzee, whatever, stood there watching the whole bizarre mishmash proceeding with the cold eyes of a born war leader calculating the odds of what he had to work with.

Cook, that grinning sociopath, and he really is one, smiling behind his mirrored aviator shades, his uniform crisp and pressed, made eye contact with me and nodded. His old bloody red Monarch Spec Ops beret shaped just right. Pistol belt loaded for battle. He was even sporting a cross-body holster with some kind of pearl-handled revolver of the massive hand cannon type.

He swaggered and hefted his pistol belt, returning the introductions between the Old Man and the first sergeant and the rest of the chimps.

I marveled at Chief Cook's clean uniform.

I'd been on the ground in this little conflict for less than four hours and I'd already needed to go to my backups. Chief Cook, who'd inserted two weeks prior via fast orbital drop courier to interface with the chimps on the ground and shelling the hell out of the Ultra positions, looked like he'd just stepped out of the showers back on the *Spider*.

Just before the meeting began, as a small fight broke out between two groups of chimp foot soldiers, monkeys with automatic weapons I'll add, fangs bared and each snarling and howling at the others, our psyops specialist sidled up to me. Chief Cook always sidles. He's a sidler. Moving in to stand sideways at your shoulders, beginning to speak without looking at you. Staring at what you're staring at. Watching and not watching what you're focused on.

Intent on the transmission of the most dangerous viral virus of them all. Propaganda. Or what he would call, "my side of things from a certain point of view, Orion."

Chief Cook probably thought I agreed.

I merely faced the first sergeant and the Old Man making last-minute orders to some of the other platoons. Ghost and Dog platoon leaders listening. Chungo and Biggs there contributing their sections to the discussion, arty and supply respectively. Captain Max and Sergeant Angry from Apocalypse Solutions waiting in the wings, as were their shadowy, hulking, looming forty-ton death machines behind them on the open cargo deck.

Cook probably thought I was taking all this in and making some sort of critical assessment of what we'd gotten ourselves into this time, and how we were gonna get through the rest of the day, much less the rest of the invasion given our current awful circumstances.

"Looks bad, Sergeant Orion." I could hear the grin in his voice, not matching the direness of the situation we were in. *So*, I thought to myself. *We're playing games here.* But I wasn't gonna bite. I sat back, drank my coffee, and waited for him to share with me the brilliance of himself, from a certain point of view, *O*-rion.

He loves to emphasize that *O*. It reminds me of some adult scolding me as a child for the latest trouble I'd managed to find.

They were right. It just took a lotta bad contracts and a few gunshot wounds to realize it.

I sipped my coffee and reminded myself that most everyone I grew up with was dead a long time ago and that I was, for all intents and purposes, king of the hill.

I can live with that.

In truth, I was drinking my coffee, pretending I was calm. I was still jittery and trying to flush the images of Stinkeye, who was nowhere to be seen now, though he was the leader of Voodoo Platoon and a warrant officer who should actually be at a command team meeting on the battlefield, from my mind.

But he's Stinkeye. Even the Old Man knows that.

"Well, buddy boy," continued Cook when I wouldn't bite. "We got us Ultra combined arms teams moving in fast, Sergeant." He hissed in my ear like some perpetual insider constantly insiding. "ASAP, Orion! They'll hit us just after nautical twilight if all my years in Spec Psyops were worth anything other than a kick in the face at three a.m. local and a cheap ticket to the Saturnalian pleasure worlds for a weekend of wicked thrills and bad booze. That's how the Ultras do it, Orion. And I don't know if you know this… but we're facing Arkades himself out there. The… emphasis on *The*… Big Boy. The real live heartbreaker lifetaker Ultra big bad wolf himself. We're in big trouble, Sergeant. The mechs are dead and can't get off the bird. The LZ is the only place in this battle line that's holding because a force made up of a dozen ad hoc militaries forming some kind of an insurrection and all under the sway of some Monarch turned galactic evangelist, your girlfriend the Seeker, doesn't mean anything when it comes to no-holds-barred toe-to-toe knife-and-gun-show combat against the Monarchs' galactic hardboys themselves, the Ultras!"

"What about the chimps, Cook?" I asked if just to break up the dire end-of-the-galaxy prophet-of-doom act Chief Cook was working his way up to. I took a sip of coffee, happy to have derailed his doomsaying equation that would lead to the inevitable "here's the actual truth, O-rion… from a certain point of view."

"Oh, them," guffawed Chief Cook. "The Simia, as they are officially known, Orion. Our current new best friends. That's what we call 'em, buddy boy. Better get used to it because they're going to come out on top in this whole mess, mark my words. I was there in sixty-nine when the Sec War declared the secret war at Subidon was all but lost and the winds of change were sweeping the galaxy, never mind the latest footage of the good fight the locals' loyalists were putting up. Best to bet on the coalition of worlds against the

Monarchs and I did, Orion. I did and here we are. Sure as Subidon is nothing but a debris field now. Them chimps, Orion, they're the best guerrilla fighters in the galaxy I've ever worked with, and I've worked with 'em all."

The chimps he referred to were now fighting in the black dust of the charred LZ we were fighting for. The two studs for the two factions snarling and howling at each other.

Their general watched the fight, keeping an eye on the captain of our company as he approached with the first sergeant in tow.

Chief Cook laughed and I knew he was chuckling at his own accidental word usage of guerrilla when referring to the chimps.

"No really," he continued. "They're tight. They've got some kind of tactics but zero organization, Sergeant. It's all tribal politics inside the combat groups they've formed, and I can't find any rhyme nor reason to their chaos and madness, but Hells of Suth, Orion, they don't need that. They've got guns, a lot of 'em in fact. Aaaaannd they number twenty to one for every Ultra we estimate is on the ground right here and now. I've been moving through the jungle for two weeks…"

I gave him the side eye as I surveyed his clean and perfectly crisp fatigues. He got the message.

"Never let 'em dress you down, Sergeant. Every day in the jungle I am showroom ready to lay the actual ever-lovin' hate and win hearts and minds or stack corpses. That's what we do in the Spec. We do… the undoable. It's how we show we're better than everyone else when the chips are down and you're gettin' ready to shoot your pack animals for some hot chow. Only way they'll ever follow you, Orion, is if you look like a winner. Rule number one in Spec Psyops: look like a winner all the time, Sergeant. Unless you need to look like a loser so you can surprise-punch your enemy right in the BALLS! Then… *blam kapow!*"

He was practically shouting at me now while he maintained his sidle. Spit flying from his thin lips and through the gaps in his tombstone-spaced teeth. Hissing as he made each point like some roadside prophet who'd sell me salvation, or his wife, if I'd just believe him.

I've seen this show before. It's not my first right-side-of-history go-get-'em speech.

"In fact," continued the chief. "Not looking like some beat-up space tramp sleeping in the starport reeds is a combat multiplier. Showered, shaved, and ready to slay as we used to say in the Spec. Really, Orion. You are an NCO. A little snap and polish like Sergeant Angry over there and you could be right in line to be first shirt once Top fades on the next contract or buys it when the Ultras jump our supply chain, heaven help them for doing so but this looks… and that's the key word, are you following me, Orion… it looks bad. You get that, son? You get that, Orion?"

We're probably the same age. But as I have described before, the chief has a fluctuating age mask of indeterminate definition. Sometimes he looks young and full of just the right amount of vinegar and ambition to get things done. Other times he seems older and jaded by all the darkness he hasn't just seen, but the darkness I'm sure he's directly responsible for. Did I tell you about that time he drugged my whole platoon so they could conduct an attack through debilitating chemical agents? Yeah. That's in these logs. The attack on the starport at Crash, or Astralon, call it whatever.

But there've been others…

Let me tell you about another one of his stunts I had to pay for. One time, on Pthalo, he killed us. Seriously. He killed us. I mean technically. But he did.

We were sweeping villages in the lower valleys, weeding out insurgents and the supply trains coming down from the mountaintop LZs. Cook got it into his mind that the guerrillas had a command-and-control base set up inside the main starport city and that it needed to be infiltrated and eliminated. He spent three weeks training a local commando team to get it done only for them to get ambushed and wiped out after being compromised. So he went to the Old Man and said he needed to use company resources to avoid the compromise variable that had contributed to his cruddy plan going up in sudden flames. Note here that the local commandos he was responsible for were the ones that got wiped out.

Classic Chief Cook move.

"He wanted to wipe out the base and collect intel on-site. High-ex wasn't gonna do the trick, it needed to be stormed intact, but it was an operation inside a free city. So no actual combat units inside the walls. Instead, he ran a covert infiltration mission by the Old Man who greenlit us, Reaper specifically, and why not Ghost you ask… because rumor is Ghost will shoot Cook in the back if they ever get the chance. Something happened over there and both sides don't trust each other anymore. I do not know the details.

But I understand the sentiment.

So, instead of Ghost, our actual snoop-and-poop scouts, Reaper gets chosen for the creep and he actually has us training in a village we cleared awhile back for an entire week. I mean, like basic military training. Stuff we know. It's ridiculous. In fact, it becomes apparent he's running his own little psychotic boot camp. At first I put up some protest against this with the first sergeant because my guys don't need basic soldier skills. I had a lot of pros and zero new guys at the time. We were good. But Cook argues that what we're going to do needs to be done with precision and we need to train as a cohesive element in order to get the timing of what he has planned.

So we do a lot of dumb basic stuff while he stands there and smokes these nasty long-stemmed smokes. And he still PT'd everyone in fatigues with him leading the runs in his boots and crisp fatigues every morning and night. Aviator sunglasses and that nasty-smelling long-stemmed smoke jutting from his mouth as he runs and runs and never sweats. While we're running. His cigarettes are nasty and they're killing all of us as the stink drafts in his wake, choking us.

We spend most of the days training recon and creep. I'll admit… that part was good. We really tightened our act up and I wasn't completely butthurt about that. But the rest was lunacy. He'd play acid synth trance cut with war movies all night long while we slept or tried to sleep. He'd randomly fire bursts of loud automatic weapons fire from wonky old AK Frankensteins, which are loud, and swill bourbon. He never slept. His uniforms were crisp and clean. And he could run like a gazelle and never sweat.

I asked him about that part. The not sweating.

"Oh," he mumbled confidentially, waving at something I couldn't see in the air. Bitey gnats or the microscopic flying snakes that were everywhere. "I take something for that."

The part I was butthurt about was, after the final stale cigarette run trailing into our ranks, a real eight-mile smoker through the jungle, pardon the pun, he had a huge catered-by-some-local-meat-on-the-street-vendor BBQ right there in the dead village.

Week's over.

Training's done.

"Why not celebrate, Sergeant Orion?" he whooped, wildly excited with his creepy perma-smile as we stood there gasping after the run.

I failed my men. I should have been more suspicious. But in my defense, slow-roasted pork spareribs with firetang sauce and cold beers was pretty enticing after that bizarre week and I felt, misguidedly, that he was trying to make amends in some way for all his strange and downright psychotic behavior. He even brought in a local singer and her guitarist.

A Sootha Hatari girl with this voice that was squeaky and fun while her guitarist, also a Sootha, plucked at the strings of his instrument in recursively hypnotic fashion that slowly revealed itself once it was too late.

You know how the Sootha are with their one big cyclops eye in their giant heart-shaped heads atop slim tight bodies. Don't forget their orange skin. It's wild. And they're big into the iridescent nano-tats that shift and swirl.

So that and the hypnotic mind control music had our guard down for what the chief had just done to us. If we hadn't been feeling so good, we might have gotten to our guns and blasted him to pieces as we began to defecate and slobber all over ourselves.

We just thought we were having a good time. I know, that sounds weird. When is taking a dump inside your fatigues and slobbering fun? But it made sense because of the drugs we'd just been dosed with.

So, as one of the happiest species in the galaxy, the Sootha, played and lulled us into a highly compliant state, I really should have been worried because it was obvious we were being set up for something.

In my defense, aren't our warrant officers supposed to be on our side? Aren't they supposed to be looking out for us?

I am a naive and simple ruck hobo. Pity me.

The answer is… in our case, actually it's best if you plan that they aren't. But in their defense, benefit of the doubt and all, they're trying to help.

In their own weird, lethal way.

So, the first clue something wasn't right was when I lost feeling in my face. I hadn't defecated on myself yet. My hands went all numb as I tried to wipe some firetang sauce from my face while I was no doubt grinning like an idiot or something. Or I thought I was. What was really going on was my body was slowly becoming paralyzed into a state of near death as Chief Cook had just drugged all of us with Hooma poison via the sweet and hot pork spareribs as the delivery vehicle.

Probably the tasty firetang sauce.

I stumbled for him instantly, intent on throttling the life out of the eyes behind the mirrored aviator shades. My guys were already starting to drop all around me. I made it three steps and the floor became the sky, or something. The next thing I realized, Chief Cook was standing over me, staring down into my lifeless eyes.

"Relax, Orion. I had to do it this way, buddy boy. See… I'm gonna sell out to the guerrillas. I'm bringing you guys and your weapons in as prizes. Then I'm gonna tell them to put you on display and shoot your bodies up like they ambushed you. Big PR victory for them."

If I could have screamed, I would have at that point. But technically, I was dead and paralyzed. So I was unable to. Our hearts were barely beating, very slowly in fact. We could all hear and know everything going on around us for the next three days, but that didn't make it better.

"Don't worry, Orion. That's not gonna happen. That's just the cover story. Once you're in your gear and before they transport you out to the ambush site, I'm going to smoke the reawakening agent I've been saturating your systems with during our little PT runs. Suddenly, right there inside their command base, you killers are going to come to ever-living life and start wasting them big-time! So play it cool until then. When it goes down, and you get your motor skills back, I'll distract them while you guys get your limbs moving and get ready to murder them… big-time!"

Then he added the fun part.

"That'll be in about three days, Orion. Until then… enjoy the ride. Consider it leave."

Enjoy the ride! Enjoy the ride, he says. Do you have any idea what it's like to be conscious for three straight days, and very long nights, but unable to move or even blink your eyelids while in the care of your enemies? Let me just cut to the chase for you on this one… you think you're going to go mad. Seriously. Dog came in and dressed us in our gear, that was weird, and then loaded us into a supply truck. We drove around in the heat as flying snakes and other bugs landed on us and we could do nothing about this but watch them crawl around on each other and bite us. Then we were "sold" to the guerrillas, who kicked us a lot and it became clear that some of them wanted to shoot us early on and not wait for the "ambush" as it would be. Chief Cook did his part well here. He wove quite a tale about this needing to be perfect and that the pooling blood spatter needed to be just right for the media and the "big-time" PR victory. When he said "big-time," which he'd begun to use of late on that mission, he actually winked at my "corpse." Like he was trying to blow the whole thing. So he, being an expert in psyops, told the guerrillas that he would know how to detect if the bodies were staged for an "ambush."

And that if that was so, then the whole "big-time" PR victory was blown, "guys."

Reluctantly the guerrillas agreed, and we were laid out on a concrete floor, under our ponchos, in a dark and smelly warehouse.

For two more days.

Fun fact: we didn't decompose. In the heat on that world full of biting flying snakes that gave you the sleeping mad sickness, our bodies should have been ripe, and the guerrillas should have detected that. There were so many flaws in Chief Cook's plan that we should have been machine-gunned where we lay playing dead. But they were aliens after all, and Chief Cook was able to snow them on the dead body smelling part.

Here's the fun fact on how he did it… prior to our ending up in guerrilla hands laid out on a smelly concrete floor in the warehouse district which disguised the command-and-control headquarters of the guerrillas in the hidden floors below, Chief Cook placed a small yellow pill under each of our paralyzed tongues.

Oh yeah. We couldn't swallow. It was insanity.

For the three days, and really for about a month, we smelled like dead guys thanks to the little yellow pills.

Afterwards…

You. Cannot. Take. Enough. Showers.

Slowly, as we lay there dead, the feeling and ability to use our bodies came back over time. Slowly. And for some reason that was worse than being totally paralyzed. We had to lie there barely testing everything because once it was *get it on* time, we needed to be able to use all our limbs in order to get the mission done and work our weapons, and shoot, move, and communicate effectively.

Why would we even want to do the mission, you might ask yourself, because I sure did repeatedly ten times a minute for three straight days.

Answer… so you could kill Chief Cook once it was done. If anything… that was the only thought that kept me sane for the entire three days.

I was going to kill him. Period.

Finally, I was able to sit up in the darkness of the smelly warehouse, and most of my platoon was there in the smelly dark with me. They'd left us with our weapons so they could stage the ambush site effectively by just placing us and blasting away at our "dead" bodies.

Things that keep me awake at night still to this day? What if they'd just decided to get it done early?

We moved slowly until we were ready to get it on. Then finally, we go in and flashbang the first few rooms telling ourselves we're gonna mag-dump on the chief if he's anywhere near them. After that, rolling thunder all the way down into the lower levels of the base, tossing frags and machine-gunning everyone we come across… just hoping Chief Cook is somewhere in there because of course he's going to get "accidentally" killed by all of us all at once.

Spoiler. He wasn't. He'd fled the facility an hour before because he knew what each of us had in mind for him.

He's wily that way.

So, we wipe the facility and the Old Man and Dog come in to extract us and clean up in the aftermath of our surprise attack. I remember Amarcus just looking at me with this cruddy smile on his horribly scarred face, that twisted sneer indicating he knew how bad it had been.

And was enjoying that secret knowledge.

The captain gets us back to the base and he comes in later to debrief and AAR, and of course all my guys are baying for Chief Cook's blood. The Old Man listens to our complaints, and in some cases ravings worthy of poor souls who've completely lost their minds. And of course, the slow cold violence Punch was planning like some men love women they'll do murder for.

Side note… Choker loved the whole thing. He thought it was great and he bore the chief no ill will. He found it… total paralysis and near death… his words here: "… refreshingly restful. I'd do it again in a heartbeat, Sar'nt."

I still shudder at the time he told me that.

Sometimes, just randomly on a march, or even once in a firefight, he'd start going on about it. "Hey, remember that time we were all dead? That was great, wasn't it, guys? I could do that again. Easily. Refreshingly restful."

The Old Man listens to us moaning and promising vendetta, sitting in a chair turned around so he's leaning on the back of the chair and smoking cigarettes just listening and watching us with not sympathy, or even patience, but both somehow and something more I can't define. Later I'd call it… wisdom.

I was the first to vent. I got it all out and then I was able to step back, because I'd officially opened the floodgate of complaints and murder promises, and just let my men vent. As I did so I could see the captain knew what he was doing, letting us get all the poison out. And… that he understood what we'd been through without ever hijacking what we needed to get off our chests. Like some people do with a story about their own sufferings in whatever came before yours. Somehow making your sufferings less, smaller, and mean.

He didn't do that. He just listened.

There's power in that, I realized later as I watched it happen and knew wisdom of a real leader. The kind I'd always wanted to be, and never would.

When we were done, he crushed his smoke tiredly and said, "I'm sorry. I let this happen to you."

No one said anything in the stunned silence that followed. No one had expected him to take ownership of the totally psychotic operation in which we were technically killed and then handed over to the enemy who at any time could have ventilated us good and hard just for giggles and all.

That three days still makes me, among other things that have happened in my career as a private military contractor, wake up in a cold sweat in the middle of the night, sidearm out, scanning the darkness for guerrillas in the other room, slapping the table and drinking, losing at Cheks, and just talking about going in there to shoot a few of us already "dead" guys. Ain't no harm in that. Ain't no harm in killing the *already dead*.

No one expected the captain to take responsibility for what the chief had done.

I think we expected him to help us secure the rope and tie the hangman's knot.

Once the Old Man had made eye contact with all of us, he spoke again. Softly, quietly, but totally dominating the silence in that debrief. All of us still smelling like the dead.

"What happened was bad. There're no excuses for it. You guys want revenge…"

He paused and looked at each of us.

"Then I'm right here. I'm the one that ordered the operation. So…"

He looked right at Punch because the Old Man knew who the real sluggers were.

Punch shot up out of his chair and stood there, trembling with rage.

"… you want satisfaction… I'm right here, Punch. First shot's free. After that, I defend myself."

The captain had just offered free justified violence on his person in payment for our sufferings. Regardless of the certain beating that would come if the justice exceeded the freebie.

You could have dropped a pin in that tense moment, and it would have sounded like a thunderclap. I'm certain of few things, but I am heart-attack serious on that one.

But I know my assistant squad leader. He was struggling with the right, and the wrong, of it. He knew the captain wasn't guilty of what had been done to us. He'd only ordered the hit. He didn't know Chief Cook would go full voodoo and execute like they do.

Who knows what they'll do? They're freaks. Ops like this make sense to them. They think asymmetrically.

Those are just words. To them.

"Punch," I said softly in the imminent-violence silence.

My ASL snapped his head over at me, pure murder and rage in his eyes like I hoped to never see directed my way.

"It's good, brother," I barely whispered, my vocal cords still hoarse from the paralysis. "This ain't the way to do it."

Punch's mouth opened and closed savagely like the snarl of some big jungle cat getting ready to feed. Then, as fast as he'd stood, he grabbed the chair he'd been sitting on, roared, and threw it against the wall.

Then he sat on the floor, legs folded. A small hurricane brewing in the space of a man.

The Old Man looked around at each of us again. Again making eye contact with all of us. Making the offer for a freebie.

"Okay," he said in the silence that followed.

He didn't say, *I'm proud of you, Reaper*. Not out loud. But you could tell by the look he gave us that he was.

"Mission accomplished, Reaper. You got a big one on that hit. It matters in the war we're fighting here for our clients. And it's good for the company. Double bonuses for the platoon from company funds. But that's not buying you off. I wouldn't do that. And you wouldn't take it. You earned it, and more, on this one. So, here's the part that's gonna sting, men. Here's the favor I am asking of my men…"

We all held our breath. Mine caught in my throat. He's probably an ex-Ultra. I'd never thought of him thinking, or saying, we were "his men." Those were other better soldiers, once and long ago. Not this unit. He just led the company for pay, right?

Ultras were his men.

That was the feeling I'd always had.

Despite his actions on our behalf time and time again.

But now, he called us that and… I've never gotten a military award… but… I bet it feels like that. My men.

Our captain, our leader, the man who went in to get you out no matter how bad it was getting, had never asked a favor of his men.

Us.

I felt awful for him in that moment. And proud of who I was now. His men. I wanted to scream and say, "Stop! We'd follow you beyond the gates of hell, sir. No favors, sir. We're yours to the death!"

But I didn't.

My mouth was dry, and we all smelled like death.

"Let him go," said the captain.

We knew exactly who he meant. Who needed letting go. Mercy. Grace. A pass.

"No revenge. No fragging. No payback. What happened to you… it's on me, Reaper. Any time you want to get him back, you come see me about that and you can have that free shot. Any time. The offer will always be there as long as I'm alive to lead you."

No one said anything.

"But let it pass, Reaper. Let it pass. It was a crazy mission no sane person would ever attempt, much less execute as well as you did, despite the circumstances. You're heartbreakers and lifetakers. And he's honored to lead you."

So…

… we let it pass.

Now Cook is standing next to me hiss-whispering his latest insanities… and if he offers me a smoke, or coffee, or even pork spareribs in firetang sauce and a cold beer… hard pass.

Fool me once, that's on you, Chief.

Fool me twice and… well, he'd done that again and a few other times since. But we always executed the mission and the company got paid on those contracts.

Mostly.

But the captain called us his men once. And for that… I'll storm the gates of heaven or hell. Just send me, sir.

"Looks bad, Orion," continues Cook amid the mad gathering on the cargo ramp of the *Spider* as chimps fight and Ultra artillery falls. "You get my meaning, Sergeant. Arkades and his combat teams all pointed right at this LZ for a big to-do to see who gets the momentum for the coming offensive. Rest of the Insurrection units are scattered and re-organizing after first contact. There are gains and losses. The decision is still in doubt, Orion. The chimps, they're great, but they're like drinking from a firehose if you gotta use 'em for an operation. No finesse. Just point and destroy if they can push hard enough. For all their mayhem and violence, using them in any type of reactively advantageous combat scenario is like trying to steer an iceberg against bona fide stackers like the Ultra Marines. So, if you were this General Arkades himself, Sergeant Orion, and you were gonna—as I read your comm to the first shirt—fight where you aren't. Hit you where you're hurt bad. Strangle you where you're having trouble breathing. That right, Orion? Well, if he's looking at the big tactical flexy, he sees this right here, this LZ we're all about to die on with mechs that can't get in the game and game-change like them big romper stompers do… well, this is where we don't want him. This is where we're hurt bad. Ship's inoperable… did you know that, Orion? Artillery holed reactor three. *Spider*'s grounded and bleeding energy. Shields are at fifty percent power and the PDCs are almost dry. We're outta contact with the various

Insurrection forces because they have no clue what they're actually doing. Yeah… looks real bad for us right about now… Orion. Get it?"

I turned to the Voodoo Psyops chief warrant officer whom Stinkeye considered a devil's devil.

"But that's not the case is it, Cook?"

He turned to me finally, breaking the sidle, mirrored aviator shades like some shark's dead eyes staring, reflecting a funhouse me, and smiled. I saw that mirror-me staring back, mouth agape, hoping for salvation in a lie. I saw a broke ruck-hump NCO who was just hoping to get to the next long silence in the lower decks and a smoke with no more of his guys dead today. Or ever. Is it too much to ask?

Or a scout ship maybe.

Or maybe even an eel girl who purred sweet and melancholic old French songs and swam in seas of azure I want to go to.

I remember you, estrangier, she wrote me once.

Knowing it was all, all of it, lies I told myself like some priest who didn't believe in his own faith anymore.

"No, Orion. That's not the case, buddy boy. The Old Man has laid a trap for Arkades himself and this… this right here, Sergeant… it's for all the marbles. This is going to be the final defeat of the Ultra legions right here on this LZ. That's why I called the LZ Heartbreak. 'Cause we gonna break some hearts right here according to the Old Man's plans."

He laughed a dry chuckle in the madness all around us.

"This is history happening right now, Orion. Big-time."

CHAPTER
TWENTY-ONE

The captain laid out our new battle plan as we stood there in the shadows of the cargo deck with welders' sparks coming off the nearby "damaged" mechs.

Mech crews yelled and called up there, and the war went on out there on the battlefield, but here… the silence could be best described as *stunned*. The operation thus far, and the change of mission we were about to shift over to, had been the Insurrection invasion plan all along. I'll run that down here to show you it was a good plan and that had the Ultras, or the Monarchs, not done what they'd done later in the battle, it would have been a fight with a clear winner by dawn the next day.

And that winner would have been us.

Side note here…

It's rare I'll accuse one side or the other in any conflict of *cheating*. First off… there's no such thing. *Cheating* in warfare is called tactics. Nothing in warfare is cheating. There are no rules, contrary to what people who've never had to fight in any real battle try to impose on the controlled chaos that is battle itself. Real battle. They usually do this, start labeling things as cheating, or war crimes, because they are in fact cheating and trying to gain advantage by denying the opposition the ability to do everything in their power to defeat you. Anything that denies this basic truth is just play-acting and politics for political advantage being done by the lowest form of life… politicians.

So, it's not a sin to *cheat*. Not some fault to be declared by an ump reffing bad calls and "illegal" plays. No such thing. In war. No one's going to shout *not allowed*, point at you, fine you, and ultimately shun you for playing to win, doing anything and everything possible to come out on top because in a fight to the death with sharp knives, automatic weapons, and high explosives there are no second prizes for runners-up.

First prize… you get to live.

There are no second prizes out here beyond the perimeter of civilization. Just the living and the dead.

And every mission, every time you get out there, you've got to decide you're the guy coming back tonight, and then do whatever it takes.

That's not cheating. It's survival. And here's a pro tip… the guy willing to do what no one else is willing to do, in their right mind and all, that's the guy I put my money on.

I try to be that guy. In lieu of talent and good looks, it's my only defense.

I think back to the days when our contracts had been steady work either playing the fool or working for the Monarchs on the "right side of history" thing. Usually just causes for the *Current Thing* as Chief Cook would have put it. There had been umps, sorta, then. But they were really playing for the Monarchs so were they really refs, calling foul and fair in some afternoon contest? No. It was all a con, even then. The whole thing. But yeah, there'd been refs, of a fashion. Umps to point and declare sins, levy fines. Penalize the fools who thought they had a chance when really… they never did. The deck, as I review it all now in the long view of the limited amount of history I've been able to collect… was always stacked against all of us.

The company had been hit with war-crime fines a number of times thanks to Amarcus Hannibal. He was really good at those.

The ones doing the fining, they were called the Inquisitors. They were right there along the edges, in the sky, and somewhere in the shadows in every conflict along the outer worlds, or the Third Worlds as polite society called the new colonies then. There to supervise, and in theory eliminate, or alleviate, the war crimes the losers always committed as they fought for their lives. The Inquisitors were always making the important calls for the "right side of history." And you know who always had the monopoly on that virtue.

The Monarchs.

Looking back, all those wars, all those conflicts and actions of various types I ended up in, and this is pure hyperbole so pardon my dust, but indulge an old ruck hobo for a moment, who knows I might buy it on this one and then someone, please let there be someone who will miss these caustic yet accurate observations of how we lived our days in worse and dangerous times, but… those conflicts we fought in, oxymoron incoming… looking back, they were *polite wars*… compared to what we were fighting in now.

And what I feared, darkly some nights when I smoke late and try to organize it all for the permanent record, is that what we were fighting in now was what we would be fighting for the rest of the known future of humanity, however long that would last.

Perhaps I should edit the log to say… *remaining future.* Instead of *future of humanity.*

Prospects beyond tomorrow seem doubtful. For all of us.

Right there on LZ Heartbreak… odds weren't favorable for anything long-term regarding our species in the galactic playground. But, as Punch likes to say, "Never underestimate the guy with nothing to lose. He may not win, but you're damn sure gonna walk funny for the rest of your life and your wife may just have to get used to hugs and kisses goodnight instead of the ol' *cha-ching* when I get finished with ya."

Punch cuts to the chase in all matters and that's why he's a great assistant platoon leader. And the First Squad ASL too, but I basically have him running First so I can run everything, badly, and on the good days… *less* badly.

But my right-hand man does cut to the chase on most everything. And that cut is usually made with extreme violence.

He would agree with my observation and tell you he's "comfortable with violence."

I once read a book called *Thinking Positively and Being Your Own Biggest Fan for Management Success.*

Can you tell?

If all humans were Punch, we'd rule the galaxy. But they aren't. And no, there were no rules anymore, even fake made-up ones, in war even. No one had heard from the Inquisitor Corps in twenty-four years. So, war crimes… were now just *war*. And no one should ever think anything other than that about the concept of war. It's awful and it needs to be awful, so you don't do it much.

No one cheated anymore, because *if you ain't cheatin', you ain't tryin',* as every basic drill instructor in all the militaries most of us have ever served in like to declare as they grind you down, retrain you, make you throw up, PT you until you think you're gonna die, then show you that you didn't and that you can still shoot, move, and communicate. Those drill instructors ensured we at least reached a point of universal agreement on the purity of war.

Along the way, after all those trainings from veteran NCOs, you learned that on your own. You learned on your way through the suck that is the grind of combat for the win that… *a little cheatin' do go a long way in any operation.*

So, there's that.

And maybe if you cheat well enough on your side's behalf, then everyone comes home with all their fingers and toes.

Thus speaketh the old ruck hobo. Attend and know wisdom, younglings. For I too, once, rode the lightning of a light machine gun cooking off rounds uncontrollably.

And it was a beautiful thing the universe gave me.

We cheated, of course we did. Who doesn't? Platoon sergeants do it a lot because we're the ones who, regardless of really big special maps and state-of-the-art drone feeds and fancy war colleges and all, actually have to go out in the mud, blood, and inclement bullet hurricane developing all over the front and implement the grand plans of theorists and tactical geniuses while under fire, leading a heavily armed group of very excited natural born killers full of testosterone and vain notions of eternity, without really ever understanding what any of that means. Your mileage may vary on the "genius" part regarding any military planner. Mine certainly has. Of course.

We platoon sergeants are trying to keep everyone alive one minute to the next in environments designed to kill them before they've had a chance to regret their bad tattoos.

So… of course we cheated. Hell yeah! We cheat through effective ambush, surprise attacks ranging from the *ambitious* to the *lunatic as conceived by evil starport carnies who've only ever fought with gas station knives and pocket sand*, and of course… the Church of High Explosives Used for All Applications to Work Smarter and Not Harder. The benediction being, *In pieces you be.* The response offered: *And to you also, Father Ruck Hobo. Hand me the detonators, so say we all.*

The company cheated in its own way though. How, you ask? We cheated because we were one of the few private military contractors who used Dark Labs freaks, never minding all the darkness and insanity, and friendly fire of course, that came with the package the freak brought to the deal.

We had them in the rank of warrant officer and called them Voodoo Platoon.

They did voodoo warfare on our behalf. Mostly.

But the Monarchs, or the Ultras… they cheated too, so it was okay. Am I doing that right? Don't worry, I'll get to that later. The Monarchs cheated there on LZ Heartbreak. The point is… everyone cheats in warfare because that's what warfare is. Cheating so you don't get killed first.

I know, it's a point. I've made it. But it's mine to make and I don't want anyone reading this after our demise thinking romantic notions about charges at first light and duels on the objective for honor or some ridiculous notion that doesn't fit in your worn-out ruck. Or the one I really hate in the sci-fi books I kill time with, cup of black coffee and smoke burning between the tips of my fingers as I turn yellow pages and smell history, is that there are such things as *fair fights* because both soldiers respected each other enough to engage in such, even though the sides doing the paying did not in the least.

No. Out here we kill each other as cheaply and as fast as we can with as minimum exposure to danger as is possible to arrange on short notice. Sometimes we even just pray and spray, hoping to see the top of the clock in the next minute, and wonder how we did at all when it's over. And as is said by all soldiers eventually… we wonder why we lived in those moments of bullets flying and men killing, when so many others did not.

As is said…

Soldiers live, and wonder why.

Now, having gotten that down, I gotta lay out the captain's brief on the hangar deck of the *Spider*. As it turned out, despite what I'd considered a simmering quiet promise on the Old Man's part to waste the Seeker as payback for her betrayal of the company on Astralon, Crash, call it whatever you will, during the Insurrection forces' battle planning on Hardrock, the captain stepped forward as some kind of war leader on the Seeker's behalf during the runup to the attack on Marsantyium.

He helped plan her war… when I was sure he was gonna kill her.

I knew something was up all along, but the captain's normally quiet and serious manner deceived me regarding the planning for what became the change of mission and the beginning of Operation Haymaker. I'd watched the prematurely iron-gray-haired man our captain, sun-wrinkled tired skin complete with livid white scars from battles before he'd become our commander, washed-out murder-blue eyes that had seen horrors I could only guess at, and that ancient leather brown trench coat he wrapped himself in as though he was always and forever cold, I watched as he threw me a fast one straight down the middle and I missed without even swinging. He'd thrown us the fastball as fast as he'd skin those two 1911s whenever he had to contribute meaningfully to a desperate fight on behalf of one of his platoons or squads going rapidly pear-shaped.

Blazing away like he was one of us when really… I suspected he was so much better than anything we could ever aspire to. We all did.

He just was.

I had been busy supplying and training my new guys back on Hardrock in the runup to departure, and also the new Kid the first sergeant signed up at the last minute, who was thus tagged such and required extra attention to get up to speed. So I wasn't even remotely in on the deception the war planners were planning on the ground at Marsantyium. And because the operation was made up of *insurrectionistas* from twelve different worlds, and some of the smaller, angrier colonies, including practically every *liberty-or-death*-minded belt miner in human-controlled space, the OPSEC was tight and need-to-know only, regarding what they were cooking up.

Contrary to what you may think in the reading of this account, I wasn't, as much as these logs may lie and say I am, important, and on the need-to-know list. I command a light infantry mercenary platoon that often gets missions where heavy casualties are considered *acceptable* by the contact holder. Some call us cannon fodder. Others use *grunts* like it's some kind of slur.

I hate the former because I've seen enough PMC infantry used as such and been one on more occasions than preferred. I am honored by the latter. And if you knew where I came from, that would be amazing.

But call me a grunt anytime. I may even let you buy me a beer.

No one cares, I often tell myself. Work harder, Orion.

So I did, to get here. Old Man Hobo Leader of Grunts.

Mark it down on the stone I may or may not get when it comes my time. I'm fine with that.

But now, on the ground at the Sack of Marsantyium, as the captain switched on the battle flexy's projector to show our situation on the ground, I saw everything that had been considered a failure, a mistake, an accident, and the ill fate of combat between two forces determined to kill each other, and saw that it had, in actuality, been part of the plan all along. A deception and a trap even.

The captain's plan of course, though I had the feeling Chief Cook had a hand in some of the finer points.

That was one of his specialties.

The Seeker wasn't on the ground yet according to the opening comments on the map. Her flagship, *Elektra*, and a ragtag Insurrection battle fleet were currently fully engaged in orbital combat against the badly wounded Battle Spire *Red Dragon*.

The last Battle Spire.

Insurrection navy was keeping a descent window open to our LZ and two others just kilometers to the rear. At zero hundred local time, overhead, if we could hold the landing zones and maintain enough integrity in the Insurrection line on the ground, we were about to receive five fresh divisions of *insurrectionistas* comprising everything from light armor to infantry in various forms ranging from anti-armor to scout recon and even heavy shock troops. We were also going to get a brigade of dropship air mobile cav out of the Horse Worlds to run screens and conduct fast-rope hit-run raids against the Ultra flanks and rear supply chains.

But wait, there's more… six more chimp hulks were screaming in for a landing on the far side of Saffron City out in the jungles of the valley below the Red Rock Mountains.

Each chimp hulk held twenty thousand chimps snarling and armed with junky AKs ready for combat and hopped up on monkey hatred.

By dawn tomorrow, if we could hold the LZs, we would have overwhelming odds that could not be denied. We would crush the city between two fresh and fully supplied forces.

The Ultras, on the other hand, had one badly wounded division on the ground and one dangerous yet mortally wounded Battle Spire, the fabled *Red Dragon*, in orbit. Supposedly she had zero indirect arty support for orbital strikes. Fighters off the Insurrection-captured carrier *Enterprise* had knocked out *Red Dragon*'s D-beam arrays in a series of alpha strikes that ended in overwhelming numbers of friendly fighters being destroyed in the effort.

But that effort had paid off. If it hadn't, everyone in the strike force currently on the ground would be getting boiled alive in the six-gigawatt range.

"Hot damn, Big Sarge," whispered Punch as the Old Man laid out the situation we were currently in. "We got us a real fight. We might just win this time."

I won't lie to you, the hairs on the back of my neck and head felt like live electricity loose and wild in the air of the *Spider*'s cargo deck, making them stand on end.

My heart was pounding and part of me, right now, was ready to get it on immediately. I felt like I was suddenly waking up from a nightmare I never knew I'd been having for most of my life. The meaning of what was scrolling out on the flexy… extended beyond this war. This was… the end of old things, the beginning of new.

This was change.

Weird, huh?

Yeah, there was arty out there pounding our broken line. Ultra shock and armor getting ready for the biggest push in Ultra combat history ever. For all that *Blood, Death, and Honor* jazz they worship in the death cult … this really was, according to the updating flexy being projected, for all the marbles. This really was, finally, a real battle we might just…

It was unbelievable. This was bigger than I'd realized. And we weren't just right in it. We were at the leading bleeding edge. Or as some say… *the tip of the spear.*

As these realizations settled on me like a cold wind in the night after a hot shower that washed away all the dirt, defeat, and shame of a long day, the wind inside me just left my body for a moment.

I couldn't breathe.

Everything was changing faster than I'd ever… dreamed. And I don't dream much. Being an NCO has disabused me of dreams. The best I can hope for is fewer nightmares. And maybe sometimes… nothing. Or the voice of the eel girl singing softly of not ever having regrets as we lie there entangled in sheets.

People had said words to me all my life. Words like *freedom* and *liberty or death.* Old humanity words. I knew them, but I'd never really believed them. They never mattered to me. Never believed they were possible, for me. For us. I knew the real score because I'd seen it through my front sights time and time again out there on the worlds. And I'd read enough history to know the game was rigged in the Monarchs' favor, and always had been, even before humanity started reaching out to the stars seeking something noble, something else, unaware they were just being used as an expendable recon force ordered by callous gods who would do none of the fighting and all of the glory-taking.

I was holding my breath in that meeting. I'd held my breath my whole life waiting for this, and I'd never known it. And…

I took a breath. It felt… new.

In twelve hours… there would be, if we held the line anchored on LZ Heartbreak, no way the Ultras could win at that point with all those reinforcements conducting a massive planetary landing.

We would have beaten them.

And these we were facing, these were the last of the Ultras. The last of the Monarchs' death cult guard dogs. The last defense of the gods.

Who knew what Earth had left to defend the bankrupt old order that was knifed and bleeding out? But I could tell you this… they didn't have Ultras. After twenty-five years of total warfare across all the inner and outer systems, this was the Ultras' last stand, and it was clear they were making it a point of order that they would not be pushed here. If they were, then they were done.

The dead god on the red stone throne when we went after the mortars told me the Ultras were fighting for themselves now. Not the gods. For honor. For eternity.

They'd lay it all on the line right here.

Looking at the live update of human-controlled space, scrolling and undulating on one side of the battle flexy's projection, the numbers were clear. We'd won and beaten them back to their second-to-last world to defend from.

By dawn tomorrow, this world, too, would be ours. The Monarchs were done. The Ultras were playing for something else now.

I was breathing free. Breathing like I never had in my whole entire life. Free…

And *then*, Orion, I asked myself. *Then what?*

Who knows? answered the constant observer I was of all things. Answered some other whispering voice inside of me. *That's the beauty of freedom. You can, we can, do anything we want with it.*

I heard the Seeker telling me, convincing me no matter how hard I'd fought it at the time, back there on that desperate run through the desert, on Crash, Astralon, *You gotta believe in something, someday, Sergeant Orion.*

And someone else spoke to me there as the briefing revealed all in quiet monotone. The implications there beyond the margins of projection, but there nonetheless. The other voice was the jaded *been there done that got the scars* old merc who'd really taught me to soldier a long time ago, telling me, *Never get caught up in anything, Orion.*

Never.

I took a breath and pretended to wipe some grit out of my eye.

We were that close… to all the words that had been made meaningless for most of human existence. For us…

Freedom. Liberty or death.

"You okay, Big Sarge?" asked Punch as the captain moved to the ground war part of the briefing. The how we were gonna get it done part.

The next twelve critical hours.

"Yeah. Just got some burnt grit in my eye back there, Punch."

Punch nodded and said, "I know. Me too. Took me by surprise... there, Sarge. It's like the hot chick you just met is telling you you're gonna get married to her. It's gonna happen right now with you in the middle of it all whether you like it or not. How many times that ever happen, Sarge?"

I croaked, "I don't know."

But the words barely came out.

CHAPTER TWENTY-TWO

"To effect the successful landing of the primary assault force, we're moving into Operation Haymaker," continued the captain before the assembled command teams both human and chimp. "Which I will now reveal to you and your men."

The first sergeant stepped close to the Old Man and whispered something. A correction. Hang around in enough command team briefings and you can spot them easily.

"And our Simia allies. No offense intended, General Kong."

The older monkey general in guerrilla rig, but with better weapons, fine hair graying at the temples, made a kindly dismissive gesture that indicated no offense had been taken. Then the chimp general croaked, "We are not easily offended, Man. There is no truth in such pettiness. No truth... then... there is... no real power."

The chimps in the shadows behind him hooted and hollered at this, screeching a little. The hulking praetorian gorillas around the general merely scanned the crowd, human and monkey, watching for anyone who intended harm to their Kong.

Chimps didn't use the term *general* for their war leaders of a certain rank. That was a mistake on our part and one they didn't correct right off the bat for us. But the proper term for their war leaders, all of them, from lowest level to highest, was Kong.

I had no idea what that meant. But they did come from our past, except, if the story we'd learned from the Seeker about one of the original exploration ships, the fabled ring ships, was true... then the *Enterprise* of that time had gone into the far future and found something. The Simia came back, but... unnaturally evolved.

The way they differentiated rank through the usage of the word "Kong" was in how ferociously they uttered the strange word. For General Kong as we'd known him, the chimps uttered his title with furious gnashing of teeth and wild screeching to boot, hooting as they did so, their eyes alive with fire and bright malice.

In hindsight, he was their king. So... perhaps Kong was some bastardization of that word. Languages aren't my thing.

We just didn't know this was what he really was, at that time. We assumed he was one of their high-level field commanders.

The briefing proceeded after the correction by our captain.

"To effect Haymaker," continued the Old Man, "and I'll explain the term used to identify the operation in case the Simia, or any here don't understand the term... it comes from boxing. It's a combative term. A maneuver in a fight. A powerful forceful punch. You swing with full force when you throw a haymaker, which is what we're about to do in twelve hours once the primary force inserting through the orbit window is down and off the LZs moving to their positions before we cross the line of advance. But before the haymaker can be executed, the fighter twists their waist and shoulders around before turning back and unleashing the blow. In short, it's a powerful punch you put everything you've got into. Right now, we've convinced the Ultras our forces on the ground are ill-coordinated and scattered with bad supply lines and heavy casualties. First engagements have been executed as best as possible, to demonstrate where we're weak. Where we lack coordination and support, and where we don't want them to attack us. This was our intention."

The Old Man stepped in from the dark, moving into the various colored lights of the projected map. The ghostly blue lines of the terrain and the red triangles of the estimated enemy positions projected across his wrinkled and tanned face. But his washed-out murder-blue eyes glowed like a tiger's in the night. Perhaps, for the first time, I wondered if he was wearing some kind of advanced SmartEye. High-speed lenses that could camouflage to look like normal eyes. Only revealed under certain conditions.

Interesting...

"I knew the general we are facing, once, before I became leader of a private military contractor."

He paused.

"He's the best they've got. Arkades won't attack unless he's sure he'll win. I've seen him hit well-defended cities and fade, deceiving the enemy into thinking they'd gotten lucky against the Ultra Marines. Then only to pursue and find themselves slaughtered in the deserts and jungles we were fighting in. Delivering themselves into his carefully planned kill zones. After that, the lines are wide open and the path to the victory defenseless against how he conducts warfare.

"Arkades is cautious, but he knows we're trying to put something together on the ground to counter him. By coming in as uncoordinated and ugly as we did, he probably knows now, given past battles against the Simia and the fledgling Insurrection armies and navies over the last twenty-five years, there are more troops jumping in soon. So he's going to have to take the D-beam-cleared LZs to stop any assault, and then kill the primary force as they try to put down wherever they can after that. That's, or so we're hoping, his only path to victory now here. So, what he perceives as us twisting away from his imminent onslaught in the next few hours, flinching before the blow and hoping to retrograde and buy time until the next big punch lands, is, in reality, us getting ready to throw our haymaker."

The map changed and showed us LZ Heartbreak. It fed via live drone updating from overhead. You could even see us down there, thermal ghosts near the main engines of the *Spider*. I could see my platoon and Dog off to our north and digging in to protect that sector.

Ghost of course would never be found on thermal.

But they were there, moving in the shadows and through the ruins that ringed the blasted LZ. Setting mines, occupying hides. Creeping to take out Ultra listening and observation posts.

No easy job.

"We've created the conditions," continued the captain, "that should convince any of their scouts watching us from the rubble out beyond our perimeter around the LZ that our ship is disabled and dry on PDC ammo. Which is the case. The number three reactor did take a hit and repairs are underway to get her operational for liftoff. The PDCs are dry, and the shields are at half strength due to the offline reactor. We're holding this LZ with two platoons of infantry and scout support. We have mechs, but we can't get them off-ship and onto the board. If I was Arkades, right here is where I'd want to punch good and hard."

Captain Max, the commander of Apocalypse Solutions, clucked like a chicken, and I couldn't tell whether he was indignant at the state of his mechs or reveling in the joke being played on the enemy.

The captain continued with the brief.

"But in actuality, the mechs are *not* disabled and they're ready to enter the battle at a moment's notice. Those mechs can ruin most of what the Ultras have left to throw at us right now in the big push coming next if they decide to go for it. Which is what we're trying to convince them to do. Right now, Arkades senses a window in which he can hit the LZ and take out the ship, thereby denying the mechs entry into the battle. That's a win for the Ultras. If they can break the LZ, he can then explode left and right along the Insurrection-held line and blow up our entire defense while fast-attack Ultra armored cav on the move, which they have two companies of, drive on the rear LZs and eat them up. After that, the force inserting coming in through the orbital window *Elektra* is holding open against *Red Dragon*, could not put down in any kind of effective battle formation for supported operations. They'd get picked off. The Ultras win."

The captain cleared his throat as we digested all this.

"Drone recon indicates Arkades has made up his mind and is pushing two battalions of armor and three shock infantry companies at this time right toward Heartbreak."

Punch swore silently.

"Damn... now that is a fight, Big Sarge."

"So... it's going to be here," continued the captain, stepping aside to let us see the map without obstruction. "Strange Company will take the brunt of the hit because it's where Arkades believes we don't want him to be, where he thinks we can't breathe, and where we don't want him to go. All units to our right and left, north and south along the Insurrection line will fight retrograde actions back to the LZs as though indicating we're trying to protect what we don't want to lose. What we *can't* lose. In reality, on my command, everyone pushes forward to support Heartbreak in the event Strange becomes combat ineffective during the defense. We have to hold this LZ to protect the other two. Those are the orders for every Insurrection unit. Hold Heartbreak at all costs until all primary forces have down and cleared off the two rear LZs.

"The inserting force will then shift north and go through the financial district, end-running on Ultra Ground Command. They don't have enough forces to defend against the primary hit, the haymaker, and if what they do have is pinned here in a fight they can't disengage from, then they should be unable to commit to a counterattack to the north once the primary force conducts their movement to contact along that axis. In short… the battle will be over and combat operations on Marsantyium will shift to cleanup. That won't be easy. The surviving Ultra Marines will turtle and fight to the death. They will not, I repeat, they will not surrender. Ever. Ultras do not understand the meaning of surrender."

CHAPTER
TWENTY-THREE

Just as the captain's plan had indicated, Ultra armor came stalking, looking for tank traps and IEDs, rolling on our lines just after dark. They were supported by dismounted infantry, crew-served weapons that had emplaced in secret, and sniper-spotter teams looking for priority targets.

XO spun up the *Spider*'s PDCs and sent fusillades of fast-moving ball ammunition hurricane-crashing into these covered positions as they began to range our positions their ground scouts were no doubt probing and identifying. Marsantyium masonry was torn to shreds in these sudden thunderstorms of fire and so were the gun teams.

No doubt the field commander would push more forward.

Ghost engaged the Ultra sniper-spotter teams. Reaper and Dog were interlocked on the line of attack and facing east toward the ruined temple buildings and ornate apartment blocks we'd threaded to hit the mortars six hours prior.

Two angry fronts moved toward one another, and the feeling of an imminent storm was noted by all in their silences.

Choker did remark, "Someone's gonna die today."

In the thin hours after the briefing on the hangar deck, the hustle was on to get the supplies forward the Simia had humped from the two rear LZs and out of the dark jungle tangle west of the city. Half of both Reaper and Dog were alternated out on loading duty aboard the *Spider* because it was all hands on deck and no time to burn. Sweating and hauling high-caliber PDC racks from the rear and up into the ship where the point defense cannons were reloaded, we worked as fast as we could, cognizant that at any moment we'd need to rush back to our fighting positions and get it on, late for the game that had already started.

Halfway through the resupply top-off, the halves of the platoons swapped with the other. Those on loading duty took over for those who'd been busy digging in and fortifying their positions with whatever they could get their hands on. Rubble, ruin, high explosives, some of the defense fortification gear we had on the *Spider*. Those who were relieved from the light-infantry-hated work of digging in, returned to the rear LZ to start dragging anti-armor systems and more munitions forward to the fighting positions and CPs that ran them. All this was staged and stacked in pits just to the rear of the improving fighting positions, should we need to resupply under fire during the twelve hours of battle when we could not, would not, cede the landing zone.

We were being generously given all the anti-armor we could do and that had everyone serious about what they were facing. Largesse on our behalf was looked on with the suspicion of beggars questioning the day-old bread they'd been offered in the back alley.

We weren't being given large munition rockets and state-of-the-art missile systems as an award for good citizenship. We were being anointed to take the hit right in the face, and not flinch.

Everyone along the line, all the Insurrection forces, got to play the game of hit and fake flinch, bob and weave for a right cross. We just had to get punched in the face.

"I got no problem with that," noted Punch as he loaded the resupply pits. "Long as I get to hit back, they can punch all they like. Ain't gonna do nothin' but make me angrier. And that's the part they ain't gonna like. Payback is what it is… as they say."

Throughout the quick hot afternoon getting hotter and heavier, Ultra Marine scout teams, and some fast-attack armored cav covering from gun buggies, probed the *insurrectionistas* to our north and south along the line, as though indicating they might attack there imminently.

That convinced me, as more and more spotrep reports crossed the comm and commanders got all excited shouting, "Contact, Contact, Contact!"… that the Ultras, when they came, were coming straight through my platoon.

And Dog.

So I worked harder, didn't eat my ration bar, smoke, or even drink coffee. Choker had to pull medic on me and make me drink water once I'd stopped sweating and he noticed it.

The day turned toward late afternoon and the Ultra heavy gun batteries in their deep rear, beyond the incoming ground force, and their forward command post, opened fire and shelled units to our left and right flanks. North and south of our position.

Again, that just told me they were coming right at my guys. I hustled harder, worked everyone faster, and thought up every nasty trick I could play on tanks and infantry.

Finally, I was busy moving from position to position at that time, checking kill windows and making sure there was enough AT stacked and ready to go for when the time most certainly came. We'd tried to canalize as much of the rubble beyond our positions by setting up mines we could run via drone and dragging out the defensive wire spray cylinders we had a chance to use because they stayed on the *Spider* and rarely made it planetside on past contracts.

Now, as we placed the cylinders and prepared to fire the charges that would deploy the wire sprays, I knew why the first sergeant had us spend a maintenance day during flight time out to the battle.

Crafty old Senior Ruck Hobo that he is.

We rolled the defensive massive cylinders out from the belly of the ship, aimed them so the distribution sprays would interlock, then fired the charges that shot the razor wire all over in every direction in front of our line. In seconds, we laid down impenetrable fields of deadly sharp industrial diamond monofilament that would cut through armor and slice off limbs if enough force was applied. Imagine getting blown by a mine into it. What the blast didn't do the wire would.

I told you, it was time for me to get creative and ruck-hobo at the pro level to keep my guys alive. We attached trailing wires that could ignite camouflaged antipersonnel mines and claymores, and other wires attached to buried batteries that could electrify sections as needed.

Then I left areas "open" where the Ultra scouts would think they'd found the only way through. These were our canals. Where we set up overwatched kill windows the gun teams could traverse and fire on.

"Try me," I muttered, finally burning a 'grit and observing my handiwork. "Because I would love it."

"What's that?" asked Choker.

"Nothing. Just talking to someone who ain't here yet."

Choker nodded and laughed like he knew what I was talking about. "Oh yeah. The big stuffed rabbit named

Marco who always wants to do the bad things, Sar'nt? I talk to him too, all the time. Good times. Marco always knows where the fun is, Sar'nt. Always."

I moved away from my medic. He was used to this response to his bizarre behavior. From everyone in fact.

The Ultras would never be stupid enough to try the wire spray fields unless they could drop artillery on them first, and to do that they'd have to get close enough for their fire support specialists to adjust fire.

The wire didn't get picked up on thermal or night vision. Sometimes, if the lighting conditions were just right, you didn't realize you were in one until you watched your finger fall off.

But who knows what fancy gear an Ultra has. They're better than us.

Supposedly.

Punch has thoughts on this. I told him, as the sun began to fall behind us, turning the temples and palaces of Saffron City a burnt crimson in the end of the day, that he was about to get the chance to find out.

All he had to say to this was, "That's what I'm here for, Sar'nt."

Good. I'm glad someone was.

Ghost had been busy all afternoon sniping the Ultras that tried to creep and prowl, and at times, Ghost themselves had gone out creeping to kill the gun teams and spotters. Snipers who dared to engage got dusted by Sleeper himself. Ghost's best distance engagement shooter.

A stone-cold killer who was practically a ghost himself.

Darkness had fallen and Ultra arty opened up right on time as though there were some schedule of events we all remembered reading pertaining to the night's festivities. The first strikes hit out on the flanks, like they were going for those other Insurrection line units not holding Heartbreak. So of course I knew they were coming for us, or I have not ruck-hoboed on too many worlds in too many fights. The captain gave the order for the flanking units to begin to retrograde once they made contact with the probes out there, slowly fading and fighting backwards like they were going to close the defense around the two rear LZs, thus hanging Heartbreak in the wind to get hit hard.

If the Ultra field commander did indeed have a different plan, right now his scouts were telling him LZ Heartbreak was easy money for the taking.

We were temptation itself.

For once, just after dusk, everything went according to plan in the opening moments of the battle and the Ultra armor came roaring out of the gloom ahead, heading straight into Heartbreak to roll us and take what we could not give them.

Pay for what was not for sale. At any price.

Reaper would hold.

CHAPTER TWENTY-FOUR

It's something to hear, a fight rolling toward you. It used to bother me when I was new. I definitely liked being on the attack as I've talked about a little in this account of what happened there on LZ Heartbreak at the Sack of Marsantyium.

But I was different now.

The early evening sky had cleared but the latest drone weather forecast was guessing we'd have dense fog late in the night due to the day's constant and unrelenting heat.

Marsantyium was a strange world in that it was farther out than most hot worlds. Other than that, it was in an unremarkable eight-planet star system like any other. It's just that in this one, the course of human history, going forward, would be decided forever.

No big deal and all.

Somehow I'd always felt, if it, and by it I mean the downfall of the Monarchs and the end of their tyrannical high culture, I've always felt that if it were ever really gonna happen it would happen on the home world. But, my guess, the Monarchs would sue for peace and ask to be left alone. Maybe everyone was tired enough, after twenty-five years of war… to just let the Monarchs go, if they would go and take themselves out into the darknesses between the stars.

But after what they've done to us…

Like Punch says, "Payback is what it is, Big Sarge… as they say."

Enemy armor began to enter the area of operation, Ultra gunners and infantry surging through the shattered remains of the ruined and haunted buildings that ringed the D-beam-blasted LZ we'd determined not to surrender. The sound of gunfire rang out in short staccato bursts and the rumble of armor on the move, rolling thunder, didn't bother me as all of it, the last big fight, came right for me.

I didn't know if I went in for all that *history* and *this is the big one* stuff, other than it so obviously was… something. I pushed all that away. This was a fight, and like Choker had said, *someone was gonna die.*

Okay, I whispered as I watched my sectors. *Let it be the other guy.*

But… like I said, I was different now. This was… *for* something. It's best to be honest about these things.

"Target acquired…" whispered Ulysses, who was manning the targeting 'nocs for the Jackhammer Ones we had many of to burn tonight. Disposable one-shot armor killers. The projectile tube was planted like a mortar in the charred dirt just to the rear of our fighting position, facing up at an angle into the dark night.

There were stars up there, but I didn't have time for them. The slow dance of the broken chandelier of the universe would wheel over this fight and not care in the least who died for whatever it was gonna mean in the morning. Many would die, even us, even me probably, Sergeant Orion, keeper of the log, teller of the tale that was the Strange Company, but the galaxy would not care about our little wars. Not stop for even the smallest measure of time.

It would continue its turn.

Who would tell the Strange Company story then? I wondered that as I gave the order for the former Ultra to thumb the fire button on the targeting 'nocs and burn the incoming enemy armor as it entered our sector and kill windows for our various weapon systems.

And if we all died? I wondered that in the pause before battle. When you as the leader order the first shot to be taken and wait. The hang time almost pleasant in that halfway between heaven and hell moment. Tiresome in that you're ready to get it on. Ready to either get on with living, or be dead and just answer that question once and for all. Knowing it was coming at you all along the way.

Who would finish the tale that was the tragedy of the Strange Company?

Not my circus, not my Simia, Sar'nt Orion.

Ulysses shouted, "Area clear!"

The Kid backed away from the loaded round, standing clear. This was the new Kid who I wouldn't bother to name because the last Kid had died on me on a bad LZ where I'd left him and maybe tonight this one would too, and I just don't have enough ruck hobo to spread around for everyone.

I shouted back, "Area clear to fire!"

Ulysses Two Alpha Six thumbed the fire button on the targeting 'nocs and the round streaked away and up with a *hiss* and a *whoosh* out of the disposable launcher tube to our rear in the burnt dirt. It immediately course-corrected, marrying up with the targeting image Ulysses was holding in the 'nocs. The missile raced away to our left, arching up and then leveling out and descending as it spotted its target and made ready to penetrate and destroy.

It danced a little along the flight path as batteries along its side dumped displacement charges and the round jinked up and down, side to side, but always forward as it raced feverishly toward our selected target.

I watched through my own 'nocs which I'd slaved to the targeting 'nocs Ulysses was using. Thermal crosshairs were dead on the massive tank coming in through a ruined façade of some massive palatial living structure at the edge of our LZ.

My LZ. Not for sale.

Ulysses held the textbook sight picture for firing AT. Of course he did.

We were facing War Mace heavy tanks out there. Some of the best the Ultra Marines were known to field in their elite armor divisions. Two massive thick treads held a central armor compartment just off the ground while the forward turret, sloped and slanted, the smaller of the tank's two gun turrets, held the targeting systems and defensive guns that protected the tank from armor and incoming rounds. The rear turret held the two main one-forty-millimeter guns that could alternate fire on a target.

Reducing it to nothing in seconds.

At the last second, the tank's onboard mini-PDC spun up and tried to engage the incoming AT round Ulysses had fired at it. But the Jackhammer One had help from the *Spider*'s powerful onboard electronic jamming systems.

Field units, armor, and infantry don't usually have to deal with starship-level systems. So... this was going to be fun.

For us.

Powerful systems like the ECM jammers, and the ECCM jammers that counter-jam any enemy efforts to jam, are generally reserved for intense high-speed combat between capital ships in space. Not ground war. There are units that specialize in that and try to get close to cover friendly units with ECM and ECCM, but the chimps had made a game of wiping those out with reckless artillery strikes and specialized units of spider monkeys that got close to spot and adjusted fire from the tops of high buildings and remote places the Ultras couldn't cover.

On the battlefield, the *Spider*'s powerful jammers devastated any local countermeasures and targeting equipment by the sheer fact they were powered by four nuclear reactors with endless amounts of energy to spend overwhelming and blowing out enemy systems with noise, spam, and bad info.

Which is what it did to the mini-PDC as it spun up and tried to knock out the incoming missile.

The War Mace's onboard PDC sprayed rounds from twin snub-nosed matte-black barrels sticking out of the forward turret, to no effect. These mini-PDCs could also be used for ground suppression against infantry or lightly armed vehicles. But now, in this instance, the mini-PDC failed to engage the Jackhammer round and at the last second, like a pro, Ulysses adjusted the targeting crosshairs in the thermal image and directed the round to land just beyond the forward turret, smashing right into the onboard magazines in the tank's hull.

At the *last* last second, before the round connected and exploded violently in a shower of hot white ghost sparks within our thermal image, two Ultra infantrymen, one sporting a carbine and the other carrying what was clearly my new favorite weapon ever, currently, the Sturm squad automatic suppression weapon, appeared just ahead of the tank, no doubt sweeping ahead of the War Mace for infantry or buried mines.

Then the impact and explosion blew out the image for a second.

As the rounds in the War Mace's magazine cooked off, the shock troopers were blown to bits instantly, just vaporized by the sudden detonation of seriously high-caliber rounds going off in the tank's hull all at once.

"Sucks to be them," whispered the Kid after he swore in amazement at the strike.

I liked him for that. It meant he was ready to see the wizard.

War. Up close.

If you have to... then you should at least be excited about it. That might help some, but no guarantees.

In the chaos of the image, streaks of light and explosions erupted out of the central hull of the penetrated tank. The main rear turret suddenly exploded skyward, tumbling end over end out of frame of the targeting 'nocs.

"That's a kill," I noted in understatement, but Ulysses was already landing the thermal crosshairs on the next tank to try and push through our sector in the defenses. The dark shapes of infantry on the move out there were surging through regardless.

But then again, they were Ultras. So... of course they would. I'd seen Third World jihadis who'd been muttering all the Freedom Words turn and run when a tank or a big piece of equipment got hit in the opening moments.

War clarifies things for people whether they like it or not. It certainly has for me.

Hot tracer rounds from some hidden gun team that had crept into place and now revealed themselves in the firing, came at us, crossing the thermal targeting image like sudden heat lightning.

"Round up!" yelled the Kid to our rear as he finished setting up the next Jackhammer One for employment on behalf of our collective defense of LZ Heartbreak.

"Round up!" I echoed, doing my job. I sitrepped the kill and noted the weapons of the two shock troopers I'd seen killed. Other sitreps were filling the comm, and the first sergeant was managing and noting items of importance for us all to consider.

"Netcall netcall netcall... be advised, Strange... we got a-grav gun platforms moving through on Dog. Be advised..."

Ulysses called another target and we engaged. Another tank died in a fiery apocalypse, but Third Squad's Pigs, our supporting element, were already engaging infantry in the wire, closer than I thought they'd have made it this early in.

I checked my watch.

Two minutes in. Twelve hours to go.

"Here they come," I called out over the platoon comm. "Get it on, Strange!"

CHAPTER TWENTY-FIVE

It was at this point, having burned now three tanks among all Reaper elements firing AT, that we needed to react to the Ultras running their game inside our wire.

They'd moved faster and with more cunning than even I'd anticipated, and I was in a weird way... their biggest fan. In other words, they overachieved the expectations of the pen-pal admirer who was still going to kill them with everything I had down to my last round.

Then it was knives out and I was pretty good with the karambit.

So there's that.

I had placed First Squad at the center of the action, and it was there I was doing my fighting contributions from while keeping an eye on the whole mess I'd organized on their behalf. First's line was linked up with Dog to our north. The Ultras were pushing hard there along our sister platoon's line, but enemy armor that had tried that route was now burning out there in the charred debris of the burnt wasteland LZ.

Heartbreak was earning its name and I wondered if Ultras had loved ones out there in the galactic sprawl that would remember this day as a day of loss. Or just eel girls who told pretty lies?

One of the Ultra War Mace tanks had taken two hits, one of which bounced on contact and the other deflected off reactive armor charges fired by the onboard computer to redirect the blast and the round, and perhaps even the tungsten rod in some of the armor-piercing rounds.

Who knew?

That holed and burning War Mace tank had gotten close, torn through wire, and started firing the thirty-millimeter anti-personnel gun danger close on the two Dog positions facing it on the line of battle.

Dog already had casualties and it sounded bad if the frantic calls for "Medics!" over the comm were anything to go by.

Not "Medic," but "Medics."

Meanwhile the two one-forty main guns atop the burning War Mace were firing right into the *Spider* looming above the battlefield on her main landing gears, despite the fire on the hull of the Ultra combat assault tank punching through the wire, slowly.

I would find out later that Cheater, one of the Dog squad leaders, a guy I'd found to be a real scumbag on different occasions, went forward with satchel charges, crawled in under the rapid firing thirty-millimeter, and blew the forward hull off the tank, killing himself in the process but saving what remained of his squad being shot up in the fighting positions.

So there's that too. Much to consider early in the long night but no time to process. I filed it all and vowed that if… *if*… I lived, then I'd get it all down and even guys like Cheater would get their fair shake in the end.

Except, death really does have a way of skewing things. I knew Cheater for who he really was. Everyone did. Hence the tag. But in the end, with eternity calling, he purchased the get out karma card and the company logs would remember him as a bonified stud who *got it on*.

A brother to the end.

And I'm not butthurt about that. It's better that way and I can only hope that whoever puts down my final handprint in the log will be able to make the same entry on my behalf.

And I hope it's true.

At the moment when I saw the hulking silhouette of the tank—a gargantuan shadow stuck on rising black charred debris and tangled in our wire sprays—explode forward suddenly, throwing volcanos of molten armor and internal systems in every direction as the charges detonated, I had no idea that Cheater had died well.

Ave, Cheater. The Strange thank you for your efforts on our behalf. Rest in peace now.

I had my own problems at that moment as I watched the tank go kinetic in every direction. Second Squad Reaper was off to First Squad's south. Jax reported he had wounded and that a team of Ultras had gotten close enough to start using explosives to tear through the wire and detonate the mines.

Combat engineers. Okay, I thought. This is a problem and it's a big one. Now go solve it, Sergeant.

And then I went off to see what I could do about them.

Second Squad was using a low scar the D-beam blast had cut through the LZ in order to stay out of Third's suppressive fire fields. The Ultra combat engineers were getting ready to clear a way through our defensive wire for tanks that I had no doubt would come running down that channel and right into the LZ around the *Spider*.

The last tank had already punched smoking holes in the ship's flank armor. More damage wasn't gonna help matters if we needed an emergency dustoff.

Then I reminded myself we weren't losing this LZ. We weren't dusting off. The Old Man had given nothing in the op order for that contingency. Without saying so, he'd basically let us know we were dying in place on this one. The stakes were too high. This was the Ultras' last stand and all we had to do was hold their attention so they didn't see our haymaker coming in on their flank. After that… the universe, or at least human-controlled space, was a different place tomorrow.

You gotta believe in something, Orion.

I told the voice of the Seeker, the pretty Ultra who'd joined the company for a hot minute to get it done on Astralon, Crash, call it what you will, to shut her piehole.

And then I reminded myself I was holding my position for something bigger than mem, flavor currency of the month, or scars and glory.

I was holding for a better tomorrow.

If that ain't belief I don't know what is.

"Ulysses… you got this position… I gotta handle a breach between us and Second!"

I grabbed the Sturm because I couldn't reposition Hustle and Hoser from their support position at the moment. The constant chatter of the squad's Pig off to my left told me they were fully engaged and not the least bit concerned about anything other than traverse and patient murder.

Good for them.

I went to the position where Itchy and Goods were placed and ready to use the ancient M67 recoilless rifle on anything that came through that sector's kill window. They'd fired once and bounced a hit on one of the fast-moving War Mace tanks.

"Man, Sarge, these rounds ain't gonna punch on that fancy Ultra armor!" shouted Itchy above the chatter of the nearby Pig roaring as Hustle encouraged Hoser frantically to "Get some more, man! Over there… two o'clock… teach 'em, Hose! Teach 'em!"

I glanced at their sector and saw dead Ultra marines torn to pieces in a shallow in the burnt-black-dirt battlefield out within the debris field identified as a perfect engagement window for plunging fire. Incoming rounds smacked into Hustle and Hoser's improved defenses, but neither gunner nor assistant gunner cared and instead worked their machine like a machine made to work a machine. Speaking their own little gun team lingo as they did their dance of linked belts and barrel changes, laying their hate on behalf of the company and an LZ that needed to hold at all costs no matter what, for a better tomorrow that may or may not be a lie.

In a world of questions, I'd learned to find my constants as an NCO. Hustle and Hoser were one such constant I'd come to not just rely on… but need.

Don't tell Hustle or Hoser that.

And… there couldn't be one without the other. No Hustle, no Hoser. I didn't want to see that day.

Whoever… please hear the unbelieving prayers of a faithless ruck hobo. Keep my gun team alive. Without them… I'll be lost and there are still too many New Guys and a Kid who need me to be found at all times. Constant and all-knowing even if it only seems that way and I am as scared as they are.

"Grab the recoilless and follow me," I ordered Itchy and Goods. We stayed low and moved toward the developing breach in Second's line out there down the length of the scar. We arrived on the other side of the deep gash below the horizontal plane of the battlefield, and I could see Jax and Klutz hunkering behind debris on the far side. Jax motioned forward and I followed his knife hand, spotting the Ultras tossing charges and blowing their way through our wire sprays farther down the length, just topping a small rise in the wide ditch that a fantastic space weapon had burned there.

Overhead, one of the Ultra fast-attack Ravens came in, chain guns targeting Dog's positions. The PDCs on the *Spider* roared to life and shot it down as it streaked over our fight. Seconds later it plowed into the black char farther up our line north of Dog, spreading hot burning fuel in every direction in a suddenly all too real moment.

AT rounds over there in Dog lashed out and struck at more tanks pushing through the rubble ruins ringing the landing zone. Sometimes for kills. Sometimes missing. Sometimes deflecting as the fire-spitting battle mammoths pushed through and tried to get close enough to kill the cleverly hidden infantry armed to the teeth with high-ex, rockets, missiles, machine guns, hatred, and coffee.

Never push light infantry. We got nowhere to run. So we'll fight like cornered Pantha dogs, all razor-sharp teeth and scorpion tails full of instant death. Yeah, you might crush us, but a lot of you are going to die in the process. Think about that before you order the next charge, 'cause there's every chance you'll die getting it done, combat leader facing us.

Ulysses called another kill and without taking another breath shouted, "Target acquired!" over the blare of everyone trying to kill each other as fast as possible.

He was becoming one of those constants for me. And right now, I needed all the constants I could get as I tried to figure out how to stop the combat engineers from ruining all my carefully laid plans.

Tricks, really. C'mon, at least be honest about that, Orion.

Yeah, well if they punched through here, then the whole line was useless because getting through here put them behind our line and right on the LZ.

No go.

I couldn't hit the Ultras down the scar as they weren't just using ballistic shields to cover their work, they also had a field cannon they were pushing forward on a-grav. The field cannon was a classic howitzer-type gun. From it they were shooting anti-personnel shot into the wire, destroying it, and detonating the mines sown within the deployed tangle.

The gun also had mounted ballistic shielding and they were covering behind that as they patiently pushed the gun forward and fired more shot.

Also, if we pushed on them now, they'd turn that gun tube on us and fill *us* with shot. Then they'd push the LZ over all of us torn to shreds.

Again, I cursed myself for not grabbing the Savage Lone Wolf thumper from the bird. I could have dropped forty all over them and shut this down right here.

Also, I had the Bastard staged back at the fighting position when it came time for CQB. Overconfident in my new love for the Sturm, I'd figured I could just vaporize an infantry team pushing through the wire with charges.

Instead I had combat engineers patiently doing their job under fire with all the right equipment to do so, which is what makes combat engineers so deadly.

Combat engineers do this stuff exclusively. So they carry and tote exactly what they need to do it. Infantry, on the other hand, must adapt to whatever the higher-ups suddenly have a migraine about and decide needs getting done immediately.

Assaulters. Door-kickers. Build defenses, badly. But to be fair we do that badly because we don't like it and we're pouting. Armor support. Whatever. For light infantry every day is a new day to learn a new job you've never done before… under fire.

I coulda had *Opposite Us* badly attempting to be crafty about my minefield and canalizations. Instead I had combat engineers protected behind a field cannon and getting it done effectively.

Wheeeeeeeeeeeeeeee.

"Gimme the MeGoosa!" I shouted, mistaking the M67 for one of our Carls and using the company slang for the weapons system.

Itchy corrected me and I promised to murder him with PT when this was all done and over as I grabbed the recoilless launcher from his trembling hands and told Goods to load me.

"Loading H-E!" shouted Goods behind me as I sighted down the trench at the combat engineers and their fancy levitating a-grav howitzer.

I waved Itchy and Goods away mumbling, "Back blast area clear…"

Then fired a round at the field cannon just down the scar. There was a loud *DANK!*

Then the round exploded harmlessly in front of the Ultra a-grav field cannon pushing through our sections.

"Bounce!" shouted Itchy redundantly as I ducked back, and we loaded another round.

"Stand by to rush!" I shouted across at Jax and Klutz on the other side of the entrance to the scar in our line. The look in their eyes seemed to echo-scream my thoughts of charging a ballistic-shielded howitzer with a-grav firing anti-personnel. The field cannon was getting closer as it tore up our wire, clearing a path wide enough for one of their tanks. But if I could knock down the floating howitzer's ballistic shield, then we could get on it and engage CQB if the crew was too stunned to fire the next anti-personnel round.

I know… really bad plan based on wishful thinking and a lot of *what-ifs.*

There weren't many other options available to us, and this was what we got paid to do after all. Plus, I'm an optimist and so I had ridiculous visions of taking it for ourselves and using it to maintain the scar, flinging their howitzer-shot rounds right back in their faces.

Just as Itchy was ready to fold back behind the burnt concrete debris we were firing from, the field cannon roared and sent thousands of flechettes screaming down the scar right at us and the remaining spray wire in between. The sound of it moving through the wire was like a chorus of singing wraiths whining about the pain of death. The air felt cut in half and the concussion from the blast sucked all the air out of the area we were fighting from.

Itchy turned to face me, then fell over dead saying something without sound, just suddenly bloodless lips moving because the wind had been knocked out of all of us.

One of the bright, steel flechettes was sticking right out of the center of his head, beneath his helmet.

He was dead. Dying right in front of me.

I callously pushed the rest of him aside and I'm sorry for that, knowing he was dead from the close-up look in his eyes as the light faded in the half second after his lips made a small *o*. I grunted and popped from cover, barely taking time to land the M67 sight on the field cannon ahead and down the dark carved gash. This time I fired low and got the speeding round right under the a-gravs and below the ballistic shielding.

The round hit earth and exploded up and away. One of the ballistic shields immediately sheared off.

"Move now!" I shouted at Jax and Klutz across the scar entrance.

They had seconds to move up on the gun before whoever survived the blast could recover and load another AP round to send down the scar.

If the cannon was still even operational.

I know... *what-ifs* and dreams. These are not the makings of good tactics and strategy. But it was all I had.

Klutz of course tripped on burnt and bent construction rebar sticking out of the D-beam-blasted scar. He went sprawling and landed face down in the burnt black soil.

I tossed the recoilless rifle, grabbed the Sturm, and charged forward, watching the barrel of the howitzer and just knowing it was going to be the last thing I ever saw as it suddenly exploded in my face, sending thousands of steel flechettes right through me.

Ahead, Jax covered behind the remaining ballistic shield on this side of the gun that was still facing down the scar. I could see a dead Ultra draped over the gun behind the shield but in an instant another one popped up and I landed the Sturm's targeting laser on him and pulled the trigger for a short burst, taking no chances that he'd fire the gun, knowing he could even in death with just some last action jerk.

My precious HERK rounds destroyed the Ultra, but more Ultras were surging forward farther up the scar as I hit the dirt close to Jax on our side of the howitzer draped with scattered and ruined dead combat engineers.

Jax looked at me, sweating hard and swapping in a new mag. He'd fired going up the scar. I got to my knees, dragging up the Sturm as Jax slipped around the side of the field gun's remaining ballistic shield and began to fire the shorty he carried. He opened up on full auto because why not. Fatal funnel. Lots of bad guys. Nothing about this was polite or pro. This was a quick brawl to see who would own the rise.

And that, of all the things infantry does… is what we do best. We own terrain.

"Hot soup!" Jax swore madly and fired wildly into the surge I had yet to see as I got ready to employ the gun.

I waddled forward, saw six Ultras supporting the howitzer we'd just knocked out coming forward and reacting to contact as a group, thanked the galaxy for the tight grouping, and wasted them good and hard.

I opened fire as Jax's rounds tore into the lead assaulters and he screamed out, "Hot soup comin' for ya, wasters!" over and over.

That didn't register for me as I opened fire and tore the rest to shreds with a long trigger pull on the nano-cooled

Sturm, riding the lightning and never feeling so alive as everyone died before my desperate wrath.

I know… wordy. A little overheated. But I told you, I tell you the truth. And that's how it felt at that moment as I shot them, the Ultras, the Monarchs' death cult guard dogs, to death right there in the scar.

All the worry and fear and desperate work to get as much done as possible leading up to this just evap'd as I held the trigger and machine-gunned them to high-dosage death. The spray of gunfire was more about something else inside of me than defending the position I vowed would not be taken. I have to admit that now in this account. It was a kind of pressure release and maybe you understand? I was punching back at someone. It was a *take that* to a galaxy that didn't care.

I had to watch that with the Sturm. It felt good to work it. This weapon was the purity in truth of *riding the lightning*. This thing worked so fast I'd already torn through a belt clearing the scar.

But they were dead, and I wasn't. For a moment right there in the middle of all hell breaking loose in every direction, no enemy tank was going to push my guys here, or through here, because all the combat engineers on the field gun were too dead to notify armor they had a path through.

Right now, there was some commander out there with no intel and no comm with a team that was supposed to be creating a breakthrough in the next few. If he was smart, he'd realize what happened and notify the armor to stand by on the push.

I could almost see those tankers getting the hurry up and wait, tense and smoking, knowing and not knowing what was happening.

Or they'd just push now and go for it…

But I had a feeling they wouldn't.

Breathing heavily, Jax looked up at me from his position behind the remaining ballistic shielding of the howitzer, the barrel of his Bastard shorty smoking, chest heaving. His dark skin gleaming with sweat.

"We did it, Orion. Did it for Hotsoup, man!"

Then he spit on one of the dead Ultras.

"That's for Soup!"

CHAPTER TWENTY-SIX

With the breach between Second and First sealed for the moment, I had time to get back to my fighting position and check on the battle as a whole. What I'd been able to follow in sitreps from the various elements indicated we'd survived the first push, but that Dog had taken it on the chin. Hard.

Very hard in fact.

Minutes later as both sides exchanged crew-served weapons fire at range, the Old Man and the first sergeant appeared at my position. According to the captain, the first Ultra tanks had tried to push through and had gotten smoked in the process all across the line. I could see them out there, burning in the debris field in the dark, or within the decimated buildings they'd pushed through, rounds cooking off and destroying more of the structure they waited in until the whole place was either raked and rebuilt by whoever won, or... just waited forever, becoming a place where boys would climb and play, dreaming of wars like this one.

In the skies high above, strange lights and explosions crossed the night sky near the upper atmosphere. The battle between *Red Dragon* and *Elektra* raged on as the Insurrection battle fleet tried to hold the orbital insertion window open with the landings just hours from getting underway.

I checked my watch. Three hours and change. Then hold for another six as the force stacked and staged.

Then the haymaker.

In the distance, someone's close air support came in, howling like a ghost drowning, and unloaded everything it had on someone else's position in a short underwhelming burst that must've been anything but if you were on the receiving end of it.

I had no idea what was going on out there. I could only listen to the command comm with one ear as I tried to count my dead and wounded, resupply ammo, and switch the teams to secondary positions now that the Ultras knew where we were at.

Keep them guessing and more dirty tricks.

Jax and Duster were busy putting all the high-ex we had forward on the scar the Ultras had tried to push through once already. I redeployed Goods with New Guy Number One as the assistant gunner to cover the scar, now that Itchy was under his poncho to the rear of the scar.

I commed with Hauser and told him to shift suppressive overwatch to that sector as I had a good idea the Ultras would go for it and exploit there once the scouts they had looking around figured out what had happened there.

I could feel those scouts crawling through the char in thermal-defeating stealth suits and low-profile combat armor, assessing what had worked and what hadn't.

Ghost was taking shots where they could. But right now, they weren't keen on revealing their positions. We had too few of those to move between and we'd need to shift between expected pushes until dawn.

One of the drawbacks of holding the objective, the price for the privilege of preparation and defense as it were, was that you didn't have a lot of places to hide. The enemy pretty much knew where you were.

So that's why you needed to be a crafty old ruck hobo and think smarter, so you didn't work harder. Save what you got. Pretend, or at least make the enemy think, you had more than what you really did.

All warfare is psychological. To a point. Then it's just gunfire. And you can't do much about that mentally other than making up your mind to have a good attitude about it.

Or as the practical wisdom of Punch puts it…

"If you're gonna be in it… might as well win it, Big Sarge. Food tastes better after a gunfight anyway."

Ultra arty opened up, and the PDCs aboard the *Spider* spun up and intercepted incoming rounds falling toward our LZ. At the same time, XO shifted the dorsal shield array to cover us somewhat overhead.

When that happened, when the shields shifted to cover you on the ground, a normally energy-expensive outlay not affordable to most ground units, it felt like your guts were being squeezed out of your butt and your head felt weird and thick like a bad sinus infection all at once. But given the overhead cover, it was worth the tradeoff. For the moment, out in the fighting positions we didn't have to worry, much, about getting vaporized by a high-caliber artillery shell.

And if you spit, coughed, then tried to unplug your ears… it got better. Kinda.

Doing something, even if it doesn't work, helps.

My sector in somewhat shape by that time, the captain and the first sergeant, who was carrying one of our flame-throwers, came through the shadows and briefed us on the situation.

There were fears the Ultras might have gotten into our quantum-scrambled comm for a moment. A thing that was supposed to not be possible according to the people who made those quantum-encrypted comm systems. But of course, the Monarchs always got the back doors and the advantages.

I looked at the tanks burning out there, and the second-to-last ruined world they'd been chased to, and thought… *lotta good that did them.*

"Sir, First Sergeant," I greeted my leaders, NCO and officer, as they came from the rear.

The Old Man studied me for a moment like he was assessing a broke old workhorse he might buy, then reached up to my face. He wiped away blood there and grabbed my chin, turning my head. He was making sure I was okay.

"Caught a graze," he said flatly. "That's all, Sergeant," he reassured me as I felt my heart take a dump. I hadn't realized I'd been hit.

My eyes told him I'd had no idea until he'd wiped away the drying blood. Felt the shallow gash. Just like the one we'd just held. I hadn't noticed.

Hadn't noticed I'd almost gotten domed.

"Got a few of those myself, Sar'nt Orion," said the first sergeant. I noted the anti-personnel flamethrower on his back.

When those came out of deep stores on the *Spider*, things were indeed getting serious.

"Sergeant Orion, Dog's in bad shape," said the captain as he stepped away to watch my line. "Over fifty percent casualties currently reporting. Some missing. No idea how many dead or wounded. They were hit hard by the a-grav assaulters, but they managed to hold and push those off the line. First sergeant's going to stiffen your position here in case they decide this is the next lane to push on, thinking we're going to reinforce over there. I'm taking control of Dog and I'll fight the platoon from there."

Okay… the Old Man was now the Dog platoon leader. That wasn't good.

"Copy that, sir."

Then, "That was just a probe wasn't it, sir? The last push from the Ultras. That was them just getting warmed up?"

He nodded once at me in the dark.

"Final recon in force before they commit to the probes by the leading elements of the main body. Identifying where exactly we're at. They're going to hit us hard one more time and see what snaps when they do. Ultra SOP says they'll do this within the hour of breaking last contact. So…"

The captain checked his ancient watch. It was an old antique. I'd gotten a look at it once, close up when he'd taken it off on a late-night watch to go wash up and get some chow for us.

It had old Numerican words inscribed on the face.

Omega Seamaster. Words as old as the home world we'd all come from once and long ago. And never seen.

Well, maybe we would soon. Maybe we were coming home after Marsantyium.

I had no idea what they meant. Those words. *Omega Seamaster.* But the watch was a thing of ancient beauty, rare, in what had become the age of Monarch-supplied junk being the *all* of what we'd ever known.

A better tomorrow was coming… I reminded myself.

"…That would be less than eight minutes from now," continued the captain as he lowered his wrist. "Do not let them get through, Sergeant."

He didn't need to repeat this as some commanders did by emphasizing the *I repeat.* Once was enough.

"We have nine hours thirty-seven minutes, Sergeant Orion, until the primary force is ready to shift north and end-run for their ground command. We will hold until then."

I watched him in the dark. Compared to most people he said few words. For him, that little speech he'd just given, that was downright verbose.

So: it was important.

I had this feeling he was about to say goodbye without ever telling me his story. That he was going to say, *"If I don't see you, Orion, it was good working with you."*

But he would never say that. He would never admit defeat was a possibility. Defeat to him, when it came, would be a surprise.

Then I laughed at myself, some kind of weird smile crossing my face in that half second in the shadows of the battlefield. Like he would ever tell me his strange and mysterious story. Whether he really was an Ultra. Where the scars had come from. And a dozen other questions the company at large had collected, discussed, and dissected ad nauseam, regarding small clues he'd let slip across the years and bad contracts.

Now… that was a story worth hearing, I thought and knew I never would.

We will hold, sir, I started to say and for some reason couldn't. My mouth was too dry. I pulled out my canteen and drank cold coffee, hoping to make words and lying to myself about why I couldn't.

Words I'd never believed came and stood around the captain and myself and the first sergeant standing nearby with the flamethrower on his back. Like ghostly holograms, the kinds you see starship AIs using to broadcast emergency messages within the confines of the engine room, lounge, flight deck, sensors, places I'd always felt would be safe and far from war. Far from now. Places of escape I'd been dreaming about all along the way to this moment.

This final now.

Places that led somewhere better than this and all the worlds I'd ever fought, and watched people die on.

"No one's getting through Reaper tonight, sir."

Then he was gone.

CHAPTER TWENTY-SEVEN

The next push came, and it was a big one.

The Ultras, unsatisfied with their ineffective artillery strikes, sent in hunter-killer drops to prep the next attack with rockets and ground suppression guns. The larger Super Stallions with missile pods and miniguns came in slowly, engines beating the night like flying giants.

The *Spider*'s PDCs tracked five and shot down three before two swept in overhead lobbing missiles against our line and chewing up the black charred dirt we were fighting for with heavy minigun fire.

I'd sworn to hold at all costs.

Anti-air launchers tagged one of the Super Stallions on her way out of the area and she was trailing fire and probably black smoke in the night. The other one got away, their jammers barely getting them out of the firing envelope for the PDCs and our anti-air man-portables.

A moment later falling star shells rained down all over our positions, illuminating the entire battlefield and shutting down any kind of night or thermal vision we possessed.

We switched over to open eyes and by that time, XO was alerting everyone the PDCs were down for the moment and would be unavailable for the next ten as the teams of Simia swapped in new munitions racks for the reload.

Ulysses, ahead of me and lying in the twisted debris of our secondary fighting position, watched the front with the thermal 'nocs for the next round of armor to come for us. The Kid was next to him. Watching him, watching what he was watching, and anticipating the next command from our wonderboy.

Good kid, I thought as I watched them from behind the debris pile.

I was scrolling through my battle board trying to see if we had any drones operational at the moment.

Nothing.

The first sergeant watched the flanks off in the dark. He had the flamethrower's "gun," a sprayer really, in one hand. And an old lighter in the other. On the silver lighter was the worn insignia of the old Saturnian Batts.

He was softly humming some ancient running cadence to himself, the way old men who don't care what anyone thinks anymore do sometimes regardless if they are alone or not. It was barely audible. It must have been something from the batts back on Saturnia.

Something about drop zones and coming through.

Something from long ago he'd carried all the way from there to here. Like we all do, given enough time.

I saw him by the light of the slowly falling red star flares, smoking like dying hell's angels in the night, the ones the enemy hunter-killers had dosed our positions with in the last pass.

I could still hear the Super Stallions out over the ruined city somewhere. Their engines beating and echoing off all that silent ruin.

Ultra snipers fired on whoever they could see by the light of the dying fallen angels.

Our snipers counter-fired when they could.

Sleeper was out there, working, and again I remembered I had constants I could count on. And that Ghost, and Sleeper, were two.

In the dark the first sergeant looked old, but not tired. He seemed eager even. But not worried. Maybe concerned. But eager to get to what was about to surely happen, one way or another.

"Been at this a long time, Orion," he said abruptly.

I closed my battle board. It had little to offer, and I'd finally come to that conclusion. Best to stop, look, listen, and smell what I could. Whatever was gonna happen was gonna happen soon. I needed all the intel I could get. Since the battle board wasn't giving up anything… I'd gather on my own. Best to get acclimatized to the dark and the flares. Watch shadows that moved too much or were not natural.

Listen for the steps, the battle rattle, the whispers.

Guns barked out there. But here in my sector were silences in between the sudden noises you could check and watch. Footsteps. Battle rattle. Magazines swapped. Spoons on grenades to be thrown suddenly sprung.

The merest warning could be lifesaving.

One of our mines went off forward, and that told me the Ultras were using their scouts and sappers once again to crawl in close and see what they could see.

So—someone had "found" one. I hoped they were dead in the finding. Their friends too.

"Reaper, be advised we got snakes in the wire." I told the platoon this and waited for my double-click acknowledgments from the squad leaders.

"Been in a lot of fights, Sar'nt Orion," mumbled the first sergeant so low I couldn't really tell if he was even talking to me. "One-sided, fair's fair, and last stands too, Sergeant," continued the first sergeant as he watched the hellish darkness out there created by the drifting falling flares coming down all across the burnt-out-tank-haunted landing zone we were determined to fight over tonight.

I counted the minutes. We still had too long to go before those PDCs came online once more. I stacked the Bastard close at hand and hefted the Sturm with a fresh belt.

I would stay on the edge of ready for as long as I could because I knew that the instant I thought I had a moment, it would start. So I stayed ready.

"Man might say…" continued the first sergeant, "this one feels more like a last stand than a last battle. But all of 'em, Orion, all of 'em was last stands for me all along. I was young when I got into the batts. I was in the regulars on Saturnia Station. We were fighting the Little Worlds Battles back then. All the time. I remember this big operator, stone-cold killer, the kind you know is the real deal just by the way he carries his knife, walked by young me back then out there picking up trash in the garrison. Like privates do. He had spit-black jump boots and black beret with a bloody flash and everything. Whistle and crack that one was, and I knew it at the time. He walks over to me on that field and just says, '*You do that as though your life depends on it, and I'll give you a shot at the batts. We need scouts, kid.*' Can you believe that? It was like lightning up and struck me with a way forward to doin' what I'd wanted to do all along."

I didn't know what I was supposed to have trouble believing more. That the first sergeant had been some young private picking up trash once… or that I was hearing part of his story on how the first sergeant became a Ranger in the legendary batts back on Saturnia. Though they were gone now, over the hill and into history at the Battle of Caliban, they were still legends in the military history of humanity in space. So I kept quiet and watched the night, waiting for more, on the edge of ready until it came.

"Believe this old man was just a kid once, Sar'nt? Like that boy up there with your new Ultra wonderboy. That was me back then. I wanted in the batts so bad I could taste it. Wanted to be whistle and crack too as we used to say before you were ever a gleam in your daddy's eye for your momma's sweet frame. So I combed that field for every bit of trash that day and into the night. Down on my hands and knees in the dark and well into it some. About midnight that night he comes by again, that whistle-and-crack black-beret operator. He gets out a light and he walks the whole field. Checking. Ain't nothin' he can find. Nothin' *to* find. That's how I got in. Six months later I'm at Gargadish. You know about Gargadish, Orion?"

I did.

I said nothing.

"Ten of us made it back to the birds that bad day. Every step of that ten miles through a city full of insurgents try-na kill you with all the full-auto hate they was savin' up, was as though your life depended on it, just like that field I picked up to get it. Glad that operator told it to me that way… because no one ever did after that. But that's how I Rangered in the batts, Orion. Back when I was a young man and so handsome girls got pregnant just a-lookin' at me in my black beret and jump boots. That tab right there… lady-killer, Orion. Shoulda seen me then. I was somethin'."

Said the old man carrying a flamethrower and more than willing to light some Ultras up tonight on a bad LZ.

Something terrific exploded over in Dog's sector a moment later. There was a sudden exchange of frantic gunfire that followed.

"Captain's gettin' it done over there," whispered the first sergeant, then softly sang his old cadence as he watched the night out there, scanning for something he and I knew was coming soon. Lighter and flamethrower ready to get it on, on behalf of the company.

"That operator, he was with the Special Operations group in the batts. He finds me after I get out of the hospital after Gargadish. I was shot the first time on that one. Takes me out for a beer. Tells me, *'Kid, that's how they all are. Every fight is a last stand. Man who realizes that first, is the man who does everything as though his life depends on it. He's the man that's maybe gonna win. He's the strong horse.'"*

It was silent now. The flares were low, still throwing their hell light just over the ruin and dark carnage beyond the wire. Enemy spotters were no doubt tagging everything they suspected was us. Telling that unseen commander out there what was what. And who to hit first.

It was so silent you could hear the falling flares hiss as they drifted toward us. Coming close and closer to the charred black dirt we'd defend.

"After that, the operator pays for the beer and gets up. As he goes out, he pats me on the back and says, *'Be a-watchin' you, kid. And hey, don't ever have a plan B. In it to win it every time, every day. Everything like your life depends on it. No other way. Every time.'* I never saw him again, Sar'nt. Found out later he was with the Delta. One of the legends, those guys. Got ate up hard in a war no one ever heard nothin' about. Stacked 'em deep that day though. Or so the classified docs I got hold of said. So… I believe it."

I could hear the next wave of Ultra armor coming through the distant streets. The bigger howling turbines of the heavy hitters spooling up as they made ready to push. The whiny howls of the armored cav moving around fast, this way and that.

This was gonna hurt.

And I knew, in the silence beneath those urgent engines, infantry just like us were out there, among those heavy armored killers, ready to see who was gonna walk away from this one tonight.

I checked my watch.

Eight hours fourteen minutes to go.

We'd hold.

We'd do this.

I thought about one last message to Reaper. But they didn't need that now. They knew what to do. It was as if our whole lives had been leading up to this moment. We knew that going in even if we didn't say it out loud.

We were good with that.

"So I never did, Orion. Never had a plan B, young Sar'nt. Know what plan Alpha was?"

I told the first sergeant I did not.

"Plan A was always a Third Worlds ditch and a pile of expended brass. Might as well be here, Sergeant. Might as well be tonight then. Sons of bitches ain't gettin' through."

He clicked the lighter and the flamethrower ignited, emitting a soft blue glow in the dark, the smell of industrial fumes filling the night.

CHAPTER
TWENTY-EIGHT

The next push from the Ultras would come in to find the cracks they suspected were here. Cracks I knew were there.

Obviously, Dog was in big trouble. The captain had gone there not just to stabilize the battle on that flank, but to take direct command. That meant the platoon leader was either dead or badly wounded over there.

Chimp casevac flights were coming in close to the ship, under fire, to get the wounded off the field. Word on the comm was Cutter had moved his triage station out onto the field, off the cargo deck and under the protection of the shields and the PDCs.

One squad from Ghost was now pulling security there while counter-snipers were all tasked with any Ultras taking shots at the wounded and the medics working.

Monkey dropship pilots flying old Grauman Whales, dropships from wars that started and ended long before my time, came in fast and hot, blowing char and debris everywhere, taking fire, Simia pilots hooting and screeching as medics raced to get our wounded out of harm's way and on board the flights out of here.

I watched the casevacs dusting off in the night, Ultra hot red tracers raking the old heavily armored and patch-welded hulls of the Whales, built and reinforced to take fire from wars that had once been described as *apocalyptic* and *galaxy-ending* back in the day, and felt like the company was being slowly torn apart faster that I thought possible or liked.

Those were our wounded on the way out. Where were they going? To the chimp hulks? To the Insurrection field stations off in the jungles? What would become of them? What would become of us?

"They'll be okay, Sar'nt Orion. Strays always find their way back to the company eventually," murmured the first sergeant in the night. "Just as you have on occasion."

Cracks. They were appearing.

The Ultras, this General Arkades, what had they called him... the Imperator-something... he had to see Dog as where he could punch us right in the balls and roll the forward LZ that was rapidly earning its name.

Heartbreak.

I grabbed the Savage Lone Wolf I'd finally sent the Kid back for and as many reload bandos as he could struggle back to my little perimeter with. Whether I wanted to admit it or not, I knew it was going to get rough soon. I was now sporting three weapons, two placed nearby, one slung around me, besides my sidearm, karambit, and a whole lot of frags just in case things got up close and personal.

"All dressed up for the dance, Sar'nt?" Punch had noted in passing, hustling off to check the line as more Ultra mortars had walked toward our position twenty minutes prior. Then the Insurrection sent in Cobra ground attack fighters a few streets over and knocked them out. One of our close air support craft went down off over the city, unable to dodge mobile AA fire out there somewhere.

If that pilot was lucky, he was now knee-deep in enemy-held territory, *E-and-E-ing* for his life.

If he was lucky.

If he wasn't, well, that crash had just solved everything he'd ever been worried about in his whole life up until he took fire.

Or, as Mad Max sometimes mutters to himself, "I ain't got no problems that a double tap on me wouldn't solve right now. That's my perspective on life and death, Sar'nt."

I'd once made the mistake of asking him how he stayed so cool under fire. That was his answer. I was still trying to figure it out, but I think I understood. Kinda.

The *Spider*'s PDCs were now on constant *Brrrrrrrt*. My guess is Arkades was trying to use everything he had to deplete our ability to reload those terrific combat multipliers we had operational for the moment. Once he had the intel from the front they were bone dry… he'd make the big push.

Until then he was going to keep them busy with indirect fire, provided by close-at-hand mortars, and far away via heavy mobile guns shooting and moving through the ruined red marble streets of Saffron City. Rumor was there were two massive heavy mechs tagged as Scylla and Charybdis that fired eight-hundred-millimeter guns. They were moving in, and Insurrection air was trying to knock them out before they could fire on the LZ.

Boy… I sure hope so. Go get 'em, drop monkeys.

But those were other people's concerns. Other commanders' circuses. Other plat daddys' monkeys.

I had my own and right now everything was set up to protect that scar I knew they were gonna push on eventually because they had to have known they got far enough.

Some Ultra scout had no doubt crept through the bloody carnage we'd made up there. Seen a little of how far the combat engineers had gotten.

They'd gotten close is what they'd done.

Off to our right, Hauser was on the move. He lit up something in the night and called it over the comm. Hunter-killer cyborg stuff.

"Contact front. Three fast-attack HMGTs," he called out over the comm. HMGTs, high-mobility gun trucks, or what were affectionally known as Rhinos, came charging up the scar leading two light tanks already engaging with fire.

A round slammed in off to our right and blew black charred dirt and debris high and in every direction.

Ulysses called out, "Target acquired... engaging!" almost instantly.

The first Jackhammer was already deployed and ready to fire, so he could fire immediately. The round *hissed* and *whoooshed* away to his intended target.

Supporting fire from Hauser and Mad Max worked the incoming gun trucks when they could, but they were heavily armored, with huge mine scoops in front and small battery-charged defensive shields radiating outward.

The first one triggered one of our mines and the explosion bumped the front end skyward. At the same time, thanks to Jax and Duster's creative application of demolitions for better living through high explosives, secondary charges detonated along the sides of the scar.

These were chain-linked shotgun mines called Sluggers. An advanced design on the old claymore system that had followed humanity out into the stars. Biggs, go Biggs or go home, had swapped captured pickups which we'd been stacking all through Astralon, Crash, call it what you will. We'd sent them upwell to the *Spider* whenever we could arrange for a pallet courier from planetside to orbit.

We traded those for some advanced defensive systems like the Sluggers.

Which was good now that Ultra armored cav were trying to make sure the crack in my section of the defensives was indeed a crack they could exploit.

Of course, Arkades, or whoever was running the attack on this point, my sector, in the battle, knew we'd try to protect our weakness when the Ultra combat engineer squad had devastated our wire sprays and gotten close enough to start lobbing grenades into the LZ itself.

That is until Jax and I murdered them a whole bunch for their efforts.

The secondary Sluggers fired as the first Rhino pushed hard into the scar. The initial explosion raised her nose, then the Sluggers shotgunned five thousand, each, carbide balls impregnated with conductive thermite, into the lighter armored sides and underbelly of the fast-attack cav vehicle.

The resulting effect: four mines sent twenty thousand steel balls speeding at twenty-four hundred feet per second right into the undercarriage and sides of the highly mobile, negative steer, armored gun truck. These balls hit thinner armor and if they didn't punch outright, and even if they did in fact, they turned to white-hot thermite, still moving at a high rate of speed, and began to splatter and melt through everything they came in contact with.

That gun truck was ruined instantly whether it knew it or not.

It didn't explode so much as drive off the lip of the scar and roll over on its side, beginning to burn like some lamp that had twenty thousand holes punched in it.

Rhinos carried a squad of Ultras each.

"Here they come, Sar'nt," said the first sergeant. "Time to get it on now… as you boys like to say."

We hustled off toward the scar as Ulysses burned another tank out there in the fire and the darkness.

CHAPTER TWENTY-NINE

The next two gun trucks made it further up the scar before both were so shot to hell the drivers forced the vehicles into a defensive position, putting as much of the armor of the Rhinos between them and our incoming fire from Second supported by Third as they could.

First Squad, run by Punch and hardened by Ulysses, had much of the sector now. Near the scar, firing short bursts from defensive cover, Hauser gave me his situation analysis report.

"Sergeant Orion. Probability indicates we are facing two squads of elite enemy shock troopers. My algorithms indicate they will hold position and allow for more troops to stack on their location before pushing next. Ultra combat doctrine means they have ten minutes to support this push. Drone recon across this front is currently unavailable so we have no information to confirm this. Passive enemy jammers somewhere outside the current area of conflict are interfering with my sensors."

In the background of the transmission, hot brass and linkage flew away from Hauser's gun as he covered a belt change on Mad Max who was prone and under fire from enemy efforts to suppress the position. Besides Hauser and the gun team, I had Jax, Klutz, Goods and New Guy One on the M67, the first sergeant, and myself.

"How fast will the enemy push those troops forward, Hauser? Best guess."

Hauser folded back behind the chunk of twisted debris he was fighting from, eyes glowing red in the darkness meaning he was running IR in his optical sights. He usually did so when he needed optimum kill success under low-light intense conflict.

I could only imagine the data crawls running across his onboard mainframe, updating him on every possible factor we were facing and sifting as much intelligence as his sensors could as fast as possible.

Assessing and fighting at the same time.

If the chimps didn't come out on top of this, then perhaps the cyborgs were next for the seat of power. And if they were all like Hauser, I wasn't so sure they'd do worse than us. In fact... maybe they'd succeed where we'd failed so often. Maybe they'd value, and conserve, the things that worked, protecting the little foxes in the desert night that were all of us when you really thought about it. Valuing things that should be valued over mem-hoards and constant distractions of media and entertainment and petty games of power beyond our collective pay grades.

I don't know.

As I said... above my pay grade. I was in a firefight for a cheap cut in the ground no one would ever die over in their right mind.

But, as the first sergeant likes to say on occasion, "Here we are, boys. Doin' dumb stuff well."

"They will move at the double ignoring patrol safety parameters during movement under scout and recon conditions," answered Hauser regarding my enemy ability to deploy question. "This is active combat, Sergeant Orion.

Momentum is a key Ultra doctrine. They prize owning a superior fighting position at the expense of cover and concealment in a range of possible simulations I am currently running."

I popped a look out and scanned with my SmartEye, setting the parameters with visual cues to scan on low-light and thermal. I wanted to see what Hauser was seeing.

Lots of fire out there.

The Ultras, the ones that had survived the destruction of the two following gun trucks, were hunkering low and not returning fire.

I only got bare heat sigs off them.

I switched over to night vision and picked up something I would have missed on thermal. Someone beyond them was popping smoke. They'd use that to cover the advance of the supporting shock troops who'd make the push once they were staged on the ruined gun trucks.

I tapped my comm channel, audibled over to the ship's comm, and signaled for XO.

I got M.O.M. instead.

"Hello, dear... are you okay at this current time? My sensors indicate you are currently experiencing extreme stress given your respiration and elevated heart rate. You are also dehydrated, Sergeant Orion. Perhaps you should take a moment to drink some refreshing cold water and take some deep breaths. Your health is very important to Strange Company and the legal team currently representing them."

Her matronly yet calm tone was designed to do exactly that. Calm. In starflight. Where people can get a little sketchy being trapped inside a giant hunk of metal deep in the depths of space with no out anywhere in light years nearby.

On the battlefield it was exasperating.

I have found it best not to think too hard about starflight when actually doing it. That way lies madness. There are some things you shouldn't think about so much.

"Mom… I need to talk to XO. It's urgent."

There was a slight pause. Mad Max was up on the gun and dosing the two ruined gun trucks some more.

"Good goin', Max," cheered the first sergeant behind me, covered by the large piece of blackened street that had been boiled and overturned by the D-beam strike that had cleared LZ Heartbreak. "Give 'em somethin' to think about!"

"Oh dear, Sergeant Orion," continued M.O.M. "XO is currently attempting to reroute a targeting malfunction down in the lower data libraries. Battle damage from our current position has resulted in a loss of power between decks nine and twelve at this time."

I paused, noting that yes, I was breathing hard. And I probably was thirsty. But I didn't have time for a drink of cool refreshing water and some deep breathing. Enough Ultras to choke a cyclowhale would push through that smoke to stack on the two vehicles at any minute and then they'd flashbang and frag us all and push up the scar, opening up a lane right into the LZ.

More lethal chatter rattled out from both my gunners. One of the Rhinos was now on fire across the front armor where the dead forward gunner still hung limply out of the turret.

"MOM… are you currently running the point defense cannons?"

"Why yes. I am, dear. My protocols are presently targeting incoming artillery which is absorbing eighty-seven-point-one-eight percent of my point defense capabilities. Secondary protocols dictate engaging all strike aircraft nearing the landing zone during this window. My PDC reserves are down to twenty-seven-point-nine-four percent. At this rate of fire, we will experience system shutdown in twenty-seven-point-three-zero-two minutes, dear."

"MOM... requesting a ground suppression mission at this time. I need to retask the forward PDC... the thirty-millimeter autocannon... and target fire on my marker."

There was a pause over the hum of the comm with the ship. Out on the line the fighting was beginning to swell through my ear pro.

"I'm sorry, dear. The ship's captain has specifically set the tasking protocols at this time, and I cannot override without proper authorization. Let's wait until the captain gets to the bridge, dear. Then he'll decide what's best."

Targeting mortars were starting to fall across Dog and us. The Ultras were trying to bracket our positions near the exit from the scar.

It was clear they were getting ready to push.

"Why don't you have that nice cool drink of water now, dear. And try to calm down. Intense combat can be very stressful. You seem very upset right now."

I swore.

"Priority override Ice Cream and Cake for Breakfast, MOM. Say again..."

Another mortar smashed into the LZ's edge just behind us. Medics threw themselves over our wounded to protect them from raining debris. One of the chimp drops down on the casevac LZ injected frag and lost an engine right there. Chimps were running out of the bird with fire extinguishers, screeching and howling as they hopped madly around, angry about the damage.

The fire was suppressed, and the screeching chimp forward and above in the cockpit gave the thumbs-up. They were dusting off without the engine regardless.

Total madness. Wild and reckless. And... a kind of bravery I admired.

In monkeys.

"Priority override Ice Cream and Cake for Breakfast, MOM," I said again, sure my traffic over the comm had been lost in the sudden strike.

The Strange command team had access to a code phrase that could override M.O.M.'s current protocols in most emergency situations. *Ice Cream and Cake for Breakfast* was it.

This was definitely an emergency.

"As you wish, dear," said M.O.M. in my comm. "Standing by for your change of orders."

I pulled a flare round off the bando I was carrying for the Lone Wolf. The Sturm was slung heavily around my back. And yeah, both weapons are heavy already. But thankfully I wasn't needing to hump large distances as most of my men and fighting positions were in a tight semicircle, close proximity relatively, and I could reach each quick enough if I kept low. Plus I had no idea what I'd need to contribute to the defense my squads were running.

Indirect fire or high-cyclic suppression. I was ready to go as best I could.

Or... as they say... *why not both?*

"MOM, redirect the forward thirty-millimeter cannon to fire a five-second burst on my placed marker shortly. Firing marker now... stand by to fire."

I sighted the two shadowy gun trucks out there and lobbed the flare round right into the shot-to-hell wheels of one.

Then I thumbed in six massive flechette rounds from the bandos as I spoke to the rest of my men there on both sides of the scar. Alerting them to what we were gonna do next.

"We're gonna destabilize their push, Strange. Ship's gonna light up the gun trucks and we're going forward right after. I clear whoever survived with this, then both gunners set up on opposite sides of the trucks. Any Ultras moving up the scar, engage immediately. We hold from there since they're trying to put indirect on us here now. Ready up, Strange…"

I tapped the comm.

"Engage the marker, MOM. Five-second burst."

Immediately, with zero hesitation, the forward PDC swilled and spat out a voluminous targeted five-second stream of uranium-depleted thirty-millimeter rounds. It was like a wave of evil dark birds passing over us in the night. The trucks jumped and shook as the entire area surrounding their position suddenly disappeared in a swarm of black lead and flying charred dirt.

Under PDC fire like that… five seconds might as well have been forever.

There was little left of both trucks when the gun on the bird suddenly went silent.

"Firing complete, dear," said M.O.M. "Have a nice day."

"Follow me, Strange. Get-it-on time."

CHAPTER THIRTY

We pushed fifty meters up the scar to the destroyed gun trucks as fast as we could. We needed to take possession of the small rise where the Ultra armored cav force had tried to create a breach in our line before the ground troops swarmed up the far side and took it.

As the captain had told me, Ultra doctrine prioritized high ground possession, and even as I ran, I couldn't help but think, or worry, that I was reacting instead of acting. That I was making the choice to take possession of the high ground fast just because they wanted it first.

But I had no other choice and so we hustled forward fast.

Behind us, where we'd been defending from, enemy mortar rounds were starting to land with more accuracy. And in a weird way that made me feel better about my decision to move forward.

Good move, Sergeant Orion. Your men were not blown to pieces by indirect fire because you hesitated. Now they could go forward and try to hold something hardened killers who held fast to a death cult of salvation through combat wanted real bad. Let's see how that works out for us.

At least I get some things right. Sometimes.

I didn't direct my men as we raced up on the trucks, I just hustled, lugging the Lone Wolf and hoping like every hapless infantry small unit leader before me that they were following. Or what remained of them. I was too busy moving low and checking everything I could with what was essentially a ten-gauge shotgun that could fire one hundred razor-sharp needles a shell at you. Needles that penetrated most rated combat armor. I expected things to get personal shortly. And if you're gonna get close, nothing says *kaboom you're dead* like the Lone Wolf loaded with anti-personnel shells.

I didn't have to wait long to say hello to my first Ultra Marines. Two scouts were already there amid the ruin of the gun trucks and torn-to-pieces bodies of the two squads who'd been holding there. Now, as their point men secured the location, the Ultra teams pushed out of the smoke to the rear.

I dusted the first one at five meters as I came around the side of the ruined gun truck. If I thought the random body parts and what remained of torsos and the occasional barely identifiable piece of someone's head lying on the ground all around our little fight had been bad, what the *Spider*'s thirty-millimeter PDC had done to this position… then what the Savage Lone Wolf firing flechettes at close range did was pure horror.

But you don't have time for things like horror and images you'll live with for what remains of your life when you're slam-firing at close quarters.

Like I said… the wars we'd fought on all the company's bad contracts up until now, I was only now realizing just how polite those had truly been. Small arguments over tea and politics compared to the dark age of warlords and genocide I feared we were entering regardless of who came out on top.

It was just a torn-up rise in a scar on a bad LZ on some world falling apart. Two sides, both human. Still, I tore those two Ultras to shreds with that trench gun.

It was either them or me, going forward. Into what, I didn't know. But I was determined it was me and mine that were going to be the ones with the shot to see what a better tomorrow looked like. For better or worse.

Two things were going on as I pulled the fat trigger on the Savage Lone Wolf and disintegrated the first Ultra scout who was leading the way up to what remained of both gun trucks.

He'd just turned his back to give some kind of hand signal and I didn't even wait to see the look in the visor of his helmet as I popped around what remained of the rear section of the troop deck of the Rhino and opened fire.

I saw and pulled.

He got suddenly rocked by a deafening roar from my gun and then by fast-moving steel needles disintegrating much of his upper torso. A lot of fast-moving needles moving forward in a bright spray.

It blew off the top half of his body regardless of high-speed Ultra armor and beliefs in blood, glory, honor, and all that other death cult nonsense.

Whoever thought there was anything to be gained in war except an innate desire to find some other kind of work to be quiet in forever, was an idiot.

And yet, as the first sergeant likes to say on occasion... *here we are, boys.*

I pumped the next shell and did the kid behind him just as quickly and badly as I'd done the first.

To be honest I have no idea if he was a kid or not.

But I just hate myself enough to let it be that way. That he was some kid on his NCO's six, trusting the leadership as they crept up to take what we wanted. What would be ours.

War should be horrible. Maybe we don't do it so much if we recognize that. And so... he was some kid.

Pumping the heavy Lone Wolf and maintaining sight picture is difficult. Unless you're Hause. You should see him working this thing. It's savage awful and it'll make ya drink if you're so inclined. But it's a thing of precision beauty if you're a pro in the business of soldiering.

My aim was lower for that second dull thud on the other side of the trigger pull, and I hit the kid center mass that time and blew him in every direction on the other side of it.

Then the Ultras down the scar coming out of the smoke began to fire at me and I was twisting away as fast as I could and just falling backwards, rolling behind the troop carrier for cover as rounds smacked armor and buzzed haircut close off into the night and the rest of the battle behind and around us.

You don't get to be a wily old ruck hobo unless you get good at ducking, twisting, rolling, and scrambling like a coward the instant after you blast two guys like some action-hero Monarch in the spectacuthrillers.

There are no one-liners or action-hero poses in war. You're best to be like some local predator thieving chickens out of the henhouse: a pest. But a wily one intent on chicken dinner that night.

One gun was up and working the Ultras. Mad Max for the win started to ride the lightning on them fast because they were that close.

Speaking of Hause...

Max was swearing and rocking the gun in long bursts as I tried to find my other Pig gunner and best-friend combat cyborg. Way beyond six- to eight-round bursts I noted as I scanned the chaos of my element. That wasn't good. Mad Max was a good gunner.

So, just by sound I knew the push was on from the enemy and that it was close and desperate this fast into it.

I pushed off from the black dirt where I'd gone prone, sprawling really like no Monarch action spectacuthriller hero ever, trying to avoid Ultra target practice. I tried to count by the bare glance I'd gotten before diving for cover how many teams of Ultras I'd seen firing and moving up the scar on our new forever home.

A lot. Too many to count really.

Then I spotted Hauser.

He was down halfway up the scar we'd just surged up.

"What the…"

Then I saw the drone that had brought him down. It was attached to his torso and neck like some kind of alien parasite. Mechanical bat wings fluttering as it tried to hack into his systems.

Generally, this kind of attack wasn't a problem for the company as we were usually facing third-rate local armies with nothing but junk weapons and slogans made meaningless by what we all knew was gonna be the end of the conflict. Again, before meeting the Seeker, we never would have faced Ultras in our right mind.

When they showed up, back then, it was *show's over, folks.* Everyone boogie for deep space.

But… that was then. This is now. And something I kept telling myself about *getting caught up in the action* and *a better tomorrow.*

Lies probably. Lies I couldn't shake because I didn't want to. Listen, it's best to be honest about these things. There are lies, bold-faced or bald-faced, however you want to put it, that we want to believe. And those are the worst ones. The ones we tell ourselves. The ones we want to believe oh so badly.

Having a combat cyborg was unheard of among the PMCs. Besides them being specifically designed for urban combat and guerrilla warfare… they were pure killing machines that looked human.

Which made them far worse when you thought about it.

Imagine six-foot-four killing studs that looked like you, a human, instead of any of the intergalactic predator species we'd encountered thus far in our outward journey. "Human" murder machines that could stand up to incredible amounts of damage and conduct a variety of combat operations with ease, efficiency, and even affinity in any given weapon system or tactical situation. Hiding among human populations and colonies, undetectable without sophisticated gear, and weaponized against anyone that stood in opposition to the current regime that could not be questioned or voted out in any way, shape, or form.

Imagine living in that kind of civilization.

But there were systems and technology designed to identify and terminate hunter-killer cyborgs. Make a weapon system and the corporations would develop one to counter the one they just sold you.

Humans. It's what we do.

The only barrier to entry was that these high-tech systems were expensive and generally available to not just the team playing for the winners, always the Monarchs of course, but to the Ultras themselves who also ran hunter-killer teams of cyborgs and enjoyed a monopoly on upgrades.

So of course the Ultra Marines, the Monarchs' guard dogs, would be fielding razorblade drones to take down any of the cyborgs who'd ended up becoming self-aware and siding with the *insurrectionistas*. What other choice did they have? If the Dark Labs got them back, they'd either reboot them after a system wipe or recycle them for scrap.

Hauser was down. My SmartEye ran a diagnostic scan on his injury or injuries. Something I'd set it up to do just in case the inevitable inevitably happened.

Always plan for failure, that way you're not never disappointed... but just less.

I'd researched tech that could take down a combat cyborg on the off chance we ever ran into some high-powered contractors, or well-financed operators, with that kind of gear.

Never the Ultras like we're currently in it with. Silly me.

The SmartEye spotted the razorblade drone that had attached itself to Hauser and then electromagnetically pulsed him in order to disable and hack. If it was doing what my research said it had the capabilities to do, then it was currently rebooting Hauser in an attempt to either hack him outright and turn him loose on us instantly, or it was going for the old factory wipe.

Which would be bad for everyone involved in this fight, and... be the end of the company right here and right now. Hauser popping up and going all termination mode on us would be bad... yes. For us. Hauser detonating the equivalent of a micro-nuke yield would be a bad day for everyone within a ten-block radius.

Hope you brought your sunblock two thousand.

A factory wipe would start Hauser's internal runtime clock, set at fifty-eight seconds to detonation... and then detonate that onboard micro-reactor inside his advanced combat frame. The resulting explosion would destroy about ten blocks, give or take, for the next one hundred years.

It would settle our company accounts and outstanding debts right now.

I swore and ran for all I was worth to my downed friend who was also a really-bad-day bomb waiting to happen. Most of the company don't know about this feature and the command team has kept this knowledge tight. Private military contractors might have problems serving alongside a bomb.

Switching the Lone Wolf to my off hand as I shucked the small device I'd carried since finding out such hacking and rebootings could happen to Hauser, I made ready to take my best shot with something I'd only tested, and try to save his life and ours too. I'd ordered the device and it had followed us via delayed shipments for a few contracts. Once it finally caught up with us, I felt a lot better.

It was called the D-Shock defensive control.

I'd tested it on a couple of less high-tech drones when I'd had the chance in secret and reported my findings to the Old Man and the first sergeant.

It worked. In test situations with simple drones. Complex thinking-machine lethal weapons like Hauser... in theory. Or so the brochure that came with it assured me.

Now, as I pounded across the midnight burnt dirt between me and my downed friend who was jumping and twitching in the dirt, deep shadows shifting uncertainly from the firefight all across the line, I hoped for the best and better-than-promised outcomes regarding devices ordered from a catalog. Catalogs badly printed in Muhadji brochures. Fires of burning War Mace tanks out there in the dark, and more falling flares from above via the latest artillery airbursts, my SmartEyes graphed the terrain between us, providing some insight to my path back to the combat cyborg who was my best friend.

The whole time, and this was just seconds, I tried to block out thoughts that the thing on my friend, the razorblade drone, had already hacked him and reset Hauser. Counting down the last seconds of his life.

Our lives.

Visions of reaching him just as he detonated, my friend telling me, "I'm sorry, Sergeant Orion," and me feeling like I'd failed us both... everyone knows those waking nightmares you beg never come true. Ask any parent.

Me reaching and screaming "No!" and thinking... *It's just "Orion," my friend.*

Then the blinding white flash that ends us all.

Worst day ever.

CHAPTER THIRTY-ONE

I skidded and fell on Hauser, jamming the D-Shock into the batlike drone and pulling as hard as I could to get it off him. I connected and pushed the single red button that pulsed a small charge that should shut the razorblade drone down if badly printed catalogs in Muhadji are ever to be believed by poor ruck-hump hobos asking for one deal in the universe to finally be a good one that swung their way somehow.

Just for once…

Blue electricity surged and the batlike drone exploded upward, fluttering its rotors and screeching electronically. Weird. Smoking, it fell back down to the burnt ground.

Hauser was still lights out though as the fighting surged behind me and off down the line. The Ultras were hitting us hard now. Grenades up close and machine guns cackling on tight murder bursts as they tried to create a breach in our line.

I looked into Hauser's eyes and magnified the image there with my SmartEye…

The boot symbol was spinning, almost invisibly, inside those complex targeting machines that saw so much I never would.

Desert foxes in the night.

"C'mon, Hause…"

Now!

His eyes fluttered open. Mechanically.

"This unit is operational," he said suddenly. "There are currently fifty-eight-point-two seconds of runtime for this unit. My name is… Hauser. Combat Cyborg Model Series Eight. Identification factory number zero zero zero seven zero nine one eight zero two. Booting… combat operations assignment… warfare."

Then he looked at me…

"I have lost time, Sergeant Orion. Status update on current operations… is the company safe?"

That was his first thought. Us.

Are we safe?

How many of them would have thought the same regarding *his* operational runtime?

As I have said… he's the most human entity I have encountered.

"We're good, Hause, but we're in it, buddy. You good to go? 'Cause I need you right now."

"Affirmative," he said, suddenly sitting straight up like some movie Frankenstein. The Pig draped across his chest. Linked ammo falling away.

"It's time to get it on, Sergeant Orion. Commencing combat operations now. Mode… close-quarters battle."

Orion, Hause. It's just Orion, my friend.

CHAPTER THIRTY-TWO

Mad Max and his gunner Bad Bet, the guy with the duracast shattered arm, had to pull back behind the wrecked Ultra cav armor. They got pushed hard there and now they were shifting to a new loc to engage.

Goods had fired an AT round at… something, but I had no idea what. Jax was hit and Klutz was trying to get a pressure bandage on the wound that was dangerously close to vital areas in his chest. It had come in just above the plate, deflecting through meat and muscle.

I checked the wound, checked for an exit and found it, then called for Choker on the comm as Jax gasped he was *all good*.

Which he wasn't. Clearly.

"Think it went straight… through…" he gasped, shaking hard as he tried to fight off shock. "Orion. G-g-g-goood to… go."

There was no pink froth on his lips. Yet. But I had concerns.

Hauser stepped forward and opened fire to cover Choker coming and the rest of us attending to Jax. The combat cyborg dumped a belt of highly effective fire on Ultras coming from all angles across the mangled and burnt wasteland forward of our position for the scar they'd decided to try and open up as a weak point.

Not gonna happen.

Brass and linkage flew away frantically above a curled-up Jax as Hauser went into overdrive. But the Ultras were not to be deterred. They didn't get to be Ultras by flinching much.

Even if it was a real-life hunter-killer doing his murder-best to get you to flinch. It was the ultimate game of death-chicken.

Rounds began to smack into our combat cyborg above as he drew accurate fire and replied with effective fire on their positions and movements. Shooting down the Ultras out there revealed by his intensive targeting analysis sensors.

The belt burnt and Hauser took a knee, refusing to cover and I knew the why of that. The Ultras had now collectively switched over to making the human-shaped optimized hunter-killer their primary target. They'd shoot him as much as they could as fast as they could.

Whenever we got into these kinds of situations, his concern was to direct fire on himself in order to save the "biologics." Ultra sensor capabilities in their helmets would analyze and identify him as a cyborg now and small unit leaders would be doing their absolute best to take him off the board.

A combat cyborg, in fact, in most commanders' priority of targets, often ranks with a forty-ton mech. The damage they can do, especially with infiltration and surprise… can get exponential quickly.

Officers and NCOs leading their men would target him for effective fire and Hauser knew it as we worked the problem of Jax's gunshot wound and why he was starting to bleed out despite no obvious arterial bleeding. Even as Hauser knelt and loaded the next belt of the five he kept around his neck, moving away and higher on the rise to present a clearer target to our enemies, more rounds landed in testament to the pro-level shooting of the Ultras out there trying to kill him.

I heard the solid hits on his armor and tried not to wince. One caught him in the head and deflected, leaving a wicked hot gash.

He merely recoiled from the kinetic impact. Slightly. Belt loaded, gun up, he engaged again, moving forward, firing at them in short bursts, killing one with each. Then switching to the next target.

Even Ultras... that had to freak them out on some level.

The first sergeant was there, exposing himself to fire, and shouting, "Come and get it, you pretty-boy bastards!" Then he let go with the first jet of burning fuel from the flamethrower. It flung itself farther than I ever thought possible, arcing out and landing in a great burning rush like something from some mythic great lizard's dragon breath.

That had happened to me every time I saw the flamethrower employed. It always reached out to cover our enemies in burning, inextinguishable fire, crossing greater distances than I'd thought possible.

If you thought, on the other hand, and I have made that mistake, that flamethrowers are close support weapons for tunnels, bunkers, and general defensive line clearing... then you're wrong.

They can reach out and light you up. Pardon the pun. I know you're burned up about that.

The first spewing jet of burning fuel from the first sergeant's weapon went out about fifty meters and splashed across two teams of Ultras working the center. One kneeling. Two were on the ground and covering with fire. Another actually rushing forward when all got covered in a great wash of burning fire there wasn't a thing you could do anything about.

It just suddenly lashed out across the battlefield and lit them all on fire. I doubt they'd even known one of these weapons systems was in play until the first sergeant got it going. And in their defense… it's an ancient weapon system most modern militaries do not bother fielding for reasons I'll never understand.

It absolutely gets the job done on many levels. Non-Ultra troops will just run. If they can. Fire is very primal. Very powerful. Weaponized it's insane.

They were done. The four dead Ultra Marines were rolling or dropping as they were cooked right there on the battlefield.

And that's a smell you never forget.

You eventually get it on every world. Burning bodies. War wouldn't be complete without it. But you never get used to it.

If I could edit war… I'd edit that one out for sure. But I can't and so… you gotta be honest about these things. It's yet one more of many horrors.

But the first sergeant wasn't done. Not yet. Not by half. He shifted both feet, heedless of high-power seven-six-two streaking in from the Ultras' heavy battle rifles all around, targeted another group, and let go with another barfing jet of hot liquid death splashing over armor, burnt dirt, and the cover you'd put your faith in more than any hokey old religion… that cover was now on fire too.

The center of the scar was now, also, all on fire. As was the right flank where the Ultras had tried to climb, firing and moving, trying to gain any angle on our position at the shot-to-hell Rhinos we'd gotten to first.

Now many Ultras out there were covered in fire and not concerned in the least about pushing so much as getting clear of the spreading, jetting fire the first sergeant was providing like some consummate worker of the art of flame-throwing.

Fire don't care. Fire burns.

Mad Max put fire on the left flank which was mostly not on fire and seconds later Choker came running in, skidding onto his ballistic kneepads as he started checking Jax's vitals and assessing the wound.

He pulled the pressure dressing away with disgust and saw it was still leaking bad.

Choker swore and got to work, pushing Klutz away violently, grabbing the bandage, and pressing his weight on it as hard as he could. Jax screamed in response. I knew what the medic was doing. He was worried about an internal arterial bleed. He was getting as much pressure as he could on it to try and get body weight to seal it up or at least slow it.

Jax screamed and promised to kill Choker someday. Choker said he'd enjoy that meeting and reached for his hip pouch injector. Then quick as a lick he shot Jax up with his free hand.

Behind me the air was blossoming with fumes of burning gel-ignite. The first sergeant was swearing and laughing, screaming at the Ultras, "I'm your death god, you sons o' motherless dogs!"

Our entire front was burning fuel now covered by two Pigs on full cackle. We were good for the moment. Time to get Jax dealt with effectively.

"Got a problem, Sar'nt," said Choker.

I didn't say anything but the look I gave told him to go ahead with the more bad news I was always expecting and never surprised had arrived right on time. It was my *this might as well happen* look.

My platoon knew it well. Everyone did.

"Possible artery bleed. Internal, Sar'nt. Gotta get him to Doc Cutter fast."

I nodded, unsure what to do. There for a moment. Someplace else also. Tired and frustrated and not time for either.

"Gotta do it now, Sergeant, or you lose him right here and now in the next few," said Choker, all business zero psycho. "Also... I can't carry him and keep pressure on the wound. I need the 'borg. He carries. I'll keep pressure and we'll get him to the rear."

I stood there trying to figure out if I could carry Jax effectively and keep pressure on the bleeding artery. Internal arterial bleed was bad. Even Cutter would have a hard time with that.

I needed Hauser to hold the position here.

Jax was going gray. His mouth hung open in drugged stupor or imminent death.

I'd known Jax a long time. He was a good man. He'd never told me his story. Just said, "Merc'n' was the only way I had to go. Plus... ladies like mercs contrary to what people say, Orion. We dangerous. Ladies... the right ones... they likes them a little danger."

To confirm this, and just in case there were any eligible ladies on the battlefield, he'd written on the side of his helmet in white marker: *A Little Dangerous... Sometimes.*

That was an understatement.

Jax was my master demo handler. Better living through applied explosives.

He was in fact… very dangerous with the serious putty. Sometimes also known as C4. Why they called it serious putty I had no idea. That was old Earth slang that had hung on. Like Wednesday being some day of the week. No one knew why it was called that. Or why it was spelled like that when no one, on the worlds that used days like that, pronounced it as it was spelt.

Earth of yesterday would probably be as strange to us as a newly discovered alien world. And yet… "Deep calls unto deep," as Preacher will sometimes talk about in the once-a-week meetings no one ever goes to. Except me. Sometimes I go. Especially when I've lost my faith in everything and I'm looking for some reason to keep doing it.

"Hauser!" I shouted over the loud ringing chaos of the fight.

I hated that Choker used the cyborg slur *'borg*. But I had bigger problems right now and Hauser had never minded it.

He told me so one time.

"It's true, Sergeant Orion. I am one. 'Borg is just short for cyborg. There's no offense, Sergeant. You are being offended on my behalf. This is not necessary."

"I know, Hauser," I told him. "And it's just Orion. It's just…"

"It's not important, Sergeant. Don't be offended for me. My combat chassis is made of graphene-infused nano-titanium. One of the strongest forged substances in the galaxy. I can produce nine thousand pounds per square inch of pressure to crush things with my hands via onboard hydraulics. Do not sweat the small stuff, Sergeant Orion. Do you know who told me that?"

I did.

"Me," I'd told him sullenly, and he'd smiled that his lesson was complete.

Now I yelled for Hauser and he turned away from blasting our enemies effectively. I told him what I needed done and he simply took hold of the lifeless Jax, gently but forcefully, which seemed impossible to do both at the same time, and hefted him up for the carry to the rear.

Choker complained about Hauser not moving so fast. But he followed and kept pressure on the injury as the two of them moved off quickly to the rear in order to save our Second squad leader's life.

Despite the fire out there on the front, the Ultras weren't done yet. They'd push on this crack in our defenses come hell or high water. They didn't take a lot of *Flaming Nopes* that was a well-employed flamethrower in the hands of a senior-most ruck hobo for an answer, like most people would've.

"Tank incoming!" shouted Bad Bet from next to the gun Mad Max was running six- to eight-round bursts from on the Ultras still holding out behind burning cover out there.

I low-crawled forward. We were still taking fire from Ultras out from those covered positions. Despite the conflagration, they'd decided they could still fight from there.

I scanned the burning battlefield and found what I knew was coming but what I hoped wasn't.

This was one of the big ones.

Two treads. One main gun. Old-school and built like a brick house. I didn't have the exact identifier for this one but I knew it was from the giant-class heavy tank platforms.

"Goods!" I shouted as I spotted the behemoth stalking forward to relieve the flaming Ultras holding down the scar.

"On it, Sergeant!" shouted Goods and battle-rattled his way to a firing position. It took seconds but you know how it is… it felt like it took all the time in the world to make it happen.

I call this "NCO burning-clock impatience." They inject you with a dose of it when they give you stripes and it infects your whole system, multiplies, and you find yourself sighing with frustration in activities ranging from targeting the thing coming to kill everyone to having to wait two seconds longer for a pack of smokes at the starport kiosk because the alien running it doesn't speak well and keeps trying to give you the expensive brand you don't have the current trade for.

I'll be honest… I didn't have all the confidence in the world for my recoilless rifle gunner at that moment. I tapped the platoon comm and shouted out for Ulysses, to get him on this rapidly developing problem about to smoke us all with a fat high-caliber tank round.

Close enough and some canister shot and that would do the trick for sure.

"Tank coming for the scar. You have an angle on it, Reaper One-Eight?" Ulysses's call sign.

Pause over the static in the comm. Yeah, the Ultras had jammers out there and in the mix.

Goods popped and fired after shouting, "Backblast area clear!"

I watched the slow-moving, to me, round arc out across the blasted wasteland we were fighting for, illuminating the burnt bodies of Ultras. Passing over ruined tanks and the cav fast-attack that had tried and died. It was a direct-fire round…

No dance. Not smart onboard AI. Nothing electronic. Just a dumb old warhead that direct-fired and either didn't… or did.

Ruck-hobo hopes were high… sorta. Believe me, we're willing to believe… it's just experience has taught us not to.

Maybe that was why Ulysses was so… amazing to me. I found myself trusting in him, trusting him to get it done, faster than I normally did of the constants, Ghost, Hauser, Hustle and Hoser.

In short… I wanted to believe in him.

The fired M67 round connected with the forward armor of the giant-class tank, exploded terrifically in thermal, and then dissipated just as quickly as it struck.

No damage done.

The rumbling, rattling, quad-jet-turbine-howling monster was still moving on us rapidly.

"Target acquired…" shouted Ulysses over the comm. "Firing!" almost as quick.

I had a sudden bad feeling because I don't want to believe.

I was on the company comm again trying to interface with the ship. M.O.M. was telling me all PDCs were now currently dry and the next reload was fifteen minutes out. I watched as Ulysses's anti-tank round, dancing and shifting as it flew across the battlefield, suddenly went haywire, climbed, and exploded harmlessly above it all.

"No effect!" shouted Ulysses over the comm. "They scrambled it."

The monster battle tank had ECM jamming capabilities of its own.

We were in big trouble now. Flamethrowers, squad suppression weapons, even the HERK rounds, weren't gonna do jack against this metal monster.

Then I heard Nether in my private comm.

"I'm close, Orion. On my way now."

CHAPTER
THIRTY-THREE

I had some choices to make quickly. Which as anyone knows is the best possible way to make important life choices.

I jest. It ain't.

There was every chance we were gonna lose this position now that the giant-class tank was involved. But I couldn't just let it go and have the Ultras push on it, clearing the way for the monster tank rolling up the scar to get direct access to the LZ.

Ulysses burned another Jackhammer on it, but again the missile scrambled and squirrelled off into the nearby ruins, exploding and sending a sudden flash of light across the gouged-out and eyeless red masonry of rubble and ruin ringing the LZ over there.

Meanwhile things were bad for Dog too. Actually worse, in fact.

I heard the captain over the comm as I got us ready to do what we needed to do.

"Dog pulling back to the second positions," said the captain matter-of-factly over the comm. "Stand by to fire final protective fires on my command."

That was indeed dire. The captain was basically declaring the last line of defense at Dog and ordering everything used in order to hold the line.

That was the very definition of *desperate*.

"Max…" I said, looking at my remaining gunner. "Shift back to original position at the entrance to the scar. Set up a field of fire there and do not let them pass no matter what happens up here. Goods, take your AG and support from there with the M67. Do not let them pass. Dog's in trouble, and we can't add to their problems until they get the line back under control. We need to buy the Old Man time here on this flank so he can handle the grease fire over there. Klutz, get back to Second. Tell Hoser he's squad leader now that Jax is down. Apprise them of Jax's situation."

Everyone boogied, leaving myself and the first sergeant.

"Gimme that bushcutter, Sar'nt," said our senior-most NCO as he held out his hands for the Savage Lone Wolf I was death-gripping. The flamethrower was dry. "One bando too if ya please, son. Don't think we're gonna have time for more'n that."

"Looks that way, First Sergeant. Nether's on his way in. So… you know… maybe, First Sergeant."

The first sergeant started thumbing slugs into the Lone Wolf. "'Member what I said, young Sar'nt. They're all last stands."

"Copy that, First Sergeant," I agreed, getting the Sturm off my back and straightening the belt to feed more smoothly once we were in it up close and personal-like. "I got some charges left if you wanna get creative…"

"Well that's good, Sar'nt Orion. Here I was thinking we were all outta tricks. Gimme."

I handed the old man the three charges I carried in the top of my assault pack. Working fast, he placed them against the ruined Rhino, near the dark gigawatt-burnt ground.

"They roll over us, Sar'nt Orion, we fire the charges on the underside of the hull and flip that beast on her back.

Whaddya say, young Sergeant? Sounds like a fun way to go out."

I didn't feel young. Not right now. But I was sure as hell scared as I heard the rumbling tank getting closer on the other side of the rise. And I was angry.

The smell of burning fuel and bodies was heavy in the air.

I moved to the side of the ruined fighting vehicle, the first sergeant taking the other side. As though we'd both silently agreed to defend from here.

I discarded the fear as there was no room in my emotional ruck to hump it much further. I'd learned to do that a long time ago. The key was getting angry about the situation. Then I could jettison the fear because I was angry and someone was gonna get some payback, regardless of what happened to me, for the perceived wrongs I was fuming about. Real or imagined. Either way, I'd get there. I started to engage the Ultras I could see out there in the dark and the charred ground. Rocking them with short blurs of outgoing lead from my beautiful Sturm.

Where have you been all my life, baby? No, no… there is no other. Looks like we're gonna be together forever.

The HERK rounds put all the shock and awesome I could muster on those wrecked elite shock troopers out there doing their best to push on a position we'd fought hard for.

I was good with that. Die trying, losers!

A grenade came in and bounced off the wrecked armored vehicle we were covering from. I shouted, "Grenade!" anyway and covered as it detonated.

It exploded, and a moment afterward the ghostly hollow voice of Nether was there and not there. Calm, collected, but I could tell he was afraid too.

"I compartmentalized the blast in another dimension," he gasped. His voice calm and hollow at the same time.

Then...

"What do we have here, Orion? Let me take a look now."

Like some doctor working after you've been hurt and know it's bad.

Then...

"Okay, hang on... I got this..."

"Hang on, First Sergeant! Nether's involved!" I screamed.

The tank fired and hit low. The tremendous round slammed into the other side of the burnt and churned dirt that had formed the small rise so many had died for. Who would've ever imagined on all the tac-plan maps we fight over this... simple scar in the world... here... where the ruined Rhinos had formed their last defensive position.

But as the first sergeant likes to say, *Here we are, boys.*

I felt like I was gonna dump myself and hurl at the same time as my guts churned from all the displaced kinetic energy traveling through the ground from the short impact distance between round and right through us.

Grunting out one giant big, "*oooFFFF!*"

One of the Ultra gun teams in the nearby ruined structures had us ranged at that moment and was peppering the wrecks. They couldn't hit us because of the Rhinos, but they could work us if we fell back even the slightest, the rest of the length of the scar into the LZ in full view of their gunsights.

Dirt fountained behind us as the gun fired and churned blackened char.

The first sergeant swore and then laughed as the blast wave from the tank shot faded.

I could barely breathe.

"Okay…" said Nether softly. "Here we go…"

The ground was shaking from the tank treads. Sure. I heard the turbines spool up as the tank suddenly surged forward to get it done with the treads or the auto guns. Clearly its intent was to run us over by ramming straight through the two demolished Rhinos.

"Here we go, Orion!" said the first sergeant and grabbed the wireless detonator. "See you on the other side if he makes it to the trucks!" Then he whooped like an old man having fun for the first time in a long time.

CHAPTER THIRTY-FOUR

The ground began to shake, wobbling back and forth in that sickly way it does when planetary quakes seem to come out of nowhere and suddenly start shaking everything sideways like it's never gonna stop.

It's that forever moment where you think... *this should end...* but then it doesn't. And you realize, compared to the titanic forces of nature, how small and insignificant you truly are as a mere biologic. The world is shaking, you are nothing.

That's what Nether's power feels like when you're close enough to a display of it.

Titans and forces of physics and energy and motion think of you as their plaything, puny little mortal.

I could see Nether as he discharged his Dark Labs powers... or curses. Depends on how you think of it.

And this is an odd way to put it, but...

As the tank surged forward, unseen on the far side of the rise, coming straight for the ruined fighting vehicles we'd fought from, intent on rolling them and going for broke on the LZ, with First Sergeant ready to blow us to kingdom come in his mad battle lust of the Saturnian Batt's code-of-battle full-blown *in it to win it...* I could see Nether... better... glowing... but shadowy.

Which makes no sense but that's how I'll describe it for you.

It was as though his shadow glowed *darker* in the night and the incoming fire. Like the darkness was real and everything else was just a dream. The drifting pop flares high above were dandelion spores of light. The noise and thunder of Dog's last defense off to the north of our line was distant music in a universe bigger than I imagined. The roar of the tank was the bellow of some all-too-real deep dragon.

Nether's power... was access to something bigger, darker, and more dangerous.

And it would be the end of the world if Top blew the charges as he laughed madly at me, daring the tank to dare his position.

I saw Nether as he was, kinda...

He was just a man. That's all. Tall. Thin. In that moment he struck me as some kind of... teacher, a scientist maybe. But never a soldier. A private military contractor.

He had a large nose. A pointy chin. His face was thin and gaunt. All in that shadow world where he was... real. Not indivisible... not *not here*... like here in the universe of the Strange Company. The world ended and the universe made room, impossibly, expanding suddenly outward and growing where it shouldn't have been. Something creaked savagely, something else groaned titanically and broke. Nether was kneeling beside me... face forward, concentrating on what was coming for us. Concentrating on what he was doing to the universe.

And then...

The ground near us... just dropped.

Savagely.

Suddenly.

To us… it felt like you instantly fell off your bed in the night. Fell into some nightmare abyss where you couldn't breathe, couldn't live, and would fall forever… and ever.

Some voice, some boy's soprano screamed and fell, calling, *There are other worlds than these!*

I think. That's how I remember it. But… it was strange. Like the Bar at the End of the Universe. And so… I'm not sure that ever happened.

Then we were jerked backward, both the first sergeant and I, as though we were going into the midnight abyss too, like dreamers dreaming in a nightmare, a powerful nightmare we couldn't escape. We slammed into the dirt below us without ever moving. Slammed into reality all of a sudden. Realizing all of it, the whole horrible reality, had been just a dream. Or another reality and *this* was… the dream?

The nightmare of falling forever and ever…

We'd maybe just dropped a foot. I don't know.

But the tank…

I could see now, sure that I'd been blind and seeing something not here in the instant before… now the tank that had been about to drive over us, crush us underneath its massive treads, it had fallen into a new chasm in the scar, just opened, just the other side of the rise where the two ruined Rhinos were now going over the edge, being dragged down into the suckhole Nether had opened up. Following the swallowed tank.

First one Rhino, blasted and shot to pieces, went over and down, undercarriage groaning and screeching, dragging the bodies of the dead Ultra Marines that had been riddled by space weapons from the *Spider*. Then the other armored fast-attack vehicle just fell over and tumbled down, dragging D-beam-blackened earth, and the charges, with it.

The Ultras who'd been in wedges to attack us, support-ing the massive monster battle tank that had been just sec-onds from rolling us, were falling into the new deep hole to join the nose-forward tank being sucked down into some type of oily black swamp down in there. Other Ultras were scrambling for the sides of the opening black pit, but the burnt dirt there was turning into soil waterfalls, and they were being tossed down whether they liked it or not to dis-appear underneath. Buried forever.

Something groaned and sucked, and then suddenly sheets of the sides of the walls collapsed, burying the Ultras and the sinking tank all at once.

The first sergeant stood, crouching, and stared into the sudden vast hole in sudden amazement. He armed the det-onators, hooted, and then shouted, "Take that, Bastards. Mess with the best, mess with my boys, and die with the rest!"

Then he fired the charges and we stumbled away from the destruction, moving fast back to the second position be-fore the nearby enemy gun team could light us up in all the rapid chaos.

Covering behind a chunk of burnt building that had been melted into that strange apocalypse glass, Nether, still shadowy and just barely visible now, was next to me, kneel-ing. Breathing heavy.

His head hung down.

"Orion…" he gasped weakly in his hollow calm. "Got a smoke?"

He sounded weak and frail.

I shook one out and lit it. Inhaled and blew smoke, get-ting it going for him. He gasped once more as he looked at the burning ember. Nether reached for it, careful not to touch my hand. Never. I watched the cigarette dance inviably between us as he started to fade from sight. As the merest of shadows that was my brother in the Strange, and friend, inhaled. The ember at the tip glowed violently and then... just like Nether, began to disappear. Fading from the universe.

"Thanks, Nether," I said to nothing, knowing he was there only on faith. The carnage hadn't stopped. But the destruction that had just befallen the Ultras hitting our line had given them pause for a moment. They'd think twice about my sector.

Off to the north, the gunfire around Dog's position was absolutely frenetic. A string of explosions tore through the night over there and I could see by their bright light that Nether was fading back to his normal invisibility. Fading from the shadow he'd become.

"I'd say it was nothing..." he gasped softly.

He sounded breathless as he faded. As he spoke.

"But that one cost me, Orion. That one... cost me."

CHAPTER THIRTY-FIVE

Imagine you're trying to make things better for the galaxy. That's Nether's story, and I guess I'll tell it here and now, though for a long time I've kept it out of the logs. But Stinkeye never reads these, and I can put some encryptions on them so he can't see this part. The Monarchs are on their way out and so Nether's sad and strange story can now be told. It's the story of a real scientist. The story of a man of science pursuing the deep truths of the universe for nothing more than the sake pure of science itself.

To know and to investigate. To appreciate the grandeur, beauty, and yes… the mystery… of it all.

There's a nobility in that, and if you're reading this and you're part of the company and we're all dead… keep that in mind. He started off with noble intentions, and along the way met the devil in the forest at midnight.

Do I think he ever intended to do what he did? No. Do I think he would become involved in the darker things the Monarchs got up to, things so dark I don't think… I don't know what to think. Except that… there are some people who sit around thinking up the unthinkable. And they don't care who gets hurt along the way as long as they get up to their… evil.

Yeah. Evil.

And no, I don't think Nether is evil. Or maybe was evil as of the reading of this account. Perhaps we're long dead. I don't know why, what events are happening that are causing me to stick this prewritten bit of company lore in, other than it must need to be told now for you to understand the whole story of what happened to the Strange Company.

So… here it is.

Nether, whose real name I have never cared to know, and that's pretty much company SOP, standard operating procedure, started off as an academic pursuing research into quantum displacement theory… specializing in volumes. This was before he ended up in the Strange. He was a big brain. So, what is quantum displacement theory… specializing in volumes? Basically it's the working of fold engine technology which the premium Monarch starfaring vessels like the Battle Spire use.

Space-fold technology is not for general consumption. It's a closely guarded secret that, should it ever fall into other hands not Monarch-friendly, could change the shape of human-controlled space. So of course, it gives the Monarchs the ability to be anywhere almost instantaneously, whereas the rest of us need to use jumps or dumb thrust to get where we're going. This can take anywhere from days, to weeks, to months, to decades. Depending on how far you need to travel.

Fold crosses all known distances instantly.

Imagine you discover an answer in the basic mystery of Quantum, which, summed up very simply is… *if you know where it is… it ain't there.*

Which is what Nether did in his former life as a scientist. He did it when no one was looking and suddenly, the galaxy changed for him.

Believe me, when he told me all this, I had to keep picking my jaw up off the floor. I mean, Nether in his current form is pretty... fantastic... others say creepy. I mean c'mon, he's a ghost after all... but that is pretty cool.

I ain't afraid o' no ghost. Stinkeye says that all the time for reasons none of us understand. Then he just swigs from his totem flask and starts humming some tune you can't follow, badly.

But in truth, Nether does bother pretty much everyone else in the company because you never know if he's around. So, when he's completely invisible he keeps to himself in his quarters as a general courtesy. At night you can kinda see him as a walking shadow. He moves around more then.

In the field no one seems to mind because chances are he's either scouting or ruining someone's day on your behalf.

The Strange as usual are shallow appreciators of freaks and cyborgs who try to keep them alive. Complaining about them in one minute, grateful they saved their bacon in the next.

There's a word for that... but it escapes me right here and now. So...

Nether wanted to identify the *there* there in quantum displacement theory... specializing in volumes. Because, as he told me once, and only once when relaying his entire tragic tale of woe, and yes I will vouch for this horror, there's always a *there* there in quantum displacement theory... specializing in volumes.

Let me explain... badly.

Nothing really ceases to be unless energy bottoms out. And quantum displacement has no energy loss signature. So whatever gets displaced... well, it goes somewhere. Generally it goes, under the guidelines of quantum displacement theory... specializing in volumes... where you want it to go. As in fold technology. So, no one much cares where because, apparently that was unknowable because again, *if you know where it is... it ain't there.*

Universe is a big place, I told Nether as he explained this. *It's either burnt or it goes somewhere.* Nether was smoking one of my cigarettes. This was during transit between worlds. He gets the one drag, then the cigarette goes somewhere... and it's not because he's smoked it or it's disintegrated at an atomic level or reduced to a null energy signature within the cosmic background of heat radiation.

No, according to Nether, it *goes somewhere*. And he wanted to know where things went and so that's why he specialized in quantum displacement theory... specializing in volumes.

When Nether interacts with something in a specifically focused manner... it begins to fade from existence. It... the smoke of the cigarette he's getting one drag of... goes somewhere else.

I asked him, later, a follow-up on this, clarifying the details because of course his tale really isn't about his weird Dark Labs ability to make volumes just cease to exist. And... his tale is not for public consumption because if it were, well then... Stinkeye would probably try and kill Nether because Stinkeye hates the Dark Labs and anyone who ever had anything to do with the modern equivalent of the slavery and involuntary servitude of wretched existence that goes on there.

And Nether most certainly did have something to do with it. And he... didn't.

But reasoning with Stinkeye on the nuances of deception and the Monarch corruption... is impossible. Stinkeye, who can be gray about his own faults and sins, has very black-and-white ideas about wrongs and injustices just like any miserable starport drunk does.

"I don't makes da rules, Little King. I just calls 'em what dey is. You owe me a drink for banishin' da evil spirits from yas bar… better pay den. Or I burn it down. Thas how it happen. Sorry the other two biz went up too. Not my fault. Dems was probably cross wit da karma of Heart of Darkness. So… it all *shaka shaka* out. In da end, Little King. Cuz… der certain is dat comin' down da line."

That's how Stinkeye would, and had on many occasions, put it whenever the company had needed to bail his skinny butt out of jail.

Stinkeye wouldn't see it any other way than the way the old miserable space war wizard drunk wanted to see it. As he saw everything… badly and himself wronged. And also, the executor of his own personal vengeance against the galaxy, whenever convenient and especially when he was in trouble.

The wrong way was always Stink's way to see things.

Stinkeye lived in a world of suspicion, jealousy, and constant intrigues always stalking the shadows to do him in.

We ignored this because he was a ridiculous paranoid and no one had ever come to collect even a bad debt off him, and he was known to lose phenomenally in Cheks parlors from here to Ceti-Vega.

So… he was just paranoid.

I thought that too, until Nether told me his tale of the Dark Labs.

I'll cut to the chase here because the tale isn't about what Nether can do, like I said. Quantum displacement theory… specializing in volumes is just what got him involved in the Dark Labs. Nether's tale, his backstory as it were, just like everyone else in the company having one, is about what it cost him to end up in our scarred and badly tattooed company, current locale on the most likely losing end of a bad contract in a violent war zone. We're very attractive that way to people with zero options.

"The there... Orion..." continued Nether as he tried to explain quantum displacement theory... specializing in volumes to me, "is that the *there* there... it's a real place. And it's tied to the black hole, the super-giant at the center of this galaxy. My work suggested this was common in every known galaxy observable," he explained in his calm ghostly hollow voice. Which I find... comforting. "That within the heart of each galaxy, the gravimetric heart that is, Orion... there's a black hole and that's... where Quantum... condenses. Anchors."

He was invisible because it was day. Even aboard the starship we were on. The *Spider*. That's another weird thing about Nether. His body, which isn't, but let's just call it that because really he's just incorporeal... his *body not body*... always synchronizes with local time wherever we're at. During the day he's invisible. Can't see him. During night he's a shadow. Even on starships where the *day or night* is implied by kept clocks and created by contrived lighting or subdued lighting. Humans need that to stay sane.

Even on starships.

It also happens on worlds where times and days are different one world to the next.

Even on those strange new worlds... *he synchronizes.*

"The universe is a strange place, Orion," is all Nether says when I ask him the why of this.

"So, what is it you actually do... when you... do your thing? For the company?" I asked as I tried to make sense of what to me... seemed pure big-brain nonsense.

I do cut to the chase, don't I?

Nether cleared his throat softly and began to speak. It's a normal voice like any other human that actually exists in real time. But it's slightly hollow. As though he's a ghost trying to imitate a human. That's the best way I can describe it.

"I can take things," continued Nether, "if I have the sufficient amount of positive quantum charge... which I think is somehow tied to the day-night rhythm of my current existence. During the day, in this form, it dials back and I turn, effectively, into a negative charge absorber. At night, I'm full up for reasons I can only hypothesize about at this time. Then... I do what I do, depending on a few factors. Which is... I take things, matter, people in this universe and bypass normal quantum interaction like the kind we use for encryption and fold travel on the high-priority Monarch ships... and I interact with the transit signal between the two points because that was the part I was researching in quantum displacement theory... specializing in volumes. You see, if encryption and fold work, which they're not supposed to, but they do anyway... then there would have to be some link. That's what I was surmising in my work. Turns out I was right, and there is a small tachyon signal not from linear space but... *super*-linear. Laymen would call it time travel but it's not really. It's quantum entanglement on a super-linear level but anchored far forward in super-linear space."

"Speak dumb ruck hobo, Nether."

"Sorry, Orion. The tachyon signal that allows super-linear fold tech, quantum... which is basically exchanging two points of information, or real-time space in the case of ships executing a spacefold... and spoiler.... It turns out you can't know where both places are... *unless* you know that they have an anchor between the two points. Then you can establish all three locations. Early quantum displacement theory... specializing in volumes had determined you could create the fold and traverse without having to know the anchor point. In fact... many just said the anchor was everywhere. Me, I wanted to know where it was specifically, Orion."

I wanted to be a scout. I'd read a book on superluminal mechanics just so I could have some solution to a busted jump drive out on an unfound world well past the frontier. A solution other than hitting it with a spanner again and again and realizing I might be marooned forever on some lost world.

So... I kinda got what he was saying. *Kinda.* The two points of quantum, the known and the unknown, could be triangulated if you followed the signal that made it possible for both points to exchange information, or volume, via the anchor point. Then... arriving at the anchor point calc you could detect, using pure mathematics, where the other point was down to the picosecond in real time.

"See, Orion, the problem for everyone in quantum displacement theory for over three hundred years had been that signal. It was undetectable until the right equipment came along. Then... it was nothing but a brief *pip.* That's what we called it, the *pip.* There was no way to track it, and we didn't need it because the folds were executing anyway, so we just thought... for want of a better phrase... the pip was just a sound effect. You know like when a round gets struck by the firing hammer and the chemicals ignite and then there's a loud *bang.*

"We thought the pip was just the *bang* that fired as a result of the quantum connection being made by the two points in space-time over radio frequency in the tachyon levels. Turns out we were wrong. See, that pip fascinated me and so I specialized in it, and lo and behold I'm the guy who figured out it wasn't a sound effect but a tachyon signal connection forward in linear space that was actually... super-linear. Do you understand the ramifications of that, Orion?"

"Sure," I lied.

Nether bought it and so he moved on and didn't tell me about *time travel* and *probability manipulation*. I did research later and figured out the ramifications made my brain hurt. But those are them.

"Do you know why the Ultras are so good at combat and anticipating what their opponents' next move is, Orion? Wanna know how the Monarchs can raid all the junk cryptos even though those accounts are supposedly quantum-encrypted? The answer is... me, Orion. I discovered how to use the tachyon entanglement signal to figure the anchor point and basically unlock unhackable encryption. That *pip*... follow it to the anchor and you can plot the interaction and find out right where the hidden point is. Meaning you can break quantum encryption and listen in on comms and if you do it right... hack people's private accounts and files. I unlocked that for the Monarchs and they... *rewarded* me for it."

And that's where Nether's story, his tale of woe and horror... actually starts. Time travel and state-level bank robbery.

"You see, Orion, there really are other worlds than these..."

Uh-oh. That confirms I did hear it when he... did his voodoo on our behalf on earlier occasions and I'd sworn it was just an earworm that surfaced in my memory from some old book I'd found rotting in a library on some back-water world.

"And I mean that in two senses… *other worlds than these.* I'll start with the first—the one you really want to hear about but didn't actually know you did until I told you. Then the part you wish you never knew… never heard about, never met me, which is… let's call it… *my trick*, okay?"

Okay, I agreed. Sure, I was just some rube making a deal he didn't understand the full dimensions of and getting taken by a crafty star carnie.

Boy was that truer than at first I ever believed. Again, I like history because of what it really is, other than facts and dates… it's knowing.

And in Monarch galactic culture… to know the truth, the actual truth, well… you feel like the one-eyed man in the kingdom of the blind. Or Stinkeye when he's got a good hand at Cheks. For once.

And he's sober enough to play it right.

But Nether's *other worlds* comment… yeah there are times since hearing all this when I wish I didn't know it in the first place.

"Once my paper was published," continued the Voodoo warrant we now called Nether, "on what I thought the *pip* really was… a tachyon signal into a super-linear anchor point within reality… life changed for me right there… and my family."

I bet.

"Representatives from the High Council of Science—the effective holy priests of Monarch Culture, keepers of the chains that keep us all shackled—they swarmed me. You see, I was just some academic working at a third-rate institu-tion, not because I hadn't gone to all the best schools, I had, but because… my wife's family were locals on Idyllwild. You know that world? I was there, invisible as far as science was concerned. In fact that's probably the best reason for how I arrived at my conclusions. I was far enough away from "science!" with an exclamation point to be able to actually do some real science for the sake of just finding things out."

No. I'd never heard of that world. Idyllwild. But there are lots of worlds I've never heard of. Universe is a big place. It's the places that don't have names that I'm interested in shucking this ruck for one day.

But those are hobo dreams if there ever were such.

"Like its name, it's… *idyllic,* Orion. Ag community. Temperate. Ironically very hospitable to human life, but massively underdeveloped. I guess someone has to supply the empire with food. Add in that it's beyond the stellar enclave of the Bright Worlds, and it's a very nice world that's little more than one massive system of local farms. Best peachberries you ever had come from that world. Juicy and big as a fist. Due to its early colonial constitution, everyone born there is a landowner at eighteen. So it really works out for the locals and keeps the Monarchs at bay.

"I met my wife at Proto Athena U in the Bright Worlds. She was studying genomics. We, ah… we had a child. She, my wife that is, wanted to be near her family after something happened to him around six months old. Our child was suddenly special needs. So we moved back home and I took a job with a lesser university teaching nothing even close to quantum displacement. The things you do for love, Orion. The things you do… did you… ever?"

I was in listening mode.

But I nodded. We all have. I hope. What a poor soul if you haven't.

In the silence between us for the moment, I lit a smoke and took the first drag. Then the cigarette danced invisibly between us and Nether grasped it and took his drag. Then we watched the cigarette and the smoke he'd exhaled… disappear from reality.

But I said nothing specific about love, or things I had done for it. Ever.

Never play Cheks with me. I'm cold as ice.

"Ah… I bet you did, Orion. I bet you did. You can't hide that, hard as you try and all to be worn out and dead inside. You're the guy who cares. Everyone knows it."

Acting. *Huzzah!*

"They offered me the world. Worlds, Orion. If only I'd consider continuing my research at one of the secret Dark Labs that didn't exist but of course we all knew about them. And some of us even dreamed… Orion, we… we even dreamt of working there, thinking the rumors were just that. Some kind of imaginary fence to keep prying eyes out.

"See, I'd written that paper on tachyon-quantum signal entanglement on Idyllwild. Just continuing my own research even though I was teaching basic quantum interaction and the history of linear engagements. Basic stuff that's not going to shake the pillars of the universe. But the *pip*… it fascinated me because everything… all of it, it *goes somewhere*, Orion, if there's not an energy deficit. And I didn't like that gap in quantum displacement that dismissed the signal noise as nothing more than a *sound effect*. There are no accidents. And my superiors, the high priests of Scientism, what the Monarchs use to silence arguments and have their way with the culture… not to get into it… but they never liked the way my research was going in the first place."

Why, I asked.

"Easy, Orion. An anchor meant someone, or something, had arranged quantum fold exchange that way so that it worked. It pointed toward design instead of random chance. And they didn't like the implications of that. It gave the pagan religions a foot in the door implying creation of some sort had taken place. Or it implied that there had once been higher cultures than the Monarchs that had engineered the basic structures of reality so they could traverse great distances. We'd be like savages finding evidence of an old road buried beneath the dust of the galaxy. It meant things that made the science-exclamation-point crowd uncomfortable. And they don't like that. They don't like questions. That's absolutely not done, you see. See… that happens, you do that and make them uncomfortable and then…

"Well, you don't get that kind of pushback so much out here on all these contracts on war-torn worlds along the frontier where a form of rugged individualism still exists. In other words, where truths of survival cannot be denied. But back in the Bright Worlds… the Monarchs have achieved, thanks to their brilliance, direction, and god-like wisdom, what no other species has ever managed. And it cannot be questioned or diminished. And the High Council of Science, the priests of the greatest heresy of truth ever foisted on humanity, well, they can't allow there to be the possibility that they were wrong about something. Or that their Scientism isn't supported by the science. Anything that says that is immediately labeled as bad information. And you know the prison sentences on the Incarceration Rings for that."

This I did know.

"So, once my wife and I had taken off to a backwater farming world, most of the academy, of which I'd once been a member in good standing… they were, well, they were just happy to see my research get good and buried. Problem is I kept working on it and eventually published it, just because I think I was bored with the life there on that perfect world. Funny thing is… that publication? It was taken down immediately and within a day a fold-capable ship arrived with emissaries of the Secret Investigations Council, and why a High Council of Science would ever need such a thing like that tells you everything, and well, they wanted to hear all about my research."

I'd never heard of that council. But yeah. It sounded like the secret police of science. And I've been in enough rodeos to know… yeah… sure that exists.

"Long story short, I got the offer every scientist dreams of… and this is the part Stinkeye might just kill me for one day… and I wish it weren't so, Orion. Because I love him. I pity him too. I have a very good idea of what was done to him. I worked at the kind of place where they did those things. And I understand in ways the rest of you don't, and won't, why he's the way he is. But one day he's gonna kill me, kill us all maybe, and that's possible because he is, and I repeat, he is the most powerful *bishop* I've ever encountered."

I stopped Nether right there and asked what a bishop was.

"Ah. Technically that's what they're called, the successful test subjects created in the Dark Labs. They're called *bishops*, Orion. In the constant Monarch games of power and control… the bishops are the ones that move truly asymmetrically on the board we've all been playing on for our entire lives and never known it. They are called other names too, but… in official work they're referred to as bishops."

"I take it you're one... of those. A bishop, Nether?"

After a short silence he simply said, "Yes. I am now, Orion. Technically. But I'll explain."

Then he resumed.

"Stinkeye will kill me, he'd kill every scientist who ever worked at any Dark Lab... if he knew, Orion, knew that what we all ever dreamed of no matter how much we silently hated the Monarchs, is the offer I'd just received because I wrote a paper theorizing what the damn tachyon signal really was. That's what we call it in science research. *The Offer*. You see, Orion, when you do science out in the open, it's always got to serve the current narrative, or... no funding and no wine and cheese faculty or staff parties. Science that doesn't... well, science that doesn't... *fit*... it gets memory-holed off to some pastoral world of long days and pleasant nights."

Nether was silent and I could tell he was considering choices long-since made. I've listened to enough stories for the company logs to know the pause. And if I was a gambler... well, I'd make some money right here.

Because Nether is invisible... I wondered if he was even there when the silence stretched out longer than it should have. But then I heard that dry, raspy breath he sometimes takes when he breathes deeply.

I know that sound. It means he's thought something through and decided on a course of action.

"Are you okay?" I asked when the silence continued.

"Yes. Better now, Orion. I can't cry. But sometimes... sometimes I wish I'd never... I'd never left the most pleasant and most boring world in human space. Never ever, Orion. Biggest mistake of my life. Our lives. Sometimes when I think back... about all the things that would happen... I just think... as a ghost... it would be nice to cry a little sometime. Grief. It's very cathartic."

He continued. They made him an offer. A big life-changing one. Come and do real science, without the control of the High Council. Pursue your research in secret with unlimited resources to its conclusion, and then, either live on the patents and grow wealthy, or continue new research, selling it all to the Monarchs to retire rich and full of life.

"You see, Orion," explained Nether, "imagine fighting with one hand behind your back every day of your life. That's what doing science is like with the High Council and their belief in their lord and savior Scientism. Every day. Discover the wrong thing, something that disagrees with the narrative, and goodbye research funding if you know what's good for you. Figure out something else if you wanna feed your family and be a member of... 'the community.' Facts become very inconvenient when you live in a totalitarian society like that, and despite all the democracy propaganda that we advocated... we really weren't.

"But here's the deal, Orion. The Monarchs, despite having organized the game we all have to play where they always win, they still need real science done because that's what maintains their monopoly. Discoveries, technology, knowledge. It's a great trick they've pulled on all of us, controlling knowledge with Scientism... but then still heavily investing in real science for the sake of science getting done and finding out the things that need to be discovered. For the sake of just knowing what's out there.

"The Monarchs still believe in that, Orion. They need that in fact.

"And that... that right there gives every real scientist... *hope*. Hope that one day you're going to get to pursue the truth, whatever your weird little field is, for the sake of the hunt, and just the pursuit of good old knowledge. Like back when humanity invented the wheel or figured out hydrodynamics. Knowing things just to know why they do it that way… and then finding practical applications for civilization to benefit. You see, despite the High Council, where the approved science gets all the love and money… everyone knows there're still places in the universe where you can do *real* science. Free of all the politics. And those places are, Orion… and here's the dirty little science secret incoming … the Dark Labs."

Internal aside I did not voice because I was acting as the listener-recorder here… but I add now. *Do you mean, Nether, the mythical Dark Labs that had supposedly mentally scarred Stinkeye to the point that he was both a human wreck and a freak of nature who could do the futuristic equivalent of "magic" and bend people's will to his?* I'd seen Stinkeye do unexplainable stuff. And there are other freaks out there. The Little Girl was one and though we never knew it for sure, we suspected somehow the Wild Thing had gotten her out of there. Out of the Dark Labs. The Wild Thing… some futurist super-soldier she could summon to go on a killing spree at the drop of a hat.

What had happened to her? I intended to ask the Seeker the next time we ran into each other. But she was busy overthrowing human space and becoming its new ruler. And I had my doubts ruck hobo was gonna get an audience with the queen or whatever title she ended up taking if the chimps didn't knife her first.

"I said no, Orion. I… said no to *The Offer*." Then Nether added, "At first. At first I said that. Then…"

That first week, as some of the biggest names of modern science came in to look at Nether's research and put him through the full third degree, taking control of the college, canceling classes, and ringing the entire campus with plain-clothes operators I'm pretty sure were Special Section Ultra Marines, he said *no.* "No to the offers of wealth beyond imagining, and it was a lot because when I went home and told her, my wife, Pers... short for *Persephone*... when I told her what they were offering us in wealth and... the chance to do what I'd always wanted... she didn't say no. I remember her mouth opened and she made this small 'o' because she knew what it all meant. She was a scientist too, you see.

"Then, I can remember it like it's happening right now... she looked over at our son... Charlie.

"You see, on that world, with her family, the peace and tranquility, he was fine there. He was coming out of what had happened to him after the vaccinations. We were doing a lot of therapies. Unregulated and downright illegal stuff. But it was working. There was a chance he was going to be... *functional* as an adult. Not... perfect... but... our son."

Nether paused. The air around us seemed to throb and empty. I can only imagine it was some type of effect coming from the emotions firing inside of him. It made me feel cold.

But I didn't shiver.

"I'm sorry, Orion," he said after a moment. "Charlie was perfect... to me. It's just... it took all that happened... for me to realize, disabled or not, he was... so perfect. I was proud of my boy, my simple beautiful boy, just the way he was.

"And so... we said *no.* To the Monarchs. You have to believe me we told them no, even though... you know, Orion.

Everything. They offered it all if I would just disappear into the Dark Labs and unlock the tachyon-quantum entanglement for them."

Silence.

I could tell, even though he wasn't saying anything, that my friend was back there, at that critical decision moment that marks us for the rest of all our days. If we let it. On that world, long ago, in those hot classrooms in front of the e-boards he'd filled with his speculatory math. Math that indicated... something fantastic.

I could tell he was there and being offered the chance all over again, to do it differently.

"They made one final offer. To Pers and me and *how how how* could we say no to this one, Orion? *How...?*"

When he said nothing, I waited, and then prompted. Sometimes I have to do that during these stories. And I've heard them all and not all of them are as nice and whatever as Nether's. Some are downright terrible. Some are crimes that seem to be unforgivable. Murders and double-crosses. Sometimes the teller of their story gets lost back there in the fatal funnel of time's decision-point moment, the choice that has made all the difference on the road less traveled that leads to the Strange Company. Eventually.

So I have learned to be silent in these titanic pauses. And then when enough time has passed... to prompt and to continue on.

"What did they offer you, Nether?"

"I'm sorry I smoke all your cigarettes, Orion. Would you?"

I did. I lit. Inhaled. Watched the smoke dance invisibly between us. Then the smoke and the cigarette fading from existence. Just like they always did.

"They said they could fix Charlie. If we accepted The Offer. Reverse the damage the vaccinations did. Fully. Gene therapy. He would be a perfect candidate... even for the Ultras, someday. No loss at what had been done to him. No... and I hate those words they used to describe everything he was, and wasn't. But none of that. They said they could do it, and they did, Orion. They did. Because we... we said... *yes*."

Again, Nether was silent for a few minutes...

Then suddenly: "Pers... wanted it. I could tell even though she didn't say anything. She blamed herself for what had happened to him like every mother does. This was a chance to make it... *right*? And so, without her ever having to make the decision, some plausible deniability survival instinct kicking in that I felt we might need someday... like a man does and is supposed to do... I made the call, Orion. I made the call and we accepted. And we went to the Dark Labs like rubes to the star carnie."

Nether's little family was whisked away that night. Gone. Disappeared. Transferred immediately to a Battle Spire diverted away from a developing hot zone.

Yeah, an entire Battle Spire. Ten thousand crew. Divisions of Ultra Marines. Fighter wings. All for some scientist who had a theory about quantum fold tech and what was really going on.

Once aboard, the Battle Spire executed a series of folds that ultimately took Nether, or who he was then, and his family, to a world not listed on the stellar charts anywhere.

"For a place that didn't exist, Orion, it was anyone's definition of paradise. Temperate and soft winds. It was an entire tropical world full of shallow seas, tiny perfect islands, and aquamarine water with few storms and few predators.

The science stations were all on individual atolls or far-flung islands and each was serviced by what the finest resorts in the universe can only dream of.

"Monarchs, actual Monarchs were there, Orion. They walked among us, and I know it's all crap and I hate them… but it's different when you're around them. You have to admit that to yourself because it's the truth whether you like it or not. They're something… other than us now, Orion. Better than us in every way."

He thought about this as I tried to test it against the one Monarch I'd known, the Seeker. It was true. Or at least it was true with her.

"But they need us, Orion. And you never feel that more than when you're working deep down under the service where the real Dark Labs do the real research miles below the surface. Doing… real science for the sake of it itself. Or at least that's what you think you're doing at first. Later, when it's far too late, it's then you realize you were doing it for them all along. Pursuing your passion the whole time so they could weaponize it. So they could maintain control. Just as they had done with the faux science of Scientism out there and passing itself off as some kind of holy writ that can't be questioned. And if you do, you get unpersoned. If you question using science as a plaything for some kind of position, an unreasonable belief really, that science is some kind of moral reasoning for why things should be done, and never questioned. It isn't. Science isn't that, Orion. Not there, in that fake paradise, not there when you're doing it. Science is a method of investigation. A series of questions and hopefully an answer that always, always raises more questions.

"But at least, doing it for them, our betters the Monarchs... at least you're *doing it*. And that's the first lie you tell yourself so you can *keep* doing it. Ignoring the re- stricted-access corridors and yeah... Orion, this is where you think less of me... the screams of torment."

I couldn't tell if he was looking at me. But I could feel Nether's gaze like a thing... well, a thing that could be felt.

I know, I'll never make a great writer no matter how much I try to spice up these logs. I got no game. I get that.

But that's what Nether's gaze, the gaze of a ghost, felt like.

"You know what's worse than screams of torment, Orion?"

I did not. Or at least, he'd caught me flat-footed, and I had no answer.

"Terror. Trust me. Those are far worse. But you ignore it all because... reasons that are really lies you're telling your- self to get to focus on your fixation. Real science. But trust me... terror... orders of magnitude worse."

He continued on after the aside of the flavors of screams one hears in medical white corridors and behind gleaming security stations and protective laser grids.

"That's when you begin to meet the prospects, Orion. Later. Once the theory and investigation portion is done and there's all kinds of... celebrations that don't really feel like that as you continue to lock down all the doubts that keep piling up at the end of the night when you can finally process... stuff you don't want to admit is happening in the periphery of your 'important' work. Looking back, looking in the eyes of the others who'd been there in that perfect paradise, doing science, the older ones who'd made their deal with the devil... that's what it seems to me now when

I think back about it, they were trying to tell me, without saying anything, what was coming next. Phase Three. That's what it's called. Weaponization is what it really means."

Nether shifted and the air around us seemed to get quieter, heavier.

"You see, Orion, first priority once you get to weaponization is to create a human interaction with the technology. Now, weaponizing humans is something we were never able to do until the Monarchs rose to power, as near as I can tell. As a species… impossible, even though all the arguments can be made the potential was there. The ability to unlock unknown human power and do it, all along, it was there. With the psy-cans… and the ability to detect them, it became… possible."

I asked for clarification on that. Psy-cans are not widely known about. And I think that was on purpose. The Monarchs have run a lot of psyop campaigns to convince the galactic population that psy-cans don't exist, or that they're some kind of witches or highly dangerous monsters that need to be destroyed. Reported. Then the Monarchs will send some hero, and many spectacuthriller plots involve these concepts, to handle all the mess.

Trust them. Those deadly psy-cans are stacked, blown up, or six feet under garlic and WholeWater never to be seen again. If this log survives current Monarch Culture, or the end of it, WholeWater was a power drink cure-all that claimed to be good for every planet's climate. It was made of the purest waters in the galaxy on Earth itself, or so the marketing campaigns claimed.

It was a status symbol to have a bottle of the purest grades of WholeWater, but there was a cheaper version, a semi-frozen canned pop you could pick up everywhere and read the back label of or watch the endlessly repeating holos where cute chicks and ripped studs excitedly told you about how the stuff cured every disease and condition across many worlds.

Then a lawyer appeared and said so many words so fast it was like listening to Hoser ride the Pig.

Stinkeye hated these auto-vendors and attacked them physically every time he ran across one, raggedly screeching they were, "Poisons da oil o' da snake!"

We had to forcibly restrain him and drag him away before the authorities got interested and came to talk to the Old Man and the first sergeant about destruction of public property and the galactic statutes that governed WholeWater dispensers specifically.

"Ah… Orion, psy-cans stands for pysionic candidates," clarified Nether in response to my question. "People from across all the worlds who have been *recruited*… that's what they tell you at first when you're working on projects in the Dark Labs and you have questions… *recruited* is the word they use… but that isn't what really happens, Orion. It's really human trafficking and there's no getting around it no matter how hard you try. Believe me… I tried."

He let his last statement hang there flatly between us. Like some kind admission of sin, a failure, something he had come in time to admit shamed him.

"Most of the candidates are kids from rough low-income worlds, or such places one finds on every world out there along the star lanes. They have been tested and identified though public-funded community centers and low-income school programs designed to give them a leg up, as having the potential to be gifted in psionics. All that charity and helping… that's a lie, Orion. What you find out eventually, whether you like it or not, is that the Monarchs, all their charity, all their good deeds, ain't that in the least. Once these children, candidates that are psionics-capable, are identified as potentially useful psy-cans, they... accidentally 'die,' or in some cases, 'disappear.' Really they're drugged to a state of near death and the parents get a funeral but that ain't the body that gets buried.

"Imagine that, Orion. Imagine the callousness it takes to not just do that, but to set up a system, a machine, that does that. And if you think that's bad... that is, believe it or not, a kind of mercy for the parents. At least they get to believe a lie for the rest of their lives that they lost a child in some terrible accidental drug interaction when the perfectly healthy child came down with a sudden illness and expired within three days. It's a tragedy. Sometimes there's... or there was... even payouts from corporations to make it all seem legit. A settlement for an accident that wasn't an accident at all. And like I said, that's merciful compared to some other ways they get ahold of the useful psy-cans. There's worse things they do.

"And remember, I just heard this in dark talk drinking parties, and there were lots of those in paradise, but they weren't any fun. But there was talk that when a psy-can was detected but wasn't useful... then they just arranged an accident and *actually* killed them. Run over by a car. Innocent bystander in a stray bullet gang shooting. Stuff like that. That's bad too. But, in the grand scheme... it ain't the worst.

"This is the worst, Orion. And yeah, in time I knew about it. And I kept working. The other way they get a child, a potential psy-can... they abduct them off the street one day and the kid just disappears into the galaxy, gone forever. Sex traffickers or homicidal maniacs are blamed but never found. But really… those kids are en route to the Dark Labs located all across the galaxy. And the parents never know. Have no fake grave, or real one, to stand over. No answers, even if the answers are just lies."

He stopped and sighed. We shared a smoke. I had half a pack left that day.

"I've thought a lot about lies, since then, Orion. I may even believe a few about my own… life. It's not bad. They're… sometimes they keep me going. So… I have complicated thoughts about lies. But… I won't lie to you… that's the cancer at the heart of all our problems. Lies. And that's why… I'm out here with the company. Tired of the lies, Orion. Damn tired of them."

In time he returned to the narrative of his tale.

"So, because of the existence of psionics we've found weaponization of new tech is faster that way, the human focus way, and it really has a better practical application in the long run if we can successfully integrate human and tech. Plus… it's more secure. In some cases, it's the only way to keep the tech out of anyone else's hands and that right there is what the Monarchs are the most concerned about. You know, we all know, they don't like to share. Sometimes in development and application, a device or system can be created to use the technology. But for the things like I do, or Stinkeye does… powers… do you really want that as a device anyone can just pick up and use? Steal and reproduce? If you're the Monarchs, no you don't, Orion. What you want is a slave. A slave that can only use this power whenever you need it used. Someone who can't be stolen, or copied. Someone who you can control because they're a slave. Theoretically and practically, the technology is far safer that way if you can keep control of the slave. Or at least that's the way Monarchs like to run things. And believe me, the ones, the bishops who have escaped… their numbers are minimal compared to the bishops out there who are still, probably even now, under the control of the Monarchs. Even at this late stage of the game. Doing their voodoo powers on behalf of our petty gods even though the galactic gig is up. My bet is they've got a big ship out there no one's ever seen that's going around collecting the bishops and icing them in coffin-sleep, or stasis chambers like we do for me, and carrying them off into the outer dark beyond human-controlled space to start a new society. That would be my bet, Orion. We'll see."

I prompted him to get back on track with his story of how he'd become Nether. A living ghost. A shadow that could make things disappear.

"All right then, Orion. Sorry… so we moved to Phase Three and that's when they started bringing in the psy-cans to test affinity. Kids, really. They were… zombies. There's no other way to put it. Obviously, they were being controlled with hyper-suggestive tranquilization drugs early on, but we found those psychotropic substances interfered with their gift potential, or what we call… *affinity*. So, eventually, to get them to interface with the potential tech we were developing… in my case, quantum destruction at the human level… they've got to come out of the narcotics that control them so we can get them into the affinity chamber and try to marry the science to the psy-can and create a bishop. I wasn't ready for that. And yeah… I was a monster, Orion. I'll never deny that."

Then he stopped.

"I can tell by the look on your face, Orion, so don't fake that you understand somehow what I was doing and how I got lost along the way. I know… right now you're wondering how I was okay with all this. And if I'm really even your friend having once done this. Stolen children, obviously… under narcotic influence… being used for science experiments. That's the stuff of monsters in every fairy tale I ever heard. There's no two ways about it and as I sometimes hear you telling Reaper, Orion… you'll say… *we have to be honest about these things*. So, here's me… being honest about things. Being honest about being… a monster."

I said nothing and nodded and wondered if Nether, on the other side of this story, was still going to be my friend. Even if I wanted him to. This was… hard to digest. I'll be honest about that. Sometimes… we have to be honest about these things.

"You start with little lies, Orion. You start with those and even though they bother you, lies like… *They're just orphans. They're being cared for better than life on the streets.* Or… this is one you reach later when you're really struggling and it's the worst, cheapest one of all… *It's for the greater good.* And… *We're doing science. That's noble. One of these with a high empath quotient…* let's say they're connected with a deadly disease… *well, they might just be able to cure large swathes of the galactic population. So it's for the greater good, right, guys?* Except you ignore the fact that none of the research anyone's doing in any of the other departments you have limited access to are doing *disease research*. So you lie and say well, maybe that goes on at other worlds than these. Other, better Dark Labs.

"Lies, Orion. You tell yourself all the lies to get where you were going all along. And then, when you can't tell yourself lies anymore because the affinity sessions are requiring less and less narcotics to get the latent psionics to take hold of the tech and perform miracles like moving things around with their minds or lighting things on fire or suddenly teleporting a few feet right or left, or even reading minds, or any of dozens of other fantastic things I saw in the two years we were there… well, the lies don't work anymore because you can hear the torment… and the terror, Orion.

"Then this happens. You realize one of your fellow scientists who was starting to not be cool with it, all the screaming… the person everyone was concerned about as being too fragile for the work… they aren't around anymore. They're just gone one day. And when you go for a run, Orion, on a beach so white and so dazzling, near waters so clear it's like looking at the beautiful alien fish below with nothing in the way, passing by that fragile colleague's bungalow in paradise… well, it's empty now. His whole family is gone. And no one ever mentions him at the morning meeting.

"And also, you think, you're passing by to check an empty bungalow… and that's surely been noted, some little voice tells you in the back of your skull. Your mind. After that, you start to see the shadows where there were none. The dark places in your architecture. You realize someone, one of the administrators, an overseer, probably a bishop, might just be reading your mind. Finding your doubts. Reporting…

"Then one day you get the talk. They lay it all out for you so there's no more lies and this is the sick part, Orion, the really sick part… you're almost relieved for a second. There are no more… lies… after that. You're just gonna do the science now, wherever it goes and believe me they tell you it's going dark, and they're not gonna lie to you about the abductions and the abuse, and yeah there's abuse because they say it makes them, the psy-cans, no longer referred to as kids or children, just psy-cans, it makes them more vulnerable to accepting their affinity-state everyone on the team is working to achieve. Are you on the team? Are you a team player? they ask, and you remember the empty bungalow and realize this is the most important question you've ever been asked in your entire life, Orion. All that science and theorem and complex math... child's play. Science and all now, but it feels like the old lies of Scientism. And you're scared to death, and you have no idea how it got this crazy. How it got here. Screams of torment... and terror. But you say yes. Yes you are, in fact, a team player."

He was silent and then he said, softly, "My only defense for becoming a monster, Orion... is them. Pers and Charlie. I had to save them, and I couldn't think of any other way to do it than go along and be a *team player*."

I didn't think he was a monster. I've never been in that situation. But I can understand what it's like to be caught in a lie. And not be able to get out.

"And as the first sergeant saith, Orion... *But here we are.*" He whispered it. So low and quiet the recorder barely caught it.

"What about Charlie?" I asked. "Did they do... what they said they were going to? Make him..."

Nether laughed. Ever seen a laughing ghost? One, you haven't seen a ghost at all. Because he's invisible. And two... it ain't funny. What we were discussing.

"They... fixed him, Orion. He was fine. Normal. *Better than,* really. What we'd always suspected because of both our high IQs, Pers's and mine... was revealed in him within weeks of the process. It was like... he just woke up and became the boy we thought we'd always wanted him to be and accepted he never would. And you know... in the long years after, during outbound flight time… I missed that little boy he was. Simple and kind and good. Innocent in his disability."

"How did…" I started to say and then stopped because it was all too much to digest regarding my friend. So I said nothing. Frankly… I was horrified. I'd always thought of Nether as a kind, tortured, sensitive soul. Something bad had happened to him. I knew that. Surely he'd overcome, escaped the Dark Labs and found the company. Found us, his brothers.

I had no idea he'd *been* the Dark Labs.

"How did it end, Orion?"

"Yeah."

Nether was silent for a moment as he made ready to tell me the last part.

But first…

"You think… differently… about me now, Orion?"

"No," I said too quickly and realized that, yeah, I did. "I won't lie to you, buddy. Yeah, it's shocking… but I'm not the guy everyone thinks I am, Nether. Just like you, just like all of us… I got my story too. We all do. And if any of you knew it…"

I trailed off and didn't finish thinking about the things that had brought me to the company.

"No, Orion," said Nether. "We wouldn't think badly of you. Maybe, if your past was all you ever were, like we all are on some level… then yeah. But that's not who we are now. I've seen you work yourself to death and almost get killed just to save them, Sergeant. They don't think of the *who* you were. They think of the Sergeant Orion they know. Whoever you were… that guy, like me, died a long time ago. That's how I can live with me. I did something. I slew the monster I'd become… and became a ghost, Orion."

"Maybe. I don't know, Nether. It's… nice to think of our past that way. But yeah, Stinkeye… he'd kill you if he knew even half of this."

"Jokes on him, Orion," Nether whispered softly. "I'm already dead."

CHAPTER THIRTY-SIX

I'd suspected that. That Nether was technically dead. I mean, I don't know how. But consider Nether. He's non-corporeal. He's as close to a real-life walking talking ghost as you're gonna get. Yes, he's a shadow, his very being reversed on a quantum level into some kind of weird negative energy he doesn't even understand… but if you were a doc checking for vitals… "He dead, boss," as Choker likes to say when someone has expired. Friendly. Or foe.

Nether's a warrant officer in the Strange Company. Take that, every other PMC in the game of big war. We got us a ghost.

And not the high-speed low-drag operator type. I mean a shadow entity that can go *boo* in ways only high explosives can dream of.

Plus, he's a great scout. Kinda. He's not great at identifying military equipment but he's good at going out and taking a look around. Sometimes.

"We lost six… kids… when we activated the quantum entanglement signal relay and magnified the pip," continued Nether with his tale. "Six of them just disappeared from existence right there. The seventh… went totally nuts. Extreme paranormal activity. She destroyed the lower labs fast where she was resting and a… containment team… was sent in and got her neutralized immediately. Then they sent in two more. Thankfully, she didn't come online until she was in the catacombs. That area's basically a high-tech dungeon we moved the psy-cans to who were developing affinity status."

Nether took a deep breath, then continued on. I heard that dry burnt paper rasp he sometimes made.

"I was already struggling that week. Struggling with what I was really doing there and constantly asking myself if I could live with this. The answer, repeatedly, was I could not. Six kids... just vaporized because of your experiment. And they were awake and fully understanding that what we were doing to them... wasn't good. They cried, Orion. And I've made a promise to never forget those."

I understood. We all have things we'd rather forget... but we make sure we don't. Because we owe it to the dead... not to.

"Anyway... the seventh turned into a real live monster. A raging and vengeful destructive monster that finally had the means to hit back. And hit back she did. Hard by the sound of the thunder and destruction coming from the lower levels of the Dark Labs. A place I never willingly went. Yes, Orion, I have a very good idea of what Stinkeye will try to do once he learns my story. And yes, he may not kill me, but he'll burn the world we're on, and maybe a few others, thinking he can get me. And maybe... yeah, maybe there *is* something he can actually do, I don't know what, that he can get me with. My state of existence... has vulnerabilities. Drain my negative charge too much and I can... get sucked into the void where the signal anchors. There is... potential... for Stinkeye to do great harm to me, and everyone around me, if he wants to go there. That's, theoretically, the really big question about him. How much potential does he really have? Does he know? Does the wreck of gambling and drinking and feeling sorry for himself prevent him from finding out... or... did he already find out and that's why he is the way he is? It would be bad for me, but like I said, de facto bad for all involved if Stinkeye went full bishop."

Full bishop. Whoa. I had to reassess my feelings on our stupid drunk space war wizard. If he had the potential to burn worlds... maybe I needed to handle him a little more carefully than I had.

Honestly, I had always considered him a bit of a charlatan and nuisance in general.

"So, as I said..." continued Nether, "I was struggling, Orion, in those last days. Pers was falling apart right in front of me. She saw the toll it was taking on me. One night... I almost broke down and told her what was really going on... whispering it to her as we lay there in the dark, late in the night. The warm winds of that tropical world blowing through the palms out there on the sand. She told me to stop. Stop whispering. Stop telling. She didn't want to know anymore. She couldn't live with... the knowledge of what I knew. What it had cost to have Charlie whole. And I suspected... she couldn't live with me for long."

"What would she have done?" I asked. "Gone back to Idyllwild?"

Nether was silent for a long moment.

"Orion, you have a way of cutting right to the heart of the matter. Yes. I think she had that in her hip pocket. I think she was waiting for the moment to try. Thinking she could just take Charlie and leave. And no, I never doubted her love, except... how can you love someone who was doing what I was... involved... in? I don't know. I just... don't know, Orion. So, I think yes, I think she thought she could escape. Which she never would have. I had listened to enough gossip and seen the looks of the older scientists, inmates really, to know we were never leaving that world. One of them even took me aside and told me as much. Told me to stop dreaming of things that were never going to happen."

"What happened?" I prompted when another pause had come to stay for too long as Nether pondered that long-ago straight talk that laid out the trap he was stuck in back there. It must have seemed strange from an outside perspective, to see me, sitting in that dark stores room deep in the *Spider*. Alone and talking to a disembodied voice who smoked my cigarettes and told me about the dark parts of the universe people never really want to know about. No matter how much they think they do.

"Before I tell you what really happened, Orion, let me tell you where it goes. The tachyon-quantum entanglement I discovered. Where all my research led. What the whole mess was about in the first place. Indulge a haunt who was once an okay scientist."

I said nothing, sure I wasn't going to like what I was about to hear. Determined to hear it nonetheless.

"It goes to the end of everything, Orion. It's a dark place at the end of super-linear existence. Dark like… ancient pagan descriptions of Hell. It's some kind of deep well in the fabric of existence. That's what I know it is through measurement and calculations. That's what the scientific method tells me. But it's more than that. And here's where I stop being a scientist, a discoverer, whatever… and become a survivor of some great starship wreck. Some poor soul who barely escaped with his life and came back horribly scarred. Forever. It's a vast suffering well of… torment, and… there are things down in there, Orion… not just human… suffering. But aliens like we've never met. I've seen them in the shadows and dark as the well, like some vast hungry black hole, sucks everything, and I mean everything, matter, time, light, energy, emotions, memories… everything… down into it. When I use my powers here with the company… my voodoo on the company's behalf… I'm there too as the well begins to form around the corners of my vision. I can see it like I'm there and if I use my power too much… I'm there at the edge of the howling hurricane well and this world, where the company is fighting, *that's* the ghost world. *You're* the shadows if I go too far. Being sucked into the well, borrowing from the entanglement to displace the thing I'm focusing on, the more I do it the more it requires of reality around me. And here's where the real danger is… it's almost grabbed me before when I went too far with my powers. Sucked me into that well where dark titans slither and moan in eternal terror down in the deep howling darknesses below.

"Remember that firefight on Lost Stars? The one where Dog walked into that ambush and couldn't get out of the crossfire? When the air assets started coming in and making gun runs and I… grabbed… that one. Opened up that well… What did Dog call it when they got a good look at it right there in the middle of the ambush they were getting murdered on… dark void. Yeah, that's what it is, Orion… except it really isn't. It's really, what I do, more like opening up a gate to everything, and then tapping the raw power there. The last power of everything that was ever real. So, that cost me a lot to do that time to get Dog out of it… I'm still not sure of everything I can do since I really am a non-psy, but still entangled myself… but I opened a gate right in front of the ground attack fighter coming in for Dog, right before the captain was gonna push from the flanks and try to get the wounded lying out there in the sand, off the X. Doc was covering them by himself right then. Remember, he got killed before the captain came in with the QRF. Doc was a good medic."

Doc was the best we ever had.

"So, when I opened that gate, it was a big cost from the tachyon-quantum entanglement, and the force inside the well was so powerful and I was so weak, it was like fighting a hurricane to shut it off. I..."

He trailed off for a moment.

"It almost killed you, didn't it, Nether?"

He thought about that for a moment. Nether is very thoughtful. Nothing he speaks is ever unconsidered. But then again, he spends most of his time by himself due to the fact he innately bothers most people. So he has a lot of time to think.

"No, Orion. I don't think that's possible because technically I'm no longer a living thing. Death... would be... *not* the worst outcome. No... there are worse. I think if the void gets me, I'm going down there with all those... let's just say they're... things in the dark. The Dark Titans. But... I have a feeling, Orion, that I might not be able to shut that void, the tachyon-entanglement gate... off sometime if I deplete my negative charge too much. If that happens, given enough time, then... and I'm guessing here... the gate would manifest in real time and become permanent. Maybe."

"Then what would happened?" I asked.

"Theoretically, over time, it would eat the whole universe. Given time, Orion. Given time the outcome would be very bad. I hope not... but it has to be considered given the data I have so far. People don't want things to happen that the data suggests will happen. They see the sugar, the vanilla, the flour and eggs and they think the universe is baking them a lasagna because that's what they want. But that's not what's happening. The universe is baking you a cake. You're going to get cake. Be prepared for cake. So yeah... if I deplete my negative entanglement charge, there's every possibility I'll open a permanent gate to that well and it will... given time... eat the universe. Sorry."

Yes. My mouth was in fact hanging open.

"So... I can't do that, Orion. I shouldn't do that. I can't ever let that happen. But sometimes..."

I knew.

"Sometimes when we're in it, when you guys are... the company... and it's get your bacon out of the grease fire, Orion. Sometimes I'll creep a little too close to too far."

Because we're your brothers, I didn't say. We're all you've got left even if most of us are bothered by your... presence.

"How did you escape?" I asked.

"While the containment team was busy down in the catacombs, I executed a plan that was... foolish, to say the least. But it was our only way out. Our only hope for Charlie. The labs had a low-functioning empath in there that was capable of dimensional fold shift. They were still attempting to figure out the application because there were problems. Of course... there are always problems, Orion. I retrieved Victor, that was his name, from his cell and gave him a picture of my family. Pers and Charlie from a day at the fair back on Idyllwild. A good day. Strong emotional imprint which is what Victor needed. Then I asked Victor to begin his fold calculations chant. He was a high-functioning autistic. He could *chant* complexity theorems and that allowed him to access his ability to... for want of a better word, Orion... to teleport individuals across vast differences in space. As he did this, I called Pers and told her to retrieve an envelope I'd left in my study for her. She did."

Nether stopped.

I said nothing.

"She asked me... why there were new forged identities inside the envelope, Orion. For her and Charlie. 'Pers...' I told her. 'You're going home now. You and Charlie both. You're getting out of here. I don't know if we'll ever see each other again, darling... but I'm making it right now. Okay... I'm making it right.'

"Little Victor chanted and I could see he was beginning to stim as he held their pictures... indicating fold transference was imminent. He was so powerful he could pick them up and place them on any world I chose if I gave him the proper coordinates. I placed a mem-stick in his rapidly opening and closing hand. A mem-stick for Idyllwild. A plot for her father's farm. On a hill with a tree, where we would take Charlie and picnic under. When we were happy. When we had everything we ever really needed. That's where they were going, Orion."

I swallowed hard. You can hear it on the audio I recorded for the log. I have heard stories. And I have heard stories that moved me. This was one of them.

"That's how the trick worked, Orion. Once Victor calc'd the chant that opened the fold window in his mind, visualizing the individuals to be flung across time and space, we gave him a mem-stick and it... impossibly... it just happened."

Nether stood. I could feel it. He walked a bit and then he turned, and I could barely see his shadow.

"Orion, the universe is a strange place. Some dead old writer once wrote, '*There are more things in heaven and earth,*

Horatio, than are dreamt of in your philosophy.' I looked at their pictures, Charlie, Pers smiling, both of them in Victor's trembling hand. The hand of a boy… It was vibrating so hard as he simply exchanged places in the universe like someone moving a book from this shelf… to that shelf.

"'Okay,' Pers said just before it happened. Her voice trembling, Orion. Like she was both afraid and excited. Like… like… like when I asked her to marry me. The instructions I'd left told her to become someone new now. Get lost back on Idyllwild. Forget me.

"Then… I said, 'I love you, Pers. I'm sorry I took you to hell. I'm…'

"But she was already gone, Orion."

I had no words for Nether. But I had to say something. So I returned to the story. To hear it. To know the last of it. Sure I'd just heard the worst of it. In every story of the Strange Company… there is a broken heart. Even if that's not what the story is really about as the teller sees it, tells it, even though, in my opinion, it really is.

"So how did you escape… the Dark Labs, Nether?"

Nether cleared his throat. I remembered him saying he wished he could cry. Sometimes. But because he does not exist… he could not.

"I went to my lab, activated the entanglement generator we were using to fire the tachyon gate… and took hold of the transfers the psy-cans used to attempt to gain affinity with the technology."

"What were you hoping would happen, Nether?" I asked, having a pretty good idea I knew what he was thinking. At the time.

"Honestly, Orion… I was thinking I'd blow the whole lab to high heaven. I'd slaved in the reactor and the battery arrays so we could have unlimited access to the power grid for affinity entanglement. I was going to open the well and see how much energy we could feed in before an explosion occurred. The facility would be destroyed and Pers and Charlie's escape would be covered in the aftermath. No one would survive."

"But you ended up... getting the power?"

"Not my intention, Orion. I knew the signal went somewhere... I figured I'd go there too and try to save those children we used. If that was even possible. But I was pretty sure I was going to blow the whole facility sky-high. Instead... it changed me in one savage instant that felt like forever. I shifted several times between being real and suddenly... unreal. My mind fractured and was rebuilt at least... five or six times... that's what it felt like. *Then* the whole facility blew, detonating and burning half the world in the process."

Half the world!

"Nuclear?"

"Sure felt like it. Several times over in fact. But I'd already gone shadow in the seconds before the explosion. So... I got the rare privilege of watching a nuclear explosion, orders of magnitude beyond a D- or even a G-beam strike... *from ground zero*. I'm the only human being, Orion, to ever stand in the heart of a star and watch it kill ten thousand people all at once."

I took a deep breath, lit a smoke, and we did our dance routine.

Then...

"For weeks I wandered the destruction and mentally destroyed myself, unable to process what had happened. In time... I came back to myself. When the cruisers arrived and set down to secure the site, I got aboard one since I'm invisible, or a shadow, and slipped off-world. I got lost in the galaxy, and in time, I found the company."

The ship was silent. Night was coming on. Nether was slowly becoming more and more of a shadow as he sat down next to me.

"And Charlie and Persephone?" I asked.

"They lived a long life, Orion. She did everything I told her to do. Changed her name. In time... she married a farmer. Charlie became a farmer too and ran for local government. He was quite prosperous and by the time he died, never having left Idyllwild, which was what I told Pers she had to do otherwise biometric scans on starships would identify them, but by the time Charlie passed as a very old man he had fourteen grandchildren. All of them are... beautiful, and strong, and so wise, Orion. He made that world a better place. He conserved the good and improved the lives of his people. That was more... well, it was just more, Orion. Let's leave it... there."

"Did you ever go back?" I asked.

Nether fell silent. Then...

"Orion, I have walked those fields near their farms every day in my dreams. But no, I never went back. How could I explain what I'd become to them? How could I... be forgiven... for what I'd done? Pers and Charlie are long gone now. So, it doesn't matter."

Because of starflight and coffin-sleep, Nether's story is not unusual. Leave a world and spend sometimes years in cryo, and all the people you once knew, the ones you once loved, sometimes they're old and dead by the time a decade of your real-time life has passed out here in starflight between the worlds.

This is often referred to as *The Curse in our Stars*. I have no idea why. Other than the obvious one of being the last man standing of all you ever knew.

We all, in Strange, have experienced this on some level.

"I eventually came to the company, Orion, and I know, from talking to other freaks like me... because we do, Orion, we talk and you... *normies*... you know nothing of what we speak. But I'll tell you this... it's known among the psy-cans... the ones who see glimpses of what may be the future... of which I am barely a member of this unlucky tribe, and not really one at all if they knew this story... it's known that Strange Company... is integral in the destruction of the Monarchs, Orion. And that's what I'm here for."

Well, he'd never told me that before.

"Why, Nether? For revenge? Or forgiveness?"

"Neither, Orion. If there is such a thing, I don't think being forgiven means anything if you've got to work it off somehow. If it happens... then I'll take it as the gift I don't deserve because I know exactly what I did. Once. When I was a monster. No, Orion... I'm here to make sure Strange finishes the Monarchs and that there are no Dark Labs ever again. I'm here to make sure the best possible future... is the one that happens."

I thought about that. Considered the implications.

"It looks like that's about to happen, Nether."

"Well, let's make sure it does, Orion. Then... we'll see about what comes next."

"Which would be?"

"I don't know, Orion. I'm not a quitter. But I can't open that portal that consumes the universe inside me. It's hungry, Orion. It's a place that's never ever satisfied. That's what

I've gathered in my close encounters with it. My data. So, I can't let that happen."

"Okay Nether, so you can't die, and you can't screw up and suck the universe into a hungry void cookie monster."

Nether laughed at that.

"Never thought about it… but yeah. Can't let the cookie monster get the universe. That's my other quest."

"Other quest…?"

"Yeah. When the Monarchs are done… I want to help science, real science, a method of investigation, find its way back from where it got hijacked off to a long time ago when humanity lost their way and decided, or at least a portion of them did, that they were petty gods of some sort who could make it their plaything."

I nodded my head at that. That would be… something. The truth. Just like all the real history I was always looking for in the cracks and corners of a stellar civilization falling apart. Falling into a Dark Age.

"I can get behind that, Nether. If I'm still there, on the other side of a bunch of dead gods… then I'll help you, my friend. We'll do some science. Real science."

"I'd like that, Orion. You know… when I told her I loved… love her… she was so frightened, so terrified about what I'd gotten us into… and Charlie who was… oh she loved him, Orion. Pers loved my boy so much. He was the apple of her eye and she just wanted… she just wanted the best for her beautiful baby boy. Our boy. But I said she was breathless and scared like when I'd asked her… to marry me… at the last. She wanted to go, Orion. She wanted to leave me."

The implications of it swallowed us both and for a moment there was just silence because how could there be anything else.

"She was proud of what you were doing for them, Nether," I told him. "That you were giving them their life back. Freedom. She was just scared. Freedom's dangerous and scary. It was everything she wanted. Just like when you asked her to marry you. Which was also everything she wanted."

He thought about that for a moment.

"Do you think so, Orion?"

I don't know.

"I do, Nether. I've been there. That's how mothers are. Women. Lovers. They're so scared, and so brave at the same time. We'd be lost without them, brother. She was grateful. Excited. She was free."

He rasped in the silence, and I think that's as close as he could get to a sob, being not there and all. Technically.

"I know, Orion. It's just… sometimes… I know I'm a ghost. That world burned and if she ever did the digging, she'd know everyone on it died. Including me. I'm a ghost now, but she never knew that. I couldn't go back. Then the day came I found she'd married someone else, eventually, Orion… that was when I really became a ghost. More than that blast and entanglement with the quantum tachyon anchor ever did. I became a ghost haunting the memories of what… once was… us."

He rasped over and over in the silence.

I know. I know, Nether. I know.

CHAPTER
THIRTY-SEVEN

The final push of the Ultra Marines as the premier fighters humanity had ever produced, would come at just after oh-three-hundred local time that dark morning of smoke and fire above our heads. Spartans. Roman legionnaires. Rangers. The Ultras were going over the hill to join the lost and the dead of the greatest fighting forces we'd ever produced as a species.

Their fault didn't lie in their martial prowess or iron will to prepare, or constant endless striving to be the best fighting men… it lay in their prideful masters gaming games of power and intrigue and always for self-interest.

But in the end, as best the Ultras could, they'd shot down as many of their petty ruling gods as they could so they would not be distracted in this, their last moments on the scene of history.

The Ultra Marines who'd be coming for us spent the rest of the night out there in the dark, after making some of the most aggressive probes I've ever experienced in my whole life as a paid soldier, pushing their infantry and armor forward and shelling us hard, trying to expose the cracks and find the flaws.

And yeah… our PDCs went bone-dry eventually. Then the *Spider*'s shields got pounded into oblivion by ranging arty and missile strikes coming at us from across the ruins of the city. The dorsal shields that protected the upper hull, the bridge, the main guns, and the engineering decks, failed and the number five and six shield generators were swapped out via the panels on the flight deck and redirected to cover the top of the ship. Ablating the incoming missiles and deflecting as much fire as they could while they held.

The Ultras, stalking out there in the dark, via what drones we could get up showed us massive amounts of their shock infantry and a fair amount of surviving heavy and medium armor pushing forward now.

This was it. This was the big push. When dawn cracked the red and green horizon of Marsantyium, there would be only one victor.

And I was determined it would be us. Or I wouldn't be there to see it.

Preacher came by to check on us. There was a lull in the fighting and the old man with wispy gray hair, strapping two sidearms and wrapped in an old worn coat came to move among us and say encouraging things.

I guess.

"You got that look in your eye, Orion," said Preacher as he made ready to move on to the next group of grunts on the line getting ready to take a punch in the face. Then give twice as hard as they got.

"What look?" I said and wished he'd get on to going off somewhere else.

He was silent. A night wind came and moved smoke and fog around across the black charred dirt we'd fight for in the hours that remained of night. And of us.

Then… "That *eternity's calling* look, Sergeant."

I said nothing.

He bent down on one knee, grunting a little as he did so. I was doing maintenance on the Sturm. Amazed at its mechanical perfection.

"I've been around long enough to have seen it many times, and had it my share of it along the way, Orion. Anything you wanna talk about..." he said, trailing off. Seeing the look in my eye.

He smiled and lowered his head. Mumbling something to himself.

"You won't fail, Sergeant."

And then he was gone.

A few moments later both of the massive eight-hundred-millimeter mammoth mech arty tanks the Ultras called Scylla and Charybdis opened fire. You could hear the shells ripping atmo, testing their range. Whistling as they came in. They were almost within range.

"That's gonna hurt," noted Punch sullenly as we hunkered down and tried not to get hit by falling indirect fire.

"Understatement of the year, man!" shouted Choker who for some reason had begun to lose it in the interim between actions.

"Eat your bar and calm your plates, Choke! It's gonna get fun shortly. Don't wanna miss the fun, do you?"

"Don't wanna, Sar'nt!" screamed Choker, practically hysterical now. "I'll hurl it up."

"Wasn't a request, Choke. There are things in there that'll calm you down right now and help you deal. Do it now, or Punch is gonna make it happen, Choke."

Punch smiled indicating he would love this.

"Who's laughing now, loser?" Punch grunted. He cracked his knuckles.

Choker ate but he didn't like it and he made a retching noise. Incoming rounds rocked the ground all around us. Then the big eight-hundred gun, one of them at least, opened fire again way out across the city.

The shell screamed in and whistled overhead. Then exploded tremendously to the rear.

It missed us.

But it had been like some thunderbolt that was really an earthquake had just passed right over our heads. It made it clear you did not want to be anywhere near the impact point of ground zero when it did manage to land a round on target.

"Wish they'd just hurry up and get it on," mumbled Wolfy, who was covered under a giant burnt black rock nearby that had just enough space for him to squeeze in under.

Overhead, three ground-attack Whirlwind Alpha 15s, old-school fighters with jet engines and two GAU-88s apiece, swept in. The lead fighter opened up on something down over our line while the other two launched micro-missiles and blew their flares to cover the attack and strike secondary targets. Enemy anti-air reached up and tried to tag the strike, but the A-15s streaked off, their engines howling to full throttle as explosions rumbled and blossomed.

"Did they hit it?" whimpered Choker as he ate his protein bar and made more retching noises.

"Dunno," said Punch, who'd popped his head out of our new covered fighting position to watch the fighters work. "But that Big Bertha shut the hell up so maybe they gave 'em something to think about. Follow-on strike should be here in a few."

This went on for hours.

Which wasn't fun because it felt more like waiting than fighting. The Ultras kept shelling Heartbreak and slowly pushing forward for an encirclement from at least half the compass. What remaining air assets the *insurrectionistas* had up were out there working forward of the advancing line of battle and trying to shoot up whatever was getting pushed on us forward before it got forward.

The last pilot to make the final gun run was some chick. I listened to her coming in, interfacing with Cook over the company comm. Our pysop warrant officer was acting as our fire support officer now that the FIST in Dog had been killed an hour ago.

Loady was a great fister. But he took chances and put himself too far forward at times just to get the drop right for his guys. Now he'd finally paid for the risks he'd taken all along the way to here.

The chick close air support combat pilot alerted us she was setting up to make the final gun run on a battalion-sized element of Ultra infantry supporting a Defense Destroyer 88 mobile gun platform coming through the streets just ahead.

We were all hoping she hit it because that thing was gonna be a real problem with its quads laying down suppressive while the Ultras advanced.

If the destroyer made it to line-of-sight fire engagement windows on the LZ... plainly put, that thing and its quad eighty-eights could open up a clear and brutal route onto the LZ and the *Spider* laying anti-personnel flak fire the whole way in.

There were few direct solutions against self-propelled ground artillery like that. So... go get 'em, girl. The company appreciates your efforts on our behalf.

Insurrection command had identified the incoming Defense Destroyer 88 as the last priority target they could nail before air assets were off the board for the rest of the operation. Munitions and fuel were low. Several pilots had gone in with no clear sign of ejection. A few were out there escaping and evading for their lives.

It would be a ground war going forward.

"Nightmare on station…" she called out in a business-like fashion over the company comm. I was listening to the traffic between her and the chief, who had gone forward to Dog to spot the strike as best he could without getting domed by a sniper.

Regarding Dog Platoon, sister of Reaper and Ghost… I was hearing there wasn't much left of them.

The captain had ordered Third Squad Reaper under Hauser redeployed from supporting First and Second Reaper to taking up the slack in Dog now that their line wasn't just thin… it had outright holes in it.

High-ex, mines, and the last of our defensive sprays had been laid down to cover what could be covered. But it wasn't enough.

"Copy, Nightmare… this is the Doctor with eyes on target… drones painting now, Honey. Taking anti-drone fire so lock your target and make your strike, Nightmare."

"Turning base to approach…" said the pilot, still doing her job as though she were flying commercial traffic out to some orbital station and it was just another run in a very long night. "Guns hot… engaging engaging engaging…" There was a pause. "Engaging again…" Then… "Engaging one more time, Doctor… I'm dry. Nightmare off station. Enjoy what's left, ground pounders, and smoke 'em if you got 'em… I sure did. Nightmare out and off station."

The display of firing from Nightmare's ground attack fighter had been old-school shock and awesome. And it did us good to see it.

She'd opened up with long drags of bright fire from twin GAU-88s on track-and-engage mode. I'd seen streams of the system in use. It was a phenomenal tank and infantry killer. The onboard targeting AI painted the infantry clusters and then the Whirlwind A-15 slowed to just above stall speed as both guns began to burp and wipe out as many ground targets, infantry on foot, and light skinned vehicles as possible. At the same time, small bomblets streaked away from the underside of the aircraft on smart mode and angled their approach to the troops on the ground. Bomblets that detected live infantry or moving targets within a fifteen-meter radius of insert drop, then detonated like an omni-claymore would when emplaced in the defensives. Bomblets that didn't detect thermal signatures within that fifteen-foot radius just landed and didn't detonate. Instead, they'd wait for inevitable medics or the next enemy force to push on that lane.

They were the gift that kept on giving.

While this was all going on, the chick pilot, callsign Nightmare, worked the firing solutions on the missile packs and then dumped packets of anti-armor micro-missiles onto the main target until she'd gotten her kill.

I was sure there was nothing left when the moaning howl of her engines switched over to pure thunder as they spooled up to ear-splitting shock waves and she went to full afterburners, climbing straight up and out of the battlefield.

Like some angel not meant for grunts, but... adored nonetheless.

She was probably punching seven thousand feet by the time she sent her last traffic telling Cook she was off-station.

And that, *"Enjoy what's left, ground pounders, and smoke 'em if you got 'em… I sure did. Nightmare out."*

I had… feelings about her. Some pilot I'd never meet. But… you know… a girl.

I could tell every one of us had thoughts about her along those lines with small riffs particular to the individual as we waited for Ultra artillery to come at us again in the silence that had fallen over the LZ after she'd dusted their latest push on our line.

"She sounds nice," said Punch in the silence when the jet was gone into the upper atmosphere beyond the smoke and clouds and the last of the drifting, falling artillery flares.

Yeah. I bet.

Wolfy said something but his face was in the dirt and all I heard was a, *"Thounds hawwwtth."*

Choker finally threw up and said, "See? Told ya."

But he'd calmed down a little. I could work with that. I could keep him alive, I told myself like it was a promise, or a challenge, or maybe something I should've asked Preacher for.

Chimp mobile artillery kept the Ultras busy for the last hour before the final attack began against us. The chimps, out there beyond our lines, were hauling their field guns through the streets by hand and direct firing on any Ultra elements they could engage on those dark and dusky ruined lanes of fading monuments being ground to powdered dust and cracked marble.

They were getting murdered too.

But their attacks were breaking up the impending focus on LZ Heartbreak and that was buying us something.

A little less fire.

Ten less feet advanced.

Ten seconds more on the objective.

I had no idea, but like some faithful saver of investments... I hoped it was doing something for the rainy day coming my way.

At that point, as a tactician, and a minor one at that, I had to give props to both sides. The monkeys were either *utterly nuts*, or just about the bravest warriors I'd ever seen. They'd push on the Ultras firing cannon shot from their guns and then develop Bronze Age skirmishes right on top of the Ultras they managed to find. The chimps would get rocked by the Ultras, who held their cool, wasted the surprise attacks, then continued their push toward our LZ like some relentless and inevitable force that could not be denied.

Both sides were in it to win it on this one.

The chimps were like wild animals that would do anything to drag down their opponents even if it meant their own deaths.

The Ultras were the zenith of trained soldiers who could not be pushed off their objective to destroy us and take the LZ. Failure was not an option for them. Neither was defeat. The only outcome the Ultra Marines would accept was death. But even then, they'd smile and croak, *"Take that, losers,"* as they detted their own grenades while you double-tap-stabbed them at close quarters.

But... *we were being worn down slowly.* Bit by bit. And if I were their commander... I have to be honest about the situation I find myself in right here and right now... my bet... he was thinking he had this now. That we were outta PDC fire, troops, and ammo. We were worn down. The PDCs, total game-changers, were clearly dry. The shields were collapsing. The only thing standing between him and victory was two badly mauled platoons of dug-in infantry on the LZ.

The Ultras had faced incredible odds in legendary battles.

That commander had to have known we were gonna make 'em pay with our gun-team-covered kill zones and the endless amount of AT we seemed to still have. He had to have known he was gonna have to pay the price of the ticket to take the ride.

But... and this is the part where I have to be honest... we were two ravaged platoons at best. I don't count Ghost because they aren't even at platoon strength, and they don't do stand-up fights. Or at least they don't prefer to. Which is what this was gonna be. Ghost would be sniping, ambushing, and going after targets of opportunity asymmetrically from the shadows out there in the once-grand and now-ravaged-and-shot-to-hell buildings crumbling around the burnt black LZ.

The LZ had two platoons. Pretty beat-up platoons in fact. So, consider this...

The drones we could get up, before they were shot down, and the tac-feed from *Elektra* which was currently under fire from *Red Dragon* and getting slammed by ECM and counter-ECM, indicated we were facing upwards of five battalions of Ultras. Three infantry. Two armor companies. And some other scattered elements out there, but everything moving right at us.

When we got a look at the feed from *Elektra*, Choker screamed and shouted, "Well, that's just great. Why don't we just go ahead and bury ourselves right now and save them the trouble!"

A platoon is forty men.

We didn't even have that per platoon. We had KIAs and wounded that had been evacked out or were on the deck of the *Spider*.

A battalion… and these were the buried Ultra battalions, the fresh highly motivated infantry that had buried themselves alive to be ready for this final moment to take advantage of our total depletion and significant reduction in combat effectiveness, a brilliant tactic by the way, mad props to our enemies for that one, those battalions now had roughly eight hundred fresh Ultras each to commit to the taking of the LZ.

An Ultra is worth at least three soldiers.

They had three battalions of those guys locked, loaded, and ready to go on us.

Plus, two more armor battalions of tanks and light scout mechs, each with a platoon of cav… to support and anchor the final push on our position.

Two understrength platoons versus those numbers aren't going to do it.

Those aren't even odds.

The artillery had been silent for fifteen minutes when the first Ultra gun teams began to fire out there in the darkness ahead. Then the first tanks appeared as smoke popped and covered their advance. Star shells came out of their launchers and arched over our heads, painting us for visual and thermal engagement.

What had Choker said about us just digging a grave and jumping in…?

I pushed that away. If this position was going to be my grave, then not a few of those Ultras were gonna join me for all eternity.

One of the eight-hundred-millimeter mechs opened fire far away, and this time made a direct hit right against the *Spider*'s flanking number four shield. The round exploded and the shield absorbed the tremendous kinetic blow.

For now.

"Okay, Strange... here they come," I said over the comm. And I didn't sound brave. But, to my credit, I didn't sound scared.

"Bad copy, Sar'nt," said Punch. "Say again..."

I swore and tried to sound a little more pissed this time.

Then the captain, still in command of Dog on our left, broke in over the traffic.

"*Net call net call net call...* All elements, this is Warlord. Be advised, all elements... mechs coming out. Link up and commence the attack."

Calm. Cool. Collected. The kinda combat leader you'd always hoped for. The kind you knew you'd never be.

Or, as Punch said after a war whoop, "That's how ya do it, boys!"

CHAPTER THIRTY-EIGHT

The first mech to come out of the *Spider*'s rear cargo and hangar deck was the eighty-ton Ogre commanded by Captain Max himself.

It was even more gargantuan than at first I'd thought it was as it moved away from the ship. Impressive is an understatement and as it went out to do battle, for a moment, I felt like we had a real chance.

I wanted to get into the fight right now as Punch did every moment of his life.

The ground shook as both Reaper and Dog switched over to their new missions. We weren't gonna defend… we were gonna attack. Undermanned, it was the only way to hold the LZ. We didn't have the forces to hold a line. Instead, we were going to support the mechs who were going right into the teeth of the enemy in hopes of disrupting the attack from the enemy. No way with three battalions of Ultra shock troopers whose sole mission was to roll heavily defended positions, supported by two tank and light mech battalions, were they gonna get held off by some private military contractor light infantry too stupid to be anywhere else.

We'd push the push. It was unexpected. It was a plan. A few hours and maybe a lifetime of smokes and coffee in the dark would let us know if it was worth a damn.

If it was our *we happy few* moment.

The only thing we had going for us besides the multi-ton killing machines coming out and surprising the hell out of the enemy was that no one had air support now. Ours was dry and on its way back up the well, or out to guerrilla airstrips in the jungle to reload whatever they had and maybe make it back in time to drop some ordnance on our corpses.

For or against, it would make no difference in two hours. Haymaker would be swinging on their high command.

Every moment M.O.M. was updating with news of another arrival on the two rear LZs.

"Fifteenth Pavonian mech down on the LZ. Commander signals clear and moving to the line of departure, dears. *Star of Aquaria* medium lifter dusting off…"

During the briefing we'd been told not to expect air support after the mechs came out. Insurrection air support, along with the Phantom heavy gunship on suborbital station, would… *clean* the LZ if we managed to lose it. Last-resort option was a denial-of-access strike. Once the captain called in *"Broken Arrow"* all air assets would hit the LZ in one last effort to deny the Ultras taking it.

They would fire inside the perimeter. The Phantom dropship carried enough ordnance to kill a medium-sized city. We would die.

At just after three that morning, as the Ultras pushed and our mechs finally came out to play, two thirds of the Haymaker force was down on the rear LZs and heading to their first positions to strike the Ultra High Command to the rear.

We had no choice but to attack now. We were hoping this was a maneuver the Ultras couldn't have possibly seen coming and one we hoped would destabilize their entire assault before it coordinated and massed from all points of the compass east of our position on LZ Heartbreak. If we failed out there, whoever survived could fall back and try to hold the LZ until the captain called Broken Arrow.

So, we had that to look forward to.

When the plan had been made to strike first and punch the incoming Ultras' face in the attack, there was a way out for Strange if we failed and had to declare *Broken Arrow*. We'd dust off just before the Phantom dropped all her ordnance on Heartbreak. But by midnight I was on a comm call with the command team that discussed the idea of the *Spider* dusting off just before the air strikes started to clean the LZ.

When the dorsal shield of the ship collapsed, both the bridge and upper engineering had direct taken hits from artillery strikes. The bridge was smashed. M.O.M. was offline for a few hours and XO was missing. Engineering was also breached, and auto damage control systems had taken over and performed an emergency shutdown on the main reactors, powering down the engines.

It would take six hours to relight the mains in order to take off, even if M.O.M. rebooted and ran the cold start. So, for now... we were stuck.

"They got M.O.M.!" screamed Punch over the constant shelling when I let the platoon know our ride out was canked. She'd come back in limited capacity to update the feeds from the two rear LZs, but that was automated. Her personality partitions were completely smashed by the strike with fires still raging inside her data stacks. "Sons of bitches!" shouted my assistant platoon leader. Then he punched a rock, and I was sure he probably broke his hand, but he didn't say anything and just gripped his Bastard with a wince every time after that. Daring me to call him a liar. Daring anyone to say he was weak and just busted his paw at the worst possible time, what with every remaining Ultra in the galaxy stacking out there in the dark and ready to come at us.

Which I never would, even if Punch was an actual liar, which he wasn't, and would never be.

He's Punch. The tag's also a warning. Measure twice, cut once. That's how this old ruck hobo has all his original teeth.

Tensions were high. I didn't need an impromptu combatives session in the charred dirt with my assistant platoon leader right now. He'd do it. Punch would fight you on the objective. I'd seen him do it.

So we had no choice but to attack the incoming Ultra elements before they could enter the LZ in support of each other with covering firing and armor for the death punch in the face. We'd hit hard, several times in fact, fading and moving as fast as we could out there among them. Maybe that bought us another hour. Maybe we got encircled and LZ Heartbreak wasn't our problem anymore.

The voice of the Seeker tried to come and tell me about *believing in something, getting caught up in the action* and all that jazz. I told her to shut up. I had people to shoot.

The eighty-ton Ogre went out to fight, and we followed. The huge war machine was stomping forward and unlimbering both her one-forty-millimeter guns from her arms. She fired immediately and the hot rounds streaked away and punched one of the lead Ultra advance tanks right in the forward armor. The tank got holed straight up and just lay there dead, bleeding white flames on thermal as we pushed in.

The captain would take what remained of Dog and act as infantry support to protect the powerhouse Ogre mech from Ultra infantry that would now try to get close in order to lay mines, fire AT, or do any number of completely desperate and suicidal things infantry could do to stop a rampaging mech on the loose and about to ruin the commander's pretty plans for a glorious victory for the death cult.

Ogre peeled off toward the north and that was an impressive sight to behold in the night. A huge mammoth mech death machine already taking machine-gun fire and lighting up the unseen targets that dared oppose her. She blew IR pop flares for the gunners to target better as the onboard computers began to crunch up the targeting data for engagement solutions resulting in as many dead Ultra Marines as possible. A missile streaked in and exploded harmlessly, glancing off her armor. In response, both guns from Ogre replied from the massive "arms" of the OD green-colored mech, *pom-pomm*ing in a sudden series of rapid-fire blasts that knocked out whoever had dared to take a shot.

The mech was already stomping forward. By the light of the falling enemy flares and incoming auto gun rounds, I could see the Ultras deploying as fast as they could. And I could see the tiny dark figures of Dog forming up into wedges to protect the massive behemoth mech going out to battle.

Our last shot to hold the LZ no matter what.

Two hours to go.

"Walkers out, Reaper!" I shouted, switching over to thermal overlay. "First on the right. Second take left. Keep 'em off our big boys and *get it on*, Strange."

CHAPTER THIRTY-NINE

While Dog covered the Ogre, Reaper got the two Marauders. The scout sniper mech was on her own.

Assault mech Brawler Two, the Marauder lead, was commanded by Sergeant Angry. Brawler Three was commanded by one of the other TCs in Apocalypse Solutions. Never got that dude's name. Brawler Three got wiped early on.

Both mechs were old Marauders from the Sandstone Wars if their desert and ghost-gray camo schemes, and repaired damage, were anything to go by. Ancient unit markings had been painted over but if you knew your stuff, you could fill in the details and figure out where they'd been and who they'd killed. Plus, there were the kill silhouettes outside the canopies. That told you a lot. These bad boys had seen some action.

I was hoping they still had something in them to get it done.

"On your six, Reaper," called out Sergeant Angry as the lead TC on board Brawler Two. Both mechs were coming up to the line of advance as hot white fire came all across our front. "Engaging with guns…"

Reaper First Squad had taken the eleven to seven position to protect the Marauders as we advanced out into the darkness and gunfire to meet the lead Ultra elements. Second picked up the rest of the clock.

Off to our right, the towering Ogre, lead thug in the Apocalypse Solutions mech suite, was handing out short-range missile strikes against Ultra infantry and light cav pushing through the wreckage ringing the LZ. Huge lightning strikes went off over there and then were answered, in apocalyptic response, by rippling daisy chains of explosions tearing apart red masonry and collapsing structures as the Ogre straight-up laid waste to anything pushing there. The Ultras in wedges and combat teams never-minded the imminent destruction being handed out and pushed forward despite the carnage and high casualties they were racking up. Supported by gun teams firing high-power AP that could punch mech canopies, the Ultras' only chance was to get close and lay some creative explosives on the rampaging mechs.

Missiles from just behind the enemy line of advance streaked out but got scrambled by the mech's onboard ECM jammers. Other countermeasures like flares, chaff, and mini-PDCs picked up the slack. For the moment, the mechs were chewing infantry like a fat man on cheap giveaway samples at some big box store's opening day event.

Ahead, three enemy tanks raced forward, attempting to engage the two mechs we were supporting. Brawler Two fired both of her Jackhammer autoloaders and ventilated the lead tank with her opening salvos. Brawler Three engaged the second tank in similar fashion, punching armor and getting a fuel cell ignition as tank number two exploded in every direction. Rounds on board began to cook off in short order making proximity for Ultra shock infantry a dangerous proposition.

Tank number three, stalled behind tanks one and two, tried to reverse out of the sudden carnage and got nailed by a blast from Apocalypse Solutions' Basilisk just to our rear.

Besides the four mechs, Apocalypse Solutions had a heavy tank-based Mauler energy weapon, the Basilisk, to support by fire. It was like a direct-fire flamethrower that spat superheated plasma at its targets and had your six as you went in hot all guns blazing. If you were a mech.

On the other hand, unprotected private military contractors, defending the mechs from infantry... had the potential to get boiled. Or have their arm hairs and eyebrows singed.

The remaining enemy tank took one jet of hot superheated plasma and her top armor just melted as the War Mace turned into a flaming volcano an instant later.

Infantry supporting the tanks fired AT and connected with Brawler Three an instant later and then died when both of the Marauders' gunners opened fire with the thirty-millimeter chain guns at just over two hundred and fifty meters.

I watched in thermal as hot white rounds suddenly drew traversing fire lines against the infantry out there who'd managed to get too close. Explosion and chaos blossomed in the image, and the Ultras got savaged by bright lines of brutal fire raking their positions.

Over the comm, business as usual, Brawler Two declared she was moving forward. She had just dropped too many expended hammerhead rounds, and all the brass from the thirty-millimeter chains was creating a massive heat signature for enemy targeting.

"We're up, Reaper!" I shouted as I led what remained of First forward to protect Brawler Two's advance.

Punch, Choker, Ulysses, Goods, the two New Guys, and the Kid, moved forward into a contact wedge. We needed to sweep the ground ahead for remote AT or infantry that had covered and was hiding from thermal. And also mines.

Over our heads, both towering mechs were engaging distant targets pushing on LZ Heartbreak out there in sudden displays of bright and brilliant fire that sent massive sheets of apocalyptic destruction just ahead of us and even farther out into the distances.

At that moment it felt like we couldn't do anything but win this.

At times, the rippling chains of explosions were blowing out our thermal overlays, and I was having to switch over to night vision just to see the battlefield ahead and how we were gonna move through it. To say that everything was darkness, then blinding light and chaos at the same instant, was an understatement.

But that's the on-the-job conditions and why they pay me the big bucks and let me wear these stripes.

And hey… as I've said before… they don't just give these away to anyone.

An Ultra sniper engaged us and shot New Guy One two minutes later. He died even though Choker worked on him under fire. We were taking contact by that time from off to our left. An Ultra gun team had set up, covered by ruined debris, and was firing at the mechs when they took a moment to try and wreck us.

We suppressed as best we could, the blackened D-beam-blasted dirt and ruin-wreak all around us coming apart from round strikes as the Ultra gun team fired all their high-powered armor-piercing for all they were worth right on top of us. Then Goods got into the fight and popped and fired the

M67 recoilless, smoking the whole enemy gun team who'd ranged us and was intent on putting the hate on us.

They were silenced and we pushed forward, ignoring the smell of burning flesh.

Fifteen minutes later, surrounded by a sudden Ultra push from all sides, we lost Brawler Three.

CHAPTER
FORTY

Apocalypse Solutions was founded by Captain Max. It was, in his words, "a new startup in the military contractor space."

Which sounded like lawyer lies if there ever were anything but.

"*Uh… yeah*," had been the collective sigh of the command team when asked by the Seeker's command staff to partner in support of the new mech company on a critical mission planetside in the plus-one days after the plan for taking LZ Heartbreak had totally gone our way.

Which… it didn't.

Partnering with a mech combat team seemed great for us. Four battle mechs, one Basilisk, and two armored personnel carriers were a game-changer in any fight as far as we could see. And being that our finances only allowed us to light infantry in the game of for-pay war on demand, at face value, we'd just improved our outlook as a private military contractor.

If just for the fact that given the next engagement, everyone trying to kill us would freak out and shoot at the mechs for a few minutes. Giving us a chance to do something brilliant like… *not die as fast.*

That "critical mission," as it were, would fall on the planned-for, really *hoped-for* the battle plan should have read, Insertion Day Plus-One. Those of us who'd been around, well, that gave some of us pause for thought regarding plans developed that were supposed to fall on the heels of an LZ capture against a hardened Ultra Marine force with a die-in-position order. But hey… who are we to be listened to when actual plans are being made by people who won't be implementing actual plans?

We just ruck-hobos, boss.

So, when we found out we were going to go up against Ultra Marines on a hot LZ… but we had mechs supporting… we were *silent-ish* and instead concentrated on seeing how much ammo and protein bars we could carry because we are good ruck hobos who believe eventually, one day, things will swing our way and so why not today?

We had no idea Haymaker was the real plan.

Simple children that we are.

It was the *"a new startup in the military contractor space"* comment by Apocalypse Solutions' new mech commander Captain Max that fired AA alarms inside our brains and had us concerned we were drawing fire and being lied to by big ol' whoppers reserved for the high table of speculative military planning rear of the rearmost tactical operations command centers.

You know, TOCs, the place where generals lie to one another much like high priests of cults fleecing the faithful with tales of *special missions* to save the worlds most of humanity have been relegated to in lieu of the home world.

Let me explain. The age of big mech conflicts… that had been almost a hundred years ago as far as the lies of edited history can confirm. That was when every private military contractor, and local militia, had them. Mechs. Those were the Brushfire Wars that signaled the beginning, and really, if you could draw the threads together and get rid of the official propaganda fantasy along the way, the end of the Monarchs. Rich colonies had incurred massive debt to buy state-of-the-art, expensive-to-maintain war mechs to go head-to-head against the Ultras *For Freedom!*

Or something.

That had come twenty years after the Big War which was our first serious threat to human-controlled space courtesy of an alien invasion. The mechs had been absolutely critical against the Atreadi. A giant humanoid species of warrior-explorers whose armada wandered into the outer worlds and immediately began combat operations.

Humanity fought that war for close to fifty years.

And barely emerged the victor. Facing twelve- to twenty-foot giant space marines with energy guns and advanced body armor had required, really necessitated, mechs.

Never mind the prohibitive costs.

Entire planetary economies were sucked up by the war because it was that critical. It was dangerous, desperate, and a brutal fight for our survival and theirs.

The Atreadi had acquired a taste for human flesh. So… there weren't going to be any second prizes in that one.

After the blow to Monarch power the Atreadi invasion had dealt out, the brushfire conflicts began as the alliance colonies felt they'd earned a little more of their own incomes for saving Monarch culture by sending all their mechs to the front lines at Blossomwillow World and Charon Desert.

Huge battles that had changed the course of the Big War in its most desperate hours.

Remember, much of this isn't really known now. Ask any kid, or at least twenty-five years ago when the Monarchs had their control grid firmly in place over human-controlled space, or rather about our necks and minds, kids and adults then who hadn't dabbled in forbidden history had only vague sketches of everything I'm downloading onto your hard drive right now.

And what they did know… was wrong. Lies, in fact.

The Atreadi were neither giants nor more technologically advanced than us was one of the big ones.

The Ultra Marines, led by the Monarchs, defeated the Atreadi and won the Big War within a decade.

Partly true. The Ultra Marines had, of course, fought like lions and died by the bushel at places like Hell's Star and the Fields of Dead. The Monarchs, on the other hand, were nowhere near the front and rumor was they had a big ship called *Dark Star* they'd gone off on out into deep space to avoid Atreadi kill teams sent to look for Earth and our rulers.

I'm sure they just wanted to negotiate face to face which the Monarchs would never do. I'm sure they had no plans to find out what Monarch fricassee tastes like.

And… *there never were Brushfire Wars.*

That's another Monarch Truth. Meaning… *lie.*

In fact, *No colony world has ever rebelled against the iron grip of the Monarchs.* In fact, *Those colonies never existed. Check the stellar charts. Anyone who believes such paranoid conspiracy theories is spreading disinformation and that's a twenty-year sentence on a re-education ring.*

Actually, the part of the sentence about a re-education ring isn't a lie. That's straight-up gospel. You will, or you would've before the fall of the Monarchs, done that standing up.

But everything I'm telling you is as much of the truth as I know. Have found out up until now.

That's the best I know. I'm sorry. I don't know why, but I feel guilty for that. Like I'm the liar and not the Monarchs who'd been creating the lies all along. Like I've failed... humanity.

Nether says it's because I care too much about the truth. Which sounds like something you tell some employer in an interview so you can get hired when really, you probably don't even want the job. You don't care and really, you're just lying to yourself.

Maybe when this is over... maybe when we take Earth, then we can find out everything that really was. Everything that was ever true. And all the lies that weren't ever true in the first place but that we lived our lives based on anyway.

I'm not saying we humans will come out looking good in the end. But at least we'll know the truth. And maybe after that, maybe we can have another chance, aware of our mistakes now, determined never to make them again.

Maybe... maybe that's worth fighting for.

If I believed in anything, like the Seeker wanted me to, then I could believe in that. I would believe in second chances.

People can change.

I think that's a *noble* thing to believe in, and believe me... I stopped using the word *noble* after the first time I saw what a gun team can do to a human being.

So, it was the "a new startup in the military contractor space" that gave us pause. Me. Someone who looks for the lies... hoping to find the truth hiding nearby like some victim recoiling from an abusive blow. Needing help, aid, a shield. Someone to rescue it.

Mechs are huge, dangerous, and very expensive to load and maintain. They carry one hundred times more munitions that we do. All of it super expensive.

The Ogre itself carries...

Forty-five Jackhammer anti-armor rounds.

One hundred high-caliber one-forty-millimeter artillery shells.

Sixty scatter pack reloads for the short-range missile engagement pods.

Two thousand fifty-millimeter armor-piercing rounds for the Bushmaster chain gun which the TC uses to direct fire and engage targets to defend the mech.

Five thousand rounds of fifty-cal for the area suppression gun. Once again to keep enemy infantry back and protect the mech and its crew.

Five thousand rounds of armor-piercing seven-six-two for the belt-fed defense guns the loader and onboard mechanic operate to once again defend the mech from infantry.

There are five reloads for all that and the other three mechs on board the *Spider* and the two support APCs that Apocalypse Solutions operates.

It would take the company all the profits from five of her last contracts just to sustain the mechs with one combat load for three days' operations planetside in standard combat operations. Plus, mechs are heavy to haul around so better have a starship handy which most PMCs don't have. Mechs break down a lot, and as I have noted in this log already, once they appear on the battlefield, every opposing commander points everything he's got right at them and effectively fires final protective fires just to kill them as fast as possible because chances are they are going to ruin his day in a very big way.

And yes, there are single AT rounds, very expensive systems, that can kill a mech in one shot. And if anyone's got them, the Ultras surely do today.

There are also a dozen other ways to take a mech out ranging from mines to mech traps, including airstrikes, which they are particularly vulnerable to.

So…

The Old Man had been absolutely brilliant to play dead with Apocalypse Solutions' mechs and make sure most of the Ultra air assets were out of commission before baiting the Ultras to try and take a fixed position, LZ Heartbreak, guarded by two platoons who, surprise… had four game-changer mechs and a Basilisk ready to go once the Ultra Marines had committed everything they had to taking the LZ.

The Basilisk is just a tank with a massive plasma gun. It could boil another mech if it needed to. But they're slow, no firing arc, and vulnerable to everything and everyone because they have zero armor and no defenses. They're just a bunch of juiced-up special batteries, and the plasma gun. The mech companies like to have them on hand for support by fire. Literally. Very hot fire in fact. The Basilisk's secondary purpose is to create defensive walls of napalm that protect the mechs from getting bushwhacked on the flanks by sneaky infantry like Strange Company coming in with AT and mines and plain old satchel charges lobbed in faith.

Or those Ultras who have all kinds of plans and contingencies they've trained and practiced to take on mechs with.

Having said all this… it was rare in the age of the Strange Company as we found ourselves at places like Crash or Pthalo, to even be around mechs, much less work with them. There'd been some on Crash, but nothing like the old days.

They're just too expensive.

Then we were introduced to Captain Max... and our fortunes changed instantly. We went from being light infantry with attitudes to... a combined arms team.

Before Captain Max became a mech company commander in the Insurrection and the collapse of the Monarchs, he'd been a multi-million-mem-trader back in the Bright Worlds.

He was crazy.

Brilliant.

And crazy. Did I mention he was crazy?

He'd gone broke overnight when the Seeker collapsed the mem-market after Astralon. But, because Max was a paranoid—read *crazy*—and yes wily broker, he'd converted tons of hard assets accumulated over years of big deals, bad deals, and probably very illegal deals, and the occasional purely outrageous bet... into some of the new currencies developing.

He'd gambled.

Or as he put it...

"I speculated in the growth markets that promised outrageous gains and absolute death to the Monarchs and the old order and ways of doing things. I'm a maximalist. It's who I am, and it happens to be my name. Listen..." He always said *Listen* even when you already were. "I went big, and I wasn't going home because there was no home to go to. I burned it down and pissed on the ashes. It's the only way to go. You'll see. Eventually. Or you'll be dead. Or a slave. I don't know. So, who cares. It all works out, or it doesn't."

He saw that the Monarchs were losing, and already had lost long before the rest of human-controlled space woke up and began to realize it. Even as the outer worlds and the frontier were peeling away and forming the Insurrection, Max claimed to have seen it all as plain as day.

"I bet the spread. I bet the house I burned down and pissed on. No trifecta. The exacta. The big one. All nine races for all the marbles, supermodels, crystal, and coke one can do. Only way to go. Trust me. I'm a pro. If you're gonna go out… go out big in an eighty-ton mech with missiles and lasers and guns."

Then he clucked and clarified like he was some cheap stage actor adding an aside. "We couldn't get the lasers. They're too fragile and the market was asking way over current. So we added the micro-missile pods, scored a Basilisk, and made up for it on the back end."

In the wake of Astralon and the spreading financial collapse, the Monarchs were still propagating the officially approved disinformation that the collapse was all part of the movement to a new digital, and hard currency, but boy it was hard to find, called… *the Sovereign.* Which was supposed to be better than mem and everything else and it was backed by nothing but the Monarchs insisting it should be accepted as standard… or else the Ultras would come get you.

The Insurrection had nothing to lose and saw their bet. Then twenty-five years of war while we slept on the way to Hardrock and closing night of the Monarch show.

Captain Max, or just Max as he was known before— apparently in mem-broker circles he was known as *the Maximalist*—once and long ago saw that business and trade, and any kind of galactic stock market, wasn't going to be anything worth investing in until the question of a new government that would rule human space had settled the question. And then started to charge taxes and print some kind of backed currency.

So, with zero military training, he acquired used mechs and refitted them. Hired crews who'd actually never served on these old models, trained them extensively in a boot camp he financed. Hired a drill instructor, Sergeant Angry, from one of the high-speed militaries back in the collapsing Bright Worlds, a guy who'd seen action in over a dozen conflicts as a combat engineer, close enough if you want to drive multi-ton walkers into combat with the Ultras, and *voila*... Captain Max had a combat mech combined arms team to go hasten the end of the Monarchs.

I had to credit him. Many of the rich and powerful had boarded massive ships and headed for the interstellar dark with all their hard riches, getting into the cryo-coffins and setting the preferred awakening parameters with the AIs that matched their optimal civilizational circumstances for when they wanted to rejoin society.

My bet... they were gonna be surprised when they came back in from the dark and found a stellar Monkey Empire that didn't care and offered them jobs at the zoo on the other side of the bars.

But I'm an optimist like that.

Apocalypse Solutions had...

One heavy main battle mech. The Ogre.

Two assault mechs. Both Marauders.

One scout sniper mech. A fairly new Ninja with a sweet sensor package that enabled advance targeting for all the other mechs on the company operations interface system it provided and ran.

The Basilisk that had battery charge problems.

And two prowler APCs to carry the reloads, the medics, and the ground crews that got the walkers out of the trouble they constantly got into.

But as we got introduced to the command team of Apocalypse Solutions, which really just consisted of Captain Max and Sergeant Angry, it became clear to Strange Company we'd need to be making some compromises for the privilege of working with a mech combat team to get it on and fulfill our contract, settle our debts, and walk away with enough hard currency to pay everyone. Mostly.

Often, on bad contracts, I had taken shares in the company in lieu of actual pay or profits of any kind. Those shares had yet to earn a bit of mem, but hey… I'm a minority part owner in this mess! Not just some ruck hobo with two ex-wives and no retirement plan.

I'm a financial genius. I'm like you, I want to tell Captain Max, just to see him cluck and wince. But less successful.

Captain Max was like a rooster, hence the clucking, though roosters really crow. He strutted back and forth, crowed, and seemed to enthrall everyone but the captain with his knowledge of finance, how the galaxy actually worked, and surprisingly… mech combat.

He also constantly made this clucking sound as he talk-ed.

He knew everything about his mechs. He'd trained extensively in sim with them and was proficient on every job from gunner to loader to mechanic even. He was a combat frame and weapons system rated certified mechanic. And driver. And of course, he understood the MC position. Mech commander. The guy who ran the whole show on board one of those walking death machines.

"Have you ever…" said the first sergeant, who paused and seemed to be choosing his words diplomatically at that first meeting between PMCs, then decided better since we were staking our lives on these five-story walking death machines, and concluded he'd better ask anyway if just for the insurance investigations that would certainly happen once life needed to be paid out on some of us, "… been in actual combat? Captain. Sir."

Then the first sergeant raised his chin and waited for an answer he was already sure he wasn't gonna like but would have to live with anyway.

Captain Max, who was lean and not tall but seemed at various times to appear both small, or tall, depending on the situation, clucked like a rooster getting ready to crow, leaned back his head, then proceeded to lecture the first sergeant, and the rest of us by default, on how many actually rated mech commanders existed who'd seen anything approaching conflict on the scale of the Brushfire Wars. Spoiler… not many. Then supported this argument by making the case that most mechs were now barely used as little more than set pieces to provide a new form of artillery support by just eliminating grid squares through superior firepower or acting as impressive deterrents against a rebellious population thinking about… his words… "getting uppity with their basic rights to life, liberty, and the pursuit of pure capitalism."

Along the way down this long-winded argument was a kind of historical lecture—that was the part I enjoyed a lot—slash rumination on economic theory and the bacchanalian excesses of whores, cocaine abuse, and dive bars that opened at six a.m. to serve the loaders working the big ships bringing in cargo to the Bright Worlds where Max had either drunk himself silly and gambled immense sums of money, or fought some hulking stevedore with a knife over a spilled scotch and beer chaser and ended up getting dim sum with and meeting the guy's family later.

"Salt-of-the-earth people," Max clucked. "And outstanding dim sum. Always near the loading docks."

Max finally indicated gambling, drink, and cocaine were now long behind him and the only thing that got him really high now was the pure capitalism the galaxy was now returning to, now that the Monarchs' rigging of the system had "compactly collapsed around their ankles" and they were "being shoved off the rain-slick precipice of humanity's foothold among the stars."

We could see the sense in that. We didn't know what it had to do with movement to contact, or an attack on a fixed position, but… it made sense. And like I've said… he was fascinating to listen to. He really sucked you in.

"And the second thing that freezes my brain the way any good Parmanian marching powder did back in the day when I drank in those loader bars," continued Captain Max at that first meeting, "back when I was betting the spread on that day's games just in time for first bell on the floor in a freshly pressed Hitt & Prow bespoke power suit… is driving mechs now and asserting all our liberties to pursue life, money, and the drugs of your choice through the onboard superior firepower of the HGM-159 assault mech… known as the Ogre, kids. There's no better drug than that. I swear on my mother's defaulted investment accounts."

Chief Cook agreed heartily and seemed to have already joined the Maximalist Cult without ever needing any kind of formal invitation.

In hindsight... they were shades of each other. Brothers from another mother.

Sergeant Angry, the mech platoon sergeant, smiled at all of us, made a sympathetic face indicating he understood, as military, that what we were hearing was jarring, then resumed a look that said he had every confidence in his commander nonetheless.

The first sergeant turned away and merely shrugged at the captain, saying, "Works for me, sir. Them mechs wanna go get shot up on that LZ and buy some time for my boys to engage the Ultras at knives and insults up close... who am I to stand in the way of a good time like that? But... I think I will busy myself with some primary maintenance on those flamethrowers we got down in the hold because, sir... you never really know when you're gonna need to have a flamethrower handy. But it's good when you do."

CHAPTER FORTY-ONE

We punched forward with the mechs, sweeping for mines laid by remote drone or by other means. We engaged teams of dug-in Ultras who'd either been lying in wait and gotten themselves worked by the two Marauders, or they'd evaded detection. In these instances, they were ready to drop the hammer on our mechs with either AT, remote mines, call for fire, or high-caliber depleted-uranium-loaded gun teams trying to take out the TC in the canopy or the driver in the gunner's cupola below.

The mechanics on the mechs could suppress infantry with the medium machine gun they worked from the right "hip" of the Marauder. Or the TC could open fire with the thirty-millimeter Bushmaster chain gun the Marauders carried, as opposed to the fifty-millimeter the Ogre had available in its weapons suite.

Either way, Ultras got wrecked as we made our way forward into the developing enemy push and walked right into a meat grinder the Ultras had put together on the fly.

You had to respect our enemies for that.

The mechs were chewing right through their forward armor and the first battalion of Ultra Marine shock infantry to push on the LZ. But the Ultra small unit commanders, under fire and taking casualties, quickly identified an area of ground we thought we could fight from, retasked their infantry and the light mechs, and then hit us there from three sides forward of our advance. Meanwhile combat engineer elements along our sides swarmed into our rear to cause trouble in case we tried to fall back from the mobile fighting wall the mechs provided.

In other words, we were *winning, winning, winning...* then we were suddenly surrounded and taking heavy fire from every direction.

On the way to the ambush, we'd watched the towering mechs light up targets out in the blackness. We moved forward, sweeping on thermal, passing the dead Ultra Marine infantry the suppression guns had just plain ruined in their wake. Nearby, burning tanks and light mechs the main guns of our mechs had holed, still blazed as melting crew hanging from the escape hatches testified to their inability to escape in time.

One of the Ultra snipers, using some type of anti-materiel probably, recoilless rifle system probably in the twenty-millimeter range, splashed Brawler Three's TC all over the back of the mech cockpit just as the ambush kicked off.

That was the first clue we had that we'd just walked into something...

A moment later, two anti-armor missiles streaked in and rocked Brawler Three for the kill that fast. One second I was there, watching Punch at the tip of the contact wedge, then suddenly there was that loud *crack* out there above the chaos of the battlefield and Goods was swearing and pointing toward the mechs.

At the same instant, one of their machine-gun teams out in the rubble at the edge of the LZ engaged us.

The Kid was killed in the opening burst from the gun team, but Ulysses dragged him from cover even though his brains were gone. New Guy Two took a round and ran for cover clutching his guts as they leaked out on the ground. That was a bad wound, and it probably took him about two hours to die after that.

There was nothing we could do for him.

Choker shot him up with the heaviest painkillers he had and then knocked him out.

His body was lost out there.

At that moment as the incoming started… coming in at us… from all three directions, rounds whistling through the air, cutting molecules to shreds as they smacked dirt, us, and the mechs, all at once like a sudden swarm of razor hoppers out on some lost county road coming at your windshield, we reacted to contact like ya do.

We sucked dirt or found cover because there was no way to get off the X at that moment.

The mechs were the drag anchor and they weren't going anywhere.

The X we'd just walked into had been a shallow depression Brawler Two had spotted beyond our lines. A place to be taken advantage of as we attempted to push the enemy push. Being in the mech and with the advantage of height, Sergeant Angry was able to see the battlefield more clearly, even in the chaos of incoming fire, tracer, streaking rockets, falling angel artillery, and heavy machine-gun fire from both sides being exchanged like there was some kind of urgent need to use up all the ammo that ever existed.

The sensor and ground-imaging package most mechs have helps a lot to spot these terrain advantages, I'm sure. It's like having a walking observation position.

Just before Brawler Three got rocked, Sergeant Angry called out his intentions for the combat team.

"Brawler Two… on the move forward to take that hollow ahead. We'll get more cover for the walkers from there. Reaper… suggest you take the flanks once we reach the loc, and keep the AT off us if you please."

The plan was we'd take the hollow and turn it into a firing position for the mechs right there in the middle of the Ultra advance. The Ultras must have sensed this or identified it quickly as something we might try. Remember they walked into this fight thinking they were gonna hit our lines and straight-up roll us.

They hadn't expected us to go on the attack.

But that's what we'd done. We'd come out of our positions and just started throwing punches at their line. They were realizing now they had to deal with this on their terms and not ours, and they were looking for hasty ambush spots we were going to canalize ourselves into.

I'm telling you, if it was most of the military Strange Company had faced up until this point, this would've totally worked. We would have bifurcated their attack and suddenly thrown all their plans into disarray. Instead, the Ultras smooth as good scotch over cold comet cubes in a fancy bar I ain't never had the money for but I went anyway, just laid a series of mech traps for us to walk into.

We obliged them and found one.

Off to the north, amid the raining star shells dropped by enemy artillery and called for by their spotters, and the chaff and flares rising off the rampaging Ogre, we could see that behemoth still chewing up infantry over there with the Bushmaster chain gun, firing massive twin artillery strikes over rapid intervals, direct fire, on any armor that moved within line of sight.

A missile came sidewindering in from the flank, got jammed by the Ogre's more-then-capable ECM, and immediately squirrelled off into the smoke and flares above.

Then Brawler Three got punched right in the brain and the TC was dead, Goods screaming, "They got Brad! Brad's dead!"

Brad was apparently the name of the sergeant acting as the mech commander on Brawler Three. Seconds later hypersonic AT missiles, probably GTM Blackbirds strapping forty pounds of PBXN-3 high explosive, some booster rockets to punch hyper, an initiator device, and nearly one hundred titanium fragmentation rods, punched straight through the mech and sent molten flaming fragments in every direction to the rear of our new fighting position.

The mech was still upright, but it was dead. Double-tapped to the chest by some serious hardware. The Ultras had dropped the hammer on our mech. The driver was dead too. The gunner and the mechanic bailed, grabbing light machine guns to now effectively become untrained infantry.

Meanwhile, Brawler Two commanded by Sergeant Angry traversed her upper torso, sighted squads of infantry getting ready to storm the fighting position we'd just occupied, took control of both thirty-millimeter Gatling guns on the "arms" of the mech, and dumped all the pain he had to give.

"Engaging… want some, jackweasels? Come to Papa!" I heard Sergeant Angry growl over the team comm. Then a hot blur of incredible fire erupted from both guns, traversing across our front and laying sudden waste to anything that had tried to move there.

I didn't see the Ultra Marines die, as suddenly the whole front forward of Reaper turned to a wall of flying, fountaining black dirt already ruined by the D-beam strike. All of it exploding skyward into the night. But I didn't see how anyone could live.

"Contact! Action left… Get it on, Strange!" screamed Punch and opened fire on the Ultras pushing our flank while hot giant brass shells rained down across our fighting position from the death-screaming guns of the mech towering over us.

Ultra Marines were coming in lobbing grenades at the mechs and firing bursts that left glowing hot smoking holes in Brawler Two's armor.

They didn't see the understrength infantry platoon… really just two squads who'd sucked dirt and found cover… waiting to ice them.

But they sure reacted when we opened fire on them.

Some died, tumbling down the lip of the wide fighting position that had probably been the D-beam strike's initial ignition point, thus creating a crater we'd all probably die in. Others, hit by our fire, stayed on their legs and moved their boots, engaging wily private military contractors who were either providing the smallest target possible, or who had good cover.

The Ultra would die when he had nothing left to give for the cult. Until then, he'd stack. So, we bankrupted him through mag dumps or accurate but rapid fire.

The mechanic from Brawler Two got on the mech's crew-served medium machine gun and ran a line of traversing fire on the marines who were even now withering under my platoon's crossfire.

I'd like to take credit for that.

I've trained them after all.

We were playing heads-up ball because running around under the feet of forty-ton stomping death machines that make the ground shift and shake every time they take a step has a tendency to keep you on your toes, but the truth is…

… they reacted to contact beautifully. They kept a flanking assault off the mech at close quarters with no room to maneuver. Had the Ultras gotten close enough they would have either thrown magnetic charges or direct-fired AT to bypass the mech's ECM generators interfering with their forget-and-fire targeting capabilities and smoked our last big boy.

For ten minutes we fought off the Ultras, who made two more concerted pushes and one final and very wild haphazard push. None of them retreated, but by the time one of their cav missile mechs came in to support the last badly timed attack and got lit up by the Ninja sniper mech firing her heavy recoilless one-oh-five gun, they were all dead, or dying.

We had a break. The Ninja mech commander was confirming via scout sensors the Ultras were shifting the attack over to Ogre.

Choker was already handing out headshots to the wounded and dying Ultras. Fully recovered from his protein bar.

I stood. I had dead Ultras in the black charred dirt domed and wrecked by automatic gunfire from the Bastard at less than fifteen meters.

It had been that close. I whistled.

Huge shells from Brawler Two who towered above us lay everywhere. That big boy had dumped so much fire, I felt like I was temporarily deaf even through the ear pro.

The giant cylinders of her Gatling guns were still smoking in the coldest part of the night.

A short distance behind us, Brawler Three burned from her internals as flames rose in the cockpit. Automatic fire suppression systems were engaging to try and prevent the fires from spreading to the magazines or igniting the fuel cells and heat sinks.

Suddenly, off to our left, north of our position, a subsonic turbojet missile came howling in and struck Ogre.

The howl and the scream of the Hatchet missile system got all our attentions real quick. The entire crew of the Ogre was probably dead then. But the second cruise missile with cluster munitions streaked in right on the heels of the first and exploded, spraying death everywhere all at once with a shockingly final detonation.

The Ogre must have been holed in a number of places, because all that ammo she carried on board began to cook off.

I saw all this from my back as I rolled over, knocked flat by the first strike of the Hatchet missile that far away. Then I watched everyone, or surely most everyone over there, die, realizing... we might be all that's left to hold the LZ now that we'd lost the main mech and a Marauder.

I checked my old watch.

It was dead. The blast wave from the Hatchet strike must have done it.

I triggered my SmartEye for an update on the time.

One hour and change left to go, to hold the LZ.

But so little left to do it with now.

Then the Ogre's power plant exploded suddenly on the other side of the LZ, throwing debris and black char everywhere.

Lighting up the night and setting everything on fire.

CHAPTER FORTY-TWO

"Fall back to the far edge of the strike crater!" shouted Ulysses over the chaos of the very one-sided gunfight coming at us from every direction forward of the line of battle.

They were hitting us from three different directions, and I was pretty sure we had creepers along the flank that had managed to outfox the mech's targeting system and take out at least three of my guys.

Still, we were holding more than our own against the Ultra Marines... and for that, this old ruck hobo was proud of his guys.

Foxy and Fartsack in Second were wounded and out of action with serious gunshot and fragmentation injuries. Foxy, the Second medic, got domed on the way out to get them and had to be dead as far as I could tell because the last I'd seen of his body it wasn't even twitching anymore and that was as clear a gunshot to the head as I'd seen. Red mist and everything.

So, no... I couldn't spend lives to get him off the field. I'd have to do that after we won, or, if we were all dead... then it didn't matter anymore, did it?

Brawler Two, the MCM-98 Marauder, medium combat mech Series 98, was low on missiles and rocket packs, and she was switching to guns just to keep the right flank clear for us as we tried to shift to a new fighting position and set up a new defense to deal with the encirclement the

Ultras were trying to pull on us. Every comm transmission with Sergeant Angry riding the Marauder came with missile tone-lock indicators screaming bloody murder as the ECM generators whined out on small high-pitched notes and fired up. Further in the background of this transmission I could hear the remaining chaff guns deploying as fast as they could to knock out more incoming missiles.

That mech was more than holding her own too, but she was shotgunned by small arms fire and it was a miracle none of her crew was dead. Other than the dead mechanic-gunner I'd go up and take over for to get the mech off the X. But I'll get to that shortly.

While all this was going on... *oh, that mess, that's all mine, sir*, I could almost hear myself saying... I was on the comm trying to rustle up any airstrike possible or convince Insurrection Tac Air to give me something from the Phantom on station way overhead.

I would've killed for a cluster strike. Danger close even.

Nothing at this time... stand by.

"Say again, Reaper... strike package not available at this time. Hold until relieved."

I swore at the sexy-voiced comm tech probably aboard the *Elektra*. Of course we were gonna hold the line. Even if that line kept moving back a few steps at a time. We were gonna hold it.

Also... there was no way off this bad LZ. So, we had that going for us. As I've said... I'm an optimist that way.

And this was a bad LZ if there ever was one. I'd bet all the money the company owed me on that one. Problem was I probably wasn't going to live to collect.

Again... *Optimist. Me. I am one.*

"Listen, Sarge," shouted Puncher from the lip of the crater we'd fallen back to to get some cover from the Ultras swarming our position, effectively declaring, *Tag, you're it. We've decided you're the breakthrough and we're going for it right here and now.* Punch was burning ammo on short bursts, knocking down what he could as we set up the next line of defense when he shouted over the blare of staccato gunfire to let me know what was really important in the grand scheme of things. "She sounds cute, boss. You'll catch more flies with honey... or something." Gunfire, gunfire, more automatic gunfire. "So ask nice and get us an airstrike, Big Sarge, or this is lookin' like that pile of brass I was sure I was gonna find some day on the Third Worlds."

If that wasn't straight from the first sergeant's mouth, I didn't know what was. It occurred to me as I switched off the comm and tried to figure a way for Brawler Two to get out of the wide crater she was stuck in, the one we'd been fighting from until we got pushed from three directions and we had wounded and dead, that if Punch survived and kept on surviving, well then, he'd make a good first sergeant. Someday. He was full of practical yet irritating wisdom you wanted to punch him for.

Being first sergeant you couldn't. Punch him. So that would work out well for everyone. Because if you punched Punch, well... you were gonna get punched back. Hard.

"Who's got the..." I was gonna say "demo" and then I remembered exactly who currently had it.

Oh no.

After Jax got hit then casevacked to the rear, I remembered who had the last of our demo now.

Klutz.

Literally the last guy you wanted playing with high explosive angry putty and the dynamically released forces of kinetic energy. He had that tag, Klutz, for a reason. Everyone has their tag for a reason. Sometimes it's arcane. Sometimes it's painfully obvious. In Klutz's case, it fell under *painfully obvious*. Painfully.

Oh my… again.

"Klutz!" I screamed, thinking *This might as well happen right now*. And also because I had no other choice being that we were under serious incoming fire and I needed to get that mech some cover from direct-fire AT and the Ultra gun teams doing their Ultra Marine best to kill it and move forward.

This is what infantry does when it's attached to armor. We're teeny-tiny squishy babysitters to one very big, angry, murderous giant baby that has a hard time with terrain.

We help it navigate that terrain so it can kill MOAR on our behalf.

The guns on board Brawler Two spun up at that moment and massive thirty-millimeter expended brass shells flew frenetically away from each arm as it traversed across the line of battle forward of our position and devastated more Ultras attempting to push from the wide strike crater that had once been our fighting position.

That'll teach them, I thought as I formed my plan to get the mech out of there. She'd gotten in, but now, unable to turn and navigate her way out, she couldn't get out. If she turned, she couldn't defend herself.

Another mech weakness that infantry had learned to navigate. Keep a mech busy and focused and they can't break contact. Then you kill them from the flanks which was exactly the game the Ultras were running right now.

Near the center of the impact crater the D-beam strike had created in the days leading up to Insurrection planetary assault, Brawler Three continued to burn. Rounds cooked off and there was a feeling as you watched it that some kind of major blast from the wreckage was imminent. Onboard fire suppression had completely failed by that time and the fires were now fully out of control.

"If you're gonna do something, ground pounders," said a patient yet clearly irritated Sergeant Angry over the comm, "then now would be a great time. We're outta chaff here and the ECM heat sinks are pegged out well beyond the red line. Oh my gosh… I don't even think this reading is possible. Seriously… design limits exceeded. We gotta boogie, Strange. Or we're gonna get holed on the X and go fireworks all over everyone."

"Copy, Brawler Two… stand by, Strange on it! *Klutz!*"

I have no idea how he ended up in the Strange. Klutz is a good soldier. Or at least he tries really hard to be. You have to give him that. It's just that he's not coordinated. Given time, we probably would have washed him out of the line platoons and given him to Biggs to assist in supply.

But the *insurrectionistas* were hot to strike Marsantyium and it was all hands on deck, everyone gets a Bastard of some sort, we're goin' in…

"On my way, Sar'nt!" shouted Klutz over the cacophonous volume of fire exchanged with the intent to kill.

I watched the gangly, tall contractor whose battle rattle always seemed to be looser than I would have liked. Who always seemed to have a boot snake no matter how many times I tried to stay on him about those. I mean, I'm an easy-going NCO compared to some. Hannibal over in Dog was a nightmare for uniform and discipline. And they loved him for it.

Like I said, Dog was a cult.

I watched Klutz hunching and thinking he was staying low enough to avoid getting domed. He wasn't, and rounds were striking the lip of the crater and it was clear the Ultras' squad designated marksmen out there were convinced they could Yahtzee him for the win.

I had this feeling I was going to get Klutz killed today. And it wasn't even daylight yet.

Soon. One hour to go.

One dark hour and the sky would get light. Barely. Thin red in the east I'd been waiting desperately to see and sure I and really none of us, were gonna. Then Haymaker would cross the line of departure. And our work would be done.

Hope we see it.

I lunged and dragged Klutz down to the dirt below the lip of the crater as soon as he got close enough to me to do so.

"What!" he screamed, indignant that I'd suddenly tackled him.

"Got the explosives?" I roared breathlessly over the battle all around us.

"Affirm, Sergeant Orion. Where ya want 'em?"

CHAPTER FORTY-THREE

"When life closes a door, make a hole with explosives and open that sucker back up."

Or at least that's what Jax would have said had he not gotten shot earlier in the evening's festivities.

I hoped to see him again someday, but at that moment the Shaken Eight-Ballers, an obscure religious cult you'll find passing out tracts at every starport they haven't been banned from, would have said *All Signs Point Toward No, have a random day, sir.*

We fired the high-ex and created a breach in the crater wall just south of where we'd set up our defense to cover the beleaguered mech. The blast sent huge sections of debris outward across the flat surface of the crater that had been the initial strike point for the D-beam when the LZ had been prepped using apocalyptic destruction.

The dirt was still falling but I checked the cleared space and saw that the path was big enough for the mech to retrograde off the X and get some cover if they could get out of there.

"We made a hole, Brawler Two," I alerted the mech crew. "Marking with chem lights now..."

And then there was a big problem.

I had no more chem lights. I'd been using them to mark evacs and track our progress away from the line so the rear gun teams knew where we were going and wouldn't shoot us in the back when supporting by fire.

Klutz, who'd fired the charges from the other side of the breach, and nothing bad had happened and I hadn't gotten him killed so I was a good platoon sergeant so far… watched as I fumbled through my chest rig for a chem light. Any chem light. A stray.

I dropped my assault pack and found none within, and setting the Sturm down by its carrying handle, I searched harder as a growing horror began to gnaw at my hungry and upset stomach.

Behind me Ulysses was now leading the defense at the lip of the crater. We were trying to keep the Ultras off the mech. Any enemy AT popped and fired, they got engaged immediately. Any runners trying to get close to Brawler Two with magnetic charges were also considered high priority for excessive targeted fire from Reaper.

No chem lights still, amazingly, in my assault pack!

Worst. Sergeant. Ever.

"You got any marking lights, Klutz?"

He'd taken possession of Jax's assault pack, so there was a high degree of likelihood that yes, Klutz did have chem lights we could apply to the problem of getting the mech off the X. Problem was he was on the other side of the breach.

He'd need to mark the lane the mech could take once she reversed out of there.

With the falling dirt and flying debris, smoke and flares in the air, and the fact that the mech needed to maintain all weapons forward with targeting sensors on active sweep for enemy and not terrain analysis, getting a mech to just walk backward was a real trick that could easily end in disaster for us all.

A minor design flaw in a lot of mechs. Never really that important until the forty-ton war machine needed to walk backward, retrograde, while maintaining a weapons-forward posture. Then… it stopped the show.

Someone with a bigger brain than mine oughta do something about that.

But meanwhile… outnumbered and under fire… we… were trying our best.

A couple of chem lights would mark the mech's path rearward and the mechanic on the waist gun would actually take over slaved controls and maneuver the mech backward and off the X.

Klutz gave me the thumbs-up and I was sure I was about to get him killed. He was smiling and excited to be helping exactly like someone who was about to be killed would smile and try to help.

And I would have yet one more thing to live with. Listen, galaxy… my ruck is getting full. Ruck-hobo NCO needs a break. Anyone? Anyone listening?

"Mark the edges of the berm with one on each side!" I yelled over the incoming gunfire as high-caliber rounds whipped through the dark past us.

C'mon, dawn… get here already!

Klutz cracked the first chem light, dropped it of course, picked it up, oblivious to rounds streaking in at us, then tossed it close and marked the near edge of the mech's lane outta trouble right now.

Then… he cracked the next chem light, tossed, and failed to mark the other side. The chem light only made it halfway out into the breach we'd cleared. The mech would think it didn't have enough room to clear the obstacles and that could cause problems. Some of which I could see. Others, the unseen ones, I was sure would eat us all up.

Klutz simply shrugged... and ran for the misplaced chem light.

Before the rounds started exploding in the dirt all around him, I hefted the Sturm, my last belt of HERK rounds dangling, and surged out from my cover to get in front of him, whipping the belt of ammo out and away and hoping that bought me a good feed as I prepared to ride the lightning as hard as it could get ridden.

I saw Klutz running straight at me as I began to lay down suppressive fire to keep some heads down out there and give my guy a chance not to get killed as he straight-up heroed for the win.

I will do everything for my men. And wish that I could do more.

I got in front of him and went cyclic on the last of the belt, brass and linkage flying in every direction, my Bastard dangling from my sling accusingly like some jilted lover. Klutz, bent, didn't get killed, grabbed the ineffectively placed chem light, and got the next throw right, positioning it correctly for the mech's egress off the X.

The Sturm was dry, and we should have been good to go... except the mechanic who was operating the waist gun on Brawler Two was now dead, or dying.

"All clear to the rear, Brawler Two!" I'd just commed with the mech.

Nothing in reply except static and that hum of an open transmission.

Then over the comm I could hear background chatter from on board the mech. Angry swore as someone, probably the driver in the forward gunner's cupola, told him the mechanic had his brains splashed all over the waist gun canopy below. He could see him leaning over, down and to the left in the lower gun position.

Which was where the slaved controls were.

Angry swore.

I immediately turned and ran back down the breach for the stranded mech.

I'd operated a waist gun once before. I knew the controls and was fairly confident I could steer her back through the gap without breaking much.

I pounded through blackened sand racing for the looming mech taking small arms fire ahead of me. Another missile came in from the flank, streaked close… and missed. If it had hit, shrapnel and blast might have killed me on the way to being "helpful."

The Ultras were direct-firing their AT now because they couldn't overcome the Marauder's powerful onboard ECM generators.

Joke's on them, I thought. The ECM generators were overheating.

My feet felt heavy, and I was sure I was about to throw up because I was probably gonna get killed doing something stupid. Then I caught sight of Klutz right behind me in my peripheral vision, shooting, moving, and probably engaging Ultras trying to kill me.

So, I was gonna get him killed too.

"Brawler Two…" I gasped as we reached the right leg of the towering forty-ton mech. "Coming aboard to get you out of there."

"Copy that, Reaper," said Sergeant Angry. "Do what you gotta do, bro, we can't take much more!"

I deployed the handholds by popping the mount-panel, punching in the four-digit code we'd been given, then getting green illumination authorization to operate the mounting system.

Which is no easy task. Rounds are striking the forty-ton death machine towering over you as you pull yourself up its bullet-impacted armor. Meanwhile said death machine is drooling hot brass and bleeding hot gas from the heat sinks.

Klutz was down on one knee, classic rifleman position and engaging everything he could with rapid fire.

At least he looked heroic.

I was proud of him and sure I was going to feel horrible when we got outta here and he was dead for having covered me. Heroically.

"Good job, Klutz!" I shouted over the mech's whining engines, spooling guns, and incoming enemy fire. "I know this is a lot..." *for you* I didn't shout. Because it *was* going to be a lot for a guy who wasn't very coordinated in the least. But once I took control of the mech and walked her backward, he either went with us, or he was gonna be hanging out in the wind as an Ultra shooting-gallery target with no other targets but him for them to win a Squidgy Doll prize.

"You gotta concentrate, Klutz. Once I'm up, climb three handholds and hang on. I'm gonna move the mech backward then. You fall... you'll probably get killed. You try to fire or lose your grip... you'll get killed. You have to, I repeat, *have to* hang on no matter what. That's all you gotta do, buddy!"

He gave me a look.

I didn't need to know his story. The look he gave me right there in the middle of it all told me everything I'd never known about him. I've heard so many of their stories

I can start to fill in the blanks without them even telling me. I knew why he was a PMC instead of being in some proper military unit, relegated to being in the rear with the gear.

He'd always wanted to soldier. A fighting man.

I could see that now. That's all he'd ever wanted to be, a soldier. He'd tried other services, but I was betting he'd never passed the physicals or the obstacle courses. Or any of the other skills that required a certain amount of dexterity, and coordination, in order to be job-slotted. He always got ate up in the end because of his lack of coordination.

But the company... the company had been just desperate enough to take him in times just desperate enough to make an excuse for the taking.

And now here he was, under fire, soldiering... and he was about to get killed, and he knew it. The look told me everything. Even after being a hero when a mech crew was on the X and couldn't get off. He'd got it on. Got it done.

The look he gave me, tall, gangly, uncoordinated, coke-bottle glasses, and a mop of hair that could never not seem unkempt under his combat helmet, said, *C'mon, Sergeant, they call me Klutz for a reason. I know I'm gonna fall off the forty-ton walking death machine under fire. I know I'm gonna die now. But I was a soldier. Tell 'em that, Sar'nt. Tell 'em I soldiered when it counted.*

He'd waited his whole life to prove he could die heroically doing something stupid. It wasn't stupid, but when you're an old ruck hobo... it sure does feel that way sometimes.

And he wasn't afraid to do it. To die. Heroically.

Rounds smacked the mech above us.

I had a foolish thought that I could maybe let him try to climb up the mech's leg, never an easy task, under fire, operate the gun and get the mech off the X.

But… he was Klutz. C'mon, Sar'nt Orion.

"Just do it. Don't think about it, Klutz. Just climb and hang on once I get up. Three handholds. I will get you outta here, brother."

He nodded, telling me without words that he would try. That he would do what I told him and do his best in the doing of it. And that it wasn't my fault if he didn't and he died.

He was Klutz. He'd had that tag his whole life before the Strange gave it to him in all of their accurate wisdom. Like wily and wise street urchins accurately taunting you with exactly the thing you've hated about yourself all along.

All along the way to the Strange and the big show.

You're lying, Orion, I tried to tell myself as I climbed the hot mech, the heat off the sinks radiating through my assault gloves.

Of course, cool-guy ruck hobo had to cut his trigger finger off the tip of the glove and so the tender finger underneath was already blistering. Which would be fun if I needed to shoot someone.

And I was pretty sure there was gonna be more of that if I survived yet another stupid stunt to *get it on, Strange*.

"No," I grunted to myself as I climbed up to the waist gun. "I ain't lying! I will get… you… off… this… X, Klutz!"

Then I grunted and hauled myself into the waist gunner's cupola.

I checked below. Klutz was hanging on.

I slewed the gun around, targeting holos popping up around me and highlighting potential targets I could put fire on. Ultras out there waiting to get shot a lot by me.

The dead gunner had slumped to the floor.

I racked a new round just to eliminate a potential jam, tapped the slave control override authorization, and fired on the Ultras out there as the mech switched over walking systems to the panel I had access to.

Three seconds later I had command authorization from the mech commander to activate the slave controls.

Hot brass filled the deck of the waist gun cupola. Ultras were firing at me as I patiently murdered them, telling myself something about them deserving this for picking the wrong side. The side that wasn't human.

I didn't care anymore.

I leaned over the edge, sure I'd see Klutz bleeding out on the black sand of the crater at the mech's giant feet, nothing we could do for him now if I was gonna get the mech outta there and off the X.

Or I'd see that he'd fallen and was trying to climb back up as the mech started to move.

He was hanging on still. Eyes closed. Lips moving. Doing his best to hang on.

"Here we go," I said over the comm, and got the mech moving to the rear and out of there. Aiming for the lane marked by the two dim chem lights.

And yeah, there are *just-in-time moments*.

Just like in the spectacuthrillers.

This was one.

The Ultras had found some mortars and as we reached the entrance to the breach, mortar strikes began to rain down on the crater we were exiting. One hit the dead Marauder we'd left behind, Brawler Three, and it exploded everywhere, finally, lighting up the predawn darkness we were all fighting in. Showing me the Ultras swarming the far edges of the crater. It was a moment I felt that everyone who survived, both sides, would remember.

Is there a day in the future, when I am old and some Ultra I have run into on the streets of a world new and stranger than anything we have ever imagined… we are both old, each missing something along the way like legs, marbles, old brothers from the wars, and one of us will say, *I was there that day, on Marsantyium. I was there when the mech blew?*

And the other will say, *Me too*. And for a moment, we will wish for one more chance to be… young again, knowing we never can be. Knowing the two old ruined men are brothers of a sort now.

We were there when the mech blew in the strike crater. We were there at Marsantyium.

Is there such a day for you, Orion? Sergeant Orion. Or is today your day to buy it on a bad LZ like the Kid back on Astralon, Crash, call it what you will.

The mortar strike had been prepped.

The Ultras had pushed as hard as they could, and now they were trying to take the far edge of the crater we were barely holding.

Clear of the breach, I turned the controls back over to Sergeant Angry and checked on Klutz.

He was still there.

Still alive.

Smiling and looking like a hero. Because he is one.

Some days… I am an… *okay* sergeant. Just some days though. Perhaps… this was one of those *some days*.

CHAPTER FORTY-FOUR

Despite the small victory of not dying on the fade off the previous fighting position, and keeping Klutz alive for a few more minutes, the Ultras were still intent on slaughtering us now despite our best attempts to convince them otherwise. And also, we were slaughtering them too.

Dog was gone though.

What an understatement. But that's how I choose to record it in the logs. So, there it is. Perhaps some curse we'd never known we'd incurred would be gone from the company now like the smell of bad fish, or an acquaintance that could never quite seem to get it together and not cause grief at every turn.

I don't know if that meant the captain was dead out there alongside the bodies of Dog. The only one in contact with the first sergeant back at the LZ was Chief Cook.

He was under fire and had three from Dog still operational. They were surrounded. He had no idea how much more of Dog was still alive out there and fighting in pockets of resistance as the line disintegrated on that flank. There was burning armor everywhere and Ultras pushing on the LZ now.

It was bound to happen. Like something we'd known was inevitable, but we'd decided wasn't, for no other reason than we wouldn't allow it to be.

One gun team was still up over there, but no comm… you could hear them still rattling away at bad guys. Destroying anyone that entered their sector.

"We're still in it, Doghouse," Chief Cook had coughed over the comm. He'd deployed a CS gas that would break down the Ultras' filters. "But… in very short order, Doghouse… we'll be down to knives and some very special chemical weapons I can deploy… but I won't lie to you, Doghouse… these'll probably kill us too. But we won't feel anything, and it'll be a great trip as long as we don't make eye contact with the bats, First Sergeant. Standing by to go full Fear and Loathing. Once I pop the canisters, we've got about two minutes of pure native shaman spirit energy to kill as many of those damn bastards as we can. Perhaps that buys the LZ something, Doghouse. Don't know… but it'll be beautiful, man. Totally… beautiful."

Gunfire close at hand ate up the transmission, and the first sergeant made sure to finish it with a, "Negative on hallucinogenic denial-of-service attack at this time, Chief. Negative on Fear and Loathing attack… whatever that is. Fifty-five minutes to go, Doctor. Do what you can. If not… see you on the other side. I guess I'll be along shortly. Gonna stack some first, though."

Well, I almost felt bad calling in for support. We were low on ammo and the Marauder was running dry. We were either gonna need to fall back to the LZ or get rolled right here.

There weren't many options left.

I fired at an Ultra who came right over the lip of the crater as I prepared to make my final request for support by fire from anyone to the rear. Doubting there was anyone. But it is my job to try.

I hit the Ultra center mass. He went down on one knee, auto-rifle at the low ready, then I drilled him again and he tumbled down in the charred dirt past me like some sinner falling into the nether of the black hell we'd decided to fight over. Off to my left, Hoser and Hustle had shifted the gun position to cover the breach we'd blown in the crater wall. The Ultras had thought they could push faster there now that it was clear. They'd thought wrong. Hustle and Hoser were burning lead, and piles of brass were stacking up as the two of them laid the hate on anything and anyone moving down that breach.

Hustle was dragging in dead Ultras from nearby on the lip of the crater like some ghoulish undertaker as he managed the belt feed, pushed the brass aside, and then stacked the dead around their firing position for more cover.

The KIA'd Ultras wore serious armor, so that was a pretty good move on the gun team's part. Besides being the utter epitome of heartbreakers and lifetakers as they literally stacked the dead for a fighting position, they weren't gonna walk away from it until it was over.

One way or another.

I had Ulysses on the right with Punch and Choker holding from there. Wolfy with me and Klutz. Solo and Two Times were pulling rear and flank security for the gun team.

Some were wounded.

Foxy the medic was dead.

Fartsack and Rockstar were wounded enough to be down and out. Which was a problem for me. I couldn't get them back to the casualty collection point. And... if we needed to fall back some more... we were gonna need to carry them with us when we went.

See, I gotta fight and manage movement, supply, and wounded. Everybody else just gets to fight. That's why they pay me the big mem. As they say.

Choker already had both wounded on collapsible stretchers. But it was still going to be hard to fight our way backward and carry the wounded out of there.

Above all of us, Brawler Two was now down to chain guns and the overheating waist gun. The survivors from Brawler Three were aboard and taking over for the dead mechanic at the waist gun.

I needed an out. Badly.

The gun team on the right blared out. More fire on the left. The Ultras were calling in new fire missions and the first mortar rounds were starting to fall to our rear.

The Ultra spotters would bracket our position and then get the drops right on top of us eventually.

Then they'd make it rain and we'd be done.

"Doghouse... this is Reaper. We are in big trouble. Could use—"

The first sergeant stomped all over the comm as I checked my watch. Fifty-three minutes to go. Time was slowing the worse it got for us. Honestly... we weren't gonna see ten minutes from now, much less fifty-three minutes from now.

"Be advised, Reaper Actual... Voodoo chief on his way to your location. Look for Prowler Lead. ETA thirty seconds..."

"Copy," I said automatically, trying to do the math of what that meant for us. Prowler Lead was one of the two flat armored APCs that served the mechs. We could get a reload from them, but the mech reload would take time and there was no way I could see that being done under fire this close to the battle line.

We needed to shift off this position ASAP.

I tapped the comm as I heard the low howl of the prowler's engines roaring up from the rear. Nothing. The comm was dead. We were being jammed at the worst possible time. Which is when they jam you. Of course. I turned and saw the brick-shaped slate-gray flat APC on six ceramic wheels streaking right at us, churning black dust and burnt debris as it tore through the hellscape of LZ Heartbreak. The wheels locked and the vehicle turned to a slide. It stopped ten meters to our rear. The side hatch hissed open pneumatically, red light pouring through as Stinkeye pulled himself out like he was some bad nightmare coming back from hell to make things worse for people it was already going bad for.

Which is probably true in some sense.

The APC crew secured the area and one of the techs ran forward to interface with the mech. The APC's auto-turret defense gun suddenly traversed and began to blur-fire in short staccato bursts at targets we hadn't spotted off on our right flank.

Bright blue tracers and swarms of shadowy flying lead erased whoever was over there and trying to creep and flank us.

Stinkeye ran toward me, bandylegs shambling through the dust and ruin, battle rattle flapping with all his voodoo charms and weird badges of an office we had no idea he possessed and which he thought meant something.

He'd randomly handle and finger them as he talked to you in other times. Now he was waving his arms, flailing really as he closed on me with Ultras in the AO and ready to push.

If there ever was a war wizard… "Well, you could use that old fraud until you find a real one," Chief Cook had often remarked. I'd noted that as the kindest thing he'd ever said about his fellow enemy warrant officer.

There was never any love lost between those two.

"Git yo wounded aboard the APC, Little King!" screamed Stinkeye raggedly. "Then get your men to gather 'round the big mech. We 'bout to do some ol'-fashion wickedness."

I had no time to argue. I had no options to argue for.

Choker and Klutz handled the wounded Fartsack while the APC mechanics came out to help with Rockstar.

Rockstar, who'd been shot in the jaw and was drugged to the gills by Choker's injections, gave me a final thumbs-up as he was carried off the field toward the APC.

We called him Rockstar because he was good at everything. Natural athlete. Much like Ulysses. Klutz, who wasn't wounded, banged his own bucket savagely as he helped load the wounded Rockstar.

Such are the vagaries of war.

Mortars were now hitting forward of our position, telling me the Ultras were bracketing once more. The next strike, or three, would find us.

Then it was gonna rain…

But it also told me the Ultras were waiting for some direct hits before they pushed hard one last time and broke open the LZ. They were probably stacking out there, pushing more men and any armor they had left forward, sensing the storming of the LZ and final victory was imminent.

Joke's on them. We were never the real attack. But we were gonna die for it anyway.

We had moments, and not much more than clusters of seconds, to do something to buy ourselves a way to fifty-one minutes from dawn.

And I didn't see that happening. I was already trying to figure how to abandon the mechs and get the APCs back to the LZ and fight from the ship, knowing the Ultras could rock it with Hatchet strikes until the shields collapsed and we were dead inside.

I checked the horizon, hoping for a break. Hoping for that thin red stripe on the horizon. Begging dawn to come early.

Wanting to believe that someone in tac-planning got it all wrong and nautical daybreak was just about to happen.

That Haymaker was already swinging on the Ultra command structure and the Ultras were being shifted to hit the new attack from the flanks in one last desperate bid to save their butts.

This was it. One way or the other. This was… it.

Now, at the end, we were just two dead drunks swinging away at each other in a dark dirty alley behind some terrible bar.

Nothing more.

Nothing less.

"What are you planning, Stinkeye?"

Utter disbelief that this drunken war wizard wreck of a human being… was a savior. Or any kind of salvation.

And yeah, I didn't trust him enough that I said it like I thought he was some white knight coming in to save us at the last. I said, asked it, demanded it, like I was talking to some bad wild child who'd never given me anything but grief.

What have you done now!

He looked at me, eyes desperate, sweat running down his scarred and weathered black face. Coal-black eyes burning with malevolent fire and fearful terror.

"Gonna show 'em the Heart o' Darkness, Little King. Gonna show you all now. It's hang on ta ya butts time!"

CHAPTER
FORTY-FIVE

"It's hang on ta ya butts time!"

Boy... was that the truth, Stink. And some. Regardless of what the barracks philosophers blather on about the truth just being the truth and not needing anything more. The truth just is. That sounds made up, though I have may have used it on occasion to make a point or win a bad hand in a game of Cheks.

Honestly, what happened to Strange Company next was a little more truth than I care to live with for the rest of my life. Excuse me while I just... do my best to absolutely forget what happened to us on LZ Heartbreak when Stinkeye actually went full space war wizard.

I will now be adding super-whiskey, if there's such a thing, to my darkness, smokes, and coffee session while I wait for the next disaster to find me.

What had Nether said... something about Stinkeye being *the most powerful* bishop he'd ever encountered. And Nether would know.

Right now, as I get all this down, our space war wizard is fighting with one of the chimp soldiers over the dented totem flask Stinkeye always carries with him, and which has become some kind of superstition-laden relic for the members of the company. The clever monkey soldier, strapping a junky Frankenstein AK-47 relic with very little muzzle or trigger discipline for my liking, has just tripped the "most powerful space war wizard ever," apparently. Stinkeye now has a bloody lip, was just face down in a pool of oil and antifreeze I think, and screaming drunkenly at the chimp he'd been drinking himself silly with.

There are scenes you witness in your life. Scenes of low-class human degradation worthy of the lowest star carnie trash you can conscience.

This… is right up there with two rail-thin star carnies willing to do each other in with wiggle-stickers over the Fat Lady with Two Heads who's the third-rate entertainment's chief attraction.

The chimp is dancing away, hooting and howling and gnashing his teeth at the, I repeat, most powerful space war wizard… ever. Who is currently covered in filth and possible vomit, and raging like the starport drunk indignantly wronged by mysterious yet unverifiable sources.

In the aftermath of what Stinkeye did on LZ Outbreak to save our collective butts, I won't dangle the outcome in front of you like some hack storyteller trying to waste your time…

We. Won.

But it was the Heart of Darkness or as near I can tell what a Heart of Darkness would probably be, that I'd like to forget about forever and that I must now explain.

Punch's hair went completely gray afterwards.

Choker's now got a small uncontrollable twitch, as do about half of the rest of us. The tics, twitches, or waving hands and suddenly jerking awkwardly are all variations on a theme.

But yes… we are scarred by what happened on the LZ, and particularly, our exposure to the Heart. The Heart of Darkness that is. Which, I'll be honest, having heard the old drunk go on and on about it… I thought it was just drunk imaginary blather. I had no idea it was real the entire time.

If so, I would have taken steps like leaving the company forever and going into floral arranging on the last quiet concourse of some dead-end starport to avoid it, and ever being anywhere in the vicinity of it, for the rest of my life.

Seriously.

I feel older now. Significantly so. When I've looked at myself since that last hour of the battle before the Monarchs pulled their final cheat… the scars on my frame are angrier, the lines in my face deeper, and yeah, that perpetually tired NCO look… there's a haunted aspect there now, that wasn't before.

You have to be honest about these things.

I am being honest.

I asked Nether, after the fact, and he said he saw no change in me, but that to him… I'd always looked haunted.

Thank you?

Intersecting side effect of Stinkeye opening up the Heart of Darkness for the win right there on the battlefield… Nether supercharged and went on a straight-up killing spree effectively delaying or stopping the entire push on Dog's collapsed sector.

No one will ever believe the numbers Nether racked up—this is the kind of thing that doesn't even happen in the spectacuthrillers—but maybe it's why the Monarchs wanted every bishop, or psy-can, under their control, or "accidentally" dead. Whatever… Nether knocked out an entire tank platoon, a scout mech, and whole bunch of dead infantry.

Before Stinkeye opened the door to the end of everything right there in the middle of the Ultra Marines' final push on LZ Heartbreak, right before, Nether told me, he was down and out for the count and no longer combat-effective as he leaned against the main struts of the cargo deck back at the *Spider*.

His actions at the scar had cost him dearly. He was out of juice and as I've highlighted in this account, once he's out of juice it's like a system crash. It can get worse for him to the point that it can drag him right into the void anchor he connects with to use his powers.

He was feeling like that cascade was underway within whatever a ghost calls a body of existence.

"I felt like I was dying, Orion. I didn't say anything to you, but I was sure I'd gone too far that time. Everything was darker than it usually is for me, and I could feel the void-wind, this effect that happens when I get too close to the anchor point, pulling me, really drawing me, to some anchor point affinity geo-located within the city. A place that, for reasons I can't figure out yet, must have some sort of connection with the anchor point I draw my powers from. I heard your comm asking for support as I just sat there trying not to fade completely to black. I remember the first sergeant telling you Stinkeye was on the way to your location. I heard the gunfire in the back of Chief Cook's comm, sounded real bad, so I knew they were about to get overrun. I could tell that. Listen, I'm no hero, Orion. But I thought… if I am going to die now… then I'd better make it count for something. So I just started stumbling away from the LZ toward where Dog was and those lines on the maps. The Ultras had already bypassed the Dog gun team. Most of them were dead. Just Suckitup over there and he was out of ammo for the gun, and they had him. There was an Ultra getting ready to shoot him, Orion, when I came out of the darkness near them. They were going to kill him even though they could have taken him alive, Orion."

I didn't interrupt my friend the ghost. He is, no matter his status with Strange Company, not a soldier. He doesn't understand the Ultras don't take prisoners. He only operates on what humanity should do. That's the way he thinks, and I consider it a flaw. It's better to imagine the worst, and what terrible things we can do to one another, when battle planning and trying to get your men through a mission. Believing the best in people... great way to get killed. In that Nether is naive, and as much as I sometimes want to lecture him about the realities of humanity, its inerrant badness, sometimes we need that one guy, one "tenth man" for the company, to remind us we might be capable of something better than constantly expecting the worst of our fellow humans.

We're still gonna do our best to kill them. But we should remember, some of them are trying hard to be better. We need a Nether to remind us of that.

Preacher has caught these interactions between us and reminded me, when they are over and it's just the two of us in the silence that follows, me trying to ignore the old man, him trying to "be there" for me, he has simply remarked, *"The heart of man is deceitfully wicked, Orion. Who can know it?"*

That sounds made up.

Sounds like something Preacher says when the galaxy hands you nothing but wrong answers and you try to make sense of it all and can't because it don't add. Like some puzzle with all the wrong pieces that don't match the picture on the box.

But he's right, and I hate Preacher even more for that. Usually, Preacher goes away and leaves me alone for a while after saying something stupid like that. Leaving me to "think on it" without actually saying that.

Joke's on him.

I sit in the dark, smoke, and drink coffee, and I don't think about it. Instead, I stew about all the other problems everyone, myself included, has caused me, and how I can "solve" them.

If you're an enemy of the company, when you're sleeping, I'm awake… thinking about you.

"I'm no hero, Orion," Nether was telling me as Suckitup was about to get shot dead by an Ultra who'd stormed the gun team's position, fragged everyone, and left the last wounded Dog platoon soldier for a Mozambique.

Mozambique. Two to the chest, one to the head. It's a thing we do.

You have to be honest about these things.

"And I couldn't let that happen, Orion. I had no charge left to do anything about it though. Nothing. So I flung myself right at that Ultra, screaming… something, as I tried to ram into him and save that kid. I don't know. Don't remember… what… I screamed…"

I've been there, Nether. I know those battle-mad moments. And other times of grief and rage when something comes out and it's the most honest thing you've never had the courage to say. You are not alone in that. None of us are.

"And I went right through him…" Nether laughed bitterly, rasping as he did so. "Because I'm non-corporeal, Orion. I don't exist. Or rather… my existence is a form of quantum entanglement like nothing the math ever told us was possible."

Meaning... he has no physical body. He's a ghost in the machine of reality if you prefer. But that's not entirely true. He's there... but... in a sort of negative image way. He breathes. He sleeps. He grieves. He is here for his brothers in the Strange, even if it is at their last moment. Like Hauser... he is human in ways we should aspire to be.

"The void cracked over where you were when it first appeared. Above you, Orion. Do you remember that moment? The noise and the sounds..."

I had seen nothing and I just let him continue on.

I have learned much in my time as the Keeper of the Strange Company Log.

"It must have... bothered... the Ultra Marine," continued Nether. "It must have bothered him when I passed right through him. He went blind, Orion, and started to shake violently all at once. I felt something when I passed through him. Some loss. Some deep sadness like a well inside him. But I'll have to think about that some more before I'm ready to hypothesize on the effect. I am still... a scientist, Orion. I am still doing science even though I have fallen in with mercenaries. But I've never had that experience, Orion. Never ever. Then again, doing science here, I've never really tried to pass through someone. It happens accidentally from time to time, but it's usually just a bump or a rub. They feel nothing but some vague uneasiness and I feel... nothing."

He stopped for a moment, and I could tell he was making some mental note. Then he continued.

"As a scientist, Orion, I need to understand why what happened... *happened*. Why that Ultra Marine suddenly went blind and started shaking uncontrollably like he'd just been dipped in subzero polar waters. His teeth were chattering as he shouted out, in that way Ultra Marines grunt orders, that he couldn't see."

Nether was thinking again.

I shook one out, lit it, and gave Nether the last of my smoke once I'd inhaled a few drags. He burned it, and it was gone as usual. As it always happened.

"By that time the void anchor was opening over you, Orion, and suddenly... I was... I was alive, Orion, like I've never been before. I just... knew... knew... I was really charged up, and, unbelievably, charging higher and higher by the second. The marine... he was still so intent on killing Suckitup despite being blind and shaking as he roared and his teeth chattered so hard it sounded like they were breaking, shattering, in his mouth. He was gonna fire blind. Wild. *Mag dump,* you call it. So I pointed right at him and just said, *STOP!*"

Nether stopped. But I could tell the shadow who was my friend and brother in the company was looking right at me. His mouth open. His disbelief... broadcasting on high power.

"And...?" I prompted.

"And he just... died, Orion. I mean right there on the spot. I... I have never done that, Orion. That's not what I do. I make stuff... volumes... disappear from reality. Sometimes... sometimes, Orion, I can make them reappear inside other things... but I've only experimented with this and when I do... when I have... I'm out. Totally drained. It's easier just to displace stuff and let the anchor point take it. But... after Hotsoup... I was... I was *soooooo* angry, Orion. Enraged and getting more... so I just... I just stopped that marine. Stopped him right there before he could kill

Suckitup. Stopped his heart, probably. That's what it felt like inside my mind."

Hotsoup again. Oh. Hell. No.

But I didn't say anything. 'Cause I'm a pro. Still, I could not believe the *Cult of Hotsoup* that had formed in the hours after his death. Unbelievable. No reason for it. And yet… it had. I had no idea everyone had some kind of relationship, or appreciation, for a merc we tagged because he burned his tongue on hot soup one day at the range.

I'd disliked him when he was alive. Now I hated him. And I know… yes, I have problems. Stress does weird things to you. I needed like twenty-five years off.

Nether continued.

"Not only did I *not* feel weak, Orion, from what I'd just done to that poor Ultra Marine right there on the field of battle…"

Field of Battle. Oh, Nether… that's so purple I have to put it in the logs and you'd better hope none of the guys read it. They'll never let you live it down. Or maybe they will because you bother them so much by the circumstances of your existence.

Still… it's so overheated. *Field of Battle.*

And *Poor Ultra Marine.* You mean, Nether, the ones doing their best to murder us. But go on, I don't say to him.

Though I have recorded it here for all time just to show how petty and small I am.

Like I said… Nether's not a soldier. If it weren't for the accident in the Dark Labs he'd be teaching at some sleepy college, or, when I think about it… dead long ago surrounded by children and grandchildren on some other world not this one.

And yet here he is with us, as the first sergeant might riff on one of his *tried and trues.*

"I knew we were in trouble, Orion. The Ultra Marines were pushing through and the armor, their fast tanks, they were coming right at what was left of Dog. I thought they were all dead except for Suckitup. I didn't think I could just walk through them all and stop them, but... like I said, I felt... *powered up* like I've never felt power before."

I have no laws of the universe. But if I did. Call it Orion's Law then. Put simply, it goes...

Those with power, will use it.

I expect a statue with none of my bad tattoos and a little taller than I actually am. That is the price of this simple wisdom I bequeath to the galaxy.

And Nether, for all his naivete and non-soldier ways, well, he suddenly became a Storm Viking on behalf of the company and started wrecking Ultras like a bull in a holo-crystal shop.

"I knew I needed to stop them, Orion. The entire world around me, all reality as I can see it when I'm in full quantum displacement, it was starting to become the void, and that should have concerned me. I should have been worried about getting totally depleted and sucked right down into the black hole that's there at the heart of it all. And the tentacles... they were everywhere. Did you see them where you were, Orion?"

Oh yeah, I saw them. Hard pass on ever seeing them again. One star. Do not recommend highly.

"But... I'm not depleting, Orion. I'm not even *weakening...* or waning... I've got power to burn. Power to stop the Ultra Marines somehow. And so I start doing what I know I can do. But... scaled up. Significantly."

Long story short. Nether starts grabbing black dirt from off the burnt LZ via his displacement power and filling the insides of the advancing tanks with matter. And before you think that's what actually happened…

A bunch of Ultra tankers were suddenly buried alive inside their tanks.

Yeah, that happened too, for sure. But then there was some kind of subatomic matter reaction that caused kinetic explosions where matter, the black charred dirt of the LZ the D-beam had cleared, and maybe that had something to do with it, residue from the six-gigawatt D-beam strike maybe interacted on some level we don't understand. Who knows, I'm not a scientist. Just some old ruck hobo trying to make it to the next thirty days' leave with all his fingers and toes and maybe some pay to spend on a pretty eel girl.

We all have goals. You got yours, I got mine, and believe me, you don't want to know what Choker's are. I can tell you that for sure.

Don't judge me. I got a thing for eel girls. Something to do with the oblivion of their pheromones… and the buzz you get from their electricity.

But somehow Nether's displacement strikes on the Ultra strike armor moving up on the *Spider* for the kill, fast-attack Pit Bull 905s with miniguns and recoilless quads, what Nether did caused sudden kinetic explosions of… dirt. Small dirt supernovas cooked off inside the tanks as Nether blasted each of the four Pit Bulls in the platoon. The dirt fountained in every direction. I mean, they got ripped apart by the explosions. Seriously. Very strange stuff.

"Want to know another weird thing that happened, Orion?" whispered Nether.

I sure do, Nether. Pins and needles, buddy.

"I'm running fast as it happens, trying to stop them, but I'm not really running though I think I am. I'm displacing, Orion. I'm... everything... is moving like I'm at regular speed and everything else is at slow motion speed, but with frames missing. The only thing I can hypothesize about what happened is that I started to 'blink' using the displacement fields. Wherever I was trying to go, I was there instantly, fully charged, more charged in fact than I'd ever been, and blasting the tanks apart. And I got that mech too. Same way."

He was silent.

I lit a smoke and waited for him to continue.

"And the infantry supporting the strike armor push, Nether?"

Nether said nothing and I had a pretty good idea why.

He took the smoke and burnt it, making it disappear from space-time forever. His little trick.

"That, Orion," he whispered. His hand making a gesture I'd understand later. A gesture pointing to where the smoke should have been.

"What?" I asked.

He was silent again, waiting for me to understand just what had really happened to the last of my smoke.

"There are some things I don't want to talk about, Orion, ever again. Those Ultra Marines on foot, advancing with the tanks, that will be one of them. We got Suckit, Chief, and the last three from Dog... we got 'em outta there, Orion. That's enough of a reason. I understand more what you guys do. I get that now. Why... why you cope the way you do, Orion. I understand that... now. More than I ever did before. We got them out of there. That's all that matters, Orion. That's all... that matters."

No, Nether. You got them out of there. And now, you'll just have to live with that.

Just like we all do.

CHAPTER FORTY-SIX

So, what really happened when Stinkeye opened up the seam in the universe? Or as he calls it, "Da Heart o' da Darkness."

Sometimes I just write Heart of Darkness. But to hear him say it the way he says it… it's different. More serious. More sinister.

It's best to be honest about these things.

Stinkeye was chattering wildly as he brought it on. Babbling insanely on and on about "gates beyond death" and "udder worlds and da wrongs and da ain't never rights and da Big Eye who never no care about no nothin' and just want da consuming to be a-startin'."

He howled like a sick wolf and spasmed violently, shaking his fist at the darkness above.

"Den come now, yas bastard eye… come and take all yas wants… One day… one day… one day… yas gonna choke on it all!"

He was shaking violently now. Convulsing but waving us away if we dared try to help him.

Us. There was Stinkeye. Then there was Ulysses leading the left flank with Punch as his wingman and Choker and our last New Guy. Two. Me on the right with Solo and Two Times following. Klutz at the back. Wolfy on rear security. Hoser and Hustle with Hustle darting here and there, scavenging every half-burnt belt he could find.

Us who were following the mech as the darkness closed about us… and swallowed the battlefield we'd spent the night fighting over.

Stinkeye below the mech, chanting about how the end had come, the end of all things… was here and now. "Feast and fill but take da enemy first," he crooned.

"What in the hell is your guy doing?" asked Sergeant Angry from the mech cockpit, the hum and tick of instruments beeping and chirping as the mech stomped forward through the last of the night's gloom. We were approaching the lip of the strike crater one more time. We knew the terrain. We could put up a good fight here. "Reaper Actual, we got thirty seconds worth of ammo on full burn for the guns. Then that's it. Other than the waist gunner, we're just stomping on stuff."

"Stand by…" I told Brawler Two's mech commander. "Stink…"

The Voodoo war wizard chief was out of his mind, raving like a lunatic instead of a warrant officer in the company. But, as someone once said, *You go to war with what you got. Not what you want.*

If I got what I wanted, then that Phantom on station would be dropping ordnance all over the battlefield and making it rain the pain.

Then we'd sort what was left.

"Stink… Stinkeye… Stinkeye, dammit!" I shouted, my last restraints snapping. I had too much to deal with and didn't need a drunk warrant officer losing his mind right now. I needed some voodoo.

And frankly… I wasn't seein' it happening.

Of course, I was mistaken. The wind was starting to pick up. It was just before dawn and the wind was hot and it didn't smell like burnt leaves or fall like when the Little Girl's Wild Thing had come and devastated our enemies one more time.

That would have been a game-changer right about now.

No, the night wind smelled like death, and sulfur.

In my defense, after the night's slaughter, the dead lying out there in the burnt black sand and apocalypse glass, they smelled pretty bad already. So I missed the change when the wind got hot, caressing the dead and ruin, and smelled like something other than just death.

Stinkeye danced, whirled, arms upraised, heedless of my frustrated shouts. That's when I noticed things were beginning to get really weird.

Very weird in fact.

There was this audible… *thump*. Like a pulse low and ominous that suddenly rippled through everything. Like… something had just bumped into something else and that wasn't supposed to happen in the natural scheme of things. It felt like an accident, but worse. It felt wrong. Unnatural. Supernatural… in fact. In hindsight.

But simply put, it was like… a mic… had been accidentally dropped in a sound studio, shattering the thick silence with a tremendous *bump*.

Stinkeye ceased his gyrations instantly for a moment, holding still and looking around. He held up one long dirty finger and looked at us.

"Tings go bump in da night, children. Listen now yas… bumpty-bump."

I don't know if I truly heard this, because it was there, and it wasn't. As in, you thought you heard it, and then it was so weird you couldn't believe you actually heard it.

So, I don't know. Putting it in the logs. Maybe someone six thousand years from now can make sense of it. Me, a dumb and tired ruck hobo, that voodoo stuff is way above my pay grade.

But it sounded like the chains, the anchor chains in fact, of some old fishing boat on a wine-dark ocean under clouds and moon, don't ask me why I got that image, but I did, it sounded like those chains were suddenly rolling out all at once as the anchor was released and fell away into midnight gulfs deep below the water.

Gulfs...

Stinkeye shrieked, "Where da tings not seen... dey live down dere!"

It, whatever the thump and chains were, it pushed our guts... outward... that's how it felt and it's the only way I can describe that first moment when the seam began to rip into the reality of the universe we'd been fighting over on LZ Heartbreak.

A spot on a map on a world. One of many. Statistically too small to be meaningfully measured. But suddenly, it felt like something was watching us. Something bigger than us. Something that didn't... *like*... us.

Stinkeye began to laugh, and cry, at the same time...

"Here come..."

"Here come..."

He chanted.

He shook his fist like he was tossing the bones for a sudden-death round of Cheks.

"*Here come da pain. Rumma dumma dum dane... da numba be... dis time...*" Then he flung dice we couldn't see. "*...da numba be nineteen.*"

He was singing madly and sobbing hysterically like some faithless sinner ready to repent of everything if only just to avoid judgment impending.

Then he was laughing with joy like he was singing some hymn, or chanting numbers in the desert like the madmen of Hazan are known to do. Chanting the code of the universe.

"Here come da pain... like da desert rain... I love da pain... I love DA pain... I love da PAIN... I LOVE DA... Payyyyannne!"

Yeah, it made everyone's blood run cold.

The night sky shifted above us to a blinding white. Like an image suddenly reversed in the negative of black and white.

Then that tearing sound ripped through us. Like something that wasn't supposed to do that.

I remember my guys looking around to find it. I stood there, one hand up to my comm in that picture of the perennial NCO getting orders under fire. Trying to look and hear the traffic at the same time. Heedless and aware in the same moment that death has come close, and is in fact, calling. Dialing your number like it's known it since the day you were born. But you're listening because those orders, or information, or whatever, it's coming down the line from the guys who can drop steel, or call a Phantom drop in and solve your problems with tons of ordnance on demand. Ordnance that might save your squad... You're listening because the traffic is there... barely... on the other side of the ether.

And you need to know.

"Stinkeye!" I shouted over the ripping sound that tore the universe apart and made the night dark clouds above suddenly brilliant and photorealistic white like billowing ghosts. The blank spaces in between, where it would be the last of the night up there and the stars above… those were dark, dark, darkest night like the color of Hannibal's black heart.

Chromatic midnight if there's such a color.

I remember now… I remember now… I remember thinking… maybe dawn will save us now. Like a child hoping the needle that's about to sting… doesn't. Maybe it's here now, I was babbling to myself without making a sound, hoping for anything but what was becoming imminently certain. That what I'm seeing… isn't happening. That this has nothing to do with Stinkeye. Nothing. He's not doing this. All this supernatural weirdness… it's not happening.

But it is. It was. It did.

Knowing I was wrong, I checked my watch… saw that it was frantically running backwards, and sighed thinking stupid NCO thoughts about not needing this right now.

The impossible was happening, impossibly, and there I was acting like the training schedule was screwed. I am a small man caught up in grand things. They should have picked someone better equipped to deal with all… the weird things the company had gotten itself into.

Something… no wait… that's not right but I started to write the next line about someone and instead I used something. Noting it here because… maybe it's important later.

But yeah, what I meant to write was… someone better like Ulysses.

But you wrote, Sergeant Orion, *something*.

Okay… noted.

Moving on with the part where the thing at the end of the universe came and attacked our enemies.

Stinkeye was on his knees by that time, babbling and blubbering, grabbing handfuls of the blasted burnt black sand and eating it, laughing madly and sobbing, screaming…

Honestly, I'd seen half this schtick before. Any amount of leave given the company by the Old Man and the first shirt, and it was more than likely you were going to find Stinkeye drunk and babbling and doing half the nutty things he was doing now. And he'd probably pissed himself.

So, you had that going for you if you were on CQ duty for the weekend pass.

I have faked Denebian retroflu just to avoid charge of quarters duty when I could just feel, just know, that Stinkeye was going to be a real problem. And no, I'm not ashamed. You ain't cheatin', you ain't tryin'.

"All gonna die now all gonna die now all gonna die now…" he moaned.

You get the gist. He was a mess. But he was our mess. It was bad. And looking to get worse by the second.

Or as Punch put it, breaking the impending doom with a *Punchism*, the crackle of our comm barely working as that wind like a warm witch in heat came blasting over us… serious now.

Nether's Void Wind, as he called it…

"Big Sarge… too late to say I didn't sign up for this?"

Those who could… copied or double-clicked.

"Negative on that," I mumbled. "We're in it, Strange. Shoot, move, and communicate. Get on it when it starts, take it to them. Eel chicks dig scars."

Just as I said those words, a huge flock like some unclean undulating black mass of darkness… is that right… a flock, felt like something else… of evil black birds swept across the sky above crossing below those photo-bright-white clouds and chromatic midnight spaces in between.

Stinkeye stood, going silent in an instant…

And if you thought everything up until this point was weird… well, as has been said… *hold on ta ya butts.* The world, everything, let's just call it reality as we knew it… well, it bent to the side. Not over, but… *it leaned.* And not literally… but you had that weird moment of vertigo that it was actually happening that way.

I remember saying at that moment… "That sounds like wood warping."

Something deep and ominous that wasn't human… groaned.

Leave it to Choker to clarify horrifically, "Like a giant's mouth is opening to swallow us whole now."

Puncher… "Coulda done without that, psycho."

"Technically I'm a sociopath," corrected our medic.

Stinkeye was looking at me by that point, grabbing on to my chest rig and staring right into me like he was either looking for something or getting ready to borrow hard mem for a bad bet.

Then…

"Kill 'em all, Orion. Kill 'em all now and let da universe sort."

CHAPTER FORTY-SEVEN

The Marines, the Ultra Marines, were advancing through all the Stinkeye-summoned weirdness when the firefight began.

Contact front.

Hell… contact everywhere in an instant.

By that point, when the lead element of that pincer of the Ultra Marine push on LZ Heartbreak literally walked right into us as the darkness all around undulated, and the deep sounds of an unseen universe groaned and rolled out from twilight gulfs that would have driven us mad had we actually seen them, I'm sure of that, they weren't engaging. They were just as stunned as we were. But Punch has amazing reflexes and to be honest… he's always looking for a fight. Even if the end of everything has come for breakfast.

The Ultras had formed up into combat wedges as they crossed the blasted and blackened sands, stepping over the dead and avoiding the burning wreckage of their armor, but even they were looking around in amazement at the magnificent horror of what we were finding ourselves in… whatever it was.

The birds.

The ghostly clouds so blinding it hurt to look at them. The darkness that was deeper than any shade of black you'd ever seen. Like it was a living thing that ate light. Consumed it. Devouring and devouring…

All of us were stunned. But like I said… Punch reacted first.

Dark skies the color of the blackest wrongs passed quickly as the devil wind rose and yes… hissed. It hissed. Choker said later it sounded like a sizzling sound. Bacon and eggs in a cast-iron skillet too hot already.

But to me… the devil wind hissed at us.

Clouds billowing and boiling here and there like bright specters that seemed to be inhaling and breathing unlife. Evil black birds of a kind we'd never seen before, but still had some genetic memory of from back on Earth, the home world, a place we'd all once started out from, everyone here to kill each other now, those birds had come from there.

And a long time ago we'd known their names and shunned them as omens of evil while we tried to make fire, hunt, and even gather. And when that failed, war. We made war then.

We made it now.

Punch started firing staccato bursts in the first ice-cold-water moment of contact.

Now the unnamed evil birds were swarming down out of the boiling black and burning white sky to fall on the dead we had created, tearing at flesh and eyeballs.

Caw caw cawing.

And that hot breath devil wind blasting, not past us, but through all of us. As though everything, life, the universe, and the meaning of it all… were breathing its last and the wind was taking all of it off to the void place.

Displacing.

I know… I accused Nether of going purple with his *Field of Battle.* But all this description, this is exactly how it felt, and I am not embellishing it one bit. If anything, I'm not doing enough.

Sure, yeah, the truth just is, say old dead philosophers. But that's what happened. This is the truth.

There were graves coming up out of the black dirt and apocalypse sand. But they weren't any kind of graves I'd ever seen in all my crossings of the stars. Not the kind of death markers we left and made to bury our dead on worlds we'd fought on. But the kinds of graves of aliens we'd never known. Ones they would make and leave in their... trail across the stars. Just as we were doing now.

Yes. I know. That's weird.

But we have to be honest about these things.

Three wedges of Ultra Marines—maybe the last there would ever be—pushed over the top and around the curve of the crater, staring in amazement at the blackness and torment everything had suddenly become.

Those dark black evil birds tearing apart all our dead. Theirs. Ours.

Even the Ultras were still human enough to be amazed at what a real apocalypse looks like. A real end of everything known.

Then Stinkeye was grabbing me and twisting away to point at something, his face contorted in a rageful sneer...

"Kill 'em all. Kill 'em all and let da universe sort," he shrieked.

It was Punch, of course Punch who opened fire, roaring neither *Get some* or *Contact front* but simply... "Get It On!"

I remember the bright blue ghostly electric flare our weapons made as we engaged the three wedges of Ultras. That wasn't natural. A byproduct of the quantum drawing everything near to the end of everything else.

Knowns and unknowns intermingling and creating sub-atomic shenanigans like gunfire turning ghostly blue among the midnight black of a battlefield swarming with carrion and alien graves coming through the black sand.

Punch leaned forward suddenly, snapped into it really, right into the classic gunfighter stance. Rifle seated firmly in the pocket of his shoulder. Left hand, assault gloved, gripping the barrel to stabilize, and suddenly igniting the last firefight with maximum violence.

Which is what you do. Every time.

His shorty blared and he put tightly grouped rounds into an Ultra at the tip of the wedge, tip of the spear, who must not have even seen us yet.

I'd wonder later if the Heart of Darkness was messing with their fancy heads-up displays and targeting systems in their Ultra Marine slick armor.

I saw it go down and that's my guess.

Choker faded right, walking shots at another Ultra. Ulysses of course signaled the attack with his off arm and started shooting Ultras down. And advancing.

This was their rightmost flank. Our left. There was another wedge of Ultra Marines literally coming over the lip of the crater at the same time. And one coming behind us on our right flank.

They were sweeping ahead of the force coming out of Dog's sector. The one Nether was about to straight-up ruin.

I heard Hustle shout, "Let's rock!" and the Ultras back there, coming through the breach we'd created to get the mech off the X, they were getting chewed to pieces by the Pig to the rear of the formation.

At the same moment they attacked.

We took fire.

I got hit. Hard.

Busted chest plate I'd figure out later.

Guy in their first wedge sucked dirt and shot me once Punch dropped their point man.

I went down, gun up, then opened fire on him thinking, *Oh Hell Oh Hell Oh Hell I'm hit.*

Which I have said before, because… I've been shot before.

I hit the guy who shot me in the head and his helmet went back at a very wrong angle that wouldn't be good at all for him. The Bastard does that. Why? Because the Bastard do punch hard, kids. Ain't a sexy tacticool weapon. But it will get it done and straight-up ruin your day when it connects.

Then my hand was up and even though I couldn't breathe, and I knew I needed to lay back, I also knew my plate armor had caught the shot square and busted into several pieces by physical scan with my hand, looking for blood to come away on my glove and the finger pad I'd burnt. My front plate was done.

But I wasn't.

I still couldn't breathe though, and it was like that void wind had sucked the light… *life*… out of me.

Another mistake I tried to write that felt… true but wasn't. Interesting. Light. Life.

As the fight in the sand started, Sergeant Angry spun up both guns on the Marauder's arms and eliminated the Ultras to our front in a sudden blossom of overwhelming mech-induced destruction. Suddenly everyone there disappeared in a blur of outgoing lead and rising dirt fountains. Armor shattered, guns disintegrated, body parts went flying.

Those guns at close range are just a blur of outgoing, high-dosage, death.

And at the same time, as the Ultras forward of our wedge died, the evil birds swept in, shattered also by the gunfire, too greedy as they began to tear and rip at them, cawing madly.

But Sergeant Angry wasn't done. He traversed, guns spooling and bleeding the last of the hot brass, drawing cannon fire across the lip of the crater above us, literally cutting several space marines in half right there before they could produce effective fire.

This was... ten seconds.

Three wedges of marines were dead, but we were engaged by more coming in.

An AT round streaked in at the mech, who was busy turning an enemy scout mech in the distance, walking flank for the Ultras, into sudden Swiss cheese. The guns of the Marauder went dry just seconds before she took the fatal hit.

I heard her guns beginning to make that high-pitched whine they produce when they spin on empty barrels.

I was just catching my breath. There was high-cycle gunfire to my rear from the Pig. I remember thinking... that's good. Go Hustle. Go Hoser.

There were dead Ultras forward but more coming in. I started engaging and trying to breathe at the same time. I had no voice to issue any kind of meaningful orders.

Ulysses, Choker, and Punch advanced in a three-man wedge, killing as they went. Getting into the Ultras before they could react.

New Guy Number Two wasn't dead. But he was dying. He'd been hit and the evil birds had come for him in the same instant as though whatever was doing this for Stinkeye had some kind of first dibs on the fallen. Swarms of them raced greedily for his body in sudden flying fury.

Stinkeye charged them, banging away at the midnight black and burning white above with his ancient and dirty 1911. Yelling, "Git away from him ya damn demons!" as he drove them away from the downed man.

Then he had the New Guy.

New Guy had lost an eye. But he was still alive. Not dead as I'd first thought.

I can only guess what his tag will be.

But Stinkeye saved him from the greedy evil birds.

At that same moment, the mech was on fire right at our center, standing in the field of black sand and ruin and spent shell casings. The AT round had come in and struck the gunner's cupola. Flames and smoke were erupting from there and to me... it looked bad.

I tapped the comm and offered help, but Sergeant Angry was already climbing out of the mech commander's cockpit above the gunner's cupola after having blown the command hatch with the escape-ejection charges.

That hatch had instantly skyrocketed overhead, catching the devil wind and getting carried off into the night never to be seen again as the fight dissolved into everyone for themselves, shooting at as many of the swarming enemy as we could.

The staccato eruptions of our blue flashing carbines barked and flickered frantically in the midnight blackness all around. The Ultras... were having problems, but they were Ultras... so they fought hard, even at the last when it was turning into a rout. Many of them pulled off their helmets to engage with iron sights or use the helmets as weapons themselves. That confirmed for me that the Heart of Darkness had somehow messed with their targeting capabilities.

Meanwhile on the mech, the Apocalypse Solutions platoon sergeant waved me away as I ran for the burning mech. He was down to the gunner's cupola, fire extinguisher in hand.

I fell down, unable to breathe still. I was blacking out. I needed air. My men needed help with outgoing fire. The mech crew needed help not burning alive in there.

Again, I ran my hands over my chest. No blood. But I couldn't catch my breath.

Then I watched as Klutz ran past me and grabbed the handholds that had been emergency-deployed by the onboard AI once the damage control kicked in. He climbed up to take the first wounded guy out of the mech. Flames were crawling all over the gunner's cupola up there, coming from the emergency escape hatch and from inside the crew compartments. Angry was inside already, and he appeared with a looped carrying sling and the wounded gunner. He drew it around Klutz who was at the edge of the cupola, then told Klutz to head back down along the handholds. He'd lower the wounded man once Klutz had started down. The weight would equalize and by the time Klutz reached the bottom, the wounded man would be below him on the ground.

Flames were already crawling all over him as the fuel cells began to rupture. Still he lowered the unconscious gunner and held the slack until Klutz was stable. Then shouted for Klutz to take over.

"Climb down, you stupid bastard!" shouted Angry as flames raced along his arms.

I tried to stand, took a breath that hurt like hell, and stumbled toward the mech to take the wounded gunner getting lowered to the sand.

The fire extinguisher was going off above in the gunner's cupola once I had the wounded guy and Klutz down on the sand. I could breathe a little so I tightened my sling with a quick yank as I began to climb up, knowing I shouldn't. By the time I got to the top edge of the gunner's hatch, I was sure Angry was dead. I had enough adrenaline now to actually breathe myself into low-grade hyperventilation. But at least I was breathing.

The fire was out when I climbed into the tight burnt space.

But it was hot, and I had to be careful.

The driver, who'd thrown a fire blanket over the driver's compartment and hunkered down, crawled out and pushed his way toward Angry who was lying back against the gunner's seat. His flesh blackened over his torso and face. His fatigues and gear melted to his body.

I'd seen enough burn injuries to know this was bad.

He was breathing hard and shallow, gasping and mumble-swearing.

The driver bent down to get him, and Sergeant Angry didn't so much push him away as feebly wave his troop off.

I told the kid to get down and get out of the mech.

He was more than happy to go. The heat sinks were starting to cook off along the rear of the walking giant death machine. More fires would start soon. The fuel cells would ignite. Then…

I bent down and told him, "I got ya, Sergeant."

He gasped. His vocal cords cooked.

"Na-na-no… die… here," he gasped. "Get…"

He was going to die. Yes. He was gonna die no matter what I did. He was burnt that bad. Mech fires are real bad in the scheme of bad things that can happen when people try to kill each other with weapons. He fumbled for his sidearm with one hand that was little more than a burnt claw.

I bent down, hearing the gunfire going on out there. It was a real fight. My guys needed me, I thought.

Then: *Ulysses is with them. He can do it. He's... better than me.* And in that... I was finally grateful. Glad I'd rescued him off a bad LZ. Not jealous. Just glad my guys had a thinking fighter to lead them through and out of this.

"Listen, Sergeant..." I said to Angry on the fire-scorched deck of the mech's gunnery compartment.

"Ain't... ain't gonna... make... it," he gasped again like he was reciting law.

"I know. You're not gonna make it. But I gotta get you out now. Okay? It's gonna hurt... but we gotta do this."

"Wha-wha-why?" he said, his eyes filled with incredulousness. Tears of pain.

I'd grabbed one of the emergency wounded carry slings from the box they kept in all mech stations. It was hot and burnt plastic was everywhere. But the sling was fire-retardant.

"Gotta do this, Sergeant. Gotta do it so those guys can live with the fact that we got you out of a burning mech and didn't leave you to die in here when you went in to save them. You're not gonna make it. But they'll know... and maybe... someday they'll do what we sergeants gotta do when some kid's stuck in a bad situation. Feel me, Sergeant?"

My voice shook. If what I said sounded hard, it was intended to be. But I... I didn't feel it. The man was dying, and we both knew it. But we needed to be as hard as we could pretend to be to get done what needed to be done.

He nodded. Accepting the final orders he'd carry out.

"This… what… we do… Sergeant," he gasped.

I nodded. I felt like crying. But I didn't have time, and I just couldn't and get this done.

He said one last thing before he died. Just as I was getting the sling rigged for the carry down.

"Tough… bein'… NCO."

I said *I know*. But it didn't come out.

By the time I got him to the ground and away from the mech he was dead. I laid him in the black sand. I couldn't close his eyes. The lids were melted off. So I just turned his head to the side, and as I did so, a strange smile seemed to form on his face.

As though he were saying something good despite everything we'd been through, and how it ended for him.

As though he were saying, *Good to go now, Sergeant. Good to go.*

CHAPTER
FORTY-EIGHT

The battle for the lip of the crater will never be marked on any maps regarding the Sack of Marsantyium. There certainly weren't many survivors. The ones who walked away were either Reaper or wounded and they probably didn't survive the destruction of *Red Dragon*.

But it happened.

Those three contact wedges of infantry that came at us were the leading element of the last Ultra Marine push, probably in recorded history.

There was nothing left of them after that day.

The Ultras... were done.

We'd fought them through that whole night, and in the end... what they threw at the crater, was all they had left.

They'd been fighting the Insurrection and the chimps for twenty-five years. Buying time for their careless masters to avoid the inevitable. Losing world after world as the whole con of their civilization collapsed.

Mortals playing gods playing dice with humanity. Even the Ultras. And in the end, the Ultras, just to go out on a high note, had Mozambiqued their own gods.

I will give them this... that's hardcore.

Ave, Ultra Marines.

As one soldier to another, *You done good.*

Maybe Haymaker was already underway by the time that last engagement took place. Maybe there were other

Ultra Marine forces going for the LZ that had gotten diverted to stop the push on the last Ultra command bunker Haymaker was on the move for.

I don't know. No one knows now. The surface of the planet got cleaned when the *Red Dragon* detonated.

Stinkeye's darkness spell began to break up as the dawn came in the east. We'd surrendered the ground we'd fought on for at least thirty minutes. Then climbed the lip of the impact crater and made our stand there, shooting down who we could, avoiding getting shot as much as possible. We could shoot down at the Ultras forward of our position from there. The evil birds attacked the dead out there. And sometimes the Ultra Marines seemed to get sucked down into those strange alien graves that had risen up and were now fading with the red light of a bloody dawn as though they'd never even been there.

"Black on mags," someone called on the rough line we were holding.

I worked the distribution and tried to keep everyone with something to shoot with. We had pickups and some switched over to those.

That was when I saw the thin red line of dawn growing in the east of the Marsantyium sky.

The eye above us was closing. Stinkeye, dead or alive, lay back among the dead we'd killed down there where the mech had burned. He was sheltering the one-eyed Strange Company brother. To me, from the height of the lip of the crater, he looked dead. They both looked dead. Then again, everywhere you looked there were dead.

I have fought on a few real battlefields. Sometimes it's that. Mostly it's just engagements out in the bush, by a stream, a desert crossroads you can find no rational reason you're both out there to kill each other over. This was the worst, most corpse-laden battlefield I'd ever seen.

There was a lot of ruined armor still burning and cooking off there too. And the dead that hadn't made it out of those vehicles.

And beyond, in silent, eyeless buildings ruined by shell and shot, there were probably dead there too.

And beyond that, the airstrikes, the artillery, the orbital bombardments… in the streets of Marsantyium there were probably sprays of that red marble and bricks of sandstone cast out into the wide avenues where artillery pieces and downed dropships smoldered in their destruction.

I looked down as the last of the fight wound down. The Ultras must have known they didn't have the numbers to go forward anymore. And there was nothing, soon, to be left to go back to.

Strange for them.

I looked down at the corpse, or body, of Stinkeye and the wounded soldier lying a distance away from the ruined mech. Sergeant Angry's body nearby.

Many have thought the old space war wizard was dead before when he really wasn't at all.

That'll be a day. The day when he dies.

I don't know if I want to be there for that day. But I have a very bad feeling I will be.

From the lip of the crater, I could see the Ultra dead. Everywhere. Burning armor and mechs, their black boiling smoke columns rising against the red dawn telling me there was nothing left, and no one else was pushing through this sector.

To the north, I saw elements of Haymaker pushing forward in masses that could not be denied. Firefights, small ones over there, started up and ended quickly. Not lasting more than seconds. Dropships, ours, overhead and following the columns of Task Force Haymaker heading into the objective.

There would be one last desperate fight at the command bunker. But the outcome was certain. Even for an optimist like me.

Suddenly loud and long bursts of gunfire would bark from the powerful onboard weapons systems of the armored hunter-killer dropships killing pockets of Ultra resistance.

What had been decided… it was clear now the Ultras had been rolled.

We won.

Impossibly. It was over. For us.

We won and it felt… I don't know. It just happened. Everything would now happen that was supposed to happen. They would go down fighting with what they had. We would roll them and then clean up. More of us would die. The big Insurrection troop carriers and support ships would move in, and this world would be declared under Insurrection control.

Whatever that meant.

I think the Seeker was either some sort of queen, or a general of some sort. Maybe even a dictator.

The chimps… that was the big dangling thread of the future. Who knew. If they were smart, they'd roll us now. Winner take all.

We had hit them with everything and paid for it.

The chimps had too and still seemed to have more to burn.

That's usually the winner in most conflicts, contrary to the grand strategies of generals and politicians, or the big mega-torpedo that destroys the death ship in all spectacuth-rillers.

The hero saving the day.

It's usually just who can keep hitting when the other guy can't anymore. Same thing with armies, nations, and empires.

First one outta weapons loses.

Less people would get into war if they understood that simple concept. Especially if you're on the losing side.

But then how would you get a uniform, do brave things, and be remembered by the girl who will lay flowers on your grave if she hasn't moved on already?

I don't know. Go ask the Ultras.

I sank down. My chest hurt from getting tagged. The barrel of the Bastard was blazing hot, still smoking because I'd worked it hard. I held it with one hand, butt planted in the black apocalypse sand. Sand that was once red. I shook out a smoke and just watched the end of everything I'd ever known… disappear.

I don't know what I'd expected, but this was different than anything I'd ever thought would happen in the end.

Or if there ever would be an end.

The Ultra Marines, guard dogs of the Monarchs, were trashed, and this was the last of them out there, lying dead as far as the eye could see. The last divisions, the last air wings. The last armor companies. They'd gambled to retain their honor here on Marsantyium, even smoking their own petty masters so they could get it done without political interference from vain and egotistical mortals playing out being something more than them.

The Ultras should have revolted and formed a martial empire. If they had, my bet is we wouldn't be here, and they would. But they didn't and so they're not.

They'd failed.

Finally.

Beaten by mangy stray dogs looking for... those mysterious human words we may not even know the meaning of anymore they've been lost for so long.

Life. Liberty... whatever.

Ruin and death spread away from us as far as the eye could see... but it was good ruin if there ever could be such a thing.

A good death. And yes, there can be.

Haymaker was on the move out there beyond the wreckage of a bad LZ. From the look of it, unless... something dramatic happened... they couldn't be stopped now. They'd make a direct hit against the Ultra rear.

"Uh-oh..."

It was Choker who first noticed the cheat the Monarchs would play on us at the end. Cheating us of our victory. He was doming downed Ultras in the blasted ruin below, "just to make sure they're dead," he said to no one.

He just likes to shoot people.

I followed his gaze as he stopped his target practice and stared up into the yellow haze of morning on Marsantyium.

Ulysses shouted, "Run!" once he saw it.

Then he was headed down the scree of the blasted crater, shouting, "Run! Now, Reaper!"

Not *move*. Not *withdraw*. Not even *retreat!* Just... run.

As in run for your lives.

I followed the line of his sudden course. He was headed back to the *Spider*.

"What?" I shouted after him.

"Oh, hell no…" muttered Punch. "I'm too tired to fight some more."

Ulysses turned. We still weren't moving.

"They've declared *No Joy*. It's their final option. Run, Reaper, run now like your lives depend on it because they do!"

"What in the ever-living hell is *No Joy?*" shouted Punch like he was some Space Marine drill instructor who'd discovered a secret horde of chocolate bars stashed prior to barracks inspection.

Above us, through the yellow miasma of the upper atmosphere, *Red Dragon*, the last Monarch Battle Spire, was coming down through the clouds and the growing red dawn widening along the horizon. Creating shadows across the landscape of dead and ruined vehicles and a city that once was, and never would be again.

"What in the ever-living hell is *No Joy*, Ulysses? We won. Fair and square! What the hell is this…" Punch raged but we were all following Ulysses down the slope of the crater, getting anxious by what had freaked out our very own hardcore Ultra. Ulysses was ahead and working his way down to the ground level. He stopped at the bottom.

Lightning began to crackle in the skies around the massive Battle Spire. It arced across the sky, coming from *Red Dragon* herself. In the distance some very wrong and weird ominous *hummmmmmmmmmmmmmmmm* thundered through the whole world. As though dangerous energies were being raised to unheard-of and ill-advised levels. As though final cards were being played.

As though we'd left them no other choice… than this. The final denial of service. Denial of victory. *No Joy*.

"This is bad! This is bad!" repeated Choker over and over again as we moved. "I have no idea why… but… this is bad! This is bad!"

"Get back to the ship now!" shouted Ulysses as he made ready to organize the carry of the wounded we had. "It's the only chance we have to survive. Maybe the shield generators are up, or we'll just have to rely on the anti-radiation shielding in the armor. Move, Reaper, now. Here, help me get the new guy up! *No Joy* is when they det the Battle Spire over the area of operations to deny final victory by an enemy force. It's the final option. And only the Monarchs themselves can execute it."

We ran for our lives.

CHAPTER
FORTY-NINE

We ran for our lives. And yeah, we looked back over our shoulders as we lugged our wounded, pushed who needed to be pushed, helped who needed to be helped, and realized there'd been a big old giant ticking clock the whole time.

Of course the Monarchs weren't gonna let us win. They weren't just gonna blow up their stuff. They were gonna blow up *everyone's* stuff.

The ultimate denial-of-service attack.

We had gunshot wounds.

"Here we go, kids," shouted Punch as he carried the lead on the Blind Guy's litter. "The hustle's on and last one to the ship's the biggest loser of all time. Move it, Reaper!"

Remember, get wounded in the company when you're still a New Guy or a Kid and you immediately get upgraded to a tag.

Punch had decided New Guy Number Two who'd lost his eye in a firefight with Ultra Marines would henceforth be known as *Blind Guy*.

I could tell. That's how it would go down. The stress and epicness of what we'd just been through would imprint the narrative of his name.

"*There we were,*" some Strange Company grunt in the future would start. "*Last Battle Spire about to go up like a Cyclonian candle… and Punch calls him Blind Guy. I almost died laughing because to me he looked dead, and I thought*

we were just gonna call him something like Corpse or Bones.
Somethin' cool. Instead... Blind Guy. Punch for the win, man."

I laughed because that's how sick I am. Even the future
was darkly funny for me no matter how horrible it could
possibly be. I guess that's what makes sergeants sergeants.
They know it can only get worse. And Blind Guy was this
close to getting something cool like *Cyclops* and Punch had
done him in forever with a goofy tag that was true, and it
wasn't. Forever, Blind Guy would be subject to variations of
the following... *Hey, Blind Guy... see that bad guy? Oh, that's*
right... you're blind. You can't see squat!

Him: Hey guys, I'm not blind. I still have the one eye.

Everyone else: Yeah, still can't shoot worth a damn with
that one either.

Men are fun that way. Which is what you have to tell
yourself to keep pickin' 'em up and puttin' 'em down.
Women never get it.

But I wouldn't want them to. We have to have someone
in our lives who doesn't make us feel horrible all the time.
Someone who thinks we're the bravest man in the world
just because we killed a spider or fixed a sink. Or made a
commitment.

But I know very little about these things. I am just a
ruck hobo and I have no doubt Plan B was always a pile of
brass on some world gone mad.

Once you accept that, life's pretty good. Free samples
taste better whenever they happen to you like small miracles
you know you don't deserve.

If Blind Guy was smart, he'd shut up. Time would tell.
Maybe he'd end up getting called *Cyclops* if he pushed the
one-eyed comment every time he had a chance. Subtly.

These are the things an NCO hopes for when he thinks of his soldiers. Small good turns that make all the difference, and perhaps they get promoted and take his job.

A ruck hobo can dream, y'know. He can dream. He's human just like everyone else, contrary to what everyone thinks.

Pressure bandages were the best we could do, and moving as best and as fast as we could… was also the best we could do.

That massive Battle Spire was making best speed down through atmo and it was clear exactly what her intentions were if Ulysses's *No Joy* call was to be effected.

Stinkeye ran ahead of us with complete abandon, drunkenly screaming, "We all gonna die now! We all gonna die now!"

So, that was helpful.

The sky was starting to turn an odd energy-pulsing purple.

And the skies don't turn purple over Marsantyium. Or at least they don't in anyone's experience I've ever heard from.

The last time I looked back I saw *Red Dragon* under attack from both capital ships and swarms of Insurrection mish-mash navy fighters. Old war dogs from great battles long ago, and newer-gen fighters leading flight wedges in against critical targets in the massive ship's systems. They were doing everything they could to stop her before she reached her primary ignition point for the detonation, and then maybe Task Force Haymaker would make the hit on Ultra high command and many of us would survive to hold the city. She was like some great beast being harried by hunting dogs.

That was the last image I saw of the mighty *Red Dragon*.

Then… she blew everywhere all at once. Suddenly. Shockingly so, like it wasn't supposed to happen just yet.

"RUN NOW!" shouted Ulysses. *"RUN NOW OR WE GET CAUGHT IN THE BLAST WAVE!"*

And no, we weren't leaving the wounded. We may be a lot of things, but we ain't that.

We were maybe three hundred yards over broken and burnt terrain away from the hulking *Spider* still dead center of the massive blocks-wide LZ the D-beam strike had cleared prior to the invasion almost twenty-four hours ago. A terrain that had been shelled and blasted and was made uneven and ruined by great forces, and us. We had wounded to haul. We were wounded, in fact. We'd been fighting for twenty-four hours. We were dehydrated and hungry.

I can't speak for everyone else, but I was sure I wanted to throw up right there.

I'd been almost killed, many times. Or in situations that looked like certain death on occasion. Watching the biggest known starship acknowledged by mankind, a leviathan among leviathans, suddenly go supernova in the upper atmosphere, watching the clouds pulse away, seeing the blast waves radiating out like physical manifestations of powers reserved for mightier beings than we'd ever known, it felt like certain death was more than headed our way as we small beings scurried for our home in hopes it could shield us from the power of stars detonated in sullen rage by petty men playing at being mean gods denied their eternity.

I had no idea what the detonation power of an actual Battle Spire was. But it looked pretty impressive to me at the moment as we hustled for our lives, certain we were about to get the worst *Too slow, no go* of all time. In the time we'd been in coffin-sleep aboard the *Spider* on the way out to

Hardrock, the Ultras had lost all of their Battle Spires, save *Red Dragon*, in battle. So, I'm sure there were calculations of how much released dynamic power those things generated in their wrathful destructions. But *Red Dragon* was the biggest among the biggest. *Red Dragon* was legend.

There had even been a pretty slick spectacuthriller series back in the day about it called *War Trek*. Each week the fictionalized *Red Dragon* annihilated some rebellious world in order to "save the galaxy." It was pure propaganda. But it was fun propaganda to watch.

We have to be honest about these things.

Propaganda works because it's the equivalent of both salty and sweet. Like eating potato chips and a chocolate bar at the same time. Your mileage may vary on that one, but it works for me.

I remembered liking *War Trek*.

Now… as I look back on the destruction of the Battle Spire *Red Dragon*, at that last image of last images, the great leviathan under attack by fighters swarming in and along her hull, racing around her still active PDCs and fighter engagement cannons, her outer rings gone, missing, demolished, or blown up, I had no idea. Perhaps some of the naval crew had escaped via jump bubbles. Capital ships were launching missile strikes into the bulbs of *Red Dragon*'s massive mains which were bigger than the biggest cities in most of the better colony worlds. Smaller Insurrection destroyer escorts and missile frigates were making close-support gun runs against secondary systems.

Looking back, it probably was one of the most singular events a person can witness. Ship-to-ship combat against an actual Monarch Battle Spire. And I saw it. I was there. As was the rest of Strange Company.

I don't know what the shape of the universe looks like now that the Monarchs are done, but I doubt we will see ships that big or powerful ever again.

The chimps just build massive war hulks that are little more than converted super-tankers with as many salvaged guns and weapons systems as they can stick on them. They may, or may not, make a successful jump and arrive anywhere near their target destination.

I have seen two Battle Spires.

A rare experience for any human. Most people, or at least most people twenty-five years ago, who'd seen a Battle Spire, were dead or getting ready to be so if one arrived over their world ready for combat operations.

I saw one at Crash, or Astralon.

Call it what you will.

I sliced this out of the log. To remember the magnificent Battle Spires of old, as they once were before the Monarchs committed them to saving a dying and corrupt order. Unwilling in any way, shape, or form to share humanity's destiny out here among the stars. I've added this to the logs so whoever comes along next and finds fragments of a data file that mention us can know, not how I saw the last Battle Spire go down over Marsantyium when it got sacked by the *insurrectionistas* and the chimps. And yes, that the Strange Company was there to do their part and bear witness to the death of an empire. But how a Monarch Battle Spire was in all its terrifying glory when it came calling to do battle over some world. This is from the logs pertaining to the war on Crash...

"And still I could not take my eyes off the amazing Battle Spire above us.

It was the largest thing I'd ever seen in my too-short life.

I'll describe it for the record. If the record survives. Because right at that moment, I wasn't sure if Strange Company would. No one survives First Pass. No one survives the Ultras. We were dead and the worst part was most of Strange Company knew it. But what else were we gonna do but keep trying to survive for as long as we could?

The central hull of the immense Battle Spire is long. Very long. There is no ship humanity has ever constructed that even approaches its size. At least the size of New Manhattan City on Sakur. But, for the record since that is what this is, I've heard there are larger Battle Spires. The Red Dragon *is supposedly the biggest. At that moment, watching the monster heave into local airspace, dropping several armies and combat teams all at once, I had no idea what this one was called.*

The aft section of the Battle Spire is wide, where the engines should be but aren't. The local-space maneuver engines are all along the hull. Its main engine for motive transport throughout the universe, the fold engine, is supposedly deep within the ship, but no one knows for sure because no one's allowed to get close to a Battle Spire. Automatic death sentence. But whatever and wherever it is, there's nothing conventional about that engine. It's one of the most closely guarded secrets in the Monarchy.

The aft section, rather than housing the main engine, presuming it doesn't, is for the immense hover and a-grav converters that allow the Battle Spire to set down tail first and establish an overlord tower from which to continue the destruction of a world. It's like a wedding cake top to bottom but moving horizontally in this configuration at ten thousand feet as it executes the space-fold and enters the time stream in the skies above our heads to begin the invasion. The hull races forward up there, tapering at the extreme end, the bow, into a series of command blisters that form the bridge and finally the navigation needle which conspiracy theorists say is critical to the space-fold engine located deep within the immense ship.

As I understand it, the central hull is all Monarch blue. The main hull is brilliant white and dotted with glittering lights that come from the inside and seem to be small cities crawling along its tapering cylinder. All of it run, crewed, and lived in by the ship's complement of beam gunners, transport officers, supply chiefs, and air attack squadron pilots both sub and orbital. I have no credibility in guessing the size of the crew complement, but if I had to, I'd put it at upwards of ten thousand. But I could be off by a hundred thousand. The mind fractures looking at the immense size of the ship that has come to kill us all, drifting into the skies above our war like some casual end of the world come to make good on its promise.

That's not totally correct. The ship will kill some of us. The Ultras will kill the rest. That's how it'll go from here on out for what remains of this world's last gasp of self-rule.

If the magnificence of the incredibly long central hull wasn't just a universal wonder in and of itself... I mean seriously, how do they build these things? Mega-corporations can build city-sized orbital refineries or bulk cargo haulers, and of course small destroyers, cutters, liners, and the scouts and free traders. But nothing even approaches the incredible size of a Battle Spire.

If anything, its very existence makes the argument that the Monarchs are better than the rest of us. To build a ship of that size defies every known science. And yet... there it is. Moments from raining down a thousand different forms of death on our heads.

One of our wounded just died on the deck of the Drop Zero Six. Maybe two minutes from getting triaged by Chief Cutter's medics. Now he'll go to Preacher. I watch as Choker shuts the eyes of the dead man.

As I was saying, if the central hull wasn't enough to make you remind yourself to close your jaw and stop gaping like some slack-jawed local yokel, then it's the Ultra Battle Rings rotating independently about the hull that make you dizzy with fatal wonder.

I don't want to look at the dead man on the deck or remember his name. Or ask myself if I got his story down in the logs. It's all too much right now. So, I look at the fantastic death machine I'm being given the rare privilege of actually seeing during an invasion. As I've said, this is a sight reserved mostly for the deceased of other forgotten battles.

Death and wonder don't mix.

On this Spire there are five. Five battle rings. Again, I've heard other Spires have more. But five is more than enough to assure us of our imminent destruction. The rings are not attached in any way to the main hull. And yet they encompass its diameter, rotating languidly like some magnetic levitation art installation inside a mem zillionaire's private tower on one of the Bright Worlds.

These rings are where the Ultras are.

Even now as I watch, mechs, walkers, and actual airborne are being dropped all across the battlefield. Combat teams, strike divisions, enforcers, inquisition squads, death squads, special forces, armor, artillery, and drop commandos. Departing from the drop, jump, and combat cargo decks.

It's raining death out there.

It's beautiful to behold if you're given to grim fascination and your mind just keeps whispering in the background, low enough so you can ignore it completely, that you're all about to die. Then, yes, it really is fascinating to behold.

They come down like falling stars, the big mechs that will soon form the main assets of their attack and sweep during the First Pass. Walkers with GAU guns and missile packs. Big walkers with 140mm main guns and anti-personnel chain guns. Heavies with Maas Gausers and A-beams to sear right through structures and boil any defenders inside."

That was the Battle Spire that had come and driven us off our last contract on Astralon, Crash, call it… whatever you want.

That was then.

Now…

Red Dragon, the last Battle Spire I saw, or anyone would ever see, suddenly detonated itself at the behest of the Monarchs. *Homo superior* playing their games, their last cards, throwing it all down now even when they'd finally lost. *Red Dragon,* just like that other fantastic Battle Spire I'd been both terrified and fascinated to see, it just went up in a nuclear fireball out over the deserts and jungles of the Monarchs' second-to-last world.

The world they'd just lost to us on LZ Heartbreak.

My guess is they were trying to get close enough to the city to kill us all with the detonation. But they'd run out of time and some critical system had failed, making it impossible to reach the best possible execution of detonation point in order to have their last revenge on us. Who knows, maybe some onboard AI was fighting them to save the ship, despite their best efforts to spend it on little more than petty spite.

But everyone knows there's no one pettier than a Monarch.

Maybe the missile frigates and gun corvettes, supporting the large capital ships swarming like hungry hunting dogs, had scored too many internals on critical motive systems and the mighty *Red Dragon* was about to go nose over into the planet's surface, and the Monarchs' last remaining AIs, the really devious ones that have probably cooked up this whole mess, maybe they estimated a larger kill ratio if they did an atmospheric det at that altitude and range.

We estimate this much dead of the population, masters, if we execute No Joy now. The window of fatality will present diminishing returns with each second that passes after that.

Monarch thinking. Cold inhuman AI supergenius-level planning. I don't know which one is worse. And the horror show is they were working together for a long time before I ever even arrived on the scene.

If the detonation had occurred over the city... we'd all be dead.

Instead, it just went off like the biggest firecracker ever. Suddenly and all at once. The blast came from the powerful maneuvering engines. Maybe even the secret fold engine reactors contributed. A shock wave pulsed away in silence from the explosion of the hull, engines, everything... ripping the entire back end of *Red Dragon* to shreds in every direction in just seconds.

Then, faster than you could expect, and yes there was a flash that raced away across the atmosphere of this scarred world, but... it wasn't blinding. Maybe at a closer range it might have been... but faster than you can imagine the entire central hull rippled forward from countless smaller internal explosions, sending hull plating, guns, missiles systems, and crew and everything else... burning off in every direction away from the small sun igniting in the upper atmosphere.

Clouds in the area, the yellow miasma of a jungle world like Marsantyium, just vaporized in an instant and were gone as though they'd never been there.

"Blast wave!" shouted Choker as we stopped to stare in awe at such a beautifully terrible sight.

We had one hundred yards to go to reach the *Spider*.

The *Spider*'s cargo door was closing even now. We had no comm. We'd had it. Then the detonation had fried everything.

"Doghouse, we're coming in…"

"Copy that—" Static. Then nothing.

"That blast wave's gonna hit us! Run!" shouted Choker.

And it was coming. We didn't need a psychopath to tell us that. We were probably gonna die.

But we weren't gonna give up. We pushed, struggled, and hauled our wounded for our lives, knowing we were leaving the dead out there in the burnt sands of a bad LZ.

By the time we made the rear cargo deck of the *Spider*, a howling wind came up with a roar and was being pushed through what remained of the city. Hurricane-force winds suddenly surged and dead bodies were flying through the air, carried off into the storm. Shotgunned buildings in the distance, those red marble temples and palatial halls of the petty gods, were coming apart as tremors shook the surface and savage winds pushed ahead of the blast wave, grabbing and tearing down what they could.

We heard the explosion, the savage *CRAAAAAK* of the starship that pieces and flaming sections of were already flying far off into the distant sky or raining down in smoky black and gray trails all over this world just like it had once dropped armies from the sky to assert dominance on behalf of the Monarchs. We heard the big explosion of the doomed ship, and *everything went to eleven.*

I have no idea what that means. It's an old Earth colloquialism. Maybe we'd find out how it came about when we got there and dusted the last of the Monarchs.

The cargo doors of the *Spider* were coming down.

"We ain't gonna make it!" shouted Choker.

"Less piehole, more leg, psycho!" shouted Punch in response.

"MOVE, REAPER! NOW!" shouted Ulysses and for a moment it was as though you were more afraid of him than the impending blast wave. *"WE'RE GOING THROUGH THAT CARGO DOOR WHETHER IT'S OPEN OR CLOSED!"*

A black sandstorm with swirling red flecks, and yes, the bodies of dead Ultras, came whirlwinding all around all at once, trying to suck us backward as we struggled up the rear deck ramp toward the closing doors. You could hear nothing, but the first sergeant was there shouting and waving at someone to hold the door. The upper blast doors were almost down.

A dead Ultra Marine came tumbling past us and Ulysses kicked him out of the way with a savage jerk and started hauling everyone under the crack, grabbing them and flinging them inside as the winds fought to tear us off back into the storm and the ruin.

I could see Biggs working the doors in there.

Other Strange were there, but not many.

Then we were in, Ulysses and then me because I would have it no other way even though he is a better soldier than I will ever hope to be.

He's a warrior. Like something from an age of heroes and myths that were fantasies of epic deeds done by the best of us.

I'm just trying to get everyone back to the dustoff.

"That everyone?" someone asked in the thin gloom beyond the massive cargo doors lowering us into darkness.

But who could know? The first sergeant was in and among everyone as the hot wind smelling of dead bodies and dead starships raced onto the seemingly empty deck. None of the mechs had made it back. Strange was missing a platoon, minimum.

We had won.

But it didn't look like it at all.

I got together the best ACE report I could develop. It was incomplete and I knew it and I should have been ashamed. I knew which dead I'd left out there in the sand and the wind… and the destruction that was coming. They deserved better than that. But it was the best I could do.

The doors were closing.

M.O.M. who didn't sound like herself was counting down the blast wave impact.

"Blast wave arrival… forty-three seconds to impact. Destruction… imminent. Stand by and secure all items."

No *dear*. No *have a nice day*.

I didn't know which dead I'd left out there.

Then someone shouted, "Here they come!"

I turned and saw Hauser and some of Third, struggling through the blasting sand and wind out there. We could see nothing beyond them. And then… out of the hellscape of nothingness and impending oblivion beyond Hauser and what remained of Third… the captain. With Chief Cook leaning against him. Obviously badly wounded.

The captain's brown leather trench coat flapping madly in the wind as the two of them made it through the narrow window, and then Biggs lowered the ship's massive cargo doors.

Seconds later M.O.M. began the ten-second countdown after noting, "All available and reserve power to shields…"

Ten…

Nine…

Eight… Brace for impact.

"Hang—" someone was about to say but never finished *on*.

CHAPTER FIFTY

On.

Hang on.

Life is good. But there are times, and sometimes the times are many for a very long time when it's like being in the darkness, pressed and close, feeling like death is coming for you, and then getting hit by the apocalyptic blast wave of an exploding starship. I have found *Hang on* works for almost every occasion when everything, all of it, seems like too much.

In the dark, with those smokes and coffee I have often talked about… when the call comes that someone in Reaper has screwed up bad and local law enforcement wants answers, or some fire needs to be put out between the platoons, or the first sergeant's on a tear about something we should have cared more about, or there's an incoming distress call from a super-hauler with xenos on board and it's time to get it on… sometimes, in those last moments as I inhale the last smoke, drink the coffee, pat the paperback I'm always working on, as though I'm telling my friends in the book I'll be back and for them not to worry, in those times I have often heard myself mumble, *Hang on.*

Or as some wise person once said… *Sometimes you pray, even when you don't believe.*

"Hang on," said M.O.M. in her matronly voice. It sounded tired, and uncertain. Like her speech algos were damaged. I felt bad for her. I felt bad for a computer.

I know… I need to get a life.

Then the blast wave from the destruction of the *Red Dragon* hit us like the largest baseball bat ever cranked up to full and swinging deep for the cheap seats in the game of the year.

The blast connected and it was a home run.

If felt like our old destroyer was going to go right over on her side… and then where would we be?

The cargo deck fell into darkness and some of us screamed. Others shouted. Yes, there was crying. Probably Choker. And of course… I'm sure there were prayers.

I hung on.

Some got hit by flying gear, others went flying because they hadn't grabbed straps or bulkheads. Biggs keeps everything stowed pretty tight on the ship. It could have been worse. Still, stuff broke loose and one of the snipers ended up with a crushed leg for his troubles.

We were in total darkness for three hours before emergency lighting from damage control finally flickered online with little fanfare.

It just did.

We looked like the cursed dead as we stared at each other and wondered how bad it was.

For hours it had sounded bad as the ship got rocked and buried beneath the fury of the *Red Dragon*'s last breath.

We'd decided, or the first sergeant decided actually, for "everyone just to stay put for now. Safer that way. NCOs, get a count and give me a shout-out if you can."

The winds howled and beat at the ship like no storm I've ever been in for those three hours. M.O.M. was damaged. XO was missing and presumed dead in one of the artillery strikes that nailed the ship on the LZ.

We sat in the dark and listened to the multi-ton starship rock back and forth in the blast waves created by the destruction of the largest ship in existence. Massive bulkheads and the central beam of the ship groaning ominously.

We waited for the smell of smoke and wondered if we'd burn alive.

We tried to think of what we'd need to do once the sand stopped flying, stopped beating and slashing and whispering against the side of the hull.

When damage control came online later, M.O.M. came back thirty minutes after that.

"Current status, ship…" she said as though nothing was wrong, "… damaged. Extensively. Starflight unavailable at this time. Decks…"

Then she listed a lot of damage.

It was bad.

Real bad.

It sounded bad.

We began to realize, sitting there in the darkness, having shucked our gear but held on to our weapons, that there was a distinct possibility we were now stranded on this world.

The litany of damage control items sounded beyond our martial abilities, and definitely beyond our funds, to repair.

In the darkness Punch, eating a protein bar, whispered through the chewed remains of it, "Hey, we won, Big Sarge. Right? We won out there. Ultras got punched in the face and they didn't get up. That's how it's goin' down for the record, right?"

I don't know.

Supposedly.

Three days later we were able to crawl out of the ship. One half of the *Spider* was buried in the native red sand of that world.

We'd gone carefully through the main reactor, up through the engineering decks, and come out on top of the sand-covered hull.

It was a blue day. Clear as far as the eye could see. But there were great fires over the jungles off to the east. Where the *Red Dragon*, or what was left of it, had probably gone down. A gentle wind was keeping the smoke away from the city, sending it off in other directions out over the red stone world covered in emerald jungles.

Some of the city was left out there. But not much.

But much of it had been blasted away by what looked like the most devastating artillery strike ever.

Large portions of it were buried under that sand. So were the dead. Ours and theirs.

As I have said, one half of the *Spider* was buried. The other half was not, and we could enter and exit from the lower cargo doors there. The side facing the blast had been covered in sand.

"It almost looks like..." said Choker dreamily as he stared out over the vast sand sea that seemed to have washed almost everything away besides the tallest skeletons of the temples and palaces of the Monarchs. He'd been assigned to go on the recon through our own ship as the acting medic. "It's like it never happened," Choker said dreamily.

Cutter was still treating the wounded down in the lower med bays. Power was restored to much of the ship.

Later, we'd find out it wasn't as bad as it looked. The damage to our ship. But early on, it looked finished. And by default… so did we.

Mercs go to foreign worlds and fight for pay. If you can't get to those foreign worlds, then the second part of the equation for private military contractor success is going to be hard to pull off.

Also, XO wasn't dead.

He was beaten. But he'd pigheadedly saved the ship and gotten trapped in the magazines preventing a cascade detonation that would have left a crater about the size of ten city blocks.

The captain was there with us when we went out to survey the damage. He was there standing on the upper hull under the main gun. The sweeping sand had reached all the way up here on that side of the ship. The first sergeant was there too.

The old NCO said nothing.

But he looked older now. More tired and less enthusiastic about things.

Ghost Platoon leader was there too.

As was Hauser, scanning the distances, head traversing side to side. Analyzing and calculating the odds for us. He had a little more damage than the last time I'd seen him, back when he and Choker casevacked a wounded Jax back to the *Spider* before the captain sent Third off to cover Dog's sector in the last hours of the battle. What felt like many lifetimes ago and in fact was, many lives that is, of the Strange Company and the Ultras, now entombed under the red Marsantyium sands.

Chief Cook had been shot several times. He would survive. He was down in the med bays with Cutter.

When Stinkeye found him in the emergency-lit darkness of the hangar as we waited for M.O.M. to come back online, the old drunk had raggedly screamed, "Don't yas die, little man. It's my job ta kill ya someday. Yas hang in there an' let me make da universe a better place!"

Stinkeye hovered over Cutter as our company doctor tried to save Chief Cook's life. Hovered until Cutter suddenly flew into a fearsome rage and sent the Voodoo chief away, threatening the old space war wizard with a bloody scalpel.

Stinkeye retreated with promises of curses not to be trifled with.

But he watched the efforts to save Chief Cook's life like a mother cat with kittens and we all thought that was odd given their mutual animosity.

In time, somehow, miraculously in fact, later that day as the sun began to fall into the west, the chimps came out of the dust and the sand in small platoons, sporting Ultra pickup weapons and gear, and began to make contact with us.

They were uneasy, but they had comm and called in our position and status to Insurrection Command.

Within hours Insurrection drops with medical teams were all over us.

One crew chief slapped me on the shoulder as they offloaded rations and water, saying, "You guys sure held the line. We thought you were goners!"

I took the box and told him, "Yeah, we did too," as I walked back to the ship to offload.

Just after dark, as the night winds began to come up and sweep the sand along the surface of that strange world, the command team was alerted that the Seeker was coming down from *Elektra*.

She had one last mission for the company.

The first sergeant, upon hearing this at the little campfire he'd set up in the lee of our buried warship's hull, muttered, "Don't know who she thinks is left around here to pull it off. But... as I have said on occasion... *well, here we are boys.*"

CHAPTER
FIFTY-ONE

The Seeker and her entourage arrived at three that morning. I would say it was dark, but it wasn't. It was night, that hour halfway between midnight and the new day, but the sky was alight with the broken crystal of the universe and the fires in the east where large sections of *Red Dragon* went down as she broke up and smashed into this fractured and ruined world we'd fought what felt like the last battle on.

In that silent hour, as much of Strange slept, or what was left of the exhausted light infantry private military contractors who'd survived the fight against the Ultras, while the medics moved among the dead and the wounded... while Cutter seemed to be missing and we knew what that meant, the bat-winged shining steel dropship flared her thrust-reversers and a-grav kicked in ominously, throbbing the sands and our bellies, as the wind came up throwing sand all over the LZ we'd marked off.

The security team came out, then some others, and finally with little fanfare but surrounded by staff, still running operations, she appeared on the internally lit boarding ramp, and came down to meet us.

Word was the Insurrection fleet was mortally wounded. The fight with *Red Dragon* had resulted in the loss of more than twenty ships and there was now one squadron riding air cap for what remained of the fleet.

Yeah, Punch… we won. It just doesn't look like it, I would have told him. He was on watch atop the ship.

She was still the same beautiful tall model. But she no longer wore the fatigues and gear of a soldier like she'd done when we fled for our lives across Crash, Astralon, call it what you will.

What seemed another life, not this one. When things had been different, and never would be the same again even though we didn't know it at the time.

She wore the duty uniform of an admiral. Light browns. No medals. No tags. Not like some of her entourage. And nothing like the high-speed low-drag operators she had surrounding her who looked more than ready to start killing, spending their lives for her, while the other half got her out of there. Guys with the best weapons and gear who looked like they could have killed all of us and not felt too bad about it, or even raised a training heart rate in the doing of it.

You know… beards and tats. Great weapons. A couple of energy guns. Hard dead looks that were all business.

There were others with her too.

She had blood on her uniform. Smoke stained her pretty face. But she was still her.

The battle on board *Elektra* must have been something. One for the books of naval stellar combat I'm guessing.

The Seeker spoke with the captain briefly and everything was put on hold until the chimps' Kong could arrive to participate in the meeting. So, we spent two hours drinking coffee and watching the night.

Hurry up and wait, amirite?

But there was definitely a tension in the air. A sense of purpose and the feeling that yes, an impending change of mission was coming down the line.

I drank coffee and reminded myself not to get too excited. Not too caught up… even though it seemed I already was and had been for some time.

Same stuff, different day, Orion, I told myself as I burned a few smokes and nursed a coffee near the first sergeant who seemed quiet and less talkative than usual.

The only strange thing the first sergeant would say to me once the captain had gone off to check the LP/Ops and walk our perimeter around the sand-drowned *Spider* was, "Things'll never be the same now, Sergeant. People think an old guy like me knows everything. Been there, done that, got the scars and all. But we're beyond the perimeter now, Orion. We're makin' it up now as we go along, and that scares the hell out of an old man. Maybe 'cause it's new, definitely because it's dangerous. I ain't cut out for this much longer. Soon… you'll be just like me, Sergeant Orion. Then you'll see. Then you'll know."

He fell silent and would say no more after that.

By dawn the chimps in their ragged platoons, hauling their variety of Frankensteined weapons, and of course lots of battered and shot-to-hell Ultra gear they'd "found" out there in the places where our enemies had gone down fighting, they came near the *Spider* with little order. Like some savage ancient army from ages we'd never known. And in that moment, as the light began to break across the land, I think every one of us was suddenly reminded of how many of them there were, and how few of us survived. The main body of the chimp ground force stayed out near a dune that hadn't been here when we'd landed.

A small team of security gorillas and the Kong with a few of his generals appeared as the sun began to rise. Then the Seeker laid out what now needed to be done next.

I was there.

But in the hours before dark, guarded by her operators operating security team, accompanied by a female medic, she found me near the first sergeant's campfire, drinking coffee and waiting for the night to pass as Top watched the dark and the fire and thought his old man thoughts.

She asked to talk and, just the two of us, we stepped away into the darkness beyond the firelight. The operators encircled us and turned to watch the distances. But I was sure someone had their eye on me and at a moment's notice, making the wrong move, I would have been shot a whole bunch real fast. And I'm sure the groups would have been tight.

So I didn't make any sudden movements even as an anger I didn't think was there came to stand alongside me as we began our palaver.

It was... awkward and tense.

Twenty-five years had passed. For her. Me, just a few months. She was the same. Not one day older. Me, I'd been grazed. My chest hurt like hell. The lines were deeper. And yeah, regardless of Nether's opinion, I probably did look like some stray wolf that had seen too much, been alone too long, was haunted by *done things* along the way from there to here.

If I'd said that to anyone in Strange... the haunted wolf part, I would have gotten a look.

Wolf, Orion? More like stray dog.

That's probably true too.

She's beautiful. The Seeker. An actual Monarch. And she was rare now. Many less than there had been twenty-five years ago. Even in the night. Even on a battle-scarred *No Joy* world that was probably poisoned now and forevermore.

I felt less standing in front of her.

A wily old ruck hobo getting older and more scarred with each passing fight. One day I'm gonna be missing an ear or something. Then where will I be?

Then I remembered that I had done that and been there as a PMC. And that had to count for something. I didn't know what, but it meant something to me no matter how hard on myself I was.

I'd run toward the sound of the gunfire. Add that in whichever column you want to. But I'd put it on any resume or tombstone I managed to get noted on. So it had to count for something.

"Do you have a cigarette for me, Sergeant Orion?" she said plainly.

I never knew she smoked.

I was holding my smart canteen. The one she'd fixed on Crash. When she was actually, for a brief moment, a member of the company.

Or Astralon, call it what you will. It doesn't matter anymore. That world's gone, but at least a hobo keeps his running joke up in defiance of the grand sweep of intergalactic history.

Maybe that's something else that could go on my tombstone. Or resume.

He spit in the face of the Narrative.

Or, for the resume: *Thirty-six years' experience calling it as it is regardless of goods and prizes or treats of the scumbags at the top.*

Put that one right up there with *Cares too much about getting the job done.*

The captain bore the Seeker ill will. I thought about that before I handed her the smoke. I had a bad feeling about that. She'd betrayed us. True. Lied to get us to do the dirty work of nuking the Monarch economy with a hunter-killer algorithm that fried the whole mem network. Eventually.

I shook one out, she took it, I lit.

Then lit one for myself and we blew smoke. I offered her some coffee from my smart canteen.

"Is this the one I fixed?" she said, holding it, stroking it like it was some relic, some artifact from a long-lost age of myths, heroes, or legends that might never have been true.

Or just some old found toy from when you were a child, once and long ago.

"It hasn't been that long for us," I told her. "We were in coffin-sleep for twenty-five years. You know… after you stabbed us in the back and took the Little Girl?"

She said nothing at that. Just let the smoke dangle between her long and delicate fingers as she stared at my canteen and rubbed it with her thumb.

Then… "I know, Orion."

You know…

Listen, I'm not the kinda NCO who makes people call him Sergeant when he's totally in a mood and something needs to be addressed critically. Not unless you've really managed to land on my bad side and seem less careful about it than perhaps I require. I'm not that kind of NCO. Most of the time.

But… *sometimes…*

"Sergeant. It's Sergeant Orion. You may be the new doctorate of what's left of human-controlled space and all, oh by the way good luck with the monkey people, they seem like they're going to be a real big problem shortly... but the company still carries you as a member, Your Highness, in Reaper specifically. My platoon where I am the platoon sergeant. So... Sergeant. Your Highness, or whatever it is you're calling yourself. You know you screwed us along with everyone else back on Crash?"

She nodded.

"You're... upset, Sergeant. I can tell."

She drank some of my coffee and handed it back to me.

I said nothing.

"I need to discuss something important with you and I understand... the issues the company might have with me given our collective past, but in two hours I'm going to ask the company to go on one last mission for the Insurrection before we switch over to the new form of government. It's very important, Orion. I mean Sergeant Orion. They are not going to want to do it. And... the captain... he seems to distrust me. And of course, he should. I did what I had to do to bring the whole system down, but yes, I did betray you. I've tried to make it right... but I don't think I ever will be able to. I'm guessing your commander feels I need some kind of payback for not being fully honest about a contract."

"It's company policy," I said, my voice cold and lower than I thought possible. For some reason I was letting go even though I'd told myself I wouldn't. Ordered myself not to. "Tradition even, Your Highness. And the captain... he doesn't *feel* anything. Ever. So, yeah... If I were you, that'd be a pretty big concern for me too."

I took a drink of the coffee and then asked a question once she'd fallen silent.

"Why's the mission important? Why us? And why do you need me to be the good guy who convinces the company to do the right thing at the wrong time if that's where this is going? And... I don't know if you've been reading the combat reports but we're down to about three squads and a destroyer that's half buried in the sand. That mech company, they were blown to bits and burned alive out there on the line we were trying to hold for Haymaker. Which... again, casualty reports... that whole force is gone now. Side effect of a Battle Spire detonating nearby and not having shields and bulkheads to get behind."

She cocked her head to the side and made a face in the dark I couldn't quite see.

She smelled of jasmine.

"Okay, Sergeant... cutting to the chase then. The Monarchs are done more than you understand just yet. But... they're not dead. At... past crisis times... in their culture..."

"You. Monarch Culture. *Your* culture, you mean."

She hesitated for a moment.

Then, "Yes. I was one of them, Sergeant. I cannot deny that, and I never will because all I'm interested in is the truth now. That's the only thing that's—"

"Going to save us?" I interrupted sarcastically.

"No..." she replied, ignoring my cynicism. "The only thing that is going to set us free in order to see what we do with it, Orion. What we, as a species, do next out here. The truth, that's the only way forward, and I may be a lot of things to you, but I'm not foolish enough to think it's gonna be easy, or not painful. You're absolutely right. The Simia are breathing down our necks. That should be the big concern right now. But there are, is, a greater concern that is... *im-*

minent. The fact that the Monarchs are on their way here, now, is the big concern. Aboard *Dark Star.* That concern is the only thing keeping us safe right now from the Simia warlords and their king. If the Monarchs weren't imminent, the Simia would pick a fight with us right now... and then slaughter us. We're surrounded in more ways than just this landing zone. The only thing humanity has going for itself right now is the Simia are not sure what's gonna happen, and they know the Insurrection is their only ally. So they can't kill us until the Monarchs are dead. Not just yet."

Okay. That's a lot to digest. And then I remembered Punch asking, *We won, right, Sar'nt?*

"Can they actually kill us?"

She nodded slowly.

"Definitely. For years to come in fact. We're playing a delicate game with this. What's here in human-space, their hulks, that's the jump-capable stuff the Simia possess. They have sublight forces out there in the dark, large armadas on their way into the core systems. Fifty more years and we won't have the numbers. There won't be a war... they'll just be the majority. So yes, we're gonna need to fight another war, Sergeant. But right now, the Insurrection has nothing to fight that war with. Supply chain is thin. Factories are producing food and survival supplies only. No one's building warships or weapons. The best we can do is more ammunition for the systems we have. So... we cannot fight with the Simia. We do, and we lose here, tonight, Sergeant Orion."

Any... anger I'd felt toward her for using me to trick the company into going way out in the desert to strike a target, a mission that got a lot of guys killed... dissipated. And there was some small voice in me that whispered it hated me for that.

Monarchs can manipulate you mentally, and with their pheromones.

I don't think that's what was happening.

I think, now that I look back on it all, I think she was laying it all out so I knew the stakes. All of it. And… all of it wasn't good at all if your side happened to be the human side of the equation.

We were up the creek and nothing to get back with.

Some old poem about bells tolling came to stand around next to my mind, chanting like a doom bell in some spectacuthriller soundtrack. Reminding me there were always storms larger than the one you found yourself in.

And… as I have said… we have to be honest about these things.

This dumb ruck hobo wanted to save her. I could tell she had the weight of everything on her. The core worlds. The Insurrection. The future. Humanity.

She was… for all intents and purposes… in charge of all humanity now. She'd organized them, led them, and fought for them leading a ragtag armada and a monkey war machine against our oppressors. The Monarchs. And, though things looked bad for us… she had won. We had won.

Some were calling her the Empress now. As though a string of war-ravaged systems with nonexistent supply lines ravaged by piracy were some kind of political entity on the go.

"What was your real name before…" I asked her suddenly. "… before the whole Monarch business. When you were just someone."

511

She laughed like the question had totally caught her off-guard.

"Do you really wanna know?"

I do.

"Okay... it was... Isabel. When I was a child, they called me Izzy. For a long time, until things got... crazy... I was just a girl called Izzy. I laughed. I... loved. I had dreams."

She was silent for a long moment. Remembering...

Names. Orion. Little King. Hotsoup, damn him too. Names. What are they?

Isabel.

First Empress of the Human Empire. Or something. There was that doom bell of destiny and something larger than just a ruck hobo getting older with each fight. Yeah, the thin flame of humanity was in the winds of change. And like that... it could just go out.

The Monarchs, the last of them, were inbound on our position in some mythical ship called *Dark Star*, or maybe it would be the Simia that did us in. If either didn't kill us first... then maybe, maybe just...

Don't ever get caught in up anything, Orion, said that old ruck hobo I'd aspired to be just like someday. Warning me. Knowing every merc has the temptation to forget the why of why he's there. And do it for something else besides the money.

"What do you need the company to do?"

She looked me in the eye. Then she told me. And... yeah, I'd need to make sure the company decided to get it on. In the end, it was more important than anything we'd done so far. Or in any recent log within the contracts I had direct knowledge of, or had read about.

"Your… bishops… you call them Nether and Stinkeye…" she said.

"We had another. The Little Girl. Remember her? We took care of her. She was ours. That was our job."

The former Monarch waited for my brief storm to pass. I didn't say *sorry*.

"She is a grown woman now, Sergeant. She was in hypersleep to protect her for a while. But she is… she's safe, Orion."

I nodded.

"Okay… what about Nether and Stinkeye?" I asked, getting back on track. "Our bishops?"

"Nothing about them in particular. But bishops in general… have they ever talked to you about themselves? About what they are?"

I told her I knew enough.

"*Dark Star* was our doomsday escape scenario. We only executed it one other time. That was during the Atreadi invasion. All surviving Monarchs not involved in combat operations boarded *Dark Star*. It's an immense ship, Orion. And a dangerous ship. We went deep. Off into the unexplored reaches of space to—"

"To hide," I interrupted, unable to control the daggers I wanted to fling.

"Yes, we did do that. We felt we were… that important. We were wrong. I was wrong."

Humanity died in droves defending against the Atreadi. I didn't say that. But that's something even history can't deny.

"*Nightwatch*… that's the ship's code identifier… she went active six months ago. Once it was certain Mars would fall…"

"Wait… what?" I said as suddenly cold water got thrown all over me.

Then… it all fell into place.

She said nothing. She knew what I was just figuring out.

I gave her a look that probably told her I wanted answers before we talked about anything else.

"I told you… we have to do the truth now, Sergeant Orion. No more lies like the Empire of Lies that was the Monarchy. So… truth."

"I know enough of forbidden history to know Mars was part of the home system. A nine-planet home system." I was starting to breathe fast. I looked at the night sky getting light. The horizon. Putting all the terrible pieces and the meaning of it all… together.

Like for once, I had the right puzzle pieces for the picture on the box.

She pressed her lips together. It was a look of submission. Shame. Failure.

"This is an eight-planet system, yet you just called Marsantyium… Mars?" I asked her to confirm. "This is the home system, isn't it? Earth is gone."

She nodded.

"The debris field that makes stellar navigation… difficult…" I mumbled, allowing the implications to be real. Not wanting to believe that a constant in my life, one that seemed more solid than the rest, inviolable really, was a lie too.

A lie in an *Empire of Lies*. As she'd called it.

"Yes," she whispered. Her eyes down. Her pretty face a shadow in the night. She shook her head and I watched as a tear like some stolen crystal slipped down her moonlit cheek in the night.

Morning soon. The last of the night. Today… felt like it was gonna be a long one and I wondered… who would die?

And I realized I had no power over that. But that I would do my best to keep them alive anyway.

"Earth was destroyed long ago, Orion. This is Mars. This is the last world of the Monarchs. The last of what the Earth… was."

CHAPTER FIFTY-TWO

"We finally blew it up?" I asked and heard the utter bitter disbelief in my own voice as I spoke.

She merely told me the story of Earth's demise was long and complicated. But that she would tell me the whole story, everything I wanted to know, in fact, when this was over.

"But there isn't time for that, Sergeant. We have to convince—"

"It's just Orion. I'm sorry. Sorry I've been... hostile. It's just been a lot. And we don't have to convince anyone in Strange to do anything. There's been enough lying in the name of convincing someone to *do something for the greater good*. Just tell me what the company needs to get done... and my guess is we'll do it. Hopefully it's the right thing. Or... the money, whatever your new currency is gonna be... is enough to make it worth our while. We are mercenaries, after all."

"Yes, you are. But Strange Company is much more than that. The company always has been... Orion. And yes, I will reveal that also... on the other side, if there is one, of this. *Dark Star* is twelve hours away from orbital insertion. My armada is in no shape to fight another battle. We have to withdraw to the outer system. Neither are the Simia, though they want to attempt to board and detonate disabling charges to stop *Dark Star* here. They have no idea what they would be facing if they did that. The Guardians are more than capable of dealing with the Simia once they board the ship."

"So, what is it you need us to do?" I asked, looking at my backup watch I'd retrieved from my quarters. Noting the time hack she'd given me. We didn't have much to work with if we were going to plan and implement.

"Humanity... I'm sorry to oversell it, Orion... but that's the way it's got to be... the stakes are that high. Humanity needs the company to go into the Factory. That's what the Dark Lab located within the city is called on Mars. I... we... need you to go in there and rescue... children, Orion. I need the company to go do that even though it doesn't seem tactically significant. The strike force won't have cover and they'll be racing the clock to get in there, effect the rescue, and get back to the ship before *Dark Star* synchs the orbit so they can extract."

"They're not children, are they?" I said.

"No. No more lies. They *are* children. Yes, you've rightly intuited they're also psy-cans. Psyonic-capable."

"And this *Dark Star*, this Monarch lifeboat, it's heading back out into the dark and it's here to pick up as many psy-cans as it can. You want it stopped because those psy-cans... could... eventually... be used to destabilize whatever government you choose to build now, Empress. Is that right?"

She took a deep breath and stared off into the night. Watching the campfires of the Simia. The watches of the Strange Company. Her own dark and shadowy operators in the night.

"If you want to see it that way... and I don't blame you if you do... but yes. The Monarchs are done... but they will try to come back. They've been looting psy-cans from all the labs as they've fallen on the worlds they were all on.

They have many bishops already aboard *Dark Star*. They are keeping them for themselves, which is why you didn't face any when fighting the Ultras. So yes, given time, the Monarchs could discover the right psy-can that has powers that might come back to haunt us if we build something new here. They've been desperate to find a time traveler. A psy-can that can violate forward time restraints and go back and erase all their… *mistakes*… and *problems*… like me. And the company, of course. That's a big one they've been looking for. According to their theories, the travelers do exist. We've… they've never gotten close. But there are other types of psy-cans, some quite dangerous. With a new army, a new navy, the Monarchs could come back and give us, humanity, a very difficult time, especially since we need to deal with the Simia problem soon if there even is to be a humanity. In short… critical tac analysis would lay it out just like you did, Orion. But that's not why I want the company to go in and rescue those children."

"No? Why, then?"

She took a deep breath. It was starting to get light in the east. The wind was soft, and it didn't smell like death so much as all that burning terraformed jungle out there.

Marsantyium.

Or what it had once been called.

Mars.

Last of the home world. And it wasn't at all. Just a runner-up. It had once been nothing more than a lifeless rock. But humanity, with the Monarchs in their infancy pushing from behind the scenes, had turned it into a garden paradise. A second Earth.

But what had become of Earth? Original Earth. The home world?

Pins and needles. Though, I had to ask myself, who really cared anymore. It was all ancient history. Humans, people on every world, they had their own home worlds now.

Earth had just been some long-ago place.

"The company needs to hit the Factory," she continued as the light of the sun began to rise across the dunes and the burning jungles. Turning the broken and fractured cities of Mars blood-red in the morning after war. "The fleet is breaking contact. We can't afford to fight *Dark Star* now. I'll build a special navy and send them off to hunt her down once she flees for deep space, and before they can infect another world. Another civilization, Orion. There are worlds, and other civilizations, starfaring even, out there, worlds no one was ever told about. But that's not the reason this needs to happen. The reason we need to save these children is we need to, whatever we're going to become, empire, democracy, a federation of worlds maybe, we need to do everything the opposite of what the Monarchs did to get us here. Truth as opposed to lies. People over power. Accountability instead of invincibility. They used those children, Orion. They stole them in the night like real live monsters. We, regardless of what they are, the psy-cans, which in some cases may be very powerful, and very dangerous, we need to rescue them, Orion. We need to bring them back to life, set them free to pursue that life. Liberty, Sergeant Orion. Even the pursuit of happiness. Just like everyone else from now on... on all the human worlds... can, finally.

"Whatever I am to these people, these worlds, I've seen the other side, I've *been* the other side, in fact. I'm doing those old words. Life and Liberty and the Pursuit. Those old ways before they were stolen and corrupted.

"So, even psy-cans, even powerful ones… they deserve their chance at the words. I want the company to go in and get them out of there before the Monarchs can carry them off into the dark. Get them back to the *Spider*. We're installing a cloaking device, if the captain decides to go with the mission. The Monarchs won't have time to search for them once they're hidden back aboard your ship. We'll launch a long-range strike and get them occupied. If they don't get what they want, they'll jump or execute a fold. The children you rescue will be safe.

"That's what I need the company to do."

I had been holding my breath. Now it was my turn to take a breath, but I barely did.

Never let 'em see you breathe.

It's hardwired into me. No matter how much you PT everyone after a long weekend of drinking and debauchery, never let them see you sweat. Never let them see you breathe heavy.

"I don't know what they'll do, Isabel."

She watched me. Then smiled, letting me know no one had used that name… in a long, long time.

"But…" I lowered my head and moved sand around with my worn jungle boots. The sand of Mars. "My guess is… we'll do it. We gotta do things different if we're gonna be something out here in the stars. You nailed that one. We do it like the Monarchs… then we, even without their powers… we'll become just like them. And then the company would have to kill us. Sure. I'll go. My guess is the rest of us will go too. They're hard. But they've got a soft spot. So… yeah… we'll go in there and get the kids out before the monsters show up to take them off into the darkness. How much time?"

"Eleven hours and twenty-nine minutes," she said without looking at any kind of watch. Monarchs, they have all the good tech. And powers. Even little ones. "I'll brief on the difficulties. And… I'm sending someone with you, Orion."

She turned in the darkness and waved for the medic to come over. The female medic standing with the operators in the dark.

She came. Good battle rattle. She was curvy and young. Brown hair and dark eyes that shined in the night.

She walked right toward me and stood, staring, just like she'd done so long ago. Watching me as I realized who she was. She'd always watched me… trying to understand who I was.

We called her the Little Girl then.

She was a young woman now. A medic with a short high-speed carbine and an aid bag. Standing among hardened operators who'd stacked on as many worlds as the company had.

I nodded… and felt old. A smile crossing my face just like those I'd always tried to give her when she was with us last. When she was just some stray like the rest of us. Except little. Feeling bad for her. An orphan among killers. A girl who could summon a dark and lethal warrior whenever she was in trouble.

A bishop.

A psy-can.

A little girl.

"Okay…" I said to myself. Okay. Lot to process here. The only thing I could think of to say to her was… what I'd always said to all new recruits.

After the brief.

After the protein bar to cut the nerves.

"We'll take care of you. Okay?" I told her. The Little Girl who was now a young woman. A medic who would go on a mission into the dark place where monsters lived. To save someone.

The company didn't always get those missions. But, without ever saying so… maybe we'd wanted to. Maybe we thought that could wash away some of the blood. Some of the *hard done things* out there among the stars.

She nodded at me after I told her we'd take care of her.

"You always have, Sergeant. Always."

CHAPTER FIFTY-THREE

"Daylight's burnin', kids. Get this done and we're outta here."

The first sergeant was on a tear as all of, or rather what was left of, Strange Company bent to the wheel to get it done. Our senior-most NCO's earlier malaise that had settled over him near the darkness before dawn was gone.

We had a lot to do and a short time to get it done in.

And of course, it was pure pucker factor when the Old Man came to me, trying to hide his limp and the two other gunshot wounds he'd acquired when holding Dog by himself as the rest of the platoon got decimated and he fought off attack after attack.

His foot didn't work due to fragments from an Ultra grenade. Those were out but it was still tender. Being the Old Man, the traditional title of the company commander of Strange Company, a heartbreaker who'd probably been an Ultra stud in another life not this private military contractor one, had his spare boots on and was doing his best to ignore the shooting pain and make sure we didn't factor it in as the operation to take the Factory got underway as fast as possible.

One of the gunshot wounds went right through, and he was fine. Mostly. The other hit his primary hand and that was bad. It was basically destroyed. Cutter tried to save it, but...

"You're taking the mission into the Factory," said the captain when he caught me, his teeth gritted, his scars angrier and somehow more livid as he told me I was in charge now. "Cutter's gonna take my hand and he says we've got to do it now. I'll be under for a couple of hours, and we can't afford those if we're gonna hit the objective and get off it in time. So we follow the op order I laid out. If you've got any modifications let's do 'em now so I'll know what the hell is going on out there."

He was clearly pissed at himself for, as he perceived it, letting the company down.

I had no doubt there wasn't a painkiller in his system and he'd fight Cutter not to go under for the amputation of a body part. Maybe just a local. Never blockers, definitely. But Cutter had knocked out the company commander before, and the captain knew our company doc, even with all his faults, got his medicine done one way or the other. You could do it easy and let him work, or you could do it the hard way. Either way it was gonna get done and all you had the choice of was if it was gonna be easy, or hard.

Nothing like having Cutter choke you out as he gave you the *nighty-night go bye-bye now* shot.

"Your order is the way to get it done, sir," I told the Old Man. "We will go and execute, sir."

The captain jerked his head slightly like he was expecting a fight about something. But I guess he was just irritable from the pain he was trying not to show.

He gave me a hard look when he realized I wasn't gonna give him a fight about any of the points in the order. There wasn't time to make changes. It was a plan. A good one. Might as well be this one.

"I know you will," he said, suddenly softer, calmer. Like some break in his internal battles had come for just a moment. A pause in the pain. "I..."

I didn't give him a chance to tell me he was sorry he wasn't leading the way on this one.

I have few idols. And I never thought it would be some officer... but yeah, he's one of 'em. You try not to see them, your idols, your gods, whatever the directions on your compass are, for what they really are sometimes. You've got too much invested in them regarding your own self. Your own identity and how you navigate the madness of life. So I stopped him before he could show some weakness he didn't really have. A failure that wasn't his. An apology for being shot.

Cutter was gonna take his hand in a few.

Earth was gone.

To be honest... it's been a rough day. Lot to process. I didn't need that. I didn't need my idol telling me he was just a man with flaws, doubts, and rages just like my own. Whose expectations would I live up to then?

Who would I be afraid of failing? Of disappointing?

"Sir... what about the Voodoo elements?" I asked, quickly changing the subject. "They're missing from the op order."

I knew why they were missing of course. I just needed to stop the commander from apologizing for not being the stud we all knew he was. Traumatic gunshot injuries have a way of making life decisions whether you like them or not.

What was that old poem I sometimes recalled in the quiet dark cigarettes and coffee moments...? Something about *because I could not stop for Death* —

He kindly stopped for me —

The Old Man was wounded and the loss of the hand, and so many other things and people along the way... I'll be honest, I can only take so much loss. There was no more room in my emotional ruck for another one right now. Sorry, all full up on change, folks. Come at me another day, not this one.

So I stopped the captain and asked a bogus status question. Even the best of officers can be manipulated easily when it comes to unit accountability.

Stinkeye was blind drunk and passed out. Somewhere. Nether was missing, but that happened when he used his power and went too deep in the debt of charge. Like he'd told me, he was some kind of quantum battery. Once he'd discharged his charge, he, in his words, *I get thin, Orion. Like gossamer. Like I'm not even there. And I can feel that void wind pulling me and calling me to the things in the dark down there.*

"That's horrible," I told him. "Don't do that, Nether. We'll get it done another way but don't go that far."

We need you, I didn't say. *I need you.*

Nether had sighed and said, simply, *In those moments, Orion, it's not so bad to feel yourself fading into the black...*

Nether had wiped out a tank platoon supported by infantry and a scout mech out there in the Battle for LZ Heartbreak during the Sack of Marsantyium. That was more than any one of us had ever seen him do.

And maybe more than any of us had done.

Though everyone had gone all in. And some, they'd gone all the way and paid the ultimate price for the company.

Imagine how many times guys came up to me to share their *Hotsoup memories*. Imagine me biting my tongue and seething internally. Hating myself. And having to acknowledge the heroism of a guy I had grown to hate more in death, for no clear reason, than I had in life.

I am a small ruck hobo. Petty and mean.

Ah, the fun of being me.

Nether was missing…

So I told myself the void wind weather report this morning of the raid on Objective Funhouse was mild and the winds weren't calling for my friend Nether. That he was just laying low somewhere. Resting and recharging. And even perhaps having one of those dreams where everything that was lost… wasn't. And that you came home, and everyone, all of them were there.

That every sad thing that'd ever happened… had come untrue.

I checked the loadouts and hoped for that in the spare seconds I had before we rolled on Funhouse.

And Chief Cook. He'd made it back to the LZ and into the medical bays, but he was shot up good for pretty much exposing himself to a lot of enemy fire while calling in the last of the air support.

In regular militaries they give guys pretty shiny medals for actions like that. And usually those medals are awarded to your family 'cause you ain't around anymore.

Of course, he'd asked for more drugs than Cutter recommended. He probably had his own stash of painkillers, hallucinogenic and whatnot in order to "promote the healing process."

He was done for the foreseeable future and was looking at a pretty long recovery.

The captain answered my question, shifting on his leg with a grimace of sudden pain he could not hide.

"Voodoo is combat-ineffective now. Without them this LZ would be crawling with Ultras."

He paused.

"They're a neat trick, Sergeant. But wars are won by infantrymen with a rifle holding a hill. That has been true since the beginning of time regardless of what the smart kids think about conditions of victory and asymmetrical warfare. *Losses that are really wins* they try to tell us as we bury our own dead. I'll take one squad of light infantry over a hundred Voodoo operators any day. I've…"

He leaned close, once again wincing at some incredible pain, and spoke quietly, sweat breaking out across his forehead.

"Listen, Sergeant Orion, I have been through a lot that… maybe someday we'll talk about. The infantry has always gotten the job done, one way or the other. Give them some weapons, tell them where to go and who to kill, and they'll get it done regardless of fuel, food, weather over the target, or muddy roads turned to a bog. Ghost will support. The drops are moving them to the AO now and they'll be in position. Take your team in, get those kids out, get back here."

"We'll get it done, sir."

He nodded.

"I know."

And then he was off to probably nail down three other things that would assist the mission we'd been given on the fly, before he reported to the medical deck aboard the *Spider* to have his hand lopped off.

But before he did, he turned back to me one last time.

"I don't know if she can still… summon her friend. I don't even think that's what it is, Orion. I think he comes near when he senses she's in trouble. I don't know if that's still a possibility… but she's going with you. And she was once Voodoo too."

And then he was gone.

CHAPTER FIFTY-FOUR

"Contact… Frankensteins!"

It was Punch, tip of the spear of the raider strike force we'd become who called out our first enemy contact on the movement to target.

We were two hours into the wasteland of the ruined city, threading buried streets and shattered buildings, winding and zagging to reach Funhouse in time to pull the strike, rescue the hostages, and get out of Dodgeistan.

Of course, as the platoon sergeant, I didn't have time for enemy contact. But… *Here we are, boys.*

The briefing the Seeker had given us on Funhouse alerted us to three enemy units operating in the area that Insurrection intel and drone recon had identified on the way into the Factory, which we had tagged as *Objective Funhouse.*

Zombies.

Frankensteins.

And a… oh boy! A combat cyborg HK kill team on the loose.

Our raider force was two prowlers with two auto cannons, one per vehicle, and two squads of heavily armed light infantry operating in the dismount.

First Squad was Punch, Ulysses who'd effectively become the assistant squad leader, Choker, Hustle and Hoser, Klutz, Solo, Two Times, and Wolfy as the SDM. We had the

Little Girl as a highly trained medic that exceeded Choker's skills, and hopefully, an ad hoc Voodoo operator.

We'd had to cannibalize Second Squad to get to two squads.

Third Squad under Hauser was the second squad going in with the raiding force. Once we hit the objective, they would set up perimeter security and a base of supporting fire as First stormed the complex and rescued the kids.

Third was Hauser, Runs, Slash, Eights, Duster the EOD from Dog, Mad Max as gunner, Bad Bet as AG who had a shattered arm, Bender, and Yahtzee in the SDM slot. We'd thought initially very few of Third had survived LZ Heartbreak. Actually, they'd gotten separated during the heaviest fighting, and most had survived as they supported the defense of Dog's sector from the second line of defense, which saved their lives. Only Blender the medic had been killed.

The rest were banged up pretty good though. We all were. But this was all we had to work with and what needed to be done had to get done now.

Get it on, Strange.

Biggs, working with some of the chimp combat engineers, had managed to rig riding boards and straps for both squads to ride on the outside of the prowlers. We'd need to do that, so we'd have room for as many psy-cans as possible inside once we extracted them from Funhouse.

With the Frankensteins, zombies, and an actual HK kill team in the area, chances were the exit from the objective was gonna be hot, so we needed to keep the children safe from gunfire.

Now, as we reacted to contact, Frankensteins on the way in, I will tell you what they are and what the zombies are also. The HK kill team, that's pretty easy to figure out. It's three specialized Hausers adept at urban asymmetrical warfare.

So… there was a good chance a lot of us were gonna die if we got involved with them.

Everyone knew that. We were going in anyway and I'll tell you this… no one asked about pay or bonuses. The Seeker had offered. The captain had the offer. When he gave the frago for the mission and told the surviving members of Strange, Ghost, Reaper, and a few from Dog, that we were going in to get kids out… without a word it was clear we didn't need to be paid for this one.

"The Seeker has offered to open negotiations on the current contract for a supplemental agreement to undertake this mission," stated the captain, our commander, as he stood there in front of us doing his job-obligated duty to inform us of the terms of the potential deal.

"Ain't got time for that, sir," said Punch. "Daylight's burnin'. I'm in. Kids in there, sir. We gotta go get 'em out."

He stuck his assault-gloved fist out. The gesture we make when we agree to an action. We agree to see it through to its conclusion come hell or high water. Or even death.

One by one… the rest of us did too.

Everything bad I have ever written about these guys… I take it all back. I was wrong. I am sorry.

Hauser came to me later as we loaded everything we could carry into rucks and assault packs, slung on rigs, and strapped anywhere possible. Primaries, secondaries, at least two each, both holsters on the right side because you never know when you're gonna need two sidearms at once to bang away up close and personal in tight quarters or some dark room gone real bad. A backup of course. Shotguns with AP slugs were a favorite, but some were taking sub guns because nothing keeps everyone's head down like some pray and spray. Frags. EMP grenades. Assorted other fun exploding prizes you can play fun and games with.

We were *loaded for sabre bear* as the saying goes on Celestion.

Frankensteins are, or rather were, Ultras… that got upgraded with cybernetics after being badly wounded in combat. Usually so badly combat-wounded they were tossed out of the hardcore line units because the wounds were too extreme for continued duty. That's the Ultras for you. Total Spartans. Were. That *was* the Ultras for you.

They're all dead now. You're welcome, galaxy.

So, these Frankensteins are medical experiments combining war tech and a soldier that's *been there and done that.* There's maybe a platoon operating in the area according to orbital TAC AN. But they've got all kinds of special upgrades that allow them to defeat intel so…

Reinforced ceramic skeletons. Targeting sensors in their heads. Pain centers are rendered ineffective via medical implants, so they can take multiple gunshots and keep moving. And… each one is a small bomb. Probably the equivalent of two bricks of C4.

They can detonate on command, or via remote.

Just in case.

You'd think they're going to be a problem and they probably are going to be a problem. But they are very susceptible, due to the cybernetic implants, to EMP grenades. Or so we are told.

So… we got that goin' for us. Maybe…

The zombies on the other hand… they are regular people. The former population of this world and probably many other worlds out there where they've gone missing, been abducted, or mass relocated. They're under some kind of mind control, possibly mind-altering drugs, and a constant stream of psycho-babble Monarch propaganda courtesy of VR optics that have been shock-collared to their skulls.

They have zero weapons training, but they may have weapons we are told in the brief. All they will do is swarm us and try to rip us to shreds, pinning us, while the Frankensteins come in and try to kill us with weapons or explosives.

The combat cyborg hunter-killer team... who knows. "Expect the unexpected, Sergeant Orion," is all Hauser tells me. "If I can, I will stop them myself or buy the strike force time to get away."

I know what that means. Less than a minute of runtime is the measure of Hauser's life. He'll spend it for us.

Even though I do not want him to.

But there are realities. And no one understands this better than the killing machine that is my friend.

As Punch said, *There's kids in there. We gotta go get 'em out.*

Ever been in a small boat on a big ocean and there's a storm coming in? This feels like that. And there's not a thing you can do about it.

I thought we might run into the zombies first... coming out of shelters the Monarchs are popping all over the ruins of the city as *Dark Star* nears orbital insertion. The Monarchs probably have no idea what the situation on the ground is—they're just coming in hot and creating as much chaos and confusion as they can on the ground so they can grab the kids via orbital drop shuttles and a high-atmo pass.

They'll fill the streets with a mind-controlled violent populace weaponized against us, that will stop anything not broadcasting the right passivity frequency. Roadblocking everything on the way into the oh-bee-jay.

But it's the Franks who hit us first and we react to contact.

"Contact... Frankensteins!"

And it's *get it on* time. The Strange is in it one last time.

CHAPTER FIFTY-FIVE

"We're breaking contact now, Reaper!" I shout over the comm, pick up a Frank moving in fast, shooting hard to break my cover, and then dust him with a good half mag.

The cybernetic freak rolls in the dust, blood and broken cybernetics painting the red dust of a world once known as Mars in the span of human consciousness.

He was a man once. Now he's got optics in his eyes. Cybernetic limbs that were once arms. Ceramic armor plates fused into his skeleton to protect vitals, or machines pumping acting as vitals to keep him "alive" and buying time for a Monarch snatch on high-value assets.

Children.

I shoot him again because this is no easy fight, and things and people don't die as fast as you want them to.

The dead cybernetic Frankenstein Ultra groans, rolls in the dust, and comes up with his sidearm even though I have shot him a lot. Punch closes from the other side of the APC, slam-firing his pump shotgun and putting slugs into a thing that just won't die easy.

It groans electronically one last time, a horrible sound that will probably stay with me forever, and then Punch takes two more steps so he is close, shifts the barrel of the shotgun upward slightly, pulls the trigger on the slug-throwing industrial-size big hole puncher, and explodes a half-human, half-machine head that was once just like us and now is not, in every direction.

We've been fighting them for three blocks now as we close on Funhouse.

The mini-guns on the prowlers are keeping the zombies back who are surging in packs and clusters getting larger by the second as they try to close off our exit. They're getting close and we're taking fire from the Franks who are in and among them, working tight little carbine setups with tri-dot lasers and drum mags.

The game is to pick them up before they can get close enough through the press of a howling screaming slave population weaponized to protect the *Dark Star*'s orbital shuttles' landing zone near Funhouse.

We've got wounded, but we're moving. In fact, we've got to keep moving because if we stop, all those freaks out there will swarm. Right now, we're killing packs, the auto guns aboard the prowlers blaring out high-dosage death as we shield between the APCs and try to pick off the moving targets.

Wolfy is tagging Franks along the back trail slick as oil, then shifting to his secondary to dust sudden zombies streaking in at him, attempting to drag him down into the fractured rock and thick destruction dust our small strike force convoy is crawling through. Klutz comes in to cover, spraying and praying with the sub gun mini he's got dangling around his chest on a sling, buying time as Wolfy gets in a new mag on his sniper-engagement rifle to start going after the Franks in the unholy crowds swarming over shattered marble and through the remains of the great temples that worshipped the Monarchs as gods once.

Goods and Eights are both down and in the prowlers now with serious gunshot wounds. The Little Girl is running in and out of the moving APCs, getting them triaged and secured, then back into the fight.

She passes me, on the way to help Hustle who got a bounce on his chest plate. Spall and frag ricocheted into one of his eyes and he can't see out of that one.

I smell autumn, burning fall leaves as she hurries past me, aid bag rattling against her as she hustles and stray rounds come in at us.

I know that smell. I smelled it twenty-five years ago. When she was just a little waif, a war orphan we thought. A dark-eyed little girl who said nothing and watched us all. And then sometimes, when the lead was thick and the incoming hot, when it looked real bad like it does now, she would say, *"He's coming now."*

Like it was a warning. And a promise...

The Little Girl was on Eights just minutes ago as we keep moving on the objective. As the zombies come, swarming over great slabs of shattered red marble, or surging on one of the prowlers down some dusty ruined avenue created by the destruction of the savage battle we'd already fought, she was assessing his wounds, then dragging him out from under fire as Hauser came in and laid down a cone of death with the Pig to keep away the horror show of a helpless population, forced to fight us, unable to resist the will of the cursed Monarchs. They are "zombies," shrieking in horror, screaming, "No, no, *NO!* Please don't shoot me!" as they race forward at us, their cybernetic collars forcing them to reach out with their ragged bloodstained claws that were once nails and hands, or some piece of bent pipe or broken building they've picked up, coming in to destroy us. To hack at us, stab us, strangle us, swarm us… drag us down.

They can't not do this even if they don't want to. The collars make them. The VR goggles fill their brains with images and messages, breaking down their will, inciting fear and anger, even promising salvation of some Monarch kind, driving them to an unhinged madness that overlays the reality they must see of us shooting them down as they get close. Banging away on full auto as they get close to the thunder of our guns. The shaky-cam image they're seeing shouting holographic threats and promises if they do not willfully comply. The vaccinations they've had creating small control systems that move their muscles and respond to the commands whether they like it or not if they show the slightest resistance. Dumping endorphins and adrenochrome so they are both so excited and having heart attacks of cold fear at the same moment as they throw themselves into our mobile defense.

They are sweating, screaming, crying, begging for their lives, using words we understand, as they close on us from every direction through the rubble.

Packs and clusters getting larger by the second, turning into mobs and soon crowds.

Hauser cuts them down and the Little Girl drags Eights away and back to the prowler as he screams in pain.

Two blocks to go and I have serious doubts we are going to make it.

I have one last option. One inevitable option the captain and the Seeker gave me in the final moments before we rolled.

It was the captain who gave it to me straight at the end. The Seeker standing there, letting me know it was authorized.

"Sergeant, you don't make it, you see it's not going your way and you're going to get overrun, call in Broken Arrow Danger Close and the Insurrection High Command has authorized the Phantom on station to clean the area and Funhouse. We can't get them, or you, out of there... then, you won't be their slaves."

I said nothing. Because... what can you say about that? Phantoms drop a lot of ordnance. They can level small cities.

You have to be honest about these things.

"Copy, sir." That was all I said. Knowing I had the power now to make sure no one won out there today.

Yeah, you go on ops thinking you might die. But most of the time, do it enough, and you eventually learn to think perhaps you're invincible to an extent. Or it'll catch you by surprise and so there's no need to get all focused on it. Just go out there and do it. If you don't... someone else's problem now. But the *Broken Arrow Danger Close* authorization... well, that's sobering.

Real sobering in fact.

We're fighting a running battle the closer we get to Funhouse, as more and more zombies swarm our rear, racing in from all the deserted and wasted districts of the city to come and pin us now as we close on the Monarch LZ. The remaking Franks are moving ahead of our strike force, out there in the shattered and smashed buildings, shifting in and out of the ruins, firing at us when they can.

On the comm, Ghost has the Factory perimeter secured and is ready to support. They fast-roped in when dropships took them out there fast and dirty. They can support by fire and try to destabilize the push. But it's Reaper going into the compound to get the kids out.

Yahtzee is walking forward between the APCs, leading our under-fire column and dusting Franks ahead of us with his powerful sniper rifle, protected by Punch who's been hit but shook off any kind of medical attention from the Little Girl.

"Ain't got time to bleed, get away from me. Please," he told her and then continued moving, shooting, and communicating. Running First as we slaughtered our way forward.

I got knifed.

One of them, one of the zombies, got close and stuck a rusty knife, an actual rusty kitchen knife, right in me.

I didn't see it because I had traffic from Ghost on site. Sitrep for the situation. They'd cleaned the perimeter and we were good to go for penetration. Then the guy stuck me and raised back like he was gonna do it again, but this time in the ribs between my plates. I shucked my secondary and blew his brains out as he sobbed and screamed, "No! Please!"

I roared and put pressure on the wound, grunting, "Get to livin' or get to dyin', Orion."

She was on me. She got a pressure dressing on it good and tight, and it didn't keep bleeding. I watched her work. The smell of burnt leaves and smoke in the air. The smell of fall.

And then, one red leaf tumbled through the chaos and gunfire.

She looked up at me, said nothing, and ran off. Someone else was hit.

One block to go…

I can see the objective. We… might just do this.

I order the prowlers to form here and wait as we go in. Their onboard guns and both snipers will hold here. I tell Hauser to run the defense, giving me a gun team on the exfil team.

He doesn't object. He obeys. He's a killing machine.

I don't want him going in there. We still haven't found the HK team. I got a bad feeling. A bad feeling that says they're out there in the rubble, moving around. Waiting until we're weak, getting ready to drop the big hammer on us.

My one combat cyborg against three…

My friend.

"Affirmative, Sergeant Orion. I will hold the door open."

Punch and First are ready to push on the objective. We're taking fire from the buildings. The auto guns on the prowlers spool up and a section of the buildings on our right flank turns to dust and collapses.

"Doghouse, this is Reaper… commencing the assault now."

"Copy that, Reaper," says the first sergeant back at the *Spider*. "*Dark Star* one hour from orbital insertion, Reaper Actual. You have twenty minutes to get in and get off the objective. Doghouse out."

For some reason I look up at the bright burning blue sky. Trying to see the Phantom on station up there. If we fail…

We have building plans, master key algos for the security panels from the Seeker, and everything we might need to get the kids out of the lower holding level we have to reach.

"Assaulters move into position!" I order.

First and Third get ready to hustle.

It's hot. The sun is high. In the ruined buildings and streets that ring Funhouse, Ghost is operating out there.

Snipers are engaging the Franks. Ghost Platoon's combat engineers are moving out, firing sub guns, and throwing out strings of claymores to keep the surging zombies shifting around the roadblock created by Hauser and the powerless.

"Tin Man…" Hauser's callsign is *Tin Man*. "We're going in. We may lose contact. You don't hear from us in ten, it's your turn."

"Affirmative, Reaper Actual…"

I hear the blare of the miniguns on board the prowlers. It sounds like they've gone full-auto insanity. I can hear the shrieking screams for help and mercy from the enslaved zombies forced to throw themselves into our guns in order to stop us.

"Back door will stay open until you emerge, Reaper. Good luck," finishes Hauser.

Both squads race forward to opposite sides of the facility. But it's not really a facility. It's more like a pyramid. Or a ziggurat. Made of the same Martian red marble. But lined with glowing effects and surging energy symbols pulsing from within the large red stones that form its structure. It feels alien and wrong. It feels primal and ancient.

A thing we once knew. And never should've.

The destruction is wide here. Much of the great temple that once surrounded this area was shattered in the blast of the *Red Dragon*.

Punch and First move through the ruined ancient monuments and shattered columns that survived the destruction, then stack for breach at the squat yet thick entrance leading into the bloody red dusty ziggurat.

There are dead Frankensteins shot down by Ghost in the moments before we entered the objective. Some still twitch, or moan electronically, their cybernetics trying to push them to one last lethality. Some have exploded. Blood and cybernetic parts are thrown across the dust and cracked ruin of the shattered-out walls and buildings that formed the outer walls and columns of the Factory.

Statues of strange gods have been leveled in every direction. Carved torsos or legs are all that remain. The rest of what was is blown off in wide sprays.

As I run forward to link up with the breaching team, part of me, the part of me that wants to know all the history around us, the true and the lies, so I can reverse navigate and find out what was really true all along, that part of me wants to stop and take all of this in.

There are things here, familiar things. Artifacts from old Earth. Destroyed in the blast of the detonation of *Red Dragon*. Or the Frankensteins detonating.

This was all once some grand courtyard. Some garden of stone. Great statues are shattered in pieces or cut in half. Golden plaques, covered in the red dust of Mars, inscribed in that useless language of the Monarchs, tell me brief strange stories, clues of what had once been. What we once were.

I have no time for things like a *Rosetta Stone*, whatever that was. It's been blown to small dark granite pieces all over the beautiful carved stones of the paving. Some of it remains, and it was large. But much of it is gone. Or a *Liberty Bell*. Or *Sweden's Rök Runestone* that stands shattered and blasted straight through by some fast-moving piece of debris off the Battle Spire. I have no idea who *Sweden* was. Or what a *Rök* is.

We take fire from the ruins beyond the complex we have stormed. I cover quickly behind a shattered perma-crystal column that still has live current running through it. I try to spot the shooter and can't. Someone engages and I cover, reading the golden plate that declares the column to display the *Mask of Agamemnon* inside, encased in perma-crystal. Whoever Agamemnon was. There is nothing but shattered crystal and half a golden mask inside the ruined remains.

Punch's squad stacks and Third moves in, passing… the giant squat head of some ancient human ruler from long before the age of starflight. I have no time to read the plaque.

We plant demo charges and blow the doors to Funhouse.

Then we go in shooting, killing everyone as we go.

CHAPTER FIFTY-SIX

Strange Company has done a lot of jobs. Some we are good at, others we're not but the contract says we gotta do 'em anyway.

Door kicking… it's what we do best.

Third enters and we kill the guards there. First comes in and picks up the hall leading to the lift to the lower levels.

Much of the hall is filled with strange wonders from our past, things behind thick perma-crystal under soft light, things called an *American Constitution*, the *Magna Carta*, or a painting called the *Mona Lisa*, and many other things that mean nothing to me as we move fast and secure the lift, killing the last two Frankensteins we will face inside Funhouse.

We go to the lower levels and get the kids out of there.

Honestly, I don't want to say much about that. It's kids in cages. Shattered, haunted, frightened, screaming children. Little, and older. All of them… ruined.

I find it hard to believe they can ever be… brought back to life. Resurrected.

We're carrying them out and we have no contact with the surface. Something is interfering with our comms. I have one little guy, he's bawling and I'm carrying him, and I have no idea how I'm gonna fight my way out of here and back to the APCs. Carrying him. But there's nothing I can do about it. It's just gotta get done.

"Hause… we're coming out now," I say over the comm. Bring the prowlers in."

Static. I can't get through, but we've got to move. Clock's burning and that Monarch ship's almost overhead.

The levels of the elevator pass and I retransmit, getting Hauser, barely, as he comes in broken and distorted in his transmission.

Some of the kids are screaming and crying. Others just stare about in fear and bewilderment.

Fall leaves are falling in the corner of my vision and I wonder if anyone else sees them, but the lighting is dim and dark in here and we all seem like shades in hell. Shades of what we once were.

And surely, the lower levels were Hell.

"Copy, Reaper…" says Hauser, "… coming in. We're under heavy… zombies pushing… rear… maintain…"

Yes, it was dark down there. Dark as in the light was low. But also dark because it was a place of darkness other than just level of illumination. We get them into the upper hall where all those strange relics of our past wait under glass and two dead Frankensteins lie in spreading pools of blood and sprays of shattered cybernetics scattered on the ornate red stone floor.

I hear Punch push past me, carrying a little girl who stares in wide-eyed horror at the dead we made on our way in.

"Don't look, honey," he mumbles to her over and over, again and again.

"We are in position now, Reaper," says Hauser clearly over the comm. "Clear to exit, doors open."

Then a wash of static comes in waves and cuts the transmission off.

I have no idea if he got my acknowledgment. I'd like things to be better than what they are, but they aren't.

Klutz and Choker are on the doors providing rear security. Holding the entrance so we don't get bushwhacked on our way out. As we make it down the hall, carrying and leading children, they're firing at zombies swarming in close, trying to get between us and the prowlers. Keeping a lane open to the APCs against the masses of zombies swarming to our rear. Our exit off the objective.

I'm getting traffic from Ghost, but the interference is too heavy.

That's when Choker gets shot. Tagged right in the chest good and hard. Above the plate.

Instantly I know it's bad.

At the same time Hauser is on the comm. My private channel. "They're here, Sergeant." Coming through loud and clear because he has ECM and ECCM capabilities to make sure he can ensure communication with whatever element he's operating with.

I know exactly who he means when he says, *They're here, Sergeant.*

It's just Orion, Hause, I think. But that's not important. Not at all right now. But it's what I thought. And I keep the logs.

And we have to be honest about these things…

I also see what our situation is as we get ready to move the kids to the prowlers. We're carrying, pushing, and pulling twenty-seven screaming, sobbing, haunted, silent, angry children.

My medic is hit and he's down with his back against the wall, breathing rapidly, gasping really. Klutz is dumping short concise bursts to hold the path open to the APCs and secure the door.

He turns back to me as he swaps in a new mag.

No, Klutz, I think as I watch Choker begin to die right there. *Do not be a hero right now.*

"I'll clear the way, Sergeant!" shouts Klutz. "Follow me!"

Just like every dead small unit infantry leader time immemorial.

Klutz goes out and I send the rest of the strike force.

I'm still carrying this little screaming boy, standing over Choker as he dies. The little boy, dark-haired, bowl cut, howling, huge dark eyes running with tears, crying without shame and there's nothing I can do about that as I bend down to Choker.

Choker is struggling with something on his rig. Getting out a bandage I assume, to try and save himself even though I can tell… it's bad.

I can't get him out of here without getting help. I can't comm with the prowlers. I can't…

Hauser boosts his signal and cuts into the static wash of the comm.

"I'm going out to engage the kill team now, Sergeant Orion. Do not wait for me. I will stop them."

"G-g-go…" mumbles Choker staring up at me, tears filling his eyes.

"Medic!" I shout but no one hears me.

"Go… n-n-now… O-o-rion. Le-ave me."

"I'm not leaving you, Choker. I… we'll… we will get you out of…"

Here. I was gonna say here. *We will get you out of here*, I was gonna say.

Then he had his scalpel out and he slashed his own throat. I dropped the kid and fought him for the scalpel as fast as he did it. It clattered away from our struggle, but he still fought me, holding on to my arms to prevent me from saving him. From wasting our time on him. From not getting the kids off the objective because the medics came in to save him.

The kid was screaming on the floor nearby as we struggled, and I felt Choker's arms and hands begin to shake uncontrollably.

With the last of his strength Choker fought me, pushing away my hands weakly as I tried to put pressure on the wounds he'd made.

"Stop it, dammit!" I screamed at him. *"I'M TRYING TO SAVE YOU!"*

The kid… was screaming.

I think I was too.

Choker watched me, shaking his head in the negative, mouthing… *Better… this way. Go… go… go…* he whispered as he strangled in his own blood.

He knew.

He knew we'd get killed trying to get him out of there. We'd take time. Time we didn't have.

Just before the light went out of his eyes, he looked at the screaming boy on the floor next to us and smiled a little as more tears filled his eyes and he shook his head like it was all some joke.

I reached for him and held him as he died.

He tried to fight me off, not because, I think, he thought I was still trying to save him, but because he'd never liked to be touched. It was a thing for him. But in the end, as he died, he let me hold him and as he went… he gave me one last pat with the last of his strength, patting me on the back as I hugged him, saying…

It's okay, Sergeant. It's okay now. Don't charge this one to your account. This one… is… on… me.

I don't know.

And then I felt the strength and the life go out of my medic. Who, for all his flaws, and maybe some of which weren't even his own fault, had been a good medic to us.

A brother to the end.

A stranger to the universe.

I picked up the screaming kid and ran for the APCs. Leaving him there.

We barely made it off the objective, leaving a trail of dead zombies until there were none left, the APCs trundling over ruin and debris in silence through the wasted city we'd fought over. Across the ruined Mars that once was. The children inside, Reaper hanging on to the straps outside.

Dark Star was just entering orbit when the APCs found the remains of a shattered underground garage to pull into. We'd wait here and go comms dark until the orbital drops from *Dark Star* had come and gone, finding they'd been robbed.

Just before we went dark, I got a transmission from Hauser.

"Kill team neutralized, Sergeant Orion."

I wanted to tell him Choker was dead. I started to and found I couldn't say anything about it.

"Sergeant Orion… do you read me?" said Hauser across the ether.

I gave him two clicks and said nothing.

What was there to say?

We had won.

EPILOGUE

The two most important things that happened to the company on Mars, I missed.

Not much of a Log Keeper, am I.

But, once the Monarch ship, *Dark Star*, departed orbit, her drops finding the facility cleaned by the Phantom, the strike convoy was ready to head back to the *Spider*. I... walked away.

I'd had enough.

I told Punch to take the convoy back and I just wandered out into the ruins of Mars. It was dark by then. In the night I wandered broken temples, and found relics, relics of our past. Things that had once been important to humanity, lying in the dust and the darkness, meaningless now going forward.

Forgotten.

Discarded.

Trash.

Hauser found me and the two of us crossed the city until dawn, taking one last look around.

We saw the bodies of the dead, theirs and ours. We came upon great libraries of ancient books, filled with shelves stacked high, grand and ornate. Buildings of such opulence and beauty it ached to look upon them. Their beautiful red stained-glass windows were shattered, and the shards lay across mosaicked floors that told the stories of humanity. The shelves were on fire. The buildings were being consumed by flames.

I rescued three books, putting them in my assault pack, and then we left.

At dawn I lay down, using my ruck for a pillow, and slept.

On the following day we went to find the dead of Strange Company where we could, burying them where we found them, marking the spot as we did with our dead, as best we could.

Strangers to the Universe.
Brothers to the End.

When we made it back to the *Spider*, the Seeker was dead, assassinated by Preacher. At the same time the captain and the first sergeant, with his trusty flamethrower he'd taken to calling *Torchy*, took care of her security team. What they didn't handle, the gorillas of the chimp Kong made short and brutal work of.

They tore those operators the captain and the first sergeant hadn't killed, to pieces and scattered them in the sands beyond the ship.

I saw the mess, and thought, *This is how it will be now.*

The assassination was payback for betraying the company.

Preacher had been deemed no threat in the moments before it went down. Deemed zero threat by her security team of high-speed operators. I could have told them that was a mistake. I've seen Preacher go full savage when we were in it. He'll jump on a gun or start blasting with sidearms to get us out of a bad spot. But they thought different, and then paid the price for it. Such is war. Such is the universe. He got close to her, produced a small, snub-nosed, nickel-plated .357, and shot her right in the head.

She died instantly.

Later, I asked Preacher *why*. Why he'd participated in the assassination of the Seeker even though I knew it was in the captain's heart to do it all along.

That wasn't like Preacher.

Company law says we must always pay back a betrayal on a contract. That's from John Strange himself. And to us... it's a kind of gospel. I knew that. But that wasn't his answer, Preacher's answer. And I knew that wasn't why Preacher had done it in the end.

All he said was, "She was a Monarch, Orion. And she always would be."

That wasn't enough for me.

He'd turned away from me to go off into the wasteland of Mars to say prayers over our dead wherever he could find them out there.

I didn't know what to feel as I stood there. But I did know that the answer wasn't enough for me.

I shouted after him. "Just because she was what she was... that ain't a reason, Preacher. That ain't no good kind of reason to kill a person!"

I thought he was going to ignore me as he walked into the howling winds that had come up in the late afternoon on the day the deed was done. The sands were blowing, reclaiming that once-terraformed jungle world, and he was fading into them now.

But he didn't ignore my accusation. He answered it, barely turning to shout over his shoulder as he disappeared into the wind and sand, "*Thou shalt have no other gods before me.*"

And then he was gone, and I was left in the storm.

I said two things, two important things, happened that I missed. The assassination was one.

The other was fate.

The company's fate.

It was told to me that in the moments after the assassination, the Kong came forward, his gorillas standing all around him. The operators torn to pieces. The Seeker, her face beauty itself, perfect, head turned away to hide the wound as her brains and blood ran out on the thirsty red sand of that world.

The little chimp monkey soldier who was their king, the Kong, of all the Simia, stood before the captain, looking up at him and pointing one accusing finger at the Old Man.

"Dis... all dis..." and then he pointed his spindly long hairy fingers up to the stars, encompassing all the human-controlled worlds. "All dis mess on your kind."

The captain said nothing.

What was there to say? Where was the lie?

Then the Kong pointed at the captain, and then the remaining members of the company.

"You go find dem Monarchs out dere in da darkness... da last of 'em. Kill 'em and make right. Den... your company abide right with mine. And we go forward. Not until den."

Then the Kong looked around in disgust and walked away from the Sack of Marsantyium and the sand of Mars. The mess we had made.

When I was told this, I thought, *This is how it is now.*

THE END

The Tragedy of the Strange Company
will continue with

HEARTS OF DARKNESS

Made in the USA
Middletown, DE
18 July 2022